More Praise for *The One*

"Really clever concept and some great characters and twists. It's a real joy to read something totally original, smart and thought provoking."

—Peter James, internationally bestselling author

"Fantastic... I can't remember the last time I was simultaneously this entertained and this disturbed. *The One* is a clever story with great pacing but it's the characters that make this a standout thriller."

—Hollie Overton, author of *Baby Doll*

"Engaging concept, craftily executed."

—Adrian J. Walker, author of *The End of the World Running Club*

"*The One* is my kind of book, one that stimulates the mind while warming the heart... Gorgeously written, and pulsing with heart."

—Louise Beech, author of *The Mountain in My Shoe*

"This will have you gripped."

—*Woman's Own*

"Exciting, addictive, and enticing, *The One* is superbly plotted...thrilling and intoxicating."

—*Becca's Books*

"A compelling read...intriguing ideas."

—*SFX*

"Original and thought provoking."

—*OK! Magazine*

"Gripping from start to finish."

—*S Magazine, Daily Express*

"Riveting... Spellbinding twists and turns."

—*Woman's Day Australia*

"This psychological thriller is a real page-turner."

—*Fabulous (The Sun)*

the One

A Novel

JOHN MARRS

HANOVER
SQUARE
PRESS

HANOVER
SQUARE
PRESS

Recycling programs
for this product may
not exist in your area.

ISBN-13: 978-1-335-00510-6

The One

For questions and comments about the quality of this book, please contact us at CustomerService@Harlequin.com.

HanoverSqPress.com
BookClubbish.com

Printed in U.S.A.

For my dad, Charlie

"To love or have loved, that is enough. Ask nothing further. There is no other pearl to be found in the dark folds of life."

—Victor Hugo, *Les Misérables*

♥ Match Your DNA

Thank you for choosing **Match Your DNA**©, the world's first **SCIENTIFICALLY PROVEN TEST** 100% guaranteed to match you with **the one and only** person you're genetically designed to fall in love with.

With **1.7 billion people already Matched**® or on our register, this is your foolproof way of finding *The One*.

YOUR PERFECT MATCH® IS JUST **THREE STEPS AWAY:**

Sign up <u>here</u> for free.

Receive our free DNA test kit – just send us the mouth swab in the provided container, and we'll use your DNA to find your Match® in our database.

As soon as we've found your Match®, we'll contact you. For a one-off fee of £9.99, we'll put you in touch with each other. 82% of customers are Matched® within 7 days.

If you don't currently have a Match – do not worry! Thousands of new customers join Match Your DNA® each week, and 98% of Matches® are identified within six months of registering.

1

MANDY

Mandy stared at the photograph on her computer screen and held her breath.

The shirtless man had cropped, light brown hair, and posed on a beach with his legs spread apart with the top half of his wet suit rolled down to his waist. His eyes were the clearest shade of blue. His huge grin contained two perfectly aligned rows of white teeth, and she could almost taste the salt water dripping from his chest and onto the surfboard lying by his feet.

"Oh my Lord," she whispered to herself, and let out a long breath she didn't realize she'd been holding. She felt her fingertips tingle and her face flush, and wondered how on earth her body would react to him in person if that's how it responded to just one photograph.

The coffee in her polystyrene cup was cold, but she still finished it. She took a screenshot of the photograph and added it to a newly created folder on her desktop entitled "Richard Taylor." She scanned the office to check if anyone was watching what she was up to in her cubicle, but no one was paying her any attention.

Mandy scrolled down the screen to look at the other photographs in his Facebook album "Around the World." He was certainly well traveled, she noticed, and he had been to places she'd only ever seen on TV or in films. In many pictures he was in bars, trails and temples, posing by landmarks, enjoying golden beaches and choppy waters. He was rarely on his own. She liked that he seemed the gregarious type.

Curious, she looked back further into his time line, from when he first joined social media during his final years at school and right through university. She even found him attractive as a gawky teenager.

After an hour and a half of gawping at nearly the entirety of the handsome stranger's history, Mandy made her way to his Twitter feed to see what he felt the need to share with the world. But all he ranted about was Arsenal's rise and fall in the Premier League, occasionally broken up by Retweets of animals falling over or running into stationary objects.

Their interests appeared to differ greatly, and she questioned exactly why they had been Matched and what they might have in common. Then she reminded herself she no longer needed the mind-set required for using dating websites and apps; Match Your DNA was based on biology, chemicals and science—none of which she could get her head around. But she trusted it with all her heart, like millions and millions of others did.

Mandy moved on to Richard's LinkedIn profile, which revealed that since graduating from Worcester University two years earlier, he'd worked as a personal trainer in a town approximately forty miles from hers. No wonder his body appeared so solid, she thought, and she imagined how it might feel on top of hers.

She hadn't set foot in a gym since her induction a year ago, when her sisters insisted she should stop lamenting her failed marriage and start concentrating on her recovery. They'd whisked her away to a nearby hotel day spa where she'd been massaged, plucked, waxed, hot-stoned, tanned and massaged again until any thought of her ex had been pummeled out of every back and shoulder knot and each clogged pore of her skin. The gym membership had followed along with a promise that she would keep up with the workout schedule they'd set up for her. Motivating herself to work out regularly had yet to become part of her weekly routine, but she paid for the membership regardless.

She began to imagine what her children with Richard might look like, and if they'd inherit their father's blue eyes or be brown like hers; whether they'd be dark-haired and olive-skinned like her or fair and pale like him. She found herself smiling.

"Who's that?"

"Jesus!" she yelled. The voice had made her jump. "You scared me to death."

"Well, you shouldn't have been looking at porn at work, then." Olivia grinned, and offered her a sweet from a bag of Haribo. Mandy declined with a shake of her head.

"It wasn't porn, he's an old friend."

"Yeah, yeah, whatever you say. Keep an eye out for Charlie, though. He's after some sales figures from you."

Mandy rolled her eyes, then looked at the clock in the corner of her screen. She realized that if she didn't start doing some work soon she'd end up taking it home with her. She clicked on the little red x in the corner and cursed her Hotmail account for assuming the Match Your DNA confirmation email was spam. It had sat in her junk folder for the last six weeks until, by chance, she had discovered it earlier that afternoon.

"Mandy Taylor, wife of Richard Taylor, pleased to meet you," she whispered. She noticed she was absentmindedly twiddling an invisible ring around her wedding finger.

2

CHRISTOPHER

Christopher shuffled from side to side until he reached a comfortable position in the armchair.

He placed his elbows at ninety-degree angles on the chair's arms and inhaled deeply to take in the scent of its leathery covering. She hadn't scrimped on quality, he thought, confident from both its smell and soft touch that it hadn't been purchased from a run-of-the-mill retailer.

While she remained in the adjacent kitchen, Christopher glanced around her apartment. She lived on the ground floor of an immaculately restored Victorian building that, according to a stained-glass mural above the front door, had once been used as a convent. He admired her taste in pottery ornaments, which were arranged on shelves built into the walls surrounding the open fireplace's chimney breast. But her choice of literature left a lot to be desired. He turned his nose up at the paperback works of James Patterson, Jackie Collins and J. K. Rowling.

Elsewhere in the room, a suede-covered square tray was placed centrally on a chunky coffee table which held two remote con-trols. Four matching place mats had been perfectly laid around it. Her use of symmetry put him at ease.

Christopher ran his tongue across his teeth, and it hovered over a sliver of pistachio nut that had become trapped between his lateral incisor and canine. When it failed to dislodge, he used his fingernail, but it still wouldn't move, so he made a mental note to inspect her bathroom cabinet for dental floss before he left. Very little irritated him more than a piece of trapped food. He'd once walked out on a date mid-meal because she had a stray piece of kale in her teeth.

A vibrating from his trouser pocket tickled his groin, not an entirely unpleasant experience. As a rule, Christopher was quite fastidious when it came to turning his phone off at appropriate times, and he loathed people who didn't extend him the same courtesy. But today he'd made an exception.

He removed the phone and read the message on the screen; it was an email from Match Your DNA. He recalled sending them a mouth swab on a whim some months earlier but had yet to receive a registered Match. Until now. Would he like to pay to receive their contact details, the message asked. *Would I?* he thought. *Would I really?* He put the phone away and pondered what his Match might look like, before deciding it was inap-propriate to be thinking about a second woman while he was still in the company of the first.

He rose to his feet and returned to the kitchen to find her where he'd left her minutes earlier, lying on her back on the cold, slate floor, the garrote still embedded in her neck. She was no longer bleeding, the final few drops having pooled around the collar of her blouse.

He took a digital Polaroid camera from his jacket and used it to take two identical photographs of her face before waiting patiently for them to develop. He placed both photos in an A5 hard-backed envelope and then slipped it into his jacket pocket.

Then Christopher scooped his kit into his backpack and left, waiting until he had exited the darkness of the garden before removing his plastic overshoes, mask and balaclava.

3

Jade smiled when a message from Kevin flashed across the screen of her mobile.

Evening, beautiful girl, how are you? it read. She liked how Kevin always began his messages with the same phrase.

I'm good thanks, she replied before adding a yellow smiley-faced emoji. I'm knackered, though.

Sorry I didn't text you earlier. It's been a busy day. I didn't piss you off, did I?

Yeah, you did a bit but you know what a grumpy cow I can be. What have you been doing?

A picture appeared on her screen of a wooden barn and a tractor under a bright, blazing sun. Inside the barn, she could just about make out cattle behind metal bars and milking equipment attached to their udders.

I've been repairing the cowshed roof. Not that we're expecting rain yet but we might as well do it now. How about you?

I'm in bed in my pajamas and looking at the weird hotels on the Lonely Planet website you told me about. Jade moved her laptop onto the floor and looked up at her bulletin board of places she wanted to visit.

Amazing, aren't they? We need to travel the world and see them together one day.

It kind of makes me wish I'd taken a year out after uni and gone backpacking with my mates.

Why didn't you?

That's a daft bloody question—money doesn't grow on trees where I'm from. *If only it did*, she thought. Her mum and dad weren't loaded and she'd had to fund her studies. She had a student loan the size of the Tyne to pay off while her housemates from uni had all left to live their dream and travel America. The constant Facebook updates made her seethe, seeing their photos of them all having fun without her.

I hate to cut this short, babe, but Dad wants me to help with the cattle feed. Text me later?

Are you kidding? Jade replied, irked that their time had been cut short after she'd waited all night to speak to him.
Love you, Xxx, Kevin texted.
Yeah, whatever, she replied, and put the phone down. A moment later she picked it up and typed again. Love you too. Xxx.
Jade climbed out from under her thick duvet and placed her

phone on its charging mat on the bedside table. She glanced into the full-length mirror which had photographs of her absent friends who were off traveling taped to the frame, and vowed to reduce the dark rings around her blue eyes by sleeping for longer and drinking more water. She made a mental note to get her red, curly locks trimmed at the weekend and to treat herself to a spray tan. She always felt better when her pale skin had a dash of color.

She slipped back into bed and wondered how different her life might have been had she taken that gap year with her friends. Maybe it would've given her the courage to ignore pressure from her parents to return to Sunderland after her three years at Loughborough. As the first member of her family to be offered a place at university, they couldn't understand why employers weren't beating down her door with job offers the moment she graduated. And while the credit card bills and loans began to mount, she had little choice but to either declare herself bankrupt at twenty-one or move back into the terraced family home she thought she'd escaped.

She disliked the angry, frustrated person she had become, but didn't know how to change. She resented her parents for making her return and began to estrange herself from them. By the time she could afford to rent her own flat, they were barely on speaking terms.

She also blamed them for her failure to get on to the travel and tourism career ladder, and for making her spend her working days behind the reception desk of a hotel on the outskirts of town. It was supposed to have been a stopgap job, but somewhere along the line it had become the norm. Jade was sick of being so irate with everyone, and she yearned to get back to the life she had originally imagined for herself.

The only bright spot in each Groundhog Day was talking to the man she'd been paired with on Match Your DNA. Kevin.

She cracked a smile at the most recent photograph she had

of Kevin, which watched over her from its frame on the book-case. He had almost white-blond hair and eyebrows, a smile that spread from ear to ear, and his tanned body was lean but muscular. She couldn't have made him up if she'd tried.

He'd only sent her a handful of pictures over the seven months they'd been talking, but from the moment they'd first spoken on the phone and Jade had experienced the shiver she'd read about in magazines, she was sure there was no man on earth better suited to her.

Fate could be a bastard, she decided, having placed her Match on the other side of the world in Australia. Maybe one day she might meet him, if she could ever afford it.

4

NICK

"Oh you guys should totally do it," Sumaira urged, a wide grin on her face and a devilish twinkle in her eye.

"Why? I've found my soul mate," Sally said, entwining her fingers with Nick's.

Nick leaned across the dining table and reached for the Prosecco with his other hand. He poured the last few drops into his glass. "Anyone want a top up?" he asked. After a hearty yes from the other three guests he extricated his hand from his fiancée's and moved toward the kitchen.

"But you want to be sure, don't you?" Sumaira pushed. "I mean you guys are so good together, but you never know who else is out there…"

Nick returned from the kitchen with the bottle—the fifth of the evening—and went to pour Sumaira a glass.

Deepak placed his hand over his wife's glass. "She's fine, mate. Mrs. Loose Lips here has had enough for one night."

"Spoilsport," Sumaira sniped and pulled a face. She turned

back to Sally. "All I'm saying is that you want to make sure you've found *the one* before you walk down the aisle."

"You make it sound so romantic," said Deepak and rolled his eyes. "But it's not really up to you to make that decision for them, is it? If they ain't broke, don't try and fix them."

"The test worked for us, though, didn't it? I mean, we knew anyway, but it gave us that added bit of security, that we'd always been destined to be with each other."

"Can we not turn into one of those smug, sanctimonious couples, please?"

"You don't need to be in a couple to be smug and sanctimonious, sweetheart."

Now it was Sumaira's turn to roll her eyes. She swigged the remainder of the contents of her glass under her husband's watchful eye.

Nick rested his head on his fiancée's shoulder and glanced out the window at the glare of cars' headlights and figures milling about on the pavement outside the pub. They lived in a converted factory apartment, and the windows were floor to ceiling—no escape from seeing the busy street outside, and what his life used to look like. Not so long ago, his perfect evening would've been made up of bar crawls around Birmingham's hip, up-and-coming areas, before falling asleep on a night bus and waking up many stops from where he lived.

But his priorities had changed almost overnight when he met Sally. Sally was in her early thirties—five years his senior—and he knew from their first conversation about old Hitchcock films that there was something a bit different about her. In their early days together, she'd gotten a kick from opening his mind to new travel destinations, new foods, new artists and music, and Nick began to see the world from a fresh perspective. When he glanced at her with her impossibly sharp cheekbones, chestnut brown pixie-cropped hair and gray eyes, he hoped that some day their children would acquire their mother's good looks and open-mindedness.

Quite what Nick offered Sally in return he couldn't be sure, but when he'd proposed to her on their three-year anniversary in a restaurant in Santorini, she'd cried so hard that he couldn't be sure if she'd accepted or declined.

"If you two are the best example of what being Matched is about, I'm quite happy for Sal and I to remain just how we are," teased Nick, and slipped his glasses down his nose to rub his tired eyes. He reached for his e-cigarette and took several puffs. "We've been together for almost four years now, and now she's promised to love, honor and obey me, I'm 100 percent sure we're made for each other."

"Hold on, 'obey'?" Sumaira interrupted, raising an eyebrow. "You should be so lucky."

"You obey me," added Deepak confidently. "Everyone knows I wear the trousers in our relationship."

"You do wear them, honey, but ask yourself who buys them for you."

"What if we're not, though?" Sally asked suddenly. "What if we're not made for each other?"

Until then, Nick had listened with apparent amusement as Sumaira attempted to talk them into Match Your DNA testing. It hadn't been the first time she'd raised the subject in the two years they'd known each other, and Nick was sure it wouldn't be the last. Sally's friend could be both belligerent and persuasive at the same time. But Nick was surprised to hear Sally say this. She'd always been very anti-Match-Your-DNA, as was he. "Excuse me?" he said.

"You know that I love you with all my heart and I want to spend the rest of my life with you, but…what if we aren't actually soul mates?"

Nick frowned. "Where's this coming from?"

"Oh, nowhere, don't worry. I'm not having second thoughts

or anything." She gave him a reassuring pat on the arm. "It's just that I was wondering are we happy to just *think* we're right for each other or do we want to *know* for sure?"

"Babe, you're drunk." Nick dismissed her and scratched at his stubble. "I'm perfectly happy knowing what I know, and I don't need some test telling me that."

"I read something online that said Match Your DNA is going to break up around three million marriages. But within a generation, divorce will barely be a thing anymore," Sumaira said.

"That's because marriage won't be 'a thing' either," Deepak retorted. "It'll become an outdated institution, you mark my words. You won't need to prove anything to anyone because everyone will be partnered with who they're destined to be with."

"You're really not helping me here," Nick said, and dug his fork into the crumbly remains of Sally's raspberry cheesecake.

"Sorry, mate, you're right. Let's have a toast. To the certainty of chance."

"To the certainty of chance," the others replied and clinked their glasses against Nick's.

All but Sally's glass reached his.

5

ELLIE

Ellie swiped the screen of her tablet and begrudged the extensive list of tasks she needed to complete before her working day was over.

Her assistant, Ula, was ferociously efficient and updated and prioritized the list five times daily, even though Ellie never asked her to. Instead of finding this useful, Ellie often felt animosity for both the tablet and Ula for their constant reminders of her failing in reaching the bottom of the list. Sometimes she felt the urge to shove the device down Ula's throat.

Ellie had hoped that by now, being her own boss, she'd have hired enough reliable staff to whom she could delegate a large proportion of her workload. But as time marched on, she gradually began to accept the label of "bloody control freak" that an ex-boyfriend had once thrown at her.

Ellie glanced at the clock. It was 10:10 p.m., and she realized she'd already missed the celebratory drinks for her chairman of operations, who'd recently welcomed his son into the world.

She doubted anyone had believed her promise to attend—she rarely found the time to fraternize—and while she encouraged it among her staff and even subsidized the company's social club, when it came to her own participation, time had a habit of getting away from her, despite her best intentions.

Ellie let out a long yawn and glanced out of the floor-to-ceiling glass windows. Her ostentatiously unostentatious office was on the seventy-first floor of London's Shard building, and the panoramic view allowed her to see way beyond the Thames below, out toward the colorful lights illuminating the night sky as far as the eye could see.

She slipped out of her Miu Miu heels and walked barefoot across the thick white rugs which adorned the floor toward the drinks cabinet in the corner of the room. She ignored the stock of champagne, wine, whisky and vodka and chose one of a dozen chilled cans of an energy drink instead. She poured it into a glass with a handful of ice cubes and took a sip. The decor of her office was as sparse as her home, she realized. It said nothing about her. But when you didn't care enough about your own decisions it was far more convenient to pay interior designers to make them for you.

Ellie's business was her priority, not the thread count of the Egyptian cotton covering her bed, how many David Hockney paintings hung from her picture rails or the number of Swarovski crystals used in her hallway chandelier.

She made her way back to her desk and reluctantly glanced at the next day's to-do list, which Ula had already compiled. She waited for her driver and head of security, Andrei, to take her home, where she planned to read her PR department's suggestions on her upcoming speech to the media about a new update to her app. This update would revolutionize her industry, so she had to get it right.

Then, at 5:30 a.m. the next morning, a hair stylist and a makeup artist would meet her at her Belgravia home ahead of the prerecorded television interviews with CNN, BBC News 24, Fox News and Al Jazeera. Afterwards, she would sit down with a journalist from *The Economist*, pose for some photographs for the Press Association and hopefully be back home no later than 10:00 a.m. It wasn't the best way to begin her Saturday, she thought.

Ellie's publicist had forewarned the news agencies that she was only prepared to discuss her work, with strictly no questions to be asked about her personal life. It was why she'd recently turned down a profile feature with *Vogue* complete with a shoot with legendary photographer Annie Leibovitz. The column inches could have been vast and picked up by publications across the globe, but it wasn't worth the expense of her privacy. That had already suffered enough over the years.

Along with being notoriously aloof about her life outside of work, Ellie also didn't want to publicly address the level of criticism her business received—she trusted her PR team to deal with any negativity on her behalf. She'd learned from mistakes of the late Steve Jobs concerning the handling of the iPhone 4 antenna issue and how much damage it had, at the time, caused to the reputation of both the brand and the figurehead.

Her personal mobile phone lit up on her desk. Few people had the privilege of that number or her private email address—in fact, just a dozen of her four thousand employees worldwide and family members who she barely had time to see. It wasn't that she didn't think about her relatives often—she'd thrown enough money at them over the years to compensate for her lack of presence—but it all came down to there not being enough hours in the day and a lack of mutual understanding. Ellie didn't have children; they did. They didn't have a multibillion-pound global company to run; Ellie did.

She lifted the phone and recognized the email address on the screen. Curious, she opened it. Match Your DNA Match confirmed, it revealed. She frowned. Even though she had registered for the site a long time ago, her immediate reaction was still mistrust that one of her staff was playing a joke on her.

Ellie Ayling. Your designated Match is Timothy, male, Leighton Buzzard, England. Please see instructions below to discover how to access their complete profile.

She placed the phone upon the table and closed her eyes. "This is the last thing I need," she muttered to herself, and switched it off.

6

MANDY

"Have you heard from him yet?"

"Did he text you or email?"

"Where's he from?"

"What does he do for a living?"

"What does his voice sound like? Deep and sexy, or has he got an accent?"

The barrage of questions from Mandy's family came thick and fast. Her three sisters and mother hunched around the dining room table, hungry for information about her Match, Richard. They were equally hungry for the contents of the four boxes of take-out pizza, garlic bread and dips spread out in front of them.

"No. No. Peterborough. He's a personal trainer, and, no, I don't know what his voice sounds like," Mandy replied.

"Show us his photo, then!" Kirstin asked. "I'm dying to see him."

"I only have a couple I copied from his Facebook profile." In truth, there were at least fifty, but Mandy didn't want them to know how keen she was.

"Oh my God, you don't want to show us them because he sent you a picture of his willy, didn't he?" her mother exclaimed.

"Mum!" Mandy gasped. "I told you, we haven't spoken yet, and I haven't seen a picture of his willy."

"Talking of willies, I'm breaking into the meat feast," said Paula, and offered a slice to her sister. Mandy shook her head. It was her firm belief that, while her coupled sisters could afford to rest on their laurels and eat to their hearts and stomachs' content, she had to be careful what she ate. It didn't matter that it was a cheat day either; according to *Grazia*, the difference between a size fourteen and a size sixteen can sometimes be just one mouthful.

Mandy selected the shirtless picture of a surfing Richard and passed her phone around the table for her family to see.

"Bloody hell, he's a fit little bugger!" Paula shrieked. "Although he must be about a decade younger than you! You have a toy boy. You're one of those cougars, aren't you?"

"So when are you going to meet him?" asked Kirstin.

"I don't know yet. We've got to start a conversation first."

"She's waiting for another picture of his willy to make sure he measures up," Karen said, and they all burst into laughter.

"You lot have filthy minds," Mandy said. "I wish I hadn't said anything now."

For once, she was pleased she had some good news to share with her family when it came to her love life. With three younger sisters, two who had settled down and married—both to their DNA Matches—she was riven by insecurities, and she'd begun to feel like she'd been left on the shelf, especially since they'd started having children. Mandy was a thirty-seven-year-old divorcee, and she was beginning to feel as if she'd never be anything else. However, since Richard had come into her life—albeit not yet in person—everything was now looking up, and all she could think about was how things were about to change for the better.

The confirmation email she'd received from Match Your DNA had informed her that Richard had ticked the box which meant that in the event of a Match, his contact details could be sent out. He would also have received a notification informing him of this as well as Mandy's contact details, yet he hadn't been in touch. The suspense was killing her. However, Mandy was old-fashioned at heart and believed it the man's job to do the chasing.

"Right, this is what you need to do," began Kirstin. "First off, send him a text. Be proactive and set a date when you'll meet in person, at a restaurant or something…one of the fancy ones like Carluccio's or Jamie's. Then make him wait a few dates before you let him kiss you, let alone anything else."

"Oh to hell with that," interrupted Paula, who took a long drag from her e-cigarette. "The beauty of being Matched with someone is that you don't have to faff around with all that game playing. You know that you two are perfect for each other, so go and shag each other's brains out."

Mandy felt her face turn scarlet.

Her mother shook her head and rolled her eyes.

"Mandy's not like you, Paula," said Karen. "She's always taken things slowly."

"And look where that's got her." Paula turned to Mandy and said, "No offense. But what I'm saying is that she doesn't need to be that slow anymore. Mum would give her right arm to be a grandmother again, and Karen and I have spent enough on designer vaginas to not want to push another kid out. And, Kirstin, yes, I know lesbians can have babies, too, but you're too busy playing the field to even think about settling down. Mandy, grandchild number four rests on your shoulders. Just think, by this time next year, you could be married and pregnant."

All eyes flashed a wary look at Paula, who quickly said, "Sorry. I didn't think."

"It's okay." Mandy looked down at the table.

Mandy had always longed for a child of her own, and when she had been married to Sean, they had had a couple of near misses. She and her childhood sweetheart had married straight out of school, saved hard, bought a house together and had tried to start a family. It had completely shaken her world to lose those babies, and this had been part of the reason why the marriage had fallen apart. Sometimes there were times at night that, with only the silence to keep her company in her bedroom, she swore she could hear her biological clock ticking. She had probably less than a decade left to conceive a child naturally, and, even then, her body was prone to complications. During the many evenings she'd spent babysitting her nieces and nephew, she'd ached to have the same for herself, someone to love unconditionally. Of course she loved her sisters' kids, but it wasn't the same at all. She dreamed of having someone she had helped to create and mold, someone who depended on her, who needed her, who would always seek her out for guidance and who, until her dying day, would call her "Mum."

The thought of becoming a childless spinster was a terrifying prospect, and as the years sped past, Mandy worried that instead of a possibility, it was becoming more and more of a probability.

"I think you're getting a bit ahead of yourself," Mandy said. "I'm going to let him make the first move, and let's see how we get on from there, okay?"

The others nodded reluctantly, and Mandy recalled how, not so long ago, she'd been wary of registering with Match Your DNA. Her marriage had become unsteady because of the miscarriages, but the final nail in the coffin had been when Sean suddenly left her for another woman eleven years her senior. He had taken the test without Mandy's knowledge and been Matched. He promptly ended their marriage, and once their house was sold, he had moved to a country chateau in Bordeaux to be with his French Match. Mandy had been left to pick up the pieces—a tiny starter home and a broken heart.

Match Your DNA was no longer the enemy—time had healed Mandy's relationship with the thought of it. And now, after three years as a singleton, she was ready to share her life with someone again, this time with someone who'd been made for her, rather than leaving it to chance. What could possibly go wrong?

She hoped her Match was thinking the same thing, although he was taking his time getting in touch. She prayed that he wasn't already married and that she wasn't about to break up a happy home, like Régine had done to her, just to get the husband and child that was rightfully hers.

7

Christopher sat at the antique wooden desk in the box room which was situated at the rear of his two-story apartment.

He turned on both computer screens and his wireless Bluetooth keyboards, and adjusted their positions until they were perfectly parallel to each other. He opened up his emails on the first screen, and on the second he flicked though several programs before clicking on the Where's My Mobile Phone? link he'd downloaded some months ago. Twenty-four different phone numbers appeared on his screen, but just two flashed in a bright green color to indicate their users were on the move. That was about usual for this time of the evening, he reasoned.

It was the penultimate phone number that piqued his curiosity. He opened a map in his toolbar and added a red ring to indicate where the user was. Her phone's GPS system offered her current location as the street where she lived.

Based on her typical pattern of behavior, Number Seven would have just finished a shift at the no-frills Soho chicken restaurant where she worked until around 11:00 p.m. She would then have caught the number 29 bus home. He predicted she would be settled in her bed within the hour before her second job as an office cleaner began in central London at 6:00 a.m. It was between those hours that Christopher's work could begin.

When narrowing down his choices, he had factored in how he would reach them, and he knew fairly well the distance between his and every one of their homes. He'd learned from the error of others like him that there should be no pattern to the location of his marks—keep everything random on the surface but in perfect order underneath. And over time he'd worked out whose property he should drive to, who'd be best served by bike and which locations would be better reached on foot.

Number Seven's flat was just a twenty-minute walk away from his house. "Perfect," he muttered, happy with himself.

But his attention was diverted from the red circle on one screen to the other, which displayed his dozens of email accounts. The email from Match Your DNA had remained unopened since it appeared in his inbox four nights earlier, when he'd been preoccupied with Number Six. But on seeing it again, he became curious as to the woman his biology had determined was best suited to him. At least he hoped it was a woman—he'd read stories about people being Matched with someone of the same sex or with people decades older than them. He didn't want to be loved by a queer or a geriatric; in fact, Christopher didn't really want to be loved by anyone. He'd wasted enough time in brief relationships throughout his thirty-three years to comprehend the amount of effort required to satisfy another person. It wasn't for him.

Yet for all the drawbacks a potential Match presented, he was still inquisitive as to whom his would be. He glanced out of the window and into the darkness of his garden and allowed himself to imagine how amusing it would be to carry on with his project while pretending to live a normal, pedestrian existence as one half of a couple.

He opened the email. Amy Brookbanks, female, 31, London, England, it read, along with her email address. He liked the fact that she hadn't given her mobile number; it showed caution. So many of the girls on his list hadn't shown that degree of foresight, and it had been—and would continue to be—their downfall. He decided that when he returned home later that night, he would send Amy an email and introduce himself, just to see what she had to say.

As predicted, on his other screen, the location of Number Seven's telephone number remained stationary. Satisfied, he turned both monitors off, locked up the room and made a beeline for the kitchen cupboard where he kept his packed bag. He put his freshly disinfected cheese wire with the wooden handles in the bag, along with his pay-as-you-go phone with her number taped to the back of it, his gloves and his Polaroid camera.

As Christopher slipped on his gloves and overcoat, he glanced at the camera. It wasn't an original from back in the 1970s because the paper required for each print was too easy for the police to trace. His camera's paper was widely available, and the camera itself was digital, boasting up-to-date features such as colored filters. Each Number on his list had used a profile picture that had also been Instagrammed, and as he closed the door to his house, adjusted the straps on his backpack and walked briskly along the quiet street, Christopher knew he wanted his Numbers to look their very best, even in death.

8

JADE

Jade looked on amused as the hotel spa's beauty therapists, Shawna and Lucy, opened their plastic Aldi bags to take out their miserable-looking lunches.

The contents of Shawna's bag consisted of half-a-dozen thinly sliced celery sticks wrapped in cling film and a pot of low-calorie piri-piri hummus, while Lucy tucked into a gluten-free seeded roll and a chicken Cup a Soup, which was still steaming from a blast in the canteen microwave.

Jade took out her Tupperware lunch box from her handbag. She'd packed a bag of pickled onion Monster Munch, a small packet of Maltesers, a doorstop-chunky ham-and-pickle sandwich and a can of Pepsi. She had no desire to replicate the diets of her thirtysomething workmates. *Bugger the bikini*, she thought, as she took a bite of the sandwich.

"So how are things going with that guy you were seeing from the club?" Shawna asked Lucy, and licked a drop of hummus that'd fallen onto one of her false fingernails.

"He's being bloody idiot." Lucy sniffed. "He told me he was taking me out to dinner last night—which turned out to be at Nando's—then spent the rest of the night staring at the skanky lass working the till. I mean, who does that when you're on a date? It's so disrespectful."

"Seriously? He is such a player."

"I know. He's coming round mine tonight, though. I said I'd cook. What about you? What about that lad with the tattoos from Tinder?"

"You mean Denzel? He says he really likes me, but then I don't hear from him in like four days. What's up with that?"

Jade shook her head and took another bite from her sandwich. "Terrible. I don't know how you put up with it. I'm so glad I don't have to go through that anymore," she said between mouthfuls. It was conversations like this that reminded her of how lucky she was to have found Kevin on Match Your DNA, but she was annoyed that he couldn't live any closer than half the world away in Australia. Before she'd received the email confirming her Match, she'd been in the same position as her workmates, only she liked to think she was more discerning with her men. In reality, she had dated just as many losers, or "stopgaps" as *Cosmopolitan* branded them.

"Yeah, you've got it easy," Lucy said. "You've found your lad."

"But it's not like he's on my doorstep, is it?" Jade replied. "I can't just pop round for dinner and a snog, can I? At least you're actually interacting with these boys, even if they treat you like shite."

"That's just how men are, though, isn't it?" said Shawna. "If you're not one of the millions on that register who've been Matched already, then you've got to make do with what you can get until Mr. Right turns up. *If* he turns up."

"Until then we're gonna have to put up with a lot of shitbags," added Lucy.

"No, girls, you're wrong there." Jade delighted in telling them what they should do. "If us lasses all got our heads together, re-wrote the girl code and agreed to *stop* letting ourselves be treated like crap, then boys would have no choice but to up their game. Until then, they're just going to keep carrying on because we let them."

"What I don't get is what's stopping you from going over to Australia and living happily ever after with Kevin?" Shawna said. "If science reckons he's the one for you, then what are you doing wasting your life here?"

"I can't just drop everything and go." Jade shook her head firmly. "Do you know how much flights to Australia cost? I've only just finished paying off *one* of my credit cards. Plus I've got my flat, my career, my family to think about..."

"Your flat's rented, you don't have a career, you have a job you hate—I know that because we all hate this place—and you see your family once in a blue moon. So when it comes down to it, you don't have any excuse."

"It's not like you're taking a bloody huge leap of faith either, is it?" Lucy continued. "You were, literally, made for each other. Tell me what you like about him."

Jade laughed. There was nothing she disliked about Kevin. Well, except his postcode. "He's funny, he makes me feel good about myself, he's kind, he has a gorgeous smile..."

"Have you been sending each other sexy selfies?"

"Of course not." Jade was adamant. "I'm not a slag." In real-ity, she'd tried once, but Kevin didn't seem keen.

"Christ." Lucy laughed. "There's enough naked selfies of me floating around cyberspace to break the internet."

Jade agreed and gave one of her raucous laughs that every-one loved her for.

"Well, if you don't do that, then you sext, right?" Shawna interrupted.

"Sext?"

"Yeah, send each other filthy text messages or talk dirty down the phone to each other? Tell him what you want to do to him when you see him?"

Jade shook her head.

"What about sexy time on Skype? Or FaceTime?"

"Kevin doesn't have either." Jade had suggested Skyping a couple of times, but he didn't have a laptop or a smartphone. If she thought her finances were bad, it was nothing compared to Kevin and his little backwater town. It was one of the many things they had in common.

"Did you say he lived in Australia or 1950?" Shawna continued. "It's not like you to let a man fob you off."

"I don't need to see him moving around and gurning like a bloody idiot to know how I feel about him."

Shawna's and Lucy's eyes met and simultaneously nodded.

"It's definitely love, then," said Shawna. "Nothing gets past our Miss Jade Sewell, but if he's as awesome as you say he is, you need to stop wasting time here and get out there and see him."

"Or you'll end up like us," giggled Lucy, although Jade could sense something in her tone that resembled a warning. "Seriously, Jade, pet, we've got slim pickings to choose from here. Every day, another fit lad gets snapped up by his Match. Me and Shawna are like vultures left picking at the bones of what's been left behind, and, believe us, it isn't canny. It really isn't. If I had a chance to be with my Match, I'd be on the next plane out of here, not sitting on the floor eating lunch round the back of a service entrance of a hotel."

"Yeah, stop making excuses," Shawna added.

"Girls like us don't do that sort of thing," Jade said, taken aback by Lucy's directness. "I can't leave everything behind and go, just like that. And like I said, a flight to Australia costs an arm and a leg."

"How much do you have left on your credit card?"

"Well, I just finished paying one off..."

"What's your card limit?"

"A couple of grand, I think."

"Then whack your holiday on the plastic. What have you got to lose? You need to grow some balls, bonny lass."

"Don't make me get my balls out and slap you round the face with them. It's just not me to chase a lad round the world."

Shawna and Lucy glared at her, both of them with their tattooed eyebrows raised as far as the Botox would allow. "It's not chasing him, honey. He's already yours."

"I can't," repeated Jade, then paused. "Can I?"

9

NICK

"I think we should do it," Sally muttered, as she lay on her back staring at the exposed beams holding up the bedroom ceiling, illuminated by the streetlamp outside.

"It usually takes you longer than that, but I'm not complaining," Nick replied, and he removed his head from between her legs and surfaced from beneath the duvet. His hand moved toward the bedside cabinet where she kept their toys.

"Not 'it' as in sex," Sally said. "I think we should do the Match Your DNA test."

Nick maneuvered himself back to his side of the bed. "Way to kill the moment, babe."

"Sorry."

"Why now? Before Sumaira and Deepak rocked up for dinner and started talking about it, you were adamant we didn't need to do it."

"Oh, baby, I still am," she said, her fingers playing with the hairs on his chest as if to reassure him. "But like Sumaira says, it'll give us a bit of added security, just to know. To really *know*."

Bloody Sumaira, thought Nick, but he didn't complain aloud. "Are you sure this isn't your way of telling me you have pre-wedding jitters?"

"Of course not, silly." Sally pulled his head down to kiss it. "But you know what I'm like. It's okay for you. Your parents have been together since the Dark Ages, while my mum's been married three times, and my dad is on his fourth wife. They're both always searching for something they don't think they have, and I really don't want to be like them. I want to know that, at least biologically, we stand a chance."

"What if it turns out our DNA doesn't Match?"

"Then we'll be mindful that maybe we'll need to put more effort into our relationship. Like John Lennon said, 'All You Need Is Love.'"

"Yes, but he also said, 'I Am The Walrus,' so let's not hold too much credence to his pearls of wisdom."

"So you'll do it?" She gave him an imploring look.

Nick couldn't say no to those puppy-dog eyes. "If it makes you happy, then yes, I'll do it. Now can I go back to doing something else that makes you happy?"

Sally caught a flash of his smile before Nick's head disappeared back beneath the duvet and between her legs.

10

ELLIE

The clock radio hit 3:40 a.m. as Ellie finally gave up trying to get to sleep.

With a busy day ahead, she desperately needed to get some rest, but her active brain didn't seem to get the message. Instead, it raced at the speed of a runaway train with what she needed to accomplish in the next few hours in order to promote her newly revamped app. Under normal circumstances she'd have taken one of the sleeping tablets her private physician had prescribed for her, but she couldn't risk feeling groggy when she needed to be on point.

Being interviewed by the world's press was something Ellie had grown to loathe since reluctantly becoming a public figure. A decade earlier, she was another anonymous worker bee, busy behind the scenes. Then the next thing she knew, the world's media was both praising her and lambasting her in equal measure. It had made her a tough cookie, and she fast gained a reputation for being someone who was ruthless in her quest to make her business one of the world's most successful. They hinted at the unscrupulous methods she may have used to get there, but with no concrete evidence, it was all just rumor. Ellie had paid enough people off to make sure the full story of her early days in business were never truly revealed.

As public appetite for her story grew, the tabloids had sifted through every piece of her private life, examining her past as if she were on trial. They picked apart her former relationships and threw enough cash at her exes that they spilled the beans on what she was like as a person, as a girlfriend and as a lover.

It made Ellie not just wary of the press but of everyone else, too, and made dating a near impossibility. And while she acknowledged it was unfair to tar every man with the same brush, each time she met someone new her barriers would go up, and she'd attempt to second-guess the motivation behind their interest. Were they only interested in her wealth? Did banging a billionaire make for good bragging rights to their friends? Or was she going to see another kiss-and-tell headline in the *Sun on Sunday*? Ellie couldn't remember a time when Bill Gates, Mark Zuckerberg or Tim Cook had been hauled over the coals for their sex lives, yet it seemed to happen to her with an overwhelming frequency.

She rolled onto her side, stretched out her legs and recalled how she had been forced to employ a legal team specifically to fire off warning shots every time she had an inkling the press was up to no good. Then, after a half-dozen successful libel cases, she became too costly to lie about, so they lost interest. Her media team became the go-to guys for all press inquiries, and she turned off her Google Alerts, Facebook and Twitter accounts to remove any temptation to discover what people were writing about her. Only when absolutely necessary would she step out publicly as the company's figurehead.

Ellie gave a frustrated groan at her lack of tiredness, threw her sheets to one side and turned on the bedside lamp. She remembered the email she'd received hours earlier, confirming a DNA Match had been identified. She'd signed up some ten years earlier, when the company was still in its infancy, and as its popularity quickly rose she had assumed it'd just be a matter of time before she found her Match.

But when the number of registered users had powered through the one billion mark, Ellie had begun to give up hope. Her Match was either in a happy relationship with somebody else, he was living in a developing country with no access to or knowledge of the test, or he was just not interested in knowing.

So Ellie had grown accustomed to spending her life alone and, in recent years, had become too consumed with work to even care. She didn't need a relationship to make her content; she could do all that for herself. What could a Match add to her life that she wasn't capable of finding on her own?

Nevertheless, she had to acknowledge that a tiny part of her was interested in who this person was.

"Sod it," she said out loud, and grabbed her phone. She opened her email, paid the £9.99 for her Match's details and waited. Two minutes later, an automated response landed in her inbox.

Name: Timothy Hunt. Age: 38. Occupation: systems analyst. Eyes: hazel. Hair: black. Height: 5ft 9in.

His description accounted for almost half the men in the Western world, she thought.

Ula. She began to type an email to her PA. Discover what you can about a Timothy Hunt, a systems analyst from Leighton Buzzard. His email address is copied below. Email me what you find out in the morning. Thanks.

To her surprise, Ula emailed her back immediately. *Does she ever bloody sleep?* Ellie wondered. Has he got a job interview with us? I can't see him on my list, Ula asked.

Sort of, Ellie replied. And make sure you find a photograph of him. Hire outside help if you need it.

Ellie placed her phone back on her nightstand and climbed back under the duvet. She turned to lie on her other side and stared at the vacant half of her bed, the sheet just as crisp and unwrinkled as when her housekeeper had laid it that morning.

And for the first time in a handful of years, she allowed herself to imagine what it might feel like to share that space with somebody else.

11

MANDY

Mandy hovered at the stone wall which surrounded the address she'd pulled from Richard's Facebook page. She watched everyone ahead of her hurry up the path, escaping the drizzle, and prepared herself to follow them.

Although she was generally a confident person in most social situations, when it came to large groups of strangers she clammed up and was prone to becoming tongue-tied. She had no idea what she would say if anyone attempted a conversation with her, so she tried to keep a low profile. It wouldn't matter if she were a few minutes late—nobody knew or was expecting her.

Mandy hadn't thought twice about throwing a sickie from work, and had told her sisters she'd be out of contact on a course. Even if they did find out that she was lying, they'd probably assume it had something to do with Richard Taylor, her DNA Match, anyway.

She took a packet of mints from her handbag and popped a sugar-free Polo into her mouth. She also took out her hand-held mirror and angled it in an attempt to check that she still resembled something presentable after the two-hour-long car journey. She ruffled her hair, hoping the damp hadn't made her curls too frizzy.

Finally, when she heard music begin to play inside, she walked slowly up the path, approached the door and braced herself for what she would confront inside.

If she were being brutally honest with herself, she didn't know what she was doing there or what she was going to get out of it. She was only aware that she and Richard were destined to share something together, no matter how complicated that might be. So she made her way inside and found a seat at the very back.

She picked up an order of service that'd been left at the end of the pew and flicked through it, trying to calm her nerves. Two guitarists played by the microphone stand at the front, singing along to a ballad that she didn't recognize. Upon finishing, a man with a sincere smile replaced them.

"Thank you, Stuart and Derek," he began. "First of all, I'd like to thank you all for coming. And secondly, on behalf of the Taylor family, I'd like to welcome you all to St. Peter and All Saints Church for a special ceremony in memory of our dear friend, Richard."

12

CHRISTOPHER

Christopher stared hard at her through the restaurant window, attempting to decipher her body language.

Amy, his Match Your DNA date, was sitting at the table with her arms folded and her legs crossed at the ankle. She looked nervous, he thought. But according to one of the many instructional YouTube videos he'd viewed, this meant she was defensive. Either one worked for him, as it put him at an advantage.

Amy glanced at the clock on her phone's display at least once per minute. She frequently fiddled with her hair or tapped her feet against the leg of her chair. She was an attractive woman, he conceded, and looked exactly like the picture she had emailed him, after having been filtered, of course.

Her long, dark hair had a slight wave to it. Fashionable black-rimmed glasses framed her eyes, and her use of makeup on her pale skin was subtle. She was of a slim build but did little to advertise it, playing it safe with trousers, heels and a plain blue top and jacket.

Christopher was aware it was perceived to be bad social etiquette to arrive late for a date, especially with a person science decreed had been made for him. But he didn't care; it was all part of the game. It was better to keep her waiting and on edge, as then he'd be in control of the situation and maintain the upper hand from the off.

As he bided his time outside the busy restaurant, he caught sight of his own reflection in the window. He'd not been acquainted with a good night's sleep for some weeks, so had bought a cover-up stick from Boots to dab at the bags and shadows under his eyes. He'd also used a tinted moisturizer he'd obtained from the bathroom cabinet of Number Four to disguise the fact his nocturnal project affected his melatonin levels; he mainly slept during the day.

While he'd found time to shave, he hadn't been able to book an appointment to get his hair trimmed, so he'd done the best he could with his side parting, using a generous helping of a product that made it look much darker than its usual reddish brown color. He smiled to himself, satisfied that, unlike many of his former schoolmates, his wrinkles were minimal, his teeth were as near to straight as could be, and his features were angular rather than plumped by excess skin. He looked at least five years younger than his thirty-three years.

Christopher straightened the lapels of his tailor-fitted jacket, holding out a little longer until Amy looked like she was about to leave, and then entered the restaurant.

His eyes scanned the generically furnished room as he pretended to search for his date. Her frustration at his tardiness dissipated the moment their eyes locked. To Christopher, it looked as if an invisible force had thrown her back into her chair, as she stammered a nervous, "Hello."

"Amy, hi. I am so sorry I'm late." Christopher apologized, shaking her hand confidently, and kissed her on both cheeks.

"That's okay, I only just got here myself a few minutes ago," she lied and swallowed hard.

"I was held up at work on a new magazine I've been working on," Christopher said as he took his seat. "And then I got stuck in traffic."

"You said in your email you were a graphic designer?" she asked. As she drank him in he could tell that she was playing it cool.

"Yes, I'm freelance, so I have a quite few projects on the go at any one time."

"Who do you design for?"

"Mainly luxury trade magazines, you know, companies that build yachts or planes and brochures for holiday destinations that you won't find at Thomas Cook," he boasted. "It's very exclusive."

She didn't look as impressed as he had hoped, and asked, "Where are you based?"

"I work from home in Holland Park which is convenient. Shall we order some drinks?"

Christopher moved his glass so it sat next to Amy's, then opened the wine menu. When the waitress arrived, he ordered the most expensive bottle on the list.

"Will you be eating tonight?"

He looked up and into the waitress's eyes as she spoke, wondering what noises she'd make if his trusty garrote penetrated her throat and severed her thyroid cartilage. It fascinated him how each one of his sitting ducks had, so far, offered a different squawk from the last.

Christopher looked at Amy and raised his eyebrows. "Do you have time for something to eat?" he asked.

"Yes, I'd like that," she replied, trying—but failing—not to appear too eager.

As they both read their menus in silence, Christopher felt Amy's eyes lift from the page to his face. He glanced at her, and she offered an embarrassed smile. Her cheeks flushed, and he looked to see if her irises widened. He'd read enough about human behavior to know that that meant she was attracted to him.

"I'm sorry, do you mind if I just quickly use the bathroom?" she asked. "You can order for me if you like. See it as your first test of how much of a Match we really are."

"Of course," he replied, and rose to his feet as she left the table.

Impersonating a gentleman came easy to Christopher, but other behaviors, like reading facial expressions and being mindful of people's emotions, he'd learned from books and online. He rehearsed several different smiles as he waited for Amy to return, and checked his mobile phone to see where Number Eight was. He hoped she would have returned home by the time he and Amy finished their desserts, as it was only a ten-minute car journey from the restaurant to her flat.

He spotted Amy slipping her phone back into her purse as she left the bathroom, and wondered if she'd called a friend to inform them her first date with her Match was going well. It was clear she was one of the 92 percent who felt an instant attraction to their pairing.

Then, as she sat down, there was something about the way her tongue ran over her lips that sent a mild rush of blood to his head, like the first puff from a cigarette or when he stood up too quickly. He dismissed it as tiredness and shook the feeling off as quickly as it had arrived.

"Is everything all right?" he asked. She was still visibly flushed.

"Yes, I just had to make a call to work," she replied. "It's been a chaotic few weeks."

"I don't think I asked you what you did for a living?"

"Oh, I thought I'd mentioned it?" Amy took a sip of her drink. "I'm a police officer."

13

Jade slept for around three fitful hours of her thirty-hour journey. Before that day, the farthest she'd ever flown to was Magaluf with the uni girls and that ended with her drunkenly getting No Entry tattooed on her left buttock.

Much of the journey from Heathrow to Bangkok, Thailand, and then to Melbourne, was spent with her fingernails embedded in the armrests of her seat, terrified that each jolt of turbulence was going to bring her plane down. That's one of the things she hadn't wanted to tell the girls when they were persuading her to come. She was *terrified* of flying. She read one of the several thriller novels she'd downloaded to her Kindle, then watched six movies back-to-back to take her mind off it. She eventually drifted off to sleep shortly before landing.

Jade had just enough time to change her outfit and freshen up before she picked up a pre-booked sedan-style hire car. She was relieved to discover Australians drove on the same side of the road. She programmed the vehicle's sat nav with the address to which she'd be traveling. It was some 250 kilometers to Echuca, Murray Basin, the place where she would begin the next phase— and the biggest adventure—of her life. As she drove along the Great Northern Highway, she sang along to Ed Sheeran and Beyoncé, and tried to keep her nerves at bay.

Jade thought about her conversation just ten days earlier with Lucy and Shawna. She'd stared at them across the canteen table, growing ever more conscious that she was morphing into them with their over-made-up faces, fake hair extensions and their obsession to stay skinny just to remain viable in an ever-shrinking dating pool. But she was grateful for their home truths. They were right. There was no excuse not to travel to Australia to meet Kevin. The only thing stopping her was the fear of the unknown. And, after she'd got the flight over and done with, Jade liked to think she wasn't scared of anything.

By the end of that week, Jade had purchased an open-ended return flight on her credit card to Australia. As Shawna was settling into Jade's sublet flat, Jade had made herself comfortable in an aisle seat on a Megabus to Heathrow, beside herself with what the next few weeks might hold.

She sent her parents a text message from the airport informing them of her plan. She assumed the speed at which they then phoned her meant they weren't supportive, although she couldn't be sure because she refused to answer. Jade knew just how quickly her fiery temper could flare, and she didn't want their negativity tainting the nervous anticipation she was feeling.

She took another glance at the picture of Kevin she had as her phone's screen saver and knew she wasn't going to be disappointed.

The three-hour car journey to Kevin's farm passed quickly, and she was on edge with a nervous excitement as she pulled the car over to the side of the road, stepping outside and stretching her tired legs. She was immediately struck by the searing heat and was glad she had lathered herself in factor fifty before setting off. Her pale skin could never handle the heat. She had no idea how it was going to fare here.

She glanced over at a sign reading Williamson's Farm, which was attached to waist-high wire fencing running the length of the dirt track road. Tall, scrawny trees framed the road with their trunks buried deep in arid soil, and in the distance, she could make out a large, white house and the roofs of outbuildings and barns which she recognized from Kevin's photos.

Jade felt her stomach begin to churn just like it had every other time she had daydreamed about what it might feel like to meet Kevin in person. Now the moment was almost upon her, and she was terrified, particularly as he had no idea she was about to appear at his home without warning.

Back at Heathrow Airport, she'd texted him a white lie, telling him she was changing mobile phone network suppliers, so she'd be out of contact for a day or two. He'd sounded agitated by the news, but she reassured him it wasn't her subtle way of trying to break up with him. Far from it, she thought to herself.

She picked up her phone and switched it to camera mode, then took a selfie of herself with Kevin's parents' farm in the background.

Hey, babe, you okay? she typed, her fingers trembling so much so that she was grateful for predictive text.

Hey! he replied, almost immediately. I've really missed you! You got your new phone sorted out?

Yes thanks.

I'm with the cows in the shed, the place reeks, man!

Aww, poor you! Guess where I am?

In bed?

Try again.

Still at work?

No, she replied and then sent him the photo she'd taken.

Her heart raced as she awaited Kevin's text. Instead, the phone rang.

"Surprise!" she squealed. "I'm here!"

"You shouldn't have come, I'm sorry," Kevin said curtly, and hung up.

14

NICK

"Don't open it!" Sally had yelled down the phone to Nick. She sounded anxious. "Wait until you get home and we'll do it together."

Sally had admitted to Nick that from the moment her smartwatch had indicated an email had arrived from Match Your DNA, her stomach had felt like it was trapped in a lift falling twenty flights. She'd called him immediately and, after checking his inbox while she waited patiently on the other end of the line, he found he, too, had received a notification.

At the media agency where he worked, Nick was supposed to be thinking of snappy, original ways to promote a new brand of intimate wipes for women, but he was instead wondering what the contents of the email might reveal.

But it was Sally's insistence on taking the test in the first place that really concerned him. He'd assumed they were content and in agreement that their future was together, but her need for scientific confirmation tapped into his recurring worry that he wasn't good enough for his wife-to-be, that their five-year age gap was too large and that he was, and always would be, too immature for her.

When Nick finally made it home, thirty minutes after Sally, she was already clutching her second glass of red wine, sitting on the kitchen island with her legs dangling over the side.

"Sorry I'm late," he began. "I got held up in a meeting and—"

"It doesn't matter," Sally interrupted and took an anxious gulp of her drink. "Can we get this over with?" She was rapping her other hand on the countertop, clearly nervous.

"May I say one thing first?" Nick asked, and perched on the island next to her. "I don't care what these results say. I could be Matched with Jennifer Lawrence as far as I'm concerned, and it wouldn't make the blindest bit of difference. You are the one I'm destined to be with, no matter what these emails tell us."

Sally smiled and hugged him, then picked up her phone and pressed the email icon. "Are you ready?" she asked, scrolling down and opening the message. Her face fell. "It says No Match."

A foreboding silence filled the room. Neither knew what to say to the other. Eventually, Nick wrapped his arm around her shoulder.

"We're going to make it work, I know we are," he offered. "Millions of couples have, and we'll be no exception. Just because we aren't DNA Matched it doesn't mean we aren't meant to be together. You still love me, right? After reading that, you still love me?"

"Of course I do." Her voice was muffled from where she'd buried her head in his shoulder.

"Then who cares what a bit of chemistry or biology says. Nothing is going to change that."

Sally swallowed hard and began to weep. "I'm sorry," she sniffed. "I just wanted to make sure we stood a chance…that we were predestined to be together."

"Fuck that, let's take a punt instead."

Sally smiled, and they rested their foreheads against each other's. She ran her fingers through his thick, dark hair, and drew his lips toward hers.

"Let's go out and get an early dinner," he suggested. "That new Turkish restaurant has opened on the high street. My treat."

Sally nodded, and Nick hopped off the island, making his way toward the coat hook on the back of the door to grab his denim jacket.

"What about yours?" she asked tentatively.

"My what?"

"Your results."

"I don't care." He shrugged. "I know what I need to know."

"And I need to know what you don't. Put yourself in my shoes—my fiancé is probably Matched with somebody who isn't me. I'd like to know who my competition is—if they've done the test."

"You have no competition."

"Nevertheless, please, babe, open it."

"Here, catch," he said as he threw his phone toward her. She caught it and searched for the email.

"Oh. My. God." She laughed loudly. She put her hand over her mouth and looked at him with wide-open eyes.

"What? Have I got a Match?"

"You certainly have." She was grinning.

"Oh Christ, please don't tell me I'm Matched with your mum."

"No, don't worry, it's not my mum," Sally replied. "Your Match is a man called Alexander."

15

ELLIE

Ellie's face felt rigid as if it'd been caked in concrete. She couldn't wait to return to her home and start removing the thickly applied makeup, layer by layer.

After a morning in front of cameras for various international TV news channels, a journalist from *The Economist* had tried to encourage her to discuss personal matters rather than just the launch of her company's updated app. But enough bullets had hit Ellie over the years to know when a writer was about to take aim. She'd dodged him by giving a polite smile and reminding him of what she was there to discuss.

As her head of security, Andrei, drove her from central London to her townhouse in Belgravia, she opened the secure internal company messaging system on her tablet and discovered a file that'd been sent by her PA.

"Timothy Hunt" read the folder, and Ellie realized it must contain the details she'd requested of her DNA Match. As her finger hovered above the icon, she was more nervous than she thought she'd be. She was anxious about what the folder might contain and just how much detail Ula had unearthed. She assumed Ula had taken her advice on subcontracting it out to the team her firm employed to carry out background checks on potential staff as well as investigate the threatening emails she often received.

She took a deep breath and opened it. There was a handful of documents: a photograph from a local newspaper of Timothy's provincial football team, his LinkedIn CV, his internet browser history from the last six months, a bank statement and some miscellaneous images. She didn't want to know by what dubious methods this information had been gathered.

Ellie clicked on the photograph of the football team first and read the caption below it, eventually locating the name Tim Hunt. She found him in the back row of the picture: a man of average build, with dark, short, receding hair, a beard and a big grin spread across his face. She immediately noted that physically he was not her usual type.

She scanned his CV and learned he'd worked his way through a succession of employers, chiefly in computing, since leaving university. His internet history was typical for a man of his age: YouTube links to 1990s music videos and *Family Guy* clips, football and Grand Prix results, the occasional pornographic site— but nothing freakish, she was relieved to discover—and regular visits to Amazon and Spotify for his films and music. He liked Coldplay, the Foo Fighters, Stereophonics and watching anything with Matt Damon or Leonardo DiCaprio in it, none of which were to her taste. His bank statement divulged his supermarkets of choice were Tesco and Aldi; he bought most of his clothes from Burton's and Next; he donated by direct debit to Alzheimer's and stray dogs' charities and put some money away toward his pension each month.

There was nothing in the file to suggest he was or had been married, that he had a current partner or any children. He had no criminal record, no bankruptcies nor any notable money concerns. His mortgage was modest, he repaid his credit card on time, and he had no student loan left. His social media presence was almost zero, with the exception of some comments on a Cambridge United FC message board.

In short, it appeared Timothy Hunt was an unremarkable man, though one with whom she shared an extraordinary link.

"Can we take a diversion to the King's Road?" Ellie asked Andrei, and within a few minutes, on her instruction, he'd purchased her a brand-new, no frills, pay-as-you-go mobile phone so she wouldn't have to give out her actual number. She hadn't used one of these since she'd been an impoverished student, and she caught herself smiling as she recalled a much less complicated time in her life.

She typed in Timothy's number and began to write a text. Hi, she said. My name is Ellie and we have been Matched up! She then paused, deleting the message. Too chirpy, she thought. Hello, I'm your Match on Match Your DNA. Would you like to meet me? Too slutty. Hi Timothy, I believe we're supposed to be spending the rest of our lives together, she typed, and then added a smiley face.

Ellie paused before hitting the Send button, then remained still with the phone in her hand, staring at it, scared of what the Pandora's box she'd just opened might contain. She didn't have long to wait—the phone's loud alert made her jump.

Ahh, the future Mrs. Hunt, what took you so long? Timothy responded and added a winking face. And please call me Tim.

He has a sense of humor, she thought, and immediately relaxed her tensed shoulders. Sorry, I was busy choosing my wedding dress, she typed and sent an emoji of a woman wearing a veil.

What a coincidence, so was I. So tell me a little about my wife-to-be, as I only know the basics. It'd be nice to find some common ground before I book the register office.

No church then?

No, satanists like me aren't welcome there.

Something we have in common, she replied and included a smiling devil icon.

What do you do for a living?

Steal their souls.

No, I said what do you do FOR a living, not WITH the living.

Sorry. Aside from worshipping Lucifer, I work in a boring office job. You?

Computer nerd.

Over the next thirty minutes, Ellie failed to notice the queue of traffic that was keeping her car stationary or the pouring rain that lashed against the window. When Andrei finally pulled up outside her house, she was glued to her phone like a schoolgirl as she and Tim continued messaging back and forth. Andrei opened the car door and then opened an umbrella.

Can I take my wife-to-be for a drink sometime? Tim texted.

I'm not sure… she replied.

I won't bite, honest. Sometimes we all need to take a punt.

Ellie bit her bottom lip and slipped the phone into her hand-bag, as Andrei escorted her into the house. She paused for a few minutes, weighing up the pros and cons of allowing a stranger into her life before making her decision. The very reason she took the Match Your DNA test had now formed into a living, breathing person. He had a name and a face and he was waiting to learn if she wanted to meet him. But she was scared. She removed the phone from her bag, then read and reread his text again before replying.

OK, I'd like that, she typed apprehensively.

Are you free on Friday night?

16

MANDY

Mandy learned much more about her DNA Match from his remembrance service than from her online research.

She felt like an impostor, sitting alone at the back of St. Peter and All Saints Church, listening to Richard's friends regale the congregation with anecdotes about his life, what inspired him and how he acted as their confidant. She discovered he was a team player both in and out of the sporting arena, a loyal pal and a shoulder to cry on. She learned that he'd played hockey and badminton for the county; he'd become a vegetarian at the age of twelve; and he'd overcome cancer when he was seventeen, his positive attitude getting him through chemotherapy. Mandy thought back to the photos of his global travels on his Facebook and wondered if it'd been his experience with the disease that had inspired him to see the world.

Richard had also run two marathons to raise money for Macmillan Cancer Support and had organized for local people with learning difficulties to take part in assault courses and exercise programs. In comparison, Mandy felt like the laziest and most selfish person, and she knew that, when her time came, she wouldn't be remembered in the same way as Richard for his philanthropy.

It had been a little over a fortnight since Mandy had learned the devastating news of her Match's death.

She'd become frustrated at still not having heard from him, so she decided to make the first move. She was careful not to mention in her introductory email that she had looked him up on social media or that she kept a folder on her computer with photographs she'd saved. But she included a picture of herself, a flattering one taken three years earlier when she was lighter, and before the frown lines from her divorce appeared, as well as her email address and mobile phone number.

Much to her disappointment, she heard nothing in return. Her first thought had been that Richard hadn't found her attractive, but then she reminded herself that if you've been Matched, looks were unimportant—supposedly. Had he been bitten by the wanderlust bug again and had gone traveling? There was no evidence of that online… Maybe he was in prison, cripplingly shy, dyslexic or had broken both his hands so he couldn't type… Mandy was clutching at straws.

It was only by chance when she clicked on his Facebook page—one of the many times that day—that she saw a message left by his sister, informing Richard's friends of the date and address of his remembrance service.

Mandy had glared at the screen, and reread the message. Remembrance? What the hell? It didn't make sense. Richard couldn't be dead. They'd only just found each other—how on earth could the one person in the world who was supposed to have been made for her no longer be living? And how had she not read about it sooner?

On further examination, Mandy discovered that while Richard's profile pictures were public, not all his posts were. She requested to be friends with him, in the hope that his sister approved it so she could learn more. And after a tense couple of days, the friend request had been approved. There, she found thread after thread of tribute messages from Richard's friends across the world, each paying their respects to a man who'd touched them all emotionally.

Grief threatened to tear her apart, and she did her best to fight it. She poured herself a glass of Prosecco and carefully scanned local newspapers online, piecing together information about his accident. While he was out celebrating a victory with a group of hockey teammates late one evening, he had become separated from them, stumbled into a road and was struck by a hit-and-run driver. He'd been found a few hours later on a roadside verge with serious head injuries.

Mandy succumbed to her emotions and began to cry and for the rest of the night—and into the early hours of the morning. She pored over photographs of Richard, aching for all he was no longer able to bring to her life.

They would never meet for that all-important first date, never would they make love for the first time. She would never hear him tell her that he loved her, build a life together or start a family. She would never know how it felt to be the single most important thing in somebody's life. Mandy's greatest fear was being realized—that she would remain where she had been since her divorce: alone, stagnating and washed up at thirty-seven.

She paced around her living room, wondering whatever she was supposed to do with her life now. She wasn't ready to accept what had happened. She needed to know more about the man who'd been stolen from her. So, having missed his burial, she decided to gate-crash his memorial.

As the tributes to Richard came to their natural conclusion, his friends made their way down the aisle and toward an open door, where Mandy could see tables laden with bottles of soft drinks, plastic cups, paper plates and napkins. She hesitated, aware that she didn't belong among the mourners, but nevertheless something compelled her to follow.

Soft rock played softly through wall-mounted speakers as a mixture of people, faces old and young, helped themselves to food and chatted. Mandy was unsure where to stand, and found herself gravitating toward a lively group of men and a young woman. She was animatedly recalling a time Richard raised money for an abandoned dogs charity by skydiving—despite being terrified of heights. Mandy hovered on the edge of the conversation, and savored the extra information she was gleaning about Richard from the woman's story. Another in the group told how Richard had persuaded some of his personal training clients to join him at London's annual naked bike ride, again for charity. Everyone had a funny memory of Richard, and as she listened to them regale these, she couldn't curtail her envy.

"Did he ever tell you about the time he got stung by jelly fish?" The words were out of Mandy's mouth before even she was able to be shocked by them.

"No." A man with a fringe that hung down to his nose said, and all eyes fell on her. "What happened?"

Her mind raced back through the photos she'd seen of Richard, and one in particular stood out where he was standing beside a large, white catamaran, preparing to jump onboard for a sightseeing tour.

"We were swimming in the ocean in Cairns," she began, "when this school of jelly fish started floating in. He saw me struggling in the water trying to get back to the beach, so he paddled out with his board and helped me to shore, even though he had to make his way through a cluster of them first and got his legs stung." She could picture everything she said with a crystal-clear clarity.

"Typical Rich," said the young woman, and the others nodded, smiling. Mandy smiled, too, and felt goose bumps running up her back—she'd gotten away with it; no one could disprove her.

"It didn't stop him from going back in the water, though," she added. "I'll always remember sitting in a restaurant opposite Sydney Harbour Bridge, drinking with him until the early hours of the morning, swapping stories about traveling. I'll really miss him." At least her final few words had a grain of truth in them.

"Sorry, we haven't been introduced," the woman said. She gently placed her hand on Mandy's arm, leading her away from the others.

"I'm Mandy," she said, and held out her hand.

"Chloe," the woman replied. "And how did you know Rich?"

Mandy tried to disguise the panic that was swiftly rising inside her. She needed to think on her feet. "We…err…met in Australia when he was traveling, then we stayed in touch when we got back."

"How long were you out there for?"

"Erm…a few months."

"And where exactly did you meet him?"

"I think he was with some friends in Cairns to see the Great Barrier Reef, and then we hung out for a bit in Sydney."

"Really? That's interesting." The woman feigned a smile. "Because I joined Rich for the Australian leg of his travels, and we were never out of each other's sight in Sydney."

Mandy had taken her fabrication too far. She felt her stomach flip as the woman glared at her with an incensed expression.

"Now you're going to tell me who you really are and why you're lying to people at my brother's memorial."

17

CHRISTOPHER

Christopher prided himself on many things—his appearance, his determination, his skills in manipulation and the fact that he allowed very little to wrong-foot him.

He liked to think he had a firm grip on his emotions. If confronted with something that diverted him from a plan he'd set out to achieve, his instinct helped him to adapt where necessary so he could maintain his objective.

However, Amy's admission that she was a police officer was a curveball. He'd been so wrapped up in keeping tabs on his other activities that it hadn't occurred to him that he should check her background. He'd taken it for granted that all women were like the ones he targeted—gullible, lacking his intelligence and too trusting. A police officer would be none of these things.

Finding one's Match had meant little to Christopher, and he hadn't planned on meeting her again. Their date had started as nothing more than a result of his mild curiosity, but now suddenly it had become interesting. Very interesting indeed.

"A police officer?" he repeated with a fixed smile. "That must be an engaging job."

"It can be," Amy replied proudly. "I'm a detective sergeant and it's hard work, especially when you're based within the Metropolitan Police. You can end up working all the hours God sends. But it's a career for life if I want it to be."

"I don't know much about the inner workings of the police," Christopher lied. "What is it that a detective sergeant does? Or is 'investigate' better terminology?"

"Either works," she said, and sipped her vodka and orange juice through a straw. "I've been seconded to the fraud squad for the last six months."

"What does that involve?"

Christopher failed to listen to Amy's response because he didn't care for the intricacies of a role in a department without any relevance to him, so he slipped into autopilot and pretended to appear interested instead. He maintained eye contact as she chatted, nodded where he thought a nod belonged and smiled where fitting. But inside, all he could dwell upon was the hilarious irony for the woman sitting opposite him to be Matched with the man who the *Sun* newspaper had branded Britain's Most Evil Killer.

Christopher was anxious to ask about the case that had dominated every television news bulletin for the past three weeks, but he didn't want to appear overeager. However, after half an hour of polite conversation, his ego got the better of him.

"So what's happening with that serial killer who's been all over the news, then?" he asked casually, cutting into his mushroom tartine. "How many women has he murdered, is it five now?"

"Six, well, six that we know about, but the team investigating is following various leads," Amy replied cagily. It was the same officially sanctioned answer he'd heard in televised police press conferences.

"You don't want to talk about it, do you?" he asked. "I'm sorry, that was inappropriate of me to ask."

"It's not that I don't want to." Amy placed her fork to the side of her plate. "Nothing makes the press go into overdrive more than when there's a serial killer out there somewhere. There haven't been many of them in recent years."

There are four active serial killers at any one time in Britain, Christopher wanted to inform her, *and you're having dinner with one of them.*

Amy continued, "There have been a lot of leaks in the press lately, so we're not supposed to be talking about the case to anyone."

"So I'm just anyone, am I?" Christopher asked, and offered his best puppy-dog eyes. This made her cheeks flush. He was determined to tease the truth from her; he'd yet to meet a person he couldn't manipulate in one way or another.

"Sorry, that's not what I meant." Amy smiled, and Christopher was pleased to see there were no crumbs of food trapped between her teeth.

"Well, let me change the subject," he said. "What made you do the Match Your DNA test?"

Amy looked him in the eye, clearly relieved to be back on a topic more suitable for a first date. "A lot of public sector workers like me take it because we don't have time to enter the dating scene. It sounds quite mercenary, but it's the best way of cutting out the middleman. You know, finding that person who's meant for you without having to go through all the nutters to get there. And you?"

Christopher's mind raced back to the books on relationships he'd highlighted with fluorescent marker pens, excerpts of what women wanted to hear from a prospective partner. He was quite convinced he'd already reeled Amy in by simply possessing the DNA that connected them, but whatever he said next needed to hit the right emotional note.

"I joined to find the other half who would make me whole," he began, and held her gaze as the books instructed. "I wanted to meet *the one* who accepts me for who I am, who loves me for all my faults and my quirks, and who will be there by my side for whatever challenges come our way."

Christopher tilted his head slightly to one side and shrugged, almost apologetically, as if to emphasize his sincerity. A peculiar feeling enveloped him for a second time, making his head feel woozy and his skin sensitive.

Suddenly the corners of Amy's mouth began to waver, and she laughed. "Are you serious?" she giggled. "You sound like you've just read that from a self-help book."

Christopher's mask slipped, and he felt something akin to embarrassment—one of many emotions he was aware existed but had rarely experienced. "Have I said something wrong?" he asked, genuinely baffled.

"No, no, oh God, oh God," Amy said. "You were being serious, weren't you? Oh I'm sorry, it just sounded a bit…cringe, that's all."

"Oh," said Christopher, still muddled, questioning whether Amazon had been recommending him the right books.

Amy leaned forward and spoke quietly but confidently. "Look, Christopher, this is how I see it. You and I have been Matched, which means we don't have to do all the things we did when we were dating other people. You don't have to stand outside the restaurant window and be deliberately late to put me on edge, you don't have to try to impress me by name-dropping the posh part of London where you live, you don't need to subtly inform me that the magazines you design aren't for people like me, and you certainly don't need to choose the priciest wine on the menu. We can move straight to the getting to know each other part and seeing what happens without the games. And right now—and this may have something to do with hormones, chemistry or the three vodkas and one glass of wine I've just drunk—but I might explode if I don't have sex with you very, very soon. Like, *now*, soon."

Christopher was taken aback. He hadn't met a straight-talking woman like Amy before; she was beginning to excite him, and he wanted to know what made her tick. The fact she was a policewoman should have scared him off, but it had the opposite effect, and he could feel himself becoming aroused by their cross-purposed interaction.

"Um, of course," he answered, and beckoned the waitress for the bill. He paid in cash, like he always did, and within ten minutes they were driving back to her house.

18

JADE

Jade removed the phone from her ear and glared at it in the palm of her hand, almost as if it were the phone that was the problem, and not the fact that her Match had just told her he didn't want to see her.

She had traveled for almost two days from England, and, as she stood at the top of his driveway readying herself to meet him, she'd wondered what the hell was going on.

She must have misheard him, she told herself, and called him back. When it went straight to voice mail, she called again. And once more, just in case.

WHAT THE HELL IS GOING ON? she texted in angry capital letters, and held the phone in front of her, waiting for a response. None came.

Jade felt the oppressive heat of the midday sun burning her exposed shoulders and neck, so she climbed back into her rental car and turned the air-conditioning on full blast. She had traveled so far, and Kevin was so close, there was no reason that she could see why he would reject her.

She contemplated the farm ahead, then turned over the car's ignition, performed a U-turn and began to drive slowly along the highway back in the direction from which she had come. She felt hurt and humiliated.

Jade pinched the skin between her thumb and forefinger to stop herself from crying. *There must be an excuse*, she thought: he was too nervous to face her and she'd backed him into a corner. She considered what her reaction might've been had Kevin suddenly turned up unannounced on her doorstep. (*Bloody elated*, she thought to herself, but then again, she knew that Kevin was a lot quieter than she was.) She had gone and put him in a very awkward position, and he needed time to process. She would give him that and then try again later. She told herself off for her spontaneous stupidity and seethed at Shawna and Lucy for having encouraged her to go along with this ridiculous idea.

She drove in the direction of a town she'd passed some twenty miles back. Once there, she would check into a hotel. Later, maybe even tomorrow, she would text Kevin and talk him around.

Are you stupid? Jade suddenly thought to herself. She blinked hard and furrowed her brow. *Why are you blaming yourself for this? Since when have you ever let a man make you question yourself? Kevin's the one in the wrong here, not you.*

Her mind raced as a whole other host of thoughts came to her mind, reasons why he might not want to see her. She had watched enough episodes of MTV's *Catfish* to know that hopeful romantics are duped all the time online by people pretending to be someone they're not. Maybe Kevin was actually a woman putting on a deep voice when they spoke, or maybe he was old enough to be her father and hadn't wanted to say? Or perhaps he didn't live with his parents on the farm but with his *wife* instead?

That must be it. Kevin was married, and that's why he hadn't wanted to Skype or FaceTime, in case his wife caught him. And he was probably talking to Jade on a secret, second phone his wife had no idea he owned. Maybe he had a child, too, or even several children with several wives, like the TV shows she'd watched about polygamists. After all her gloating that Kevin was different to all the scumbags Lucy and Shawna dated, it turned out that he was just the same. She punched the steering wheel in frustration.

The more thought Jade gave it, the more credible her theories became, and, in turn, she became even more furious. What a nice cozy setup Kevin had with his loved ones here in Australia and a girlfriend he would string along in another country. As long as he was cautious, how could he ever get caught out? It wasn't like his Match would travel to the other side of the world and turn up at his house out of the blue, was it?

"She sure as hell would," Jade muttered, feeling her temperature rise alongside her confidence. She jammed on the car's brakes and skidded to a halt, and after another hasty U-turn she was speeding back toward the farm, then down the dirt track toward the white buildings ahead, spitting gravel and dry earth in her wake.

The white wooden single-story farmhouse with the silver corrugated iron roof sprawled out in several directions ahead of her. A handful of cars and trucks were parked in front of it, their windows wound down but empty. For a farm, and a dusty one at that, everything looked surprisingly clean and polished, and not as impoverished as Kevin had her believe. A hosepipe lay next to a row of colorful flowers planted in pots. There were more hanging from baskets attached to eaves. Jade was certain the place had a woman's touch, but there were no swings or slides or children's toys that she could see, so maybe the Williamsons hadn't started a family yet.

Several hundred meters away, she could hear the cattle braying in a huge shed, and, way into the distance, she thought she could just about make out a large flock of sheep so far away, they looked like tumbleweed glued to a painting of the horizon.

Jade turned to face the house and didn't even need to take a deep breath before marching toward the porch door, clueless as to what she was going to say but determined to make her mark regardless. She rapped the knocker until she heard footsteps shuffling inside. Eventually the door opened and a face appeared.

The man standing before her looked just like her Match, but she knew what she felt in her gut was true.

"You're not Kevin," she began, and took two steps backwards.

19

"Very funny, who am I really Matched with?" Nick asked.

"I'm not joking. Look here." She held out the phone so he could read. "It says 'Nicholas Wallsworth. Your designated Match is Alexander, male, Birmingham, England. Please see instructions below to discover how to access their complete profile.'"

"Give me that," Nick said, and snatched the phone from her hand, unamused by her prank. But when he read the email himself, he realized Sally wasn't kidding.

"You're gay." She laughed. "My boyfriend, strike that, my *fiancé* is gay!"

Nick reread the email, then put his phone down on the kitchen counter. "This is bollocks," he said. "They've either made a mistake or someone is having a laugh at my expense."

"Well, it's 99.9999997 percent accurate, which is far more reliable than a lie detector test."

"Well then, there's still margin for error, and if there's margin for error, then errors must theoretically be possible. And this is the proof that an almighty fucking error has been made."

"Babe, don't get angry," Sally said, stifling her laughter. "But that would make you the first person in the world to be mis-Matched—the only person out of about one and a half billion who've registered. I think you need to face facts, my darling, you are a gentleman who enjoys the company of other like-minded gentlemen."

"Oh be quiet, Sal." Nick was becoming irritated. "This Match Your DNA crap is just a money-making scam, otherwise they wouldn't charge you a tenner to tell you who you've been Matched with. Horoscopes are more credible than this."

"Hey, it's not a problem," Sally teased. "I've always wanted a gay BFF, and it turns out I'm about to marry mine."

Nick rolled his eyes. "I'm not gay, all right?"

"Bisexual, then? I don't have a problem with that. You know I had my moments with girls when I was in uni."

"I think I'd have known about it by now if I were. You don't just get to the age of twenty-seven without a single moment of attraction to another man and then suddenly you're bisexual or gay because you've licked a cotton bud and a test says you are."

"I didn't realize you were so homophobic."

"I'm not! Believe me, if I were one or the other, you and I would not be living together and about to get married. It'd open up a new world of opportunities for me, and I'd be out there trying to stick my dick in a whole load of new places."

"You're taking this very seriously."

"I just don't want you thinking that I'm a secret closet case, because that'd mean our whole relationship was a lie. And this is the most honest relationship I've ever been in."

"Oh, honey, come here. I'm only teasing," Sally said. "I don't think you're gay, but you must admit, it's kind of amusing. You're like that old R. Kelly song... 'Your mind's telling you no, but your body—'"

"You are not funny." Nick topped up Sally's glass with wine and took a large gulp himself.

"Well, I don't know how else to react other than to joke about it, because apparently we are not destined to be together. And while the man of my dreams has yet to make himself known, the man of your dreams could be living in the next street to us. He lives in Birmingham, too. What kind of strange coincidence is that? We may even already know him..."

"Don't be silly. And there is no 'man of my dreams'..."

"Not according to the email..."

Nick rolled his eyes.

"Shall we see if we can find him on Facebook?" Sally continued.

"What?"

"Come on, let's see if I can find my competition."

"No, I don't want to."

"Are you scared you might develop a little bit of a crush on your future husband?"

Nick shook his head. "Look we don't even know his surname."

Sally took the phone from his hand and within three swipes of the keypad, paid the £9.99 required for more details. "Name: Alexander Landers Carmichael," she read out loud. "Age: thirty-two. Occupation: physiotherapist. Eyes: gray—like mine. Hair: dark—like mine." She smiled. "Height, five foot eight—again, like me. Babe, you do have a type, don't you? He sounds like my double."

"With three exceptions—two breasts and a vagina."

"That should be enough information to find him on Facebook."

"I don't really think I want to—"

"Oh come on, it'll be fun."

Sally typed in Alexander's name and scrolled down through the list of postage-stamp-sized pictures that appeared. "What are the chances of there being four Alexander Carmichaels in the Birmingham area? I'll use his middle name as well—there can't be that many Landers."

"Just the one it seems," Nick replied, pointing at the screen.

They simultaneously squinted at the thumbnail photograph and Sally tried to click on to his profile. However, Alexander Carmichael's privacy settings wouldn't enable anyone who wasn't his friend to look any further. But even from the small picture, both recognized he was a handsome man. His lantern jaw sported dark stubble, his hair had a slight curl and touched his collar, his lips were full and his eyes were wide and warm.

"I've got to hand it to you, babe," Sally said. "Your DNA has really good taste in men."

20

ELLIE

Andrei opened the car door for Ellie, and she followed him along the canal towpath and into the building ahead.

"You don't have to come inside, I'm sure it'll be okay," she told him, fairly sure there was little danger lying in wait for her in the provincial pub.

"This is what you pay me for," Andrei replied in his husky Eastern European accent, and went inside to scout the room regardless. Throughout his three years in her employment, he had proved he was worth his weight in gold, having taken punches and even a broken bottle thrust into his chest for her. Ellie turned her head to see the other two members of her security detail in a car parked behind the one she'd arrived in.

"Okay," she conceded, "but don't let him see you. Be subtle. I don't want you scaring him off."

"Subtle is my middle name," the six-foot-five-inch hulk replied, his tongue placed firmly in his cheek.

Once given the all-clear via text, Ellie entered the Globe

country pub in Leighton Buzzard and glanced around with trepidation. Back in her early post-university days she'd often frequent similar pubs to take advantage of their cheap Sunday lunches with all the trimmings. It had reminded her of home. Now when she went out of an evening, it was all pompous wine bars, exclusive members-only clubs and grandiose dining.

She spotted her DNA Match sitting alone at a two-seater table with a partially drunk pint glass in front of him. Tim, too, looked anxious, as his eyes flitted around the pub until they met Ellie's. Ellie hoped he hadn't recognized her from the newspapers. She'd deliberately dressed down in a casual pair of jeans and blouse and had tied her hair back. She'd kept her makeup to a minimum and left her expensive jewelry in the safe at home.

A broad grin spread across Tim's face as he waved. As she arrived at the table, he stood up to shake her hand, drew her in close and gave a peck on the cheek. She went for a second kiss on the other cheek, but caught him clean on the nose instead. Both laughed and after the initial introductions and pleasantries, Tim went to the bar to get her a drink. He returned to the table with her Hendrick's gin and tonic and a second beer for himself in his hands. Two packets of salt-and-vinegar potato chips dangled from his mouth.

"Sorry, but I'm starving," he said, dropping them onto the table. "I've got a massive workload on, so I came straight from work and skipped my dinner. Help yourself." He opened up one packet and offered her some.

"Thank you." She smiled, and took a couple of chips to be polite. She could picture the horrified expression on her personal trainer's face if he were to witness her eating carbs after 6:00 p.m.

The conversation between them flowed just as easily as it had by text message, as if they were two old friends who hadn't seen each other for some time and who were picking up where they'd last left off. They swapped stories about their dreadful dating histories, Tim tried to convince her that Quentin Tarantino was the greatest film director of all time while Ellie extolled the virtues of a macrobiotic diet. They shared barely any interests, but neither seemed concerned. He spoke about his work as a freelance systems analyst and computer programmer, while she told him she was a personal assistant to a CEO in London. She was too scared she would intimidate him if she revealed her real job, and was so convincing about her role that she began to believe her own mistruths.

"So do you believe in this Match Your DNA thing?" asked Tim, a few hours into their date.

"Yes. I take it from your tone you're not convinced?"

"I'm not going to lie, I was a bit unsure at first," he said, "and I only signed up because one of my mates convinced me to. Now he's pissed off because he still doesn't have a Match after two months, and I found you within a week. But even then, I wasn't sure if it was the real deal—it sounds too good to be true, doesn't it? That there's only one person in the world who's, like, really, completely, linked to you through your DNA and who you're supposed to fall head over heels in love with… But then you walked into the pub, and I thought my stomach had just fallen out of my arse."

He smiled as Ellie stared at him, partly in wonder at why such opposing personalities had been Matched and partly because he was the least pretentious man she'd ever met, let alone been on a date with.

"Honestly, Ellie, when I saw you come into the pub, I let out the longest fart, I thought I was going to fly across the room like a deflating balloon."

Ellie couldn't help but laugh along with him.

"I mean, it could be love or the beer might be off," he joked. "Who knows?"

"So was it love at first fart?"

"I reckon I did feel something and sorry if that makes you

feel awkward or if you're not thinking the same, but I'm really glad you agreed to meet me."

"So am I," replied Ellie, and she felt something warm inside her stir. Whether it was the four gin and tonics or the unlikely but endearing Match sitting in front of her, instinct told her that the landscape in her world had suddenly tilted.

21

MANDY

"I'm sorry," Mandy mumbled, overcome with feelings of nausea. "I really need to go."

Suddenly the last place she wanted to be was at the remembrance service for a man she'd never met. She'd never expected to be questioned by his sister as to why she was making up anecdotes about him.

She felt the walls closing in on her and regretted coming. But as she was about to hurry away, Richard's sister, Chloe, grabbed Mandy's arm.

"No," she said firmly. "You need to tell me who you are and why you're lying about you spending time with my brother when it never happened."

"I—I—" Mandy stuttered.

"Were you even friends with Richard?"

Mandy said nothing.

"I thought not. You're, what, ten years older than him? So you didn't go to school together. Are you one of those horny older women he trained at the gym who kept trying it on with him? Or are you some weirdo who gets her kicks from crashing funerals for people you never knew?"

"No!" Mandy was eager for Richard's sister not to think badly of her, though she understood how it looked. "I'm none of those things."

"Then who are you and why are you here?"

Mandy closed her eyes tightly. "We were DNA Matched."

"What?"

"I did the Match Your DNA test a few weeks ago, and I found out my Match had also done the test. But when I...wanted to meet him..." Mandy paused, feeling like an idiot. "He'd...he'd died. It was Richard."

Chloe paused and eyed Mandy up and down. "You're lying again."

"I promise you, I'm not. Look." Mandy opened her handbag and showed Chloe a printout of the email confirming their Match.

"Why are you here?" Chloe's tone softened as she digested the information before her.

"It sounds daft when I say it out loud, but I wanted to say goodbye to him. I've spent the last few weeks mourning a man I've never met, and I wanted to find out more about him. Everyone here has these great memories of your brother, and I have nothing, just a name and some pictures I found online. When I was listening to them talk about him, I got carried away and made up my own story. I'm sorry, it was silly and thoughtless, and I'm old enough to know better. I didn't mean to upset you."

"I think I get it," said Chloe, taking two glasses of wine from the table and passing one to Mandy. "So what do you want to know about Rich?"

Mandy's cheeks reddened. "Now I'm talking to you, I don't really know where to start."

"That's our mum over there, let me introduce you..."

"No!" said Mandy, panicking. "I don't think I'm ready for that."

"Well, why don't you leave me your contact details, and we can stay in touch for when you are." Chloe handed her phone to Mandy. "Maybe you could come round to the house and meet her sometime?"

Mandy nodded, and apprehensively typed her telephone number. "I should be going," she said. "It was nice to meet you. And I'm so very sorry about Richard."

"I'm sorry, too," Chloe replied. "I'm sorry for the both of you."

Mandy kept her head down as she passed Richard's mother on her way out of the church and hurried back toward her car. What had begun as a way to learn more about her late Match was supposed to have given her closure.

Instead, something told Mandy it was only the beginning.

22

CHRISTOPHER

"You fucking bitch!" Christopher yelled, trying to pry his throbbing, gloved thumb from the inside of her mouth.

She continued to clamp down upon it until Christopher thought she was going to hit the bone. But he couldn't let go of the wire around her neck until the job was done.

His ninth killing over a five-week period was supposed to have been as straightforward as all the others, and, just as he had with the other women, he'd done his homework on his latest target and had carried out a full recon on where she lived.

Security cameras were the potential downfall of any criminal, so he ruled out girls whose properties were located near to areas of high concentration, such as those where they were affixed to lampposts, shops, schools, offices or blocks of flats. Other cameras to avoid included CCTV on buses and in bus-only lanes, taxis, tube stations, speed cameras or vehicle number plate recognition systems. As long as Christopher steered clear, there was no reason why his presence in such vicinities should ever be flagged up after an event.

Once outside Number Nine's house, he'd double-checked her location on his GPS, and after waiting patiently for a period of time to make sure she was alone, he put his plastic overshoes over his own trainers so as not to leave any unique marks. He'd picked the lock of the back door using his same trusted kit and entered the flat, closing the door quietly behind him.

Once in position, he'd removed a white billiard ball from his backpack and dropped it to the floor, so it landed with a real thud. He'd stood in place with his hands gripped around the cheese wire's wooden handles, waiting for her to open her bedroom door to investigate the noise.

Number Nine's death should have followed a familiar, fail-safe pattern. Once she was in front of him, he would spring into action, forcing the last breath of life from her lungs with his garrote, arrange her still-warm body with gruesome symmetry across the kitchen floor and take two Polaroid pictures of her. Numbers One to Eight had been too stunned to put up much of a resistance, other than to clumsily claw at the wire to try to lever it off. The element of surprise combined with his strength and determination were always too powerful for them to surmount. He only stopped when he felt the wire sever their skin and begin to slice through muscle. If he allowed it to go any deeper, it would be too messy, and he didn't have the inclination to spend the remainder of his night in the midst of a full-scale clean up.

However, Number Nine took a twist when, much to his consternation, it was the bathroom door that opened after the billiard ball dropped—she had not been asleep in the bedroom as he'd assumed. He had jumped from the shadows, and she saw him face on. She had been too slow to prevent the wire from encircling her neck, and he'd moved swiftly behind her to pull on it with force. She was still wearing her heels, and their lack of grip against the tiled floor made her lose her footing. She slipped backwards to the floor, knocking Christopher off balance, and he'd fallen down with her.

In the confusion, the wire became slack, and she managed to slide her fingers under it, allowing her to continue breathing. She'd also turned her head, found his thumb and sunk her teeth into it with a vice-like grip.

"Fuuuuuck!" Christopher yelled from behind his mask and balaclava, and for the briefest of moments, he considered releasing his tight grip, the pain in his thumb increasing. He pulled her head backwards and pounded it against the kitchen floor. By the time he heard her skull crack, her jaw had loosened just enough for him to pull his thumb from her mouth. He slammed her head twice more against the floor until the blood pooled in the grouting between the tiles, and he knew there was no coming back for her.

He hurried across the kitchen to the stainless-steel sink, removed his glove and rinsed his wound under the soothing cold water. He took a tentative look at it; it wasn't as bad as he'd first thought, but it was deep enough to require stitches. He held his fury at bay long enough to wrap his thumb in a tea towel before taking two photographs of her with his Polaroid camera.

Then he stood over her body, lifted his foot and slammed it down on her face. Her nose crumbled like a soufflé. He began kicking her, incensed at her for having the audacity to fight back, and he only stopped when her ribs were in too many pieces to break any further. He took a bread knife from the kitchen counter and stabbed her in both eyes, turning the blade around in identical clockwise motions in each to spoon out any remains and wipe them across her face. She did not deserve to lie on the mortician's slab like the others, resembling someone who'd died peacefully in their sleep. He'd seen to it so that whichever poor sap of a relative had to identify her body would only remember her as the bloody patchwork of fragmented bones Christopher had created.

He felt exhausted and badly wanted to abandon the girl, return home and crawl into bed, but there was much left to do. He found a tube of strong adhesive in a kitchen drawer and sealed the wound on his thumb, bandaging it with some gaffer tape which would do until he could get home and dress it properly. After bleaching the sink free of any traces of his blood, he mopped the floor thoroughly of both of their bloods and stuffed her mouth with a cloth.

He grabbed a rolling pin from the countertop and, with much more force than necessary, smashed her teeth into tiny fragments. He pulled the cloth containing her teeth from her throat, folded it up neatly and put it in his bag. He didn't want anyone finding his DNA in her mouth.

Suddenly his phone vibrated; it was Amy calling.

"Hiya," she began, "what are you up to?"

"Not much," Christopher lied. He held his phone between his cheek and his ear as he poured bleach into Number Nine's mouth, letting it spill over the sides. *That should destroy any lingering traces of me*, he thought.

"You're not having a wee are you? I can hear running water."

"No! I was just cleaning my teeth."

While he wanted to get off the phone and complete his cleanup operation, Christopher was vaguely aroused by talking to his girlfriend at the same time as staring at the gruesome remains of the woman he'd just murdered. It was as close as the two women could ever be without being in the same room.

"I'm sorry I couldn't make it tonight, but are we still okay for tomorrow?" she asked. "Work's been hellish."

"Yes, that sounds good."

"Are you all right? You sound preoccupied."

"I'm just tired. I need a good night's sleep."

"Good, because when I see you next I'm not going to let you

out of the bedroom all night," she said in a flirty tone. Christopher smiled at the thought.

After they hung up, Christopher scanned the room, satisfied with the success of his cleanup operation. But while he didn't want to ever return to this botched job, he knew he'd have to come back in a few days to finish it off and leave his trademark.

He swallowed a couple of painkillers he'd found in Number Nine's handbag to relieve the pain in his thumb and left her house silently in the direction of his home. He took a detour up a quiet street of new-build four-story flats. He checked to see that he'd not caught anyone's attention and went around the back and found the door to the ground floor apartment, which was still unlocked.

The smell emanating from the room would've been over-powering to most, but malodorous scents, especially those of decomposing bodies, didn't bother Christopher. He swiveled the torch to shine it in Number Eight's face. Putrefaction had begun in her shoulders, head and neck, and on the right-hand side of her torso. It had left her skin a blotchy dark green, and her size six frame was now bloated by the accumulation of gas inside her, pushing out her belly and her tongue, and giving her eyes a bulbous appearance. Her veins had marbled, turning them browny black, and the skin on her arms and legs was blistering.

Christopher removed the photograph of Number Nine he'd taken an hour and a half earlier and carefully positioned it on her chest. Once back outside, he withdrew an aerosol can from his backpack and in one swift maneuver, sprayed black paint over a stencil on to the pavement. He stood back to look at his work—the effigy of a man carrying a child across water—and he smiled to himself.

It wouldn't be long before Number Eight was found, he thought. Because by now, everybody knew the calling card to look out for.

23

JADE

The man standing behind the open door to the farmhouse was definitely not Kevin, but they shared a likeness.

He was probably in his mid-twenties and looked a little older than Kevin. He, too, was startlingly handsome and sported blond hair, but it was darker and straighter than Kevin's. His blue eyes sparkled in the same way her Match's had in photos, but this man had a more angular nose and thinner lips. He looked apprehensive at her clear readiness to attack.

But despite her rage and also surprise, Jade managed to keep her wits about her and remained cautious. She kept a safe distance between herself and the stranger. Her car door was unlocked and she'd kept the keys in her hand in case she needed to beat a hasty retreat or even stab him with them.

"Who are you? You sure as hell are not the man I've spent the last seven months talking to," she barked.

He stared at her with a mixture of curiosity, fascination and fear. His mouth opened and closed several times as he struggled to formulate a sentence. She recognized from the way his chest quickly rose and fell that something was troubling him and that she had the upper hand. He was no threat to her, she decided. In fact, the only thing that was, was the sun. She thought of her poor white shoulders. "You'd better let me inside," Jade continued, momentarily forgetting she was asking to enter the home of a complete stranger.

The man nodded and moved to one side, and she made her way through the porch and into the cool, air-conditioned living room. The cold temperature was heavenly against the back of her sweaty neck.

As the door behind her swung shut, Jade noticed a wall of framed family photographs above a piano. They looked like your average, normal unit, and it gave her a little reassurance that she'd not just invited herself into a scene from *The Texas Chainsaw Massacre*. In one picture was a middle-aged man with a woman and two teenage boys, one of whom was the older version standing uncomfortably in front of her. The other was a youthful-looking Kevin.

"Are you Kevin's brother?" Jade asked, and the man nodded.

"Mark," he mumbled.

She turned her temper down a notch. "So where is he hiding, then?"

"He's gone into town," Mark replied softly. "I don't know when he'll be back." He struggled to maintain eye contact and kept looking behind her to an open doorway, shuffling from foot to foot.

"I don't think you're telling the truth, Mark, so don't treat me like a bloody fool. Do you know who I am?"

He nodded.

"Then you'll also know just how far I've traveled to be here to meet your brother. And if he's told you anything about me, then it's that I'm no pushover and I don't like being taken for a ride. So I'm not leaving here until he's had the guts to talk to me face-to-face. I don't care if he has a wife or a girlfriend. I want the truth from him. And I'm not setting foot out of this house until I get it."

Mark looked baffled, and he again began to mumble unintelligibly.

"It's okay, Mark," came Kevin's voice from the doorway.

She turned her head quickly to face her DNA Match, and her mouth fell open at his appearance.

"Hi, Jade. Not quite what you were expecting, am I?" he asked.

24

NICK

The midday traffic was at a standstill, and frustrated drivers were blasting their horns as Nick and Sally arrived at Birmingham's Colmore Circus.

An accident in the Queensway tunnels had reduced four traffic lanes down to one, and there were ceaseless drilling and thumping sounds coming from construction workers who were erecting a new multistory building on the concrete ashes of a recently demolished office block.

Nick raised his head to look at their destination and spotted the name emblazoned in red-and-black lettering across two third-floor windows—"One-2-One Physio." With his advertising and marketing background, he mentally ripped apart the dated choice of font and graphic.

"Why am I doing this?" he asked Sally again.

"Because we both need to know if there's any spark between you and this man."

"That's ridiculous," Nick argued, as he had frequently since learning he'd been DNA Matched with a man. "I'm a hetero-sexual bloke who isn't physically attracted to men. First off, there will be no spark, and, secondly, in the remotest chance possible there might be, how can one even fucking measure or quantify what a spark is?"

"You told me the night we first met in the bar that you knew there and then that we'd end up getting married," she said. "You said that you felt your heart flutter. Now, for my own peace of mind, I need you to meet this guy to find out if your heart flutters for him, too. Otherwise you'll spend the rest of your life wondering."

"No, babe, *you* will spend the rest of your life wondering. I will spend it wondering why on earth I've apparently been Matched with a guy when it's a woman I'm head over heels in love with."

"There's no 'apparently' about it, Nick. It's science, and science is based on fact, whether you believe it or not. You have to do this."

Nick took a deep breath and took Sally's face in his hands and kissed her deeply on the lips. While outwardly he was giving the appearance of not caring to meet his Match, inside Nick had a growing curiosity about the man he supposedly shared a link with.

"Well, let's get this over with." He sighed.

"I'll be in the Costa over the road when you're done."

Nick gave her a halfhearted smile, pressed the buzzer on the door, and once it opened, made his way up three flights of stairs to the reception desk.

"Hi." He smiled nervously at the young receptionist who had a tattoo of a rose on her hand. "I've got an appointment with Alexander at 2:30."

"David Smith?" she asked, glancing at the schedule on her screen. Nick nodded, pleased he'd changed his name. If Alexander had also requested the contact details of his pairing, Nick hadn't wanted to forewarn him they were about to meet face-to-face. "You need some physio on your neck and shoulder, is that right?" she continued.

"Yes."

"Okay, just fill out this form, and Alex will be with you in a few minutes."

Nick sank into an armchair and began to complete the brief questionnaire about his bogus ailment. Along with his name, he'd also made up the whiplash he'd received in a recent non-existent car accident.

"David?" a deep but friendly voice with an accent Nick couldn't quite place came from behind him. Nick turned to find a smiling Alexander standing in the doorway.

"Y-yes," Nick stammered.

"I'm Alex," he began and held out his hand to shake Nick's. "Come in and let's take a look at you."

Nick followed him into a room and perched on the physio-therapy bed as Alex sat on a fold-up chair opposite.

"So, tell me about the pain and what caused it," Alex asked.

As Nick began, he hoped Alex wouldn't ask him to go into any further detail about the accident as that was as far as he'd rehearsed his lie. But instead, Alex ran through some general questions about Nick's health and work habits while Nick tried his best not to stare. Even Nick could admit that, like his photo had indicated, Alex was incredibly good-looking.

"Right, if you want to take your T-shirt off for me and lie down face up," Alex said, and squirted some sanitizer into his hands. Nick suddenly felt very scrawny compared to Alex's broad chest which burst from his V-neck T-shirt.

"I'm just going to feel around your neck and shoulders for a moment," Alex explained and stood behind him.

Oh fuck, oh fuck, oh fuck, Nick thought to himself, bracing himself for Alex's touch, hoping his body wouldn't betray him, like his nipples standing to attention or his penis twitching. He reminded himself that when he was drunk he'd often embrace his male friends, and it'd never sparked a sexual reaction before. He closed his eyes and prayed as Alex's hands made contact with his shoulders. And then...nothing. All he felt were Alex's fingers poking around, digging into knots, manipulating his neck into different positions and requesting him to tilt it in various directions. Nick breathed a sigh of relief.

He turned around and lay facedown upon the bed at Alex's request, putting his face through a hole, and Alex's hands made his way down his patient's spine, aligning certain vertebrae with an audible crack where necessary. Despite the occasional moment of discomfort, Nick felt relaxed enough to make small talk.

"So, are you an Aussie?"

"No, a Kiwi. I'm from New Zealand."

"Ah, how long have you been over here?"

"About twenty months or so, although my visa's running out. My old man's not doing so good so I'm heading home soon."

"Oh, sorry to hear that. Are you going back for good?"

"That's the idea. We're just in the process of sorting out my girlfriend's permit to work in New Zealand. She's a Brit."

He has a girlfriend, he's not gay, thought Nick, reassured that they were in the same boat. The same, straight, positively heterosexual, boat.

As Alex continued to manipulate and maneuver his way around Nick's shoulders and neck, they made small talk about work and where they socialized. Nick learned that they occasionally frequented the same bars, but had little else in common. Alex was the sporty type, playing amateur rugby most weekends—he'd proudly displayed a photo of his team, Solihull Rugby Club, on the wall of his office—or spending time away with his girlfriend hiking or rock climbing. The closest Nick came to exercise was running for a bus when he'd overslept.

"Right, mate, that should just about do you for today," said Alex. "You were a bit knotted, but it wasn't too bad back there.

Give it another week, and, if the symptoms persist, make another appointment to come and see me."

"Great, thank you," replied Nick, throwing on his T-shirt and jacket. As he got to his feet feeling a little light-headed, he spotted Sally through the window, three floors below in the coffee shop. He smiled to himself, reassured that this hiccup hadn't spoiled their plans. The person he was destined to spend the rest of his life with was sitting on the opposite side of the road, and not standing in the same room as him.

After shaking hands, Nick made his way toward the reception desk. He held his phone up to the machine scanner to pay, realizing how foolish he'd been for even worrying about the possibility of being gay. This was proof, he told himself, that the DNA tests were a con.

He glanced toward the treatment room just as Alex turned his head. And suddenly, as their eyes made contact, Nick felt himself take a sharp, involuntarily gasp of breath. His heart began to beat wildly, and he could feel eyes widen. His stomach felt like it was about to turn over, and by the look of sudden bewilderment on Alex's face, he could tell he was feeling exactly the same thing.

"Here's your receipt." The receptionist smiled, breaking Nick free from the spell. He hurried down the stairs and out of the building in a panic.

He stood on the pavement for a moment, leaning against the wall and hoping the gentle summer breeze might cool down his flushed face. *What the hell was that?* he asked himself.

When his sharp, shallow breaths gradually became deeper and his heartbeat began to self-regulate again, he made his way toward Sally.

"Well? How was it?" she asked anxiously, as he sat himself down on a stool beside her.

"Yeah, fine, but he's not my type." Nick smiled, and forced himself to laugh.

"So I'm not about to lose my fiancé to a man?"

By the tone of her voice it sounded like she was trying to make a joke, but he could tell her question was genuine.

"Did you honestly think that might be the case?"

"No. Well, maybe. A little. Yes."

"Of course not," he said reassuringly, comforting her with a peck to her forehead. As she stretched her arms out and wrapped them tightly around him, Nick's eyes glanced across the road and up three stories to the clinic, where he knew he'd left his heart.

25

ELLIE

There must be something wrong with him, Ellie thought to herself, as she read another of Tim's text messages.

Barely an hour of their waking days passed without one sending the other a message. At the vibration of the phone in her pocket she would will meetings to move faster just so that she could read what he had to say next. She'd already cast aside her pay-as-you-go phone number and given him her private contact details, and while there'd been no instant physical attraction to Tim when they'd met at the pub days earlier, there was definitely something about his presence that she found endearing.

Tim had been self-deprecating about his choice of a career as a systems analyst—"dull as hell" is the expression he'd used—while Ellie was more ambiguous about hers. She'd informed him she worked for a large company in the City, but when he inquired specifically what the firm did, she was deliberately vague, informing him it had something to do with economics and had left it at that. She knew if their friendship were to flourish into something more, she couldn't lie to him forever.

But for the time being, she enjoyed pretending to be a regular person and hoped he'd not ruin it by looking her up online.

It had been an age since Ellie had taken any real notice of a man, after a long line of disappointments. Her last few dates were only interested in using her as a networking opportunity or as someone to pitch potential business investments to. Others, be they on dates one, two, three or four, inevitably found a way to bring up the subject of her wealth. It was an instant turnoff when she realized their own insecurities had left them in fear of being emasculated by her, and it turned out that many men believed an independent, rich and attractive woman like herself was a threat who required controlling.

Back in her twenties, Ellie believed she could fall head over heels for someone even if she hadn't been Matched with them. After all, it'd been happening for thousands of years before the gene had been detected. But as time marched on and she passed the threshold of her thirties, she'd lost faith that she could ever find common ground with somebody who was not genetically Matched to her. She'd experienced sparks on dates, but they'd always fizzled out after she'd learned their true intentions. She found herself wondering what Tim's angle was, and now she was trying to find fault, becoming almost disappointed when there was nothing about him to criticize.

I'm going to be working in London on Tuesday. Do you fancy joining me for dinner before I get the last train home? Tim texted.

Yes, that'd be lovely, she replied and felt a rush of warmth inside.

While she had yet to experience that immediate love that 92 percent of Matches reported experiencing within the first forty-eight hours, Ellie still felt that Tim was something special. No two couples were the same, and, in some cases, all-consuming love could take weeks, so she wasn't worried. The longer she spent in his company, the more she would feel herself thaw.

But whether he was special enough to reveal her secret to, she had yet to decide.

26

MANDY

The front door to the modest detached house that Richard had once called home opened as soon as Mandy set foot on the driveway.

Chloe stood in the porch, a beaming smile across her face. This was a very different version of the suspicious woman Mandy had crossed paths with at the memorial service.

"Come in, come in." Chloe ushered, and Mandy nervously followed her through the hallway and into an open-plan kitchen. A woman she recognized from the church was perched on a stool by the breakfast bar. There wasn't a lot of resemblance between the siblings, or mother and son for that matter, but there was something about the way they looked at each other that somehow told Mandy she was supposed to have been a part of this family. She could feel the pull of her Match even here.

Behind the frames of the woman's glasses were the eyes of a grieving mother who was still coming to terms with the loss of her child. Mandy held her hand out to shake hers, but instead, the woman grabbed her by the shoulders and held her in a tight embrace. "Thank you so much for agreeing to come," she whispered in her ear.

"Okay, Mum, you can let go of her now. Mandy, this is our mum, Patricia," Chloe said.

"It's lovely to meet you," said Mandy.

"And you, and call me Pat," she replied, looking her son's Match up and down. "Richard would have just adored you!"

Mandy felt herself blush.

"Look at her, Chloe. She's beautiful, isn't she?"

Chloe nodded from the other side of the breakfast bar where she was preparing their cups of tea. Mandy glanced around the kitchen and dining room, looking at the family photographs which covered the top of a sideboard. Pinned to a cork notice board was an order of service she recognized from Richard's memorial next to his medal for completing the London Marathon. She could feel Pat's eyes absorbing her, but it didn't make her uncomfortable.

"Richard wondered what you'd look like," Pat said eventually. "When he did the test, he wondered who'd been chosen for him and where you'd live. I don't know if Chloe told you, but he loved to travel, and I think he'd have gone to the ends of the earth to be with the one he was Matched with."

"I'm only about two hours away, just outside Essex." Mandy smiled. "So he wouldn't have needed to travel far. Do you know why he did the test?"

"For the same reason everybody else does, I think. I know at twenty-five he was young, but all he ever wanted to do was settle down and have a family of his own. The test wasn't around when Richard's dad and I met, of course, but we were together for twenty years before he passed away, and I don't think we argued once. Richard wanted the same kind of relationship. He didn't want to leave it to chance."

"What did you think when you found out what had happened? About the accident…" Chloe asked and passed a mug of tea to Mandy.

"It sounds silly when I've never even met him, but I was devastated," Mandy admitted. "I guess it's like when people find out they can't have children…the choice has been taken out of their hands, and they mourn the loss of something they never had. I felt like that. Sounds ridiculous, doesn't it?" The thought of children sent a pang through her. Despite what had happened in the past, she had taken many tests and found that she was indeed able to conceive. She'd always thought herself lucky that she wasn't one of those poor women she spoke of. But now she'd lost everything—Richard, the chance of ever having kids, a future…

"Don't be silly," Pat said to her and placed her hand over Mandy's. "You have lost exactly the same thing as us. It's just that we were fortunate to have him with us for his whole life. What you've lost, well, it's just so unfair."

Pat's words gave her the reassurance she needed that she wasn't letting her emotions get the better of her. "I didn't think anyone else would understand," she said quietly, and swallowed hard.

"Would you like to see his bedroom?"

"Mum," interrupted Chloe. "Give her some time. She's only just got here. It might be a bit much to take in."

"No, it's all right, I'd love to." Mandy nodded and followed Pat toward the stairs.

"Richard moved out to go to college, then came home, and left again when he went traveling," Pat explained. "Chloe used to joke that we should have had a revolving door installed for him because he was always coming and going. Then when his personal training business took off he saved up for a deposit on a flat." Pat opened the door ahead of her. "Go on in and have a look around if you like. I'll give you some privacy."

Richard's bedroom was tidy and spacious. Mandy made her way toward a wall decorated with hundreds of photographs of his travels around the globe: Australia, Asia, South America, Eastern Europe and even Alaska. Next to his bed was a wardrobe which housed his shirts and trousers, all neatly pressed, she found. Mandy ran her fingers over a chunky-knit jumper and drew it up to her face to smell—but all she could detect was fabric softener.

She moved toward an armchair in the corner of the room which had a scarf draped over the back. She picked it up and inhaled deeply, desperately wanting to feel a connection with him. Suddenly, Mandy's legs felt like they were about to give way as the scent of Richard's aftershave and him hit her. She couldn't fully describe the sensation, but she later likened it to sinking into a warm, soapy bath or falling into a strong, reassuring pair of arms.

Then suddenly, to her surprise, Mandy found herself beginning to cry. Looking at photos of Richard and meeting his family was one thing, but actually breathing in his scent was something completely different altogether. It knocked her for six, and she had to steady herself against a chest of drawers before leaving the room. Closing the door behind her, she had to wipe the tears from her red-rimmed eyes.

There and then she knew that she was more deeply in love with a dead man than she could have ever thought possible.

27

CHRISTOPHER

Christopher opened the sash window to let the smoke seep out from the kitchen and into the air outside. He cursed himself for using too much chili oil in the skillet.

The filet steaks were too burned on the outside for his liking, so he heated up a microwaveable bag of peppercorn sauce and closed the kitchen door, so Amy couldn't hear the bell ping. He'd already encouraged her out of the kitchen, boasting that steak, home-made sweet potato wedges and sauce were his signature dish, one of the many lies he'd used on her. He couldn't help himself; something within him needed others to be impressed by him: his actions, his appearance, his work—and now his anonymous killings. Tonight, it was his food's turn to take center stage.

His wounded thumb—savagely bitten by Number Nine—still ached under the bandage five days later, but Amy had had no reason to doubt him when he told her he'd clumsily trapped it in the bathroom door.

Christopher blamed sleep deprivation for the overcooked meat. Since he'd met Amy, it was proving nigh on impossible to grab more than a few hours at a time. She stayed over at his house on alternate nights as it was much closer to her job at the Metropolitan Police's HQ, and her sexual appetite was almost as insatiable as his. This meant that the time he'd usually spend monitoring the whereabouts of the rest of the Numbers on his list had to be crammed into the nights he spent alone.

Amy was proving to be an added complication in an already complicated life. He'd had girlfriends before, but she was truly different for the fact that in the three weeks since their first date, he had yet to fantasize about killing her. She was his Match, and he considered that someone like him could possess genuine feelings for anyone. Her presence was throwing him off-kilter, yet there was a quality about her that made him *want* to keep her around, at least for the time being.

Christopher removed the cooked potato wedges from the oven and arranged everything symmetrically on their plates. He added organic salad leaves and a splash of balsamic vinegar, and carried their dinners to the table in his dining room. He then dashed back into the kitchen—an act completely out of character— to hide the empty food packets at the bottom of his pedal bin.

"You're a dark so-and-so, aren't you?" Amy said. He returned to find her standing in front of his bookshelves, her head tilted to one side, reading the titles printed on their spines. Each shelf was color coordinated and placed in size order. "*Inside The Mind Of A Serial Killer, The Zodiac Killer, Serial Killers Anthology*," she read out loud. "Plus four books on Jack the Ripper and two on Fred and Rosemary West... I'm sensing a theme here, Chris."

"I like to know what makes people tick," he replied matter-of-factly, and poured two glasses of wine, making sure their levels were identical. "Human behavior interests me. Even if it's dark."

He recalled reading many biographies about Peter Sutcliffe, the Yorkshire Ripper, who'd murdered thirteen women back in the 1970s and '80s, right under the nose of his unsuspecting wife. Christopher had wondered how he'd gotten away with it and what fulfillment he'd gained from taking such a risk. Had he truly loved his wife, or in Sutcliffe's world of paranoid schizophrenia, had she been the anchor that'd kept him from setting sail into complete insanity?

He had begun to spot parallels in their lives, all bar the mental illness. He knew one of the many advantages he had over Sutcliffe was that he didn't need such ballast as he wasn't insane, far from it, in fact. All the studies and tests he'd taken proved he was operating well above the average person's level of intelligence. His killing spree was a challenge, not a compulsion.

"Even your choice of fiction is macabre," Amy continued, "*Hannibal Rising, American Psycho, We Need To Talk About Kevin,* Donald Trump's autobiography…"

Christopher had read and watched many depictions of psychopaths, but he had very little in common with them. So many like him had had their images misused, misrepresented, exaggerated and caricatured by novelists and scriptwriters because they were easy targets and shocked audiences. *American Psycho*'s Patrick Bateman, Hannibal Lecter, *Gone Girl*'s Amy Dunne or the malformed soul of Cathy Ames in *East of Eden* all had varying degrees of psychopathic traits, but none like his.

Only the eponymous Tom from the novel *The Talented Mr. Ripley* bore any resemblance to him, with their shared love of the finer things in life and how the manner in which they attained them showed a clear lack of guilt. But Tom's machinations resulted in a curious mix of triumph and paranoia, while Christopher's did not.

Suddenly Amy's attention was drawn to a white book that had no name on the spine. Christopher's heart raced, and he held his breath as her hand pulled it out a couple of inches farther. The danger-seeking side of him had deliberately left it there and had wanted her to remove the book and open it, but his dominant controlling side knew that it would be game over for her if she did.

"Your meal is getting cold," he said, and Amy left the book where it was and joined him at the table. "Why hasn't your serial killer been given a name?" he asked, firmly cutting into his steak.

"What do you mean?"

"Well, most serial killers are given a nickname, either by journalists or by the police. The Yorkshire Ripper, the Zodiac Killer, the Angel of Death...this guy hasn't been given one."

Christopher was genuinely insulted that his efforts had not yet been rewarded with a moniker. It made him question why nine dead women—and hopefully another to add to the list the next night—weren't enough to be taken seriously.

"I don't know," Amy replied. "It's usually the media. Would you like to come up with one yourself?"

"Isn't that a bit distasteful?"

"Coming from a man with twenty books on his shelves about serial killers? You're an expert."

"You need to tell me what you know about him first before I pick a name."

"Well, this comes from my DI who's been having meetings with all departments this week, just in case anything about the suspect sounds familiar. The psychological profiles tell us he's male, aged between twenty and forty. He prefers to target single women living alone. His MO is always the same. He breaks in through a ground floor door or patio doors by picking the lock—their doors are almost always quite old and security lapse—he kills them in the kitchen, then lays their bodies out, arms to their sides and legs straight. Then he gives himself anywhere between two and five days to kill another woman, returns to the scene of the last crime and places a photograph of the most recent victim on her predecessor's chest. He leaves no DNA that we know of, so he is methodical, but while the women targeted are only in the London area, he seems to be taking a scattergun approach to where they live, which makes it harder to narrow down where he might strike next."

Christopher felt the butterflies in his stomach circle in a swarm and take off en masse, making his entire body buzz with excitement. He'd never heard anyone speak in person about his work in such detail before; his only interaction with others on the subject had been via anonymous web message boards.

"We think he leaves the photographs either to taunt us, or to show he has no plans to stop," Amy continued. "And he leaves the same spray-painted image on the pavement outside each one of the victims' homes to identify she's inside—it looks like a man carrying something on his back."

"Yes, I saw the picture in the *Evening Standard.*"

"He's like a ghost in the way he just vanishes and then appears again."

"The Ghost Killer."

Amy shook her head. "That's a rubbish name for him."

"The Silent Killer."

"Isn't that carbon monoxide?"

"The Cheese Wire Strangler."

"The word 'cheese' sounds like you're trivializing what he does." Amy stopped abruptly. "How do you know he uses cheese wire?"

Christopher paused briefly, realizing his error. All the reports he'd read about the murders had stated wire had been used to strangle the victims, but not specifically wire used to slice cheese.

"It stands to reason," he said, thinking on his feet. "If you're going to strangle somebody with wire that tough, you're going to need handles to hold on to, otherwise you'll risk severing your own fingers."

"We think it's cheese wire, too," Amy said.

Good, she'd bought the lie.

"Based on the width and depth of penetration, and the chemicals left in the victims' wounds, it's cleaned regularly between killings."

"Do you know where the weapon's from?"

Amy nodded and ate another mouthful of steak.

"And I bet it's been available to buy across the country for years, hasn't it?"

"Yes and it's been on the shelves for a decade at least. You've done your homework, haven't you?"

Christopher nodded. Amy had no idea just how much homework he'd done or how happy she'd just made him.

"Well, if you come up with a name for him, you should mention it at work," he urged. "How often do you get to come up with a nickname for a serial killer?"

"Probably about as often as I spend time with one."

28

The man standing before Jade was most definitely Kevin, but clearly the pictures he'd sent her had been taken some time ago.

This was not the Kevin she had traveled so far to see. His face was youthful, but his eyes had lost the sparkle that'd been captured in so many of his photographs. He was almost completely bald, all bar some soft wisps of hair covering his scalp. His arms were sinewy—his tracksuit bottoms and T-shirt had probably once fitted him but now hung loosely like they'd been thrown onto a scarecrow—and his skin was pale and gaunt. In his left hand, he held a portable drip which was attached to a metal frame with wheels. Jade took in his appearance from head to toe, both astonished and confused by it. Her initial anger toward him rapidly dissipated.

"Do you mind if we sit?" Kevin smiled, and she nodded, too lost for words to reply. She followed him into a spacious, brightly lit reception room with huge windows that overlooked miles and miles of fields, stretching as far as the eye could see. Kevin steadied himself against the arm of a chair and slowly lowered himself into it.

"I'm sorry I asked you to leave when you called, but you kind of took me by surprise," he began, the youthfulness of his voice belittling his appearance. "The last thing I expected was for you to fly over here to see me."

"I only decided a few days ago," whispered Jade. "I… I'm… sorry."

"Wow—do you know that in the entire time we've known each other you've never said sorry?" Kevin teased.

"It's not a word I'm used to."

"I'm kidding, and you shouldn't be the one who's apologizing. It should be me. I haven't been honest with you about everything. Well, I guess that's pretty obvious. There's no easy way to say this, Jade, but I have lymphoma. It's now at stage four which means…well, it ain't good."

Jade found it difficult to maintain eye contact with him. She couldn't make the connection between the man she had fallen in love with by telephone and text message and the sliver of a person sitting before her.

"I was diagnosed a year ago, before you and I were Matched," he continued. "I wanted to know if my perfect girl was out there somewhere, and a few months later it turned out to be you. And I did consider leaving it at that and not giving out my contact details—it wouldn't be fair on you—but it's human nature to be curious, and, when you spend so many hours of the day stuck in hospital or in this house like I do, it's all you can think about. I really couldn't stop myself from wanting to find out more about you. It was selfish and I'm sorry."

Jade nodded and conceded that if their roles were reversed, she, too, would want to know everything about her Match. "How much…" Her voice trailed off, deciding what she was about to ask was insensitive, even for her.

"How much longer do I have left?" Kevin continued for her. "Probably not much more than a month or two."

"What about the photos you sent me?"

"They were taken last summer."

"And this is why you didn't want to Skype or FaceTime? A few minutes ago I was going to tear strips off you. I was convinced you were married with kids."

"Ha!" He laughed. "I don't reckon I've got a Buckley's chance at marriage."

Jade suddenly realized it meant the same for her, and she began to feel very, very alone. She might eventually go on to fall in love with someone, but it wouldn't be with *the one*. It wouldn't be with Kevin.

She offered him a sympathetic smile but no hollow words; there was little she could say that would make the slightest bit of difference.

"Listen," Kevin continued, "I understand if you want to leave, I honestly do. Because if I were in your shoes, I'm ashamed to say I'd probably seriously consider it. You didn't sign up for this."

Jade gritted her teeth and curled her toes up inside her trainers. She wouldn't permit herself to become upset in front of him.

"Neither did you, Kevin," she replied. "So if you don't mind, I'll hang around a little longer so we can get to know each other in person. How does that sound?"

Kevin gave her a nod. He could barely suppress the grin that was spreading across his face.

29

NICK

"I thought you'd quit the smokes?"

"I have. Well, I had. It's just been a…peculiar…few days."

"What's wrong, is it the S&D account?"

Nick paused to take in the view of Birmingham's city center from his spot on the office building's fire escape. He could hear the warning bells of the trams making their way up New Street, while below him rush hour commuters bustled along Corporation Street toward the train station.

Rhian had been leaning against the railings puffing on her vaporizer when Nick appeared. He, too, had an e-cigarette in his desk drawer, but today wasn't a day for half measures.

He'd promised Sally he'd given up as a New Year's resolution. It would be another lie to add to the rapidly growing list. He'd also promised that he was still 100 percent sure Sally was the only one for him, that they could live happily ever after and that he hadn't given Alex a second thought since he'd met him. In reality, he was all Nick had thought about.

"Yes, it's the S&D account," Nick told Rhian. "The MD is getting confused about the message he's trying to get across. It's such a ball-ache."

"Well, start channeling your inner Don Draper because you'll need to pull something out of the bag."

In his three years at the agency as a junior copywriter, Nick had yet to be beaten by an account he'd been assigned to manage, even though he worked on many obscure products he hadn't previously heard of or even dreamed had existed. His work in making market leaders of a new yeast infection cream and a herbal remedy for erectile dysfunction had won him the office nickname of The Genital Giant, which quietly amused him. He prided himself on being able to sell anything to anyone with a smart tag line, but this week he'd been too preoccupied to make a pubic lice lotion palatable.

He'd tried his hardest not to allow his mind to wander toward Alex, and had come close to convincing himself that the emotions he'd stirred in him were imaginary. But while Nick made a living persuading consumers to buy into something they hadn't realized they needed, he knew he couldn't fool himself. He had truly *felt* something, and it wasn't like anything he had ever experienced before. And he was convinced Alex had, too.

Nick slept very little in the days after their meeting, and his constant fatigue made him impatient and ratty with Sally. He found himself sniping at everything she said or did, from her innocuous requests to pick up more kale from the little Waitrose on the way home to what new box set they should begin on Netflix.

Something in Nick's heart had deviated from the path it had been following, and it was making him nauseous. Or maybe at that moment it was the cigarette that made him want to vomit; he couldn't be sure.

As Rhian headed back inside the building, he took one long,

last drag right down to the filter and stubbed the cigarette out on the metal step. He sniffed his fingers and turned his nose up at the smell. Stinking clothes and skin—he hadn't missed these by-products of being a slave to nicotine.

His mobile rang, and he looked at the screen—the number was withheld but he answered it anyway.

"Hello, Nick Wallsworth speaking," he began.

There was a pause that Nick assumed meant an automated message was about to begin, inviting him to talk to someone about claiming a PPI refund, and he prepared to hang up, until he heard a voice that he recognized immediately.

"Hi," Alex said.

Nick's heart went from zero to sixty in a second. He felt part terrified, part thrilled.

"It was you, wasn't it?" he continued. "Who came to see me."

"Yes," Nick whispered, his mouth suddenly dry. Neither spoke for a moment before Alex broke the silence.

"Why didn't you tell me who you were?"

"In case you thought I was mad. And because I don't believe in the whole Match Your DNA thing."

"Neither do I. Well, I didn't until…"

"…until I was leaving…"

"…and you felt something, too, didn't you? It wasn't my imagination, was it?"

"No, mate, it wasn't." Nick felt his body shiver, even though he wasn't cold. "I'm sorry I lied about my name. How did you find me?"

"I got the Match Your DNA email, and I knew my Match was a guy. Then as you were leaving I just knew it was you. I paid to access your details and guessed you'd used a different name."

"Sorry."

"It's okay. I probably would have done the same myself."

There was another break in the conversation as both men fell silent. Nick steadied the hand he used to clasp the phone to his ear to stop it from trembling.

"This is awkward, isn't it?" said Alex.

"You're not kidding."

"It's bullshit, though, right? The test results, bullshit."

"Yeah, of course. Total bullshit."

"How has it happened?"

"Some glitch or ghost in the machine or something."

"That sounds about right."

"Do you think we should get together and talk about it? You know, over a couple of beers sometime, if you think that's a good idea?" Alex asked.

"How about now?" Nick caught himself saying.

"Okay, say in half an hour in the Bacchus Bar in the arcade?"

"Yeah, sure. See you there."

Alex was the first to hang up, and Nick froze, waiting for his head to stop spinning, before he hurried back to his office to grab his coat.

30

ELLIE

"Sorry, they look really pathetic, don't they?" Tim looked sheepish as he presented Ellie with the bouquet of flowers lying on the bar in front of him. "I didn't pinch them from a cemetery, honest."

"No, they're lovely," Ellie replied, glancing at the poor selection of wilting white carnations and red roses, their stalks wrapped in brown paper. She appreciated the gesture, though.

Tim raised his eyebrows like he didn't believe her.

"Well, they're a tiny bit pathetic, but it was a very sweet thought." She smiled.

"I've been carrying them around all day which is why they're battered. I bought them this morning in case I couldn't find another florist."

Ellie was touched by his naïveté in thinking there might only be one flower seller in London.

He'd already been waiting at the restaurant when Ellie arrived several minutes late. She'd gone against her security chief Andrei's wishes and had set off alone by taxi, despite his protestations that now, with a serial killer loose in the city, the need for him to escort her was more important than ever. The venue of their second date, this time in a quiet street near London's Notting Hill, had been chosen by Tim: a family-run French brasserie whose decor hadn't seen a lick of paint since the Thatcher government.

He sat on a bar stool, peeling the label from his bottle of imported beer, waiting for her to arrive. From the pavement outside, she spotted the dark suit he was wearing. His hair was slicked down into a side parting, and he was nibbling at his fingernails. He appeared to have made more of an effort this time and looked much more nervous.

His apparent anxiety made Ellie's body tense. She wondered if Tim had discovered who she was and, as a result, felt under pressure to make a better impression. It wasn't what she wanted from him at all—time and time again she'd witnessed firsthand the lengths some men went in their quest to compete with her, or others who had assumed that by showering her with expensive gifts they would win her heart. As much as she admired a strong female role model like Madonna, Ellie was no material girl.

"Can I get a Hendrick's gin and tonic please?" Tim asked the barman as Ellie took a seat by his side. She liked that he'd remembered her favorite brand. "You look really nice," he said, taking in her black top, knee-length skirt and black leather boots.

"So do you," she replied. "Is that a new suit?"

"Yes, how did you know?"

"You left this on the pocket." She grinned and tore off a price tag. However, as she pulled, she ripped away part of the pocket from the seam, too. "Oh no, I'm so sorry!" She covered her mouth with her hand, panicking.

"That's all right," he said, and tried to pat the pocket back into place.

"I feel awful—you've gone to all this effort—"

"Oh really, I haven't."

"Flowers, a new suit, aftershave...but you don't look as relaxed as when we met last time at the pub. Is everything all right?"

"I'm sorry." Tim sighed. "But I have a confession to make."

Damn it, Ellie thought, and felt her stomach sink. This was it. *He's done his research and now he thinks I'm out of his league.*

"I told my mate Michael about our first date, and he had a right pop at me," Tim continued.

"I'm not sure I understand?"

"He said that even though we'd been Matched, I should have brought you flowers and taken you somewhere nice, not to my local pub. And that I should've dressed up a bit, hence the new clobber. It's been a while since I've been on a date, Ellie. The last few were off Tinder and Plenty of Fish, and I was the only one who seemed to bother making an effort. So I went the other way with you. Then you came in looking fucking amazing, and I realized I'd got it wrong. With the others, on the rare occasion I did meet someone I was really attracted to, it was never mutual, and I always ended up being friend-zoned pretty much straight-away. But when we met, I definitely felt something more than just a bloke fancying a bird on a date—and something told me you and I weren't going to end up just as mates. And now I'm a bit nervous about that because I don't know what's supposed to happen next. I don't want to scare you off, I don't even know if it's possible to scare your Match off... By the way, feel free to interrupt me at any point before I sound like a total bell end."

"Honestly, Tim, I liked that you were yourself," said Ellie, unsure of when she had last met someone who wore his heart on his sleeve quite so openly.

"But when you get all those London City types in their Hugo Boss suits and Rolex watches trying it on with you, then you find you're Matched with some provincial pleb—"

"Believe me," Ellie interrupted, "I had a far better time with you in your local than I would've with one of those types in The Ivy."

A look of relief passed across Tim's face. "Can we start tonight again?" he asked.

"No, I'm secretly enjoying the awkwardness of it."

"Then let's go and see if our table's ready. That way I can drip some soup down my shirt or spill wine over my lap, and we can really make a night of it."

"Well, at least you're not having another one of your 'love at first fart' moments."

"You don't want to know what happens on my 'love at second fart' moment."

Ellie laughed. There were many things about Tim that Ellie found endearing: like the way his lips curled up at the sides a second before he'd break into laughter, the small gray flecks of hair peeking out from his beard, how his left ear stuck out a little farther than the right, the way his entire face turned a deep shade of crimson when he became embarrassed.

While it was neither love at first nor second sight for her, she was sure of one thing. There was *something* about him she was falling for.

31

MANDY

Mandy listened intently as Richard's mother, Pat, recalled anecdote after anecdote about her son, filling in the many gaps in Mandy's limited understanding of her Match and his life.

It was the second time they'd met in a week, this time in a garden center coffee shop in a village halfway between their respective towns.

"The women he trained at the gym loved him," chuckled Pat. "He was a handsome lad, but there was something about his personality that they adored, too. I think it's because he gave them attention and listened to them. They might not have got that from their husbands. And, of course, some of them took this to mean he was more interested than he actually was."

Mandy understood what it was about Richard these women were drawn to; the more she heard about him from those who knew him best, the deeper she was falling for him, against her better judgment.

She clung on to Pat's every word as she described his childhood days in the cubs, how he'd inherited his sense of adventure from his father and how, no matter where in the world he'd been, Richard had always stayed in regular touch with his family by email or by phone. She spoke of how, when Richard was just nine years old, he had lost his dad to a sudden heart attack and had immediately stepped up as the new man of the house.

"I think Chloe told you about his cancer, didn't she? The one that inspired him to go traveling?"

"She mentioned it, yes."

"Well, he was seventeen when he found a lump in his testicle, and at first he didn't say anything…the last thing a teenage boy wants is his mum to know he has anything wrong down there. But when he finally did admit it, I dragged him to the doctors and within a couple of days he was in hospital having the lump removed. It was malignant, and he had to have a few sessions of chemotherapy, but within six months he was as right as rain."

"That must have been horrible for you."

"It wasn't a great time, no. But it sparked a huge change in Richard. I think something inside him knew his time on earth might be limited, and he wanted to make the most of it. And who can blame him? He was right, after all, and he managed to cram more into his years than many other people do in a lifetime."

"Certainly a lot more than me," said Mandy. Richard's sense of adventure put her lack of one to shame. She couldn't help but wonder what sights of the world they might have witnessed together if fate hadn't intervened.

"What about you, Mandy?" Pat suddenly asked. "Here I am rambling on about Richard and what he was like, and I haven't once asked you how it makes you feel to hear my stories?"

Mandy removed her fingers from around her mug of coffee and glanced at the customers around them lifting potted plants and sizing them up. An elderly couple caught her attention as they sat side by side on a bench holding hands and silently watching brightly colored fish swimming in a pond. She and Richard would never get the chance to grow old together.

"When you talk about him, it makes me feel that there's so much I've missed out on," she replied. "A family man who wanted a family of his own...that's my idea of a perfect Match. I feel torn—I'm so pleased to have been Matched with him, yet I feel so sad that we weren't even allowed to meet or be together. They say you can't miss what you've never had, but that's not true. I miss him so much, and I never even knew him."

Pat placed her hand on Mandy's. "For what it's worth, I'd have been proud to have had you as my daughter-in-law."

Mandy looked away and had to bite her lip to stop it from trembling, but it wasn't enough to stop the many tears cascading down her cheeks.

32

CHRISTOPHER

The extra shot Christopher added to his espresso put a pep in his step.

He was still buzzing from the smooth, uncomplicated kill of Number Ten in the early hours of the morning, and wasn't tired enough to go to bed. There were too many plans to be made which were swirling around his head. So he put on a pair of shorts and a tight sleeveless vest and slipped on his trainers—lacing them up so the loops were identically sized—and left his house for a run. When his thoughts became jumbled, exercise helped to balance his mind.

Christopher relished being the object of attention, and he didn't care from which source it came. His killings were anonymous, so he searched for it from other means instead, such as wearing his best tailor-made Savile Row suit and test-driving cars he had no intention of buying, or making appointments to visit multimillion pound turnkey properties he couldn't afford. He'd often walk around the gym changing rooms naked for longer than necessary, showing off his toned physique that he was confident other men would envy. And when he ran, he purposely wore no underwear, so passersby could see his penis in his shorts bouncing from side to side.

His top-of-the-range Nikes pounded along the busy London pavements and took him toward the greenery of Hyde Park. As he ran, he questioned what it was about his condition that made him seek this attention, and with it the challenges and complications. Life would've been much simpler if, after he killed, he'd leave their homes and wait for them to be discovered. But he'd chosen to make things more interesting by taking a risk and returning to the scene of the crime to leave his trademark: a photograph of the next victim and the spray-painted stencil outside.

It was an original spin, he thought, and was sure to capture the interest of the press and public who, when it came to their serial killers, liked a calling card—films and books had raised the level of expectation, and he was happy to deliver to his audience. The race would always be on for the police to identify the next girl, in the hope that with each kill, Christopher would become a little more careless and leave a clue. So far, they had nothing to go on.

His aim was always to return to their houses within two to three days to leave the photograph and stencil, and, as luck would have it, so far his victims had yet to be discovered by that point. He looked on his returning to the scene of the crime as a bonus: a chance to take one final look at his handiwork.

Christopher turned the volume up on the MP3 player strapped to his arm and ran to the beat of his Spotify playlist. Adele was the next artist to shuffle on and he wondered why all killers depicted in television dramas only ever listened to angry, shouty, heavy metal music—in the same way that all fictitious black criminals only ever listened to rap. Nobody ever killed or robbed a bank to the sounds of Rihanna or Justin Bieber.

He ran across the road and past a parade of shops, recognizing the doorway of one in particular. He never picked his subjects randomly, but based on strict criteria. They were young, single women who were on the dating scene and who lived alone. They occupied older properties with no burglar alarms and front doors with old locks. They all lived a distance from their families and, London being so large and anonymous, they didn't know their neighbors. It would always take a day or so before a person's absence was noted by a friend or work colleague, and eventually reported to police.

He looked at the doorway and remembered the Lithuanian girl who lived there—he'd chatted to her online a few times and she'd made his long list. Then he'd discovered she was advertising for a flat mate. Christopher knew what a thrill he'd get from killing two girls in one night, but the amount of risk involved wasn't worth taking, so he'd removed her from his list. She'd never know how lucky she was.

Laying the blame for multiple killings at the door of "a man with psychopathic tendencies" was about the only thing the experts in the media had been correct about. His diagnosis wasn't news to Christopher; off his own bat he had filled in the test questionnaires years earlier to gain a greater understanding of who he was.

"Psycho" was a term first given to him during his schooldays following the purposefully overzealous rugby tackle that broke a boy's collarbone; the hockey ball hit with such gusto it blinded a girl in one eye; and the pouring of bleach into the school's pond to see how long it'd take for the newts to rise to the surface belly-up. The nickname didn't bother him because he wasn't entirely sure what it meant. Nevertheless, it seemed to give him a reputation of a boy to be feared, which he enjoyed.

Christopher now realized his parents must have been aware there was something different about their youngest child, as they'd had him tested for both autism and Asperger's. When the results came back negative, they swept his oddities under the carpet and concentrated on helping him to fit into society as best he could. When he had told them he struggled to feel anything, from sympathy to love, they taught him to mimic acceptable behavior instead.

As Christopher reached his teenage years, he fixated on how people reacted to circumstances beyond their control and, specifically, to scenarios created by him. Once, he took the neighbors' toddler from their garden and left him in woodland two miles away, just to see how the child's parents might react once they noticed he was missing. Frantic, it turned out. He wondered why he couldn't feel the same sort of terror, or why empathy was a foreign word to him.

It also didn't come naturally for him to detect fear in a facial expression; he couldn't identify sarcasm, and he didn't feel guilt, shame or remorse. Even when his parents walked in on him, aged fifteen, screwing another neighbor's daughter in the conservatory, he had simply turned his head to look at them until they left. He had expected to continue, much to the girl's horror.

When his schoolmates began dating and finding girlfriends, he was only interested in what would result in an orgasm, neither the foreplay nor the cuddling afterwards. Love seemed like a waste of time and energy, for minimal reward.

It was only when Christopher reached his early twenties that he examined in detail what the word *psychopath* meant. There were others out there like him, which meant that Christopher was normal, just a different type of normal. And the words that'd been chucked at him like stones over the years like "callous" and "cold-hearted bastard" finally made sense.

He completed Robert Hare's 1996 Psychopathic Personality Inventory, and of the twenty questions asked to determine psychopathic behavior, his point tally totaled thirty-two, well above the average.

Christopher learned that some scientists believed a psychopath's brain wasn't wired properly, that they possessed weak connections among the components that made up their emotional system, and those disconnects were responsible for Christopher being unable to feel emotions deeply.

That satisfied him. He liked that he was not to blame for his lack of impulse control, and, if he were ever caught for his crimes, then that would be his excuse. He'd gain entry to a high security mental hospital with attention lavished on him by those who wanted to study and learn more about him. There were worse ways to live out your life than being in demand, he thought.

He cut across Hyde Park and, after a while, left the grass and trees behind for the streets and large Victorian townhouses of Ladbroke Grove. He stopped to purchase an energy drink from a street vendor and smiled knowingly at a gay couple fixated by the movement in his shorts.

Minutes later, he paused outside a health food store on Portobello Road and looked up at the first floor flat above it. He double-checked the app on his smartphone to make sure the tenant, Number Eleven, was still at work, then used his picks to unlock her front door and familiarize himself with the layout of her home. Little had changed since the pictures had been posted on Rightmove, and he surmised that his next killing should be quite straightforward.

As he poked around and worked out his kill position, he furrowed his brow. Something wasn't right. Usually, from the moment he entered the premises of a name on his list, he'd feel a flicker of excitement, a moment of anticipation of the kill to come. But today he lacked his usual enthusiasm.

Instead, he thought about how time-consuming this project was becoming, time that could be spent elsewhere, like in the company of Amy, for example. An unfortunate by-product of meeting her was that she had stimulated him in ways no other women had—neither those he'd dated, nor those he'd killed.

But none of his research told him why.

33

JADE

In stark contrast to his brother Mark's reaction, the rest of Kevin's family couldn't have been more welcoming to their surprise visitor from the other side of the world.

When Kevin's parents, Dan and Susan, returned from a trip to town to buy supplies, neither could contain their joy at finding the pale, British girl with the fiery red hair and feisty personality they'd heard so much about sitting in their living room. Instantly they recognized her from the photographs Kevin had shown them, and once they'd gotten over the initial surprise, they bombarded her with questions about herself and insisted that she stay the night at least.

"How long are you in Australia for, love?" Dan asked. They had just sat down to supper in the dining room.

"We have a guesthouse out back with an en suite, so you won't have to share with these filthy buggers," joked Susan, glancing at her sons. While she spoke to and about them in the same manner as she had probably always done, Jade sensed that beyond her jovial facade lay a deep sadness.

"Thank you. I'm not sure how long I'm staying," Jade replied, and she genuinely wasn't. The fairy-tale romance between her and Kevin wasn't playing out how she'd imagined, and the easiest thing to do would be to beat a hasty retreat at the first opportunity. But each time she looked at Kevin, the besotted expression on his face said what his words had not. He desperately wanted her to stay. "A week or so probably, if that's okay?"

Dan served up plates full of cold meats, potatoes and salad, while Mark helped to bring the dishes to the dining table. Kevin was the only member of the family who didn't tuck in. Instead, he picked at a small portion on his plate. "I struggle to keep my food down," he told her later. "The cancer's in my digestive system, so food doesn't sit properly."

Jade had yet to come to terms with hearing the C-word and struggled to associate it with Kevin. She had to stop herself from recoiling when it was mentioned, even though the rest of the family didn't bat an eyelid and continued as normal. She understood they'd had a much longer adjustment period to come to terms with it than she had.

"It's because of you that we've had him for longer than the doctors first thought," Susan told Jade as they were drying the dishes.

"How so?"

"After we were told it was…terminal, he did like many people do and sank into a depression. Well, who can blame him?"

"I'd be as angry as hell."

"He was at first, too. He thought he had his whole life ahead of him only to be told it's not going to last as long as he'd assumed…" She paused and turned her head away from Jade, as if she had suddenly just relived the moment the awful news had been delivered all over again. She cleared her throat and continued.

"It was pretty bad, Jade. None of us knew how to react or how to help him. Then, at the darkest time of his life, he discovered he had a DNA Match, and it didn't matter that she lived in a different country or that he'd probably never meet her face-to-face. Just knowing you were out there and being in communication with one another was a reason for him to continue."

"I had no idea about any of this—"

"And he should have told you. I told him you deserved to know, but he didn't know how to bring it up. For him, you were a welcome distraction from it. When you and he were texting or talking, he'd forget about what was happening to his body. He became a different person… He was my little boy again." Susan clasped Jade's hand firmly. "Thank you," she whispered. "Thank you for being my boy's friend, and thank you for coming to see him."

"I'm glad I came." Jade smiled. It had been a long and extraordinary day, and as it caught up on her, she suddenly wanted to cry. It wasn't a feeling she was used to—she hated people thinking she was weak—so she swallowed hard and kept the tears down. She meant it, she thought; she was pleased she had met Kevin and already she felt close to him.

But there was just one problem—she knew that on meeting her Match, she wasn't in love with him.

34

NICK

It turned out the feeling Nick and Alex had shared in Alex's clinic wasn't a fluke.

The moment he spotted Alex in the trendy Birmingham bar, Nick was scared his legs might give way beneath him before he'd even reached the table. The two men politely shook hands and gave each other awkward smiles.

"Can I get you a drink?" Nick asked.

"Sure, another one of these, thanks, mate," Alex replied, and lifted his bottle of lager.

Nick nodded and headed to the bar. As he ordered their drinks he noticed Alex's reflection in the mirror behind the spirits. Sally was right when she'd commented on Alex's handsome appearance. Even as a straight man, Nick could appreciate he was a good-looking guy. He was much more masculine than him and held himself confidently. He was the kind of guy women flocked to, and for some reason this thought made him feel funny inside. He checked his phone to see if Sally had received the text he'd sent telling her he'd be late home because of a client meeting. It was a plausible lie, he thought, as he often had to wine and dine existing and prospective clients. OK babe, luv u. He read her reply. He didn't respond.

Nick returned to the booth with their bottles, sat down and took off his coat.

Neither knew where to begin.

"So how've you been?" Nick said eventually.

"Good, thanks, pretty busy at work, you know. You?"

"Yeah, same here, same here."

Both men simultaneously looked down at their drinks, unable to maintain any prolonged eye contact and risk a repeat of what they'd felt the first time they'd met. Two choruses of an old Oasis song played in the background before either of them said another word, both feeling cripplingly self-aware.

"Actually, things aren't good," admitted Nick. "There's no easy way for me to say this without sounding like a total idiot, but I need to get this off my chest before I back out. The more I try not to think about it, the more it becomes the only thing I can think about at all. It's about what happened…the first time we met."

He paused, realizing how ridiculous he sounded. He looked at Alex hoping for confirmation that he might be feeling the same, but Alex's face gave little away. *In for a penny, in for a pound*, Nick thought and continued regardless. "That feeling I got when I looked at you as I was leaving. I've thought it through a thousand times since, and I still can't explain it properly. None of it make sense. I'm not gay."

"I'm not gay either," Alex replied.

"So why do we have this link?"

"I don't know."

"I've not so much as kissed a guy, not even for a laugh or when I was drunk."

"Me, neither."

"So if neither of us are into blokes, then what's happening here?"

"It's simple. The test is fucked up, they got us mixed up with other people," Alex said resolutely.

"That's what I said. I even emailed them to check, but they sent out this standard reply saying the test isn't flawed and to date they haven't had one mis-Match. But, anyway, it doesn't explain what I felt. What I think *we* felt. Are we in denial or something?"

Alex shifted uncomfortably in his seat and took several gulps from his bottle, before leaning forward and, with a lowered voice, said, "Mate, all I know is that something inexplicable happened after I gave you physio. I didn't feel anything when we met, when you took your T-shirt off, when I touched you or when we shook hands afterwards, but then... I dunno... *something* happened."

Nick breathed a sigh of relief, pleased to hear Alex describe what he had felt, too.

"What was it like for you?" he asked.

"Honestly? Like a thousand small explosions going off inside me all at once, but not in a bad way... It was like they woke me up. I suddenly felt more alive than I've ever been before, and that's the only way I can describe it, as lame as it sounds."

"No, no, it's cool. I know what you mean. It was exactly the same for me."

"But why you and me? From the conversation we had last time, do we even have anything in common? I love sport, you love computer games. I'm going back home to live in New Zealand in a couple of months, and you enjoy your city life."

"And we both have girlfriends."

"And we both have girlfriends," Alex agreed.

"So why am I sitting here with butterflies the size of eagles circling my stomach, and I can barely look at you, and then when I do, I can't take my eyes off you?"

Nick shuffled his leg and felt his knee briefly brush against Alex's. For a split second, he felt like goose bumps were spreading to each pore in his body. A moment later, Alex slid his leg back over so their legs remained touching.

They looked at each other square in the eye, neither needing to say a word to know what the other was feeling.

35

ELLIE

On Ellie and Tim's second date, time passed as swiftly as the click of a finger as they tucked into their meal.

Ellie had dined in yam'Tcha, Le Sergent Recruteur and Tour d'Argent—three of the most critically acclaimed restaurants in Paris—and Jean-Christophe Novelli and Hélène Darroze had even cooked for her in her own home, but she couldn't remember a meal she'd appreciated more than the one she was sharing with Tim at this modest brasserie. It certainly wasn't the menu she found appealing—everything she'd ordered had either been cremated or doused in garlic—but she ate it without complaint as she welcomed the effort he'd made in organizing their night.

Tim was a kind, genuine man, the sort she hadn't met in a long, long time. Was she attracted to him? Yes, she decided, but not in the way she'd expected to be. Ellie had spent enough time in the company of couples who'd met through Match Your DNA to know what two people who were head over heels in love looked like. She and Tim didn't have that. She had erected so many barriers over the years that theirs was likely to be a slow-burner rather than an all-consuming, all-guns-blazing relationship.

With the meal completed and their coffees drained, Ellie had allowed Tim to pay before he held her vintage Alexander McQueen coat open for her to slip her arms into. She suddenly felt guilty for wearing it in his company, as it had likely cost more than what he'd earn in a month. In fact, she knew for sure that it did, as her private detectives had disclosed to her Tim's bank statements. But while she regretted intrusively checking up on him, she knew she shouldn't feel guilty for buying nice things. It was her hard-earned money to do with as she pleased, and, in the same way she encouraged Tim to be himself when he was around her, she should be true to herself also. And she was a girl who loved her clothes.

Tim held open the door as they left, and she gave in to the urge to entwine her arm inside his, immediately feeling the radiating warmth of his body. Suddenly he stopped in his tracks and offered her the widest beam, then leaned toward her for a kiss. Ellie closed her eyes, and as their lips met, she felt the unexpected release of pheromones she had heard about surge around her body, making her nerves twitch and her heart flutter. For a second, she thought she might have even seen stars.

But her moment of elation was brought to an abrupt halt when she heard a female voice shriek from behind them, "You fucking bitch!"

Together they turned to find a scowling, middle-aged woman hurling something in their direction. On instinct, Tim tried to step between the woman and Ellie, and was hit with the brunt of a whole can of red paint, which was now all over his face, shirt and jacket. A generous amount also hit Ellie, too, splashing against her arms, hair, cheeks and the restaurant window behind them.

"You've got blood on your hands for what you've done," the

woman yelled at Ellie, before throwing the can into the gutter and scurrying away along the road into the night.

Ellie remained frozen in place as a stunned Tim wiped the paint from his face.

"What did you do?" he asked, his voice filled with disbelief.

The shock had rendered Ellie immobile. It wasn't the first time she had been subject to an attack, although most of the others had been of a cyber or verbal nature, with the exception of the religious nut who'd stabbed Andrei with a broken bottle. It was precisely for this reason she had hired him and his team to escort her in public. Only that evening, she'd needed to remind herself what it felt like to be a normal person going on a regular date. As she and Tim had kissed, Ellie's defenses were down, and she was lost in the moment.

Now, though, all she felt was the thick gloopy paint dripping down her cheeks. She was aware Tim had just asked her a question, but she was too dumbstruck to acknowledge it. Instead, she stared back at the onlookers who'd stopped to gawp at the spectacle.

With the crowd around them growing, Tim leaped into action, pulling her by the arm toward a nearby black cab that'd just dropped off a fare. The driver glared at the paint-splattered pair and was about to refuse them entry when Tim pulled a fistful of £50 notes from his wallet and shoved them through the passenger window. The large bills seemed out of character for a man on Tim's wage, but Ellie was too concerned by the assault to question it.

"That'll pay for the cleanup," he said and opened the door, ushering her inside, not giving the driver an opportunity to change his mind. "Where do you live?" She was still too stunned to respond.

"Ellie," Tim said sternly. "I need to get you home. Where do you live?"

"Three-four-five Fullerton Terrace, Belgravia," she whis-

pered, and Tim repeated it to the driver, then pulled out a hand-
kerchief from his pocket and gently wiped away some of the red
paint from her lips.

"Are you all right?" he asked gently.

"I just want to go home," she said, feeling humiliated and
ashamed. She couldn't make eye contact with him.

"Do you know that woman?"

"No."

"We need to call the police."

"No," Ellie repeated, more forcefully.

Tim waited for a further explanation, but none was forth-
coming. She could sense his frustration. She looked out of the
window so she didn't have to see the disappointment on his face.

"Just who are you, Ellie?" he persisted. "Why would someone want to do that to you?"

She remained silent for the rest of their awkward fifteen-
minute journey to her home. As the cab pulled up outside her
large, white, four-story townhouse, she assumed that Tim was
wondering how a PA could afford to live in such a sought-after
postcode. But she was in no mood to admit the truth.

She got out of the cab while Tim paid the driver. By the time
he'd been handed his change, Ellie had rushed up the steps to
her front door and held out her key card to it. It opened to Andrei standing inside. He took one look at his emotional employer
and was about to launch himself at Tim, still standing on the
road, but Ellie stopped him as she entered, and Andrei shut the
door, leaving Tim out in the cold.

36

MANDY

Mandy could not get enough of her niece Bella, who sat in a high chair around her parents' dining table, surrounded by a group of other small children who were all unable to comprehend the celebrations before them.

Bella's chubby legs kicked with excitement as the lights dimmed and her mother entered the room with a pink birthday cake decorated with a large candle with the number one. Everyone gathered around to sing "Happy Birthday," and Mandy caught eyes with her sister Karen, who was trying hard to hold back her happy tears. As Bella's aunty Paula helped her to blow out the candles, Bella blew a huge spit bubble and reached out to grab the cake.

Mandy adored all three of her nieces and nephew, and she always jumped at the chance to play with them. Since they'd been born, she had spent more on designer label clothes for them than on anything she bought for herself. But she had a secret she was too embarrassed to admit: each time she bought something for them, she also purchased an identical one for the child she hoped to have. She had two suitcases and a duffel bag under the bed in her spare room crammed full of tiny outfits that would never be worn.

However, lately she was finding it increasingly difficult to be around the children—the thought of not being able to have a child with her DNA Match, as her sisters had, made her feel physically sick. Even if she soon met someone to start a family with, he would never be Mr. Right because Mr. Right was dead. She worried she wouldn't be able to love a baby she'd had with someone else in the same way she might have loved a child she'd made with Richard. And she was quietly beginning to resent Paula and Karen for having everything she dreamed of. If Kirstin could find a nice girl to settle down with, she'd be next, and the wedge that separated them would expand yet further.

"Right, missy, come with me," Paula said and grabbed Mandy firmly by the arm, frog-marching her out into the garden, and into the plastic Wendy house that belonged to Bella. Inside, they crouched to sit on the small furniture and Paula produced a pack of cigarettes from her pocket, a wicked glint in her eye. "Just what are you playing at?"

Mandy feigned innocence, though she knew exactly what her sister wanted to know.

"Richard, your Match. You promised we'd get to meet him today. Then at the last minute you suddenly say he's 'busy with an urgent personal training booking.' Who needs a personal training session urgently? Come on now."

Mandy swallowed hard. She'd told her family almost everything there was to know about Richard with one exception—that he was no longer alive. She stared at Paula, unsure what to say.

"It's been two months since you met the love of your life, and we haven't seen hide nor hair of him." Paula blew smoke out the open window. "So what's wrong with him?"

"There's nothing wrong with him," Mandy said and took a deep drag. She hadn't realized she'd needed a cigarette that badly until she felt the smoke hit the back of her throat.

"Is there a massive mole on his forehead? Tattoos all over his body? Is he missing a limb? Is he a foot shorter than you? Is he black? You do know that even our old racist grandfather could get his head around Richard's color if he knew you were happy—"

"No, no, it's none of those." Mandy wished it were that easy.

"You think we're going to scare the poor boy off, don't you?"

"Well, you girls can be a bit full-on sometimes..." Mandy wasn't ready to share the story just yet, so she said, "He's quite shy. I'll introduce him when I think he's ready."

"Okay, fair enough." Strangely Paula seemed satisfied with the explanation. "But let's not leave it till Bella's second birthday before I get to meet my brother-in-law-to-be."

"No, of course not," Mandy said, aware that her lies had an expiration date.

37

CHRISTOPHER

Christopher wasn't sure how to react when Amy walked through his front door and threw her arms around him.

He couldn't read her facial expressions, so he responded by mimicking her movements and wrapped his arms around her in response. It appeared to be the correct move.

"It's been a horrible day," she began quietly, releasing her grip and making her way through the hallway and into the living room. She unzipped her boots, discarded them in the corner of the room, and tossed her keys on a circular wooden side table. Christopher straightened each key and her footwear when she wasn't looking.

"They found another girl last night," Amy began, pouring a large measure of vodka into a tumbler from his drinks cabinet. The splash of tonic was less generous. *Wrong glass*, he thought, but it didn't seem appropriate to point that out. "South London this time."

"Why has this one upset you?" he replied, and attempted to rein in his fevered anticipation about the conversation to come.

"Because he upped the ante this time. The poor girl had been beaten to a pulp, her teeth were smashed in, her ribs were broken and bleach poured down her throat. He stabbed her in the eyes."

It was a necessity, thought Christopher.

"It wouldn't surprise me if he'd raped her, too," Amy added.

Christopher was offended by the suggestion. "Gosh," he replied instead. "How do you know all this? I didn't think you were working on that case?"

"I'm not, but a handful of us were asked to conduct some door-to-door inquiries today because it's all hands on deck until they catch him. This was his ninth victim. Can you believe it Christopher? Nine poor girls."

They'll find Number Ten soon, Christopher thought and folded his arms in satisfaction.

"Before we talked to her neighbors, the DI leading the case showed us the pictures of the girls. I've never seen so many bodies relating to one case."

Christopher only just contained a smile at the thought of how the police were discussing the fruits of his labor. And, even better, they were being discussed with someone he was close to.

"All the others had just been strangled," Amy said. "But this attack was personal, like he knew her…like he really wanted to make her suffer. It's totally changed our psychological understanding of him."

That wasn't the plan, thought Christopher, *but it's a useful little diversion.*

"In what way?" he asked.

"Well, there's no doubt that he's an evil fuck-up," she replied, making Christopher bristle. "But now it appears he's a vindictive one, too. Not only does he focus on women, but it seems that he has a deep, ingrained hatred of them as well, which is why this attack was so vicious. I don't know, maybe his mum abused him as a child or something."

Christopher forced himself to keep a straight face—she couldn't have been further from the truth. He identified himself as a primary psychopath, one who had been born with the condition—or *gift*, as he'd come to think of it—as opposed to being a secondary psychopath and a product of his environment. His environment had been perfectly suburban, with two parents who often told him they loved him, even if he couldn't actually feel it.

He dealt with their premature loss to cancer and heart disease as matter-of-factly as losing a pet rabbit. He remained in sporadic contact with his brothers, specifically Oliver, the eldest. Try as he might, Christopher never got to grips with the importance of money, and it was Oliver who'd assisted him with his share of the substantial inheritance each son received. With the correct investments, it gave Christopher a regular monthly income that was enough for him to take on graphic design work only when he wanted to.

"Did they find a picture on her of the next victim?" he inquired. He hated the word "victim" because it implied they were innocent in all of this. In his eyes they were volunteers, as they had offered him their telephone numbers when they chatted on dating apps; they'd made themselves too available, and there were consequences in doing so. None of them had Matches; they were all seen as second-class citizens, pitied by those who had found true love.

But it was a win-win situation for all involved—when this was over, he'd be happy with his continued anonymity while the "victims," as Amy called them, would be rewarded by being part of a case that would go down in British criminal history. They'd become the subjects of books, featured in TV documentaries and dramas, and the case would be theorized for decades.

They'd have accomplished so much more in their deaths than they ever could have hoped to in their pedestrian lives.

"Yes, there was another photo," Amy replied, and took a seat at the dining room table, propping her head up with her hands. "It's pretty much a certainty she's dead, of course, but there's no indication of where the body could be. We're now playing the waiting game, hoping that somebody's going to spot a stencil painted on the pavement."

"Why can't you release her photo to the media?"

"Because none of the newspapers or television channels will show the face of what's probably a dead girl. Thankfully the internet doesn't have such high moral standards, and every victim is now online. We've done an artist's impression of the latest girl for the papers and TV, so maybe that'll speed things up."

The spray-painted stencils left by Christopher had certainly captured the public's imagination, he realized. He had reached Number Five before the police had linked them, but in making it public, there'd been a smattering of copycat paintings around the capital.

Investigators had yet to connect all the women with the same dating app, UFlirt. It was an offshoot of Match Your DNA, designed for those who'd yet to find a Match to meet others in the same, lonely boat. Back when he was making long and short lists, Christopher experimented with other apps and found some of the girls were registered there, too, so maybe it was too difficult for the police to narrow it down to one common link.

Even when the police examined their phones, they would find no link to Christopher among their messages. He had created more than one hundred email addresses, assigned to dozens of untraceable burner smartphones, hidden away in a disused freezer in his basement.

He'd used software downloaded from the dark web to keep tabs on their texts, photographs, social media, cloud storage devices and GPS locations, but he had never spoken to them again.

It seemed incredible to him that people were stupid enough to store their entire lives on five inches of plastic for anyone to poke about in.

"I just don't think I'll ever understand it," said Amy. "I don't think I'll ever get my head around why someone could be compelled to take so many lives. What's the point?"

For the challenge, Christopher thought to himself. *For the fun of it. For the history books. For having the balls and ambition to decide to be a serial killer rather than fall into it or be compelled to do it. To actively choose this life and then to actively stop it. Because nobody has ever done it like this before. And because there's no other feeling quite like being in control of someone else's life.*

"I don't know," he instead replied, and thought it best to comfort her again. He stood behind her and wrapped his arms around her shoulders, bringing her toward him. "Maybe it's because he simply *can*," he added, kissing the top of her head. "So he does."

Amy clung to the security of her boyfriend's strong, warm arms for a moment as he remained behind her, wishing he could have seen the expression on her face when she first saw a photo of what he was capable of. Even he might have identified what revulsion looked like.

38

JADE

Jade was awake for much of her first night in Australia and not just because of the jet lag.

Coming to terms with the news of Kevin's terminal illness and the realization that she didn't love him had left her bewildered; angry at him and even more angry at herself.

In the quietness of the farm's guesthouse, she turned on the bedside lamp and logged on to the Wi-Fi to research whether this was normal—not feeling anything for her Match. She knew there was a love between them, but she hadn't experienced the deafening, booming, colorful fireworks or rainbows that the films and TV programs she'd watched depicted. Fictional couples with a DNA Match always fell hook, line and sinker for one another the instant they came into contact. Why wasn't it happening to her?

She checked the official Match Your DNA website: The emotions felt between two Matches can vary from couple to couple, it read. For some, it happens in an instant; for others, it can take several meetings or several days before the connection is made. This can sometimes be due to the mental capacity of a couple or an individual, or an illness which can affect the production of pheromones and receptors. A change in a Match's body clock can also affect the way they process their emotions.

Jade began to feel a little better about herself, knowing her predicament wasn't uncommon. She'd begun to worry it was Kevin's condition and how little he resembled the photos that were delaying her feelings, and the fact that she was a shallow, superficial cow. Now armed with new knowledge, she felt much more relieved. It would happen; she just had to wait for it. Although in the long run, she acknowledged that it would be hard being head over heels in love with a man who wouldn't see out the summer.

Suddenly there came a gentle knocking on her door. "Come in," she replied and propped herself up on her elbows. The door slowly opened, and Kevin's smiling face appeared.

"Hey," he said. "I saw your light was still on. Do you want to come and see something?"

"Sure," she said. The clock on the wall read 3:56 a.m.

"I'll meet you by your car in fifteen minutes. Bring a jumper. Early mornings are cold as ice out here. Oh, and your keys of course."

Kevin was already standing by the car and leaning against his walking frame when Jade appeared. "Let's go," he said chirpily.

He directed them as she drove along the dirt track driveway and back onto the highway. They traveled for around ten minutes until they reached a flat region by the side of the road.

"You can't come to Australia without seeing the sun rise," Kevin said. "It's like nothing on earth."

They sat together, listening to a playlist of soul classics as the darkness gradually lifted and was replaced by a purple-and-orange hue.

"How often do you come out here?" she asked.

"Quite a lot when I was first diagnosed," he said. "Then I went into a dark place for a while. I was angry at everything, especially thinking that everyone else would have a lifetime of sunrises and sunsets, while mine were limited. Then I began to understand that being here to see any sunrise was a major accomplishment. It means I've lived for one more day."

Jade instinctively placed her head on Kevin's shoulder, where it remained until the sun rose and he'd long drifted off to sleep. His hand was cold, his skin parchment-like, and she wondered how he might have felt to the touch before cancer started eating away at him.

While the intense Match Your DNA love was still undoubtedly missing, there was no doubt that she felt relaxed around him. They'd shared so many intense conversations by phone that she'd come to see him as a best friend as well as her Match. Maybe that was more important than anything else, she thought. Maybe when you took it back to basics, that's what love really was: just being there for someone when the sun rises and sets.

Jade arrived back at the farm with her sleeping partner and was greeted by his brother who opened the passenger door and unclipped Kevin's seat belt. He scooped him into his arms and carried him back into the house as Jade looked on, suddenly feeling the first pangs of something that she couldn't identify.

39

NICK

Nick nursed the steaming polystyrene cup of hot chocolate he'd bought from the kiosk a safe distance away from the grass pitches. He'd contemplated buying himself a burger, too, until he spotted the filthy fingernails of the man serving behind the counter.

It was the first rugby game he'd ever attended—his school had been keener to teach hockey than rugby—and it was as cold as hell outside. He pulled the gray cashmere scarf Sally had bought for his birthday tightly around his neck and his hoodie up over his head to keep his ears warm.

What am I doing here? he wondered, having no clue what the game's rules were or what the state of play was on the pitch. All he knew was that he could barely keep his eyes off the one player in front of him.

Nick's eyes moved from Alex's calves to his thick, tree trunk thighs and then his solid torso. He almost willed himself to be turned on by Alex's physical appearance so their Match might start making sense. If they had been predetermined to be together, surely he'd feel at least a mild sexual arousal? But there was nothing.

On a whim, Nick had decided to spend his morning watching the game. He'd recalled the framed photo of the team on the wall of Alex's office and had searched online for their fixtures list to see when they were playing next. The location was a community rugby pitch in Birmingham's suburbs, but, aware of how creepy it might appear if he suddenly turned up unannounced, Nick stood a distance away from the other supporters to watch Alex from afar.

A week had passed since they'd met at the bar, where they'd stayed for much of the evening, becoming acquainted with one another. They'd both grown steadily drunk, gradually discovering more things they had in common, from artists to architecture, from travel to rock music. The only subject both were reticent to go into any detail about was their relationships with their partners. And as the conversation flowed, neither of them brought up their Match again, although it wasn't far from their thoughts.

Their time together had only been cut short when Alex's girlfriend, Mary, called asking when to expect him home. For the briefest of moments, Nick felt jealous.

They had parted with a polite but lingering handshake, each secretly fearing that this touch might be their last. Neither suggested meeting again, nor keeping in contact; however, it seemed to be enough, for now, to know the other was out there, albeit leading their lives independently of one another.

In the meantime, Sally had arranged for her and Nick to take a surprise trip to Bruges. The first Nick knew of it was when on a Friday afternoon, she turned up at his office with two suitcases, Eurostar tickets and printout confirmation of a hotel she'd booked. There'd been a distance in their relationship recently, and he felt that he'd let this business with Alex come between them. But the way Sally had arranged their sexy getaway made him feel as if she were trying to make up for something, too. She was much more distracted than usual, and he could only assume it was that she was upset he had been Matched. He tried to put the thought to the back of his mind.

In Bruges, her sexual appetite was almost insatiable, and, when they weren't sightseeing, they were in bed. Part of him wondered if she suspected he had seen Alex again and that she was trying to compete. But neither mentioned his name.

On their return to Birmingham, Nick didn't just *want* to see Alex again, he *needed* to. It had been eight days since they had last been in each other's company.

Suddenly his thoughts were interrupted by a rugby ball flying through the air which smacked him square on the shoulder. "Shit," he yelled in surprise. The crowd in front of him parted and left him exposed.

"Pass us the ball, mate?" a stocky, shaven-headed man yelled through his gum-shield, and, just as Nick threw it clumsily in the player's direction, Alex saw him. Nick looked back apprehensively, promptly regretting his decision to crowbar his way into Alex's private world.

But when Nick saw the smile slowly creeping across Alex's face, his own didn't lag far behind.

40

ELLIE

Tim had a bowl of cereal in his hand when he answered the front door.

Ellie could just about imagine how it looked to him, to discover a tall, shaven-headed burly man standing rigid alongside a nervous-looking Ellie. Two black Range Rovers with tinted windows were parked on the curb outside Tim's modest semi-detached home. She didn't know if he could make out the shapes of people in both of them.

"Hi," Tim mumbled, and swallowed his mouthful of breakfast. His shirtsleeves were rolled up, and a yellow tie hung loosely around his neck. He looked taken aback by her sudden appearance, probably wondering how she'd gotten his address.

"Hello," Ellie said. "I'm sorry to turn up unannounced. Do you have a few minutes before you go to work?"

"I've been trying to talk to you for the last few days, but you've been ignoring me."

"I know and I'm sorry. That's why I'm here to explain. Please?"

Tim moved to one side. Andrei was the first to enter. He removed his dark glasses and scanned the entrance hall and various rooms before he let Ellie follow. Tim frowned at the man-mountain, then at his DNA Match.

"He's my security detail," she offered, almost apologetically.

"In that case I should make you aware of the family of ninjas living in the dining room and the barrels of mustard gas I've been cooking up in the conservatory."

An unamused Andrei shot him a disapproving glance.

Ellie had taken four days to muster the courage to approach Tim after the events of their second date had culminated in red paint being hurled at them. She'd bunkered down in her London townhouse since and remained there, embarrassed and deeply humiliated.

Had Tim been just a run-of-the-mill date, she'd have made sure to never see him again. However, he was far from ordinary. Besides, she liked spending time getting to know him, and the kiss they'd shared shortly before the attack was nothing short of wonderful.

Ellie was accustomed to public speaking, and thousands of people had attended some of her keynote speeches around the world. But, try as she might, as she had in her many rehearsals in front of the bathroom mirror, she still didn't know how to begin to explain to Tim what had happened.

"Can I offer you or your pet giant a coffee?" Tim asked, eyeballing Andrei.

"That's what I call him." Ellie laughed, trying to lighten the mood. "Andrei the Giant. You know, like the famous French wrestler? He was in *The Princess Bride*? It's one of my all-time favorite films…"

Tim shook his head and made his way into the living room, muting the sound of breakfast television presenters with the remote control. He put his bowl down on the coffee table and invited Ellie to sit.

"So what happened the other night?" he asked. "Why did a complete stranger throw red paint at us and yell that you have blood on your hands?"

"Because that's what many people think," she replied. "You've probably guessed by now that I haven't been completely honest with you about who I am or what I do for a living."

"Uh-huh."

"The surname I used on my DNA profile is my mum's maiden name, Ayling. My actual surname is Stanford and I don't work as a personal assistant to a CEO. I actually work for myself. And what I do is a little…controversial."

"What, are you an arms dealer or something?"

"No, no," she said. "Nothing like that." Ellie paused and took a deep breath. "Tim, I am the scientist who discovered the Match Your DNA gene, and a lot of people hate me for it."

41

MANDY

Many family birthdays, anniversaries, girls' nights out, work leaving parties, meals out and get-togethers passed, and Mandy declined them all.

Each time an invitation came, she mustered up an excuse as to why she was unable to attend, often citing that she had plans with Richard some one hundred miles away. She was telling the truth, at least in part, as she was choosing to spend more and more of her time with his family rather than her own.

From the tone of their voice mail messages, she guessed that her mother and sisters were finding it increasingly frustrating. They had once been a tight-knit unit, brought on by the death of their father more than a decade ago, but now Mandy was trying to pull away, and the rest couldn't understand why. Of course, they thought that she had found her Match and expected her to be at her most open, but Mandy just couldn't tell them. Not yet.

Spending time with them didn't nourish her in the same way spending time with Pat and Chloe did. She felt more and more alienated from her family; two of her sisters were in the midst of the love and happiness that Mandy could never have, and she doubted they'd be able to understand what she was going through. And her mother, though she, too, had lost the love of her life, was too old-fashioned to truly understand how strong a Match bond could be, and what it's like when it's taken away. Richard's family filled the void.

"If you want to have a few drinks, then why don't you stay over?" Pat had texted the evening before. So with a packed overnight bag, she spent the evening with them watching DVDs, drinking wine and leafing through an album of Richard's baby photos.

Not for the first time, she wondered what their baby might have looked like.

When they finally retired to bed, Mandy found herself wide awake in the guest room, unable to sleep. She closed her eyes and, as she did most nights, she pictured a future they'd never have. She imagined walking through her parents' front door on Christmas Day arm in arm, and how he'd be the center of her family's attention. Her fingers clenched the duvet, and she squeezed it hard in frustration.

On her way back from the bathroom, Mandy spied Richard's bedroom door slightly ajar. Hesitantly, she opened it, but the room was empty. She entered, quietly closing the door behind her, and turned on a lamp.

Curiosity got the better of her, and she slid open the drawer of his bedside cabinet and peeked inside. There were toiletries such as moisturizers, hair products and deodorants, along with an open pack of ten condoms. She flipped the lid and counted— just four remaining. She immediately wondered who'd been the lucky girl—or girls—with whom he'd used the missing ones. The thought made her heart sink.

She was envious of a woman she couldn't even put a face to. She looked under his bed and found his threadbare army-green backpack from his traveling days. The torn airline and coach labels were still attached, but there was nothing inside. She removed occasional pieces of clothing from his chest of drawers to press against her skin or to run her fingertips across and inhale; each one made her nerve endings tingle.

Then, in the bottom drawer, tucked way at the back, she found a scuffed mobile phone, several models out of date. Mandy turned it on, assuming the battery would be dead, but there were two bars of power left, and it was so old it required no pass code.

She was aware that she was invading Richard's privacy, but she didn't care, her thirst for more knowledge about him was unquenchable. The more she learned, the more she needed to know.

Most of his old text messages were from personal training clients or friends organizing nights out. They revealed very little about him, other than he had a wide circle of friends and grateful clients.

However, his photos were dominated by images of one person in particular: a young woman, in various states of undress. She was nearer to Richard's age than Mandy's and was far prettier, she thought. Mandy fought away the pangs of jealousy. She frowned, wondering who the girl was, and continued to flick through his pictures quickly, hoping the photos of this girl would cease.

That was when she stumbled across a naked selfie of Richard.

She held her breath and felt her heart racing, unsure what to do next. She swiped from right to left to see half a dozen more explicit pictures of her Match. She was surprised at how well endowed he was, and unashamedly pinched the phone's display to get a closer look. She suddenly experienced a sensation she hadn't felt in quite some time—an overwhelming arousal.

She found a three-minute video clip and her face flushed red. It was of Richard, pleasuring himself, in that very room on the bed where she sat. Mandy couldn't hold herself back any longer. She double-checked the bedroom door was closed, turned down the volume on Richard's phone and lay back, in exactly the same position as he had. Slowly and silently she slipped her hand down the front of her pajamas and began to touch herself, closing her eyes and envisaging how it might have felt to have Richard inside her. It wasn't long before she felt every muscle in her body clench, and she erupted at the exact same moment as the image of her Match.

She replaced the mobile back in his drawer and lay on the bed, smiling and waiting for her light-headedness to ease. But instead of returning to her own room, she drifted off into a deep sleep, and only awoke hours later when she heard the sound of the door hinges creaking and Pat's face appeared.

"Oh, I'm so sorry." Mandy immediately apologized. "I couldn't sleep, so I came in here."

"It's fine, darling," Pat replied and gave her a warm smile. "You can stay with Richard as often as you like."

"You'd like children of your own, wouldn't you?"

Pat's question caught Mandy off guard. They'd been sitting in a park close to Pat's house, staring at the rolling countryside surrounding them. Mandy had been telling her about her failed marriage and how it had left her at the brink of despair, but she had focused her gaze on a young mum with two small children, and the conversation tapered off. The excited kids were taking it in turns to throw bread to the ducks in the pond, giggling each time the birds quacked.

"Yes, I'd have loved my own family," Mandy replied, with a resigned smile.

"You mentioned that you have nieces and a nephew? Do you see them often?"

"I see them a lot. Well, not so much lately… My sisters tell me I can spend as much time with them as I want, but it's not the same when they're not your own."

"It can be, if you allow yourself."

"Not for me. I actually fell pregnant with Sean, my ex-husband, twice, but miscarried both times, the first a few months after we got married, and then a couple of weeks after he left me for his DNA Match. I thought that was it for me, that I didn't stand a chance of being a mum with someone I really loved, until I discovered I had Richard. Then my imagination went into overdrive." Mandy gave a quiet laugh. "We were going to buy a little old cottage in a village together—somewhere that needed doing up from scratch that we could work on together—and the first room we'd do up was the nursery. And we'd time it just right so that I'd fall pregnant as we were finishing the place, and I'd be the mum I always saw myself being. Now that opportunity has been taken away from me."

Pat paused before she spoke. "Not necessarily," she said. "Come with me. I want to show you something."

As Mandy followed Pat along a steep path and up a hill, she wondered what she meant. After ten minutes or so, they stopped and squinted across the horizon.

"You can see the whole of the town from up here," she began. "Do you see that steeple right in the distance? That's the village where Richard Senior and I married—in St. Mary's Church. And down there? That's where my Richard went to primary school. Then if you look over to the right, next to the large chimneys, that's the Fox and Hounds pub where Chloe got her first weekend job when she was studying for her A levels. So much of my family's life is wrapped up in this one little viewpoint."

"It must be important to you."

"It is to all of us. Richard in particular loved it up here; he'd come up on his mountain bike and stay for ages. This is where we scattered his ashes—so they were free to blow across the town that made him. Not all of them, though, the rest we scattered at our cottage in the Lake District."

"That's lovely."

Pat turned to her and looked her in the eye. "But just because Richard's no longer with us, it doesn't have to mean it's the end of my boy, though."

"What do you mean?"

"I've told you before, Richard always wanted children of his own. Like you, he was a natural with kids, probably because he was a big kid at heart."

Mandy nodded. He sounded so perfect for her.

Pat continued looking out over the vista before them. "Well, when he found out he had testicular cancer, we didn't know how bad it was going to be. So he went to a sperm bank, just in case further down the line he couldn't have a family the natural way. He had to give three or four samples—I remember he joked about it being more enjoyable than a visit to a regular bank. Mandy, the samples are still in storage."

She turned her head to look at Pat, who continued to stare into the distance.

"I think you understand the opportunity I'm offering you," she continued. "If you would like to have my grandchild—Richard's baby—then I'm giving you that chance."

42

CHRISTOPHER

Christopher watched Amy's shoulders rise and fall as she slept in his bed.

He disliked having his personal space intruded with spooning and cuddling, so the moment she drifted off to sleep, he moved his arm from over her waist, slid his body to his side of the mattress and lay on his back with his head turned. Observing her as she slept was one of the headiest experiences he'd ever had with another person.

In the faded light, he could just about make out the bright tattoo of a butterfly that rested below her neck, something he detested almost as much as her taste in cheap rings and bracelets. But those things aside, there was little about Amy he'd change. By this stage of a relationship, he'd have normally found a multitude of reasons to have called time and cast her adrift. However, he had another plan for Amy.

Slowly, Christopher's arm reached the edge of the bed and his hand stretched to the floor below. His fingertips silently felt around until they connected with the wooden handles of his cheese wire where he'd purposely left it for this very reason. He gently pulled it over the soft bristles of the carpet, up the side of the mattress and on to the duvet. With both hands on the handles, he held the wire above him and stretched it as taut as possible. He turned his body to its side, so he was again spooning Amy and slowly lowered the wire parallel to her neck. He could feel his heart beating stronger and stronger with every centimeter he drew it closer to her skin. Finally, when it reached a position he was familiar with, he let it rest.

Christopher had gained an incalculable amount of pleasure since his killings began, but he'd always chosen strangers. The closest he'd come to those on his list were generic messages via UFlirt. "Banter," as they insisted on calling it, would pass to and fro until he'd cajoled them into giving him their telephone numbers. None had the forethought to understand that, by willingly offering up their digits, they were handing him a key that unlocked the door to their entire identities.

Amy interrupted his recollections with an audible, post-coital sigh, and Christopher wondered what she was dreaming about. He never dreamed, or at least if he did, he never remembered them. He was sure he wasn't missing out, though, because dreams were unattainable; what was the point in doing anything if there was no chance of success?

The sex between Christopher and Amy was unlike anything he'd experienced before. He'd had no substantial urge to pleasure the seventy or so women he'd slept with since losing his virginity at the age of twelve; it was—and had always been—only about his own gratification. But Amy was an exception, and he reveled in the fact that he was the one who could make her groan and who could take her to the edge, only to pull back until he was ready for her to succumb. He relished being in control of her orgasms, but then he also readily gave into her taking charge and not allowing him to climax until she gave him permission. He had never relinquished dominance like this in any aspect of his life, yet it felt perfectly normal to do so with Amy.

This left him conflicted—normal was not something Christopher aspired to be; he believed his brain was wired in such a way that was much more powerful than "normal." It was a gift that enabled him to do anything he wanted to, without fear and—to date—without consequence.

He moved closer toward her so that there was barely anything between his nose and the back of Amy's head. He inhaled deeply and took in the lemon seagrass scented shampoo she'd used the night before. That was his favorite—he liked it when she smelled of citrus.

With one swift maneuver, the wire would be wrapped around her neck, and she'd be clawing at it like all the others had.

"Why are you so fidgety?" Amy mumbled, to his surprise.

"Sorry, I thought you were asleep."

"I was, but I sensed you weren't. What's wrong?"

"Nothing. I just can't sleep and got to thinking about those women you've been investigating."

"The victims."

"Yes." He swallowed, still finding the word distasteful.

"And what were you thinking about them?"

He wanted to say that he could recall every different scent and brand of shampoo each girl had used as he jolted their heads backwards once the wire was wrapped around their necks. And how since he'd begun all this, he understood a person's beauty was transient because within just a few days of biological decay they all looked identical: bloated, discolored and eaten inside and out by their own bacteria.

"I was wondering what went through their heads when they knew they were about to die," he replied. "What would you think about?"

Amy paused before she answered. "Probably all the things I

wished I'd accomplished while I'd had the chance. What about you?"

"The same," Christopher lied.

He lifted the wire back above her head and lowered it down to where he'd left it under the bed. Knowing he could strangle her at any given moment gave him more pleasure than would the actual act itself.

But while Christopher was aware he was making good progress in the project he'd began all those months ago, there was a fly in the ointment. He'd met a woman he liked, and, for the first time in his life, he was falling in love.

And that had not been part of the plan.

43

JADE

Just over a week into Jade's Australia adventure and Kevin's health was deteriorating quickly.

He was losing his appetite and spending more and more time sleeping in his bedroom. Despite the ninety-five-degree temperature outside, Kevin often complained he was cold and layered himself in baggy clothing. He swallowed so many tablets each day that sometimes, when she listened closely, she swore she could hear him rattle.

Jade was resentful that their time together was slipping through her fingers, and she wasn't prepared for it to come to an end. So while he was awake, she did all she could to engage him in conversation and spend time being with him. They spent much of their days talking about their lives before she left England and before he was diagnosed with cancer. Hours passed as they lay sprawled across the sofa in his bedroom watching classic 1980s Brat Pack films on Netflix, and they grew so comfortable with each other that there were times when Jade forgot her moments with Kevin came with a time limit. When she was reminded of it, she couldn't help but imagine how her life would change when he wasn't around anymore, and she felt herself becoming sullen.

In the beginning of their relationship, when Jade lived in blissful ignorance of Kevin's condition, talking to him had become an integral part of her everyday routine, and she planned her mornings and evenings around it. She'd set her alarm so she could wake up earlier than necessary and talk to him as they ate together—her, breakfast and him, supper. And she'd always record anything on TV that was broadcast after 10:00 p.m. to watch later, so they had more time of an evening.

Jade was used to her heart fluttering when he texted her or when her phone lit up with his call. And she knew that when the unavoidable came, she would miss that. But what she had yet to figure out was if it was Kevin she'd miss or the knowledge there was someone in the world who was made for her.

As Kevin slept, Jade would lie beside him with her head on his stomach as it rose and fell with shallow breaths. And during the long periods when Kevin was out of action, she'd offer to help his parents, Susan and Dan, around the house, or drive into town to run errands for them. They taught her how a dairy and sheep farm operated, taking her out in the truck to help round up the sheep, or teaching her how to affix the milking equipment to the cows. It was a whole world away from the one she'd been stagnating in in Sunderland. But she now saw that the city wasn't the problem; it was her. Something about the quiet farming life agreed with her, and she felt like she could finally relax into who she was.

Jade was astonished at how close she could feel to people she had only met two weeks ago, and she desperately wished there was a way that she could remove the pain they felt as they watched their son struggle. The more time she spent around them, the more she felt that they were sanding away her rough edges.

It also made her think of her own parents, and the sadness and frustration she'd put them through in recent years. She had spent so long harboring this unnecessary animosity toward them for making her move back home after she left university, and only now did she understand it was for her own benefit. They were good, solid, working class Northerners—her father a mechanic on a car factory assembly line and her mother a baker—and she had repaid their pride and values with brattish behavior. She felt ashamed of herself.

Like Kevin's cancer and Susan's and Dan's pain, there was something of her own she wished she could remove, too, but it wasn't something she could ever share with her new adoptive family.

However, as each day passed, her affection became all the more consuming.

44

NICK

"To what do I owe this pleasure?" Alex asked Nick as they drove away from the rugby club ground in Alex's car.

Nick clenched his fists to stop his hands from tingling at the smell of Alex's damp hair and recently applied aftershave.

"Honestly? I don't know," he replied. "It was a spur of the moment thing. I remembered who you played for, and I read up about them online, and the next thing I know, I'm waving Sally off to spend the weekend with her mum, and I'm on my way over to see you play a game I don't even understand. Have I stepped over the line?"

"I should say yes, but, no, you haven't."

Nick was pleased to hear it. He sat and pondered his next question, trying to phrase it properly in his head before posing it. "This will sound really tragic, but I have to ask—have you thought about me much since we saw each other last?" He looked away and waited for Alex to reply, hoping his answer would be positive.

"What, do you mean have I thought about you over the last eight days, eleven hours and, let me check, forty-seven minutes? Yeah, you could say I have a little."

Both men smiled.

"Now can I ask you something?" Alex continued. "When we spoke on the phone the first time, you told me you took the Match Your DNA test even though you didn't believe in it. So why do it?"

"My girlfriend, well, my fiancée, wanted me to. We're getting married soon, and she wanted to reassure herself we were genuinely suited."

Nick noticed Alex edge ever so slightly away from him when he said this, as if the news had come as an unwelcome surprise.

"And when she found out that you were Matched with a guy…?"

"She found it hilarious. But it was Sally who insisted I meet you, which is why I made that appointment with the fake name."

"Why didn't you just tell her to back off?"

"It was important to her… I don't really know why, and I guess, even though I didn't want to admit it, I was a little curious about you, too."

"Most women wouldn't have let us anywhere near each other, let alone encourage it."

"Sally and I have always had an honest relationship with no bullshit… We tell each other everything."

"So she knows where you are right now?"

Nick averted his eyes. "I think you already know the answer to that. Where does Mary think you are?"

"Out for drinks with the rugby boys after the game. She's not expecting me home until tonight."

The streets of suburban Birmingham were quiet for a Saturday afternoon as Alex's Mini Cooper made its way out toward the M6.

"Where are we headed, then?" asked Nick.

"Mate, I don't have a fucking clue."

45

ELLIE

Tim hiked his eyebrows. "Are you kidding me?" He let his body sink into the soft cushions of his sofa as he digested Ellie's revelation—it was she who'd discovered the gene which formed the heart of Match Your DNA and had used it to build one of the world's most successful businesses.

Then, much to Ellie's surprise, Tim began to chuckle, which developed into a full-on laugh. She was puzzled by his reaction and glanced at Andrei who stood in the corner of the room, hoping for reassurance, but Andrei simply lifted his broad shoulders and shrugged.

"So let me get this right," Tim said, wiping his eyes. "You're telling me that I've been on two dates with the person who is my DNA Match, and it turns out she was the person who invented it?"

"Well, *discovered* it is probably a more accurate description, but yes." Ellie nodded.

"And the company? As in, the company that's bigger than Facebook, Amazon and Apple…all that belongs to you?"

"Most of it, yes."

He shook his head and ran his fingers through his thinning hair. "You couldn't make this up."

"I'm sorry I didn't tell you the truth before now," Ellie said earnestly. "I honestly wasn't sure how to."

"No, I get it, I really do. You didn't trust me, and that's fine because, given your situation, I'd probably have kept *shtum*, too."

Ellie gave a nervous half smile but didn't appear convinced that he was okay with it. Tim placed her hands inside his, and immediately she felt that familiar sensation return. It spread throughout her body as it had when he'd kissed her on their disastrous second date.

"Look, Ellie, you could be working behind the checkouts at Lidl and I wouldn't give a flying fajita. I mean, the fact you could afford to own Lidl and still have change to buy Morrisons and Tesco doesn't matter to me either. But you need to see it from my perspective—my first date in yonks is with the person who single-handedly reinvented the concept of dating. It's bloody hilarious."

"So you're not angry with me?"

"No, of course I'm not. But I still don't get why that nutter outside the restaurant threw red paint at you? We looked like we'd spent the evening clubbing seals to death."

Ellie sighed. She hated thinking about this side of her job. "Because not everyone is pleased with the consequences of Match Your DNA. While my discovery has Matched millions and millions of people around the world, it's also broken up an awful of a lot of couples who thought they were made for each other and it turned out they weren't. And I get the blame for that—more often than you can probably imagine." She paused, trying to gauge his reaction before continuing. "And getting to where I am today, it's not been easy. Like most large businesses, sometimes corners had to be cut and people felt they were hurt, but it was all for the greater good to get us to where we are today... I don't want you to think badly of me."

"Can you give me a little credit to come up with my own opinion?"

Ellie hesitated. "That woman with the paint... I wasn't honest when I said I didn't know her. Do you remember that incident in Edinburgh seven years ago when a man started stabbing shoppers in the city center?"

"Didn't he kill, like, half-a-dozen people before the police got him?"

Ellie nodded. "The killer was her son. He had mental health issues and had been living under her supervision until he found his Match. His Match was already married, and, well, once she learned of his problems, she left him and went back to her husband. Her Match started stalking her, and then one day stabbed her to death in the shop where she worked before attacking random people. It was awful."

"And his mum blames you?"

"Yes. We've told her—through the courts—that we can't be held responsible for who takes the test, but she refuses to accept it."

Tim nodded, appearing to understand her. "I'm sorry for upsetting you. Let's move on to a lighter subject. Take me back, how did you discover this DNA thing?"

"Thanks," Ellie said, feeling more at ease. "It started twelve years ago when I hadn't long left university. I was carrying out some freelance research work at a lab in Cambridge, examining the links between DNA and depression. One day I was thinking about a conversation I'd had with my sister Maggie about why she married her husband, John. She was adamant it was love at first sight, and even though they were only fourteen when they met, they knew they'd end up spending the rest of their lives together. I'm a scientist, so by nature I'm skeptical about that kind of thing, but it did get me thinking—what if she was right? What if love at first sight actually exists? Perhaps there's something tangible inside all of us that we've been confusing with sexual attraction. Having not experienced it myself, I couldn't imagine how you could just look or talk to another person and immediately *know* they're the one."

"This isn't going to get too science-y, is it?" Tim laughed. "I failed all my exams in anything that involved Bunsen burners or dissecting frogs."

"No, I'll keep it simple," Ellie said. She was used to explaining this in layman's terms. "When you see someone for the first time, you know if you fancy them or not. Well, I began by looking at what it is that appeals to different people, like whether it's their face, their body shape, how they carry themselves, etc. And then I looked to see if there was more to it than just an instant attraction… What about those people who ended up paired with someone completely against their usual type? I wondered if there was an element, or a gene, that makes our entire body react, bypassing what our brain is telling us. Can we be intrinsically linked—scientifically—to another?"

Tim sighed dramatically. "In my spare time I question how the Galactic Empire built the Death Star without the rest of the universe noticing. Meanwhile, you're out there finding genes nobody knew existed."

"I'm sure your questions are just as important as mine." Ellie smiled. "Anyway, this is the science-y bit, so stay with me. It's important I give you an idea of the scale of what I was up against. We have roughly 100 trillion cells in our bodies, and inside each of them are two meters of DNA—if you unraveled them all, they'd stretch to the sun and back a hundred times."

Tim's eyes widened. "I'm still with you."

"And the sun is 98 million miles away from Earth… Well, we already knew women produce pheromones and men have receptors that bind the pheromone molecules, and that can create an attraction between the two. But *I* discovered that when certain people are brought together, there's a variable gene inside us that allows both sexes to produce pheromones *and* have receptor genes. Two heterosexual people, two gay people—it doesn't matter. Once the right Match is made, it's set in stone. I examined the DNA of hundreds of couples, and those who shared that same gene are the ones who'd say they'd fallen for each other the moment they met. I expanded my search globally to include thousands of volunteers in my database, and kept finding the same thing time and time again—only one other person shares that gene with you. And that person is your DNA Match."

"I thought the idea of all animals was to shag around and propagate the species?"

"That's what men like to believe. But when you break it down to basics, then, yes, it is."

"But say you're an eighty-year-old woman and your Match is an eighteen-year-old man—there's not much propagating going to happen."

"You're right. Every single person produces their own personal pheromone—it's like a unique fingerprint that remains the same for the rest of your life. And it's the luck of the draw as to whether your Match is with someone who lives in the same country or whether it's someone in a Brazilian favela. Likewise, you could be Matched with someone around your age or be decades apart. It's actually intergenerational Matches that have helped to cause a drop in birth rates around the world. And the gene is largely responsible for falling numbers of one-night stands and STIs."

"Maybe it's nature's way of balancing us out. We're close to finding cures for cancer and AIDS, so now nature is trying to keep us under control with love."

"There've been stranger theories."

"So you don't think that true love can exist between couples who aren't predestined?"

"No, no, of course it can. What I am saying is that my discovery can help you find that person you are linked to. Should you choose not to be with them, you can still fall in love with someone else. But I found that those who have been Matched often feel something deeper and more complete. The other person is literally their other half."

"And how did you turn all this into a business?"

"Once I realized the ramifications of what it might mean, it scared me so much that I sat on it for a while. It was a huge responsibility. I didn't want to get it wrong. Because once the news got out, I'd be changing the way people thought about their relationships forever. It'd be like telling the world I could prove there was no God or that aliens existed—people wouldn't believe me or they'd be scared. I got many, *many* scientists—and I'm talking dozens—to go over my research to prove I wasn't a crackpot. And when every test came back positive, there was no denying it. Some old uni friends who were now hedge-fund investors helped me to register Match Your DNA as a trademark and get biological patents for Australia, Europe, Japan and the USA. And then, after an announcement in *The Lancet*, the story went viral."

"I think I remember reading about it somewhere, but I didn't take much notice of it at the time."

"Thousands and thousands of people did, though, and got in touch wanting to send me their DNA. We sent them testing kits so they could do it for free, but to turn it into a viable business we had to start charging for the results."

Tim nodded. This part he would know. "Do people always feel love at first sight?" he asked.

"Studies show that 92 percent feel an instant, arrow-to-the-heart attraction within the first forty-eight hours of meeting. With the other 8 percent, it can take longer. But that can be down to psychological issues, anything from a mental illness like clinical depression to emotional problems, like whether they have trust issues or have built up barriers. There are a few other mitigating factors, as well. People might fight those feelings, but once they're in their Match's presence eventually, nature will always prevail."

"What about a regular person and someone with a genetic disorder like Down's Syndrome? Can they be Matched?"

"Yes."

"Wouldn't that be a bit…weird?"

"Shouldn't people with learning difficulties have the chance to find love, too?"

"Yes, what I mean is, well, what I'm saying is…"

"That society isn't ready for that yet, and, yes, that's unfortunately true. But that's out of my control." Ellie was surprised that Tim hadn't read about any of this in the news. It was something that was frequently discussed, with human rights charities constantly on her case.

"We live only about fifty miles apart. Surely the chances of us being Matched must be miniscule?"

"They're not as small as you think. We found that 68 percent of people are likely to be Matched with someone in their own country. We don't know if that has to do with the fact that hundreds of generations ago we were all more closely related—small differences in our DNA can even tell us which continent we originated from. It could be that our genes are more likely to be attracted by others from a similar environment or it could be just coincidence."

Ellie waited for Tim's next question. She'd anticipated he'd react like this, as many others before him had. It almost felt like she was being interviewed, but she was used to people's curiosity and was happy to indulge Tim's.

"You mentioned how your discovery has affected so many people's lives for the better and for the worse," Tim continued. "How do you get your head around that? If it were me, I don't know if I could deal with the responsibility."

"It's hard sometimes," Ellie admitted. "I've had hate mail and death threats from people whose partners have left them to be with their Match, and from people with no Match who think it's my fault. For every ten Matches we put together, three regular couples will split up. We've put thousands of dating sites out of business across the world, but on the flip side we've given so much work to divorce lawyers and relationship counselors. We've boosted the wedding industry as people are more willing to commit knowing they're made for each other," she said, almost by rote.

"So you don't feel any kind of guilt or responsibility?"

"No. Why should I?"

Tim ignored her. "How do you stop kids from taking the test, or pedophiles being Matched with them?"

"Each country has its own laws based on the age of consent, and here in Britain, it's sixteen. Our servers run a search through the International Criminal Database, too, and warn those who get a Match if they have a criminal record. Privacy laws mean we can't reveal the exact crime, but we are allowed to rate the severity on a scale of one to five. But sometimes people slip through the net—if they've never been charged with a crime, there's nothing we can do, which is why there's about forty pages of legal disclaimers on our website. I admit, it's a gray area, and I have a huge legal team that deals with the lawsuits, but so far not one case has got past the first couple of court appearances. We're not to blame for the results. It'd be like suing gun manufacturers on behalf of anyone who's ever been shot. It's not the fault of the weapon, it's the user. I've provided the tool to change your life, but I can't be held responsible if you abuse it. I usually take my security team with me to avoid situations like the paint incident." She gestured to where Andrei still stood silently in the corner of the room. "But the night you and I met for dinner, I insisted on going alone. I just wanted to feel like a normal person again."

"And, up until she attacked you," Tim said, "did you feel normal with me?"

Ellie blushed. "Yes, I did."

"I know you're one of the 8 percent who haven't felt that lightning bolt yet, but just for the record, I'm already there."

Ellie's cheeks went a deeper shade of red, and she tried to prevent a huge smile from spreading across her face.

"Andrei, would you mind looking away for a moment?" Tim asked, and turned his head to kiss Ellie.

For the first time since they met, an overwhelming wave of euphoria began to charge its way through her veins like an electrical current.

46

MANDY

After three nights with little to no sleep, Mandy had stopped off at Tesco on her way home from work and picked up some over-the-counter sleeping tablets.

She hoped that a solid night's sleep might offer her some perspective on Pat's unexpected and remarkable offer to carry Richard's baby. Instead, the pills left her feeling sluggish and unable to think clearly the next morning.

Regardless, she went through the motions. She crawled out of bed when her 7:00 a.m. alarm went off and dragged her weary bones into the shower. Then, with a generous application of foundation and under-eye cream to make herself look less zombie and more office worker, she set off for work.

Mandy had started work as a team leader for an energy supplier's telesales division four years ago, and she hadn't treated it as anything other than a job, and certainly not a career. Lately, she was finding it an increasing struggle to gather the motivation to turn up for work each day. In fact, after "meeting" Richard, she struggled to put her broken heart into anything anymore. Her work, her family and her social life were all suffering, and today, instead of trawling through spreadsheets of data, she'd been staring blankly at her cubicle's front partition wall.

Barely a couple of hours would pass without Mandy feeling the need to look at the photos of Richard she had on her phone, picturing herself in another life, traveling the world with him, marrying him and beginning her much-craved family together. She'd even forwarded the footage of him masturbating to her own phone. Now it was in her possession, and she could pretend he'd made it only for her.

She asked herself what Richard would do if he were in her position, working in a job he hated with no light at the end of the tunnel. *He'd just leave*, she thought to herself. *He'd pack up his bags and go traveling, in search of a bigger and better adventure.* But Mandy didn't have the guts to simply quit her job, although, of course, his mother had offered her the opportunity to go on a very different adventure. Her mention of Richard's frozen sperm had come out of the blue and opened up a whole new potential path—if she dared.

"Don't answer straightaway," Pat had advised her on the hillside. "Take your time to think about it and what it would mean to you to have his baby. Talk it over with your family, but no matter what they say, remember that you'll always have Chloe and me on your side. We are your family, too, now."

Having a child with a man who truly loved her was all that Mandy had ever wanted, and, until recently, it hadn't seemed possible. Even though they'd never had the opportunity to meet, she knew how she felt about him based only on being around the remnants of his life. Was that enough of a foundation to have his child? Of course it wasn't. The rational side of Mandy's brain knew what she should do. How would she ever explain to her mum and sisters she was pregnant with the child of a dead man she'd never met? Was this really how she wanted to become a mother? What would her child think when it became old enough to understand? Could she do it alone?

Could she do it? She was certainly tempted.

"Mandy, can I have a word?" The voice startled her. She turned to see her line manager, Charlie, a young man that she suspected was barely out of his teens but had the ability to patronize as well as any man double his age. She followed him into a large Perspex cube where a desk with three chairs sat next to a whiteboard. He beckoned her to take a seat and shuffled some papers he was holding.

"I've been looking at your team's figures, Mandy, and if I'm honest, they've been slipping." He stroked his bum-fluff goatee to emphasize his disappointment. "Over the last two months, we've seen a consistent drop in leads from you guys, and, as a result, sales have stalled. Is there anything you'd like to tell me?"

Like what? she asked herself. *Like the love of my life is dead and I'm considering having his baby?*

"No," she replied instead. "I have a few personal issues I'm dealing with at the moment. I'm sorry if it's affected my work."

"It has, it has," Charlie said. "The thing is, Mandy, I've been looking at your file, and I see that you *could* have a potentially lengthy career here. If you keep your head down and work harder, get these figures back on track, there's no reason why this should hold you back. Why, you could even be promoted by this time next year. I mean, you're quite a bit older than the other girls here, and your documents say you have no husband or family to speak of. You might as well have something to aim for, mightn't you?"

Charlie looked at her with an encouraging expression. Clearly he expected her to feel motivated by his words and didn't realize how inappropriate his comments were. Mandy stared back at him in disbelief. What Charlie didn't know was that he'd inadvertently just made up Mandy's mind for her, as well as providing an escape route.

"Thank you, you patronizing little prick," Mandy said as she rose to her feet. "You have definitely given me something to aim for. And it's not going to come cheap."

"What I mean, what I was trying to say was…" Charlie began to backtrack, but Mandy wasn't prepared to listen. Instead, she stormed out of the room, and headed down the corridor in the direction of the HR department.

Within two hours she had negotiated a generous voluntary severance package, including a bonus on the provision she wouldn't take Charlie's sexism or intrusion into her private life to an industrial tribunal. Then after walking down five flights of stairs, out of the building's revolving doors and toward her car, she pulled her mobile from her pocket.

"Hi, Pat, it's Mandy," she began, trying to contain her excitement. "Yes, I want to do it. I want to have Richard's baby."

47

"Are you ready?" Amy shouted up the stairs to Christopher.

"Yes, just give me a moment," he replied from his office, where he was looking at the chart on his computer screen to double-check where Number Thirteen was. He was happy to find that she'd stuck to her schedule and was exactly where she was supposed to be. He liked it when they were creatures of habit, as it made his job that much easier.

Faceless contacts and downloadable programs and software buried deep on the dark web provided him with the means to learn everything he needed to know about the women he targeted and more, and it all began with a mobile phone number. That would lead to a name, age, address, occupation, medical history and employment records. He could determine almost anything from their blood types to what they'd last purchased on eBay. Their lives were no longer their own to live, and Christopher would be the one to determine how much time they had left.

Early on, he was aware secrecy and anonymity would be the key to his success. On the off chance Amy might use his computer without asking, she'd only have access to a guest profile he had set up in her name. His own profile had a password cipher program he'd been assured would take months to crack by even some of the most experienced individuals.

A virtual private network made sure that Christopher's IP number, his computer's unique identifier, was buried at all times. He ran all his online data via an encrypted virtual tunnel that stopped all websites from tracking his online activity. Each email he sent and received went through a program that encrypted and decrypted, and he used unlimited aliases and disposable addresses to register with UFlirt, the only app installed on each of his dozens of phones.

It was the Tor network that allowed him to access the deep web, where millions of websites and pages were created anonymously, and individuals communicated privately. Even for Christopher, it was an eye opener as anything from drugs to firearms and pedophile pornography were available to purchase for the right price. It was there where he'd bought a package of smartphones for a fraction of British prices using darkcoins, a more discreet version of bitcoins. Then he had the phones couriered from somewhere in Eastern Europe to a PO Box he'd set up in London.

"Chris!" Amy shouted again. "Come on, we're going to be late!" He narrowed his eyes; he loathed the abbreviation of his name, but she was using it more and more.

By the time the couple found a parking space two streets away from the restaurant in Bow, they were ten minutes late. And while not being on time for an allotted appointment often made Christopher irritable, it didn't matter so much if Amy was with him.

"This menu looks lovely," she said, flicking through the pages of the leather-bound book. She smiled at Christopher, and he felt his stomach perform somersaults. He smiled back at her and meant it.

"It earned superb reviews in the *Guardian*'s *Weekend* magazine," Christopher replied. "That's why I suggested it."

He began to feel anxious, and his muscles were tense, but he disguised it from Amy. Tonight was going to be the most important night of their relationship, and he'd managed to keep his preparations under the radar. He had booked the right table in exactly the right spot, and now all he had to do was to wait for that special moment.

As they glanced over the list of traditional British foods with a modern twist, their waitress appeared with bottled water and glasses.

"What would you recommend?" Christopher asked politely. His mouth was dry, so he took a large gulp of his water. He wasn't listening when she read from the specials board, although he picked up on something about a toad in the hole with chili spiced sausages and ham hock soup. He was more interested in focusing on the silver hoop in her pierced septum and how much pain she'd be in if he ripped it out.

He liked the way a dimple appeared when the waitress laughed, as Amy made a joke about a courgette dish with a name prone to innuendo, and how she tucked her short, dark hair behind her ears and cocked her head to one side like a dog as she listened.

It was the first time Christopher had ever permitted his two worlds to collide. The light with the dark, the sun with the shade, his girlfriend with Number Thirteen.

48

JADE

Jade could pinpoint the exact moment the touch paper caught light and the fireworks began to explode throughout her body.

She was making her way toward her rental car to head into town and pick up some groceries when, through the bedroom window, she spotted Kevin being helped to dress. Without warning, it was as if the floor had given way beneath her, and she felt herself falling. She struggled to catch her breath, and her body felt as light as a feather. She wasn't sure when she landed. The only thing she could be certain of was that time had frozen, and the only two people in the world who mattered were the two of them.

There had been times when they'd been around each other that she'd felt occasional jabs and twitches, but she hadn't been certain what they meant. Now that she'd felt the full blast of it, she knew exactly what they were, and thinking back she could see what was going on. It was as if as soon as she let down her guard and began living in the moment the sensations became more frequent. She also began to feel other unusual reactions around him. But this…well this was something she had only ever read about.

As she watched them make their way out of Kevin's room, through the house and into the courtyard, their eyes locked on to each other, and she knew that she'd been hit by a lightning bolt. It had taken much longer than she had anticipated, but then again, they were in exceptional circumstances. But now a deeper connection had been made between them. It wasn't just a crush, she wasn't feeling sorry for him, and it wasn't because of Kevin's illness. It was bigger than that, and wasn't something that was going to burn out after he did. It was love in its purest form—and it scared her to death.

"Are you okay?" Kevin asked.

"Of course," Jade replied. "Why?"

"You're looking a bit flushed."

Jade smiled but found it hard to maintain eye contact. Because it was Kevin she was supposed to have fallen in love with, not the man who was escorting him: Mark.

49

NICK

Everything Nick assumed he knew about love, from his first schoolboy crush on Britney Spears to Sally, the only woman he'd ever asked to marry him, was wrong. What he had felt for them, plus the numerous other girlfriends he'd dated over the years, was nothing compared to how he felt when he was in the presence of Alex.

Nick's life might have been enviable to some. He lived with a woman he adored in an apartment with ever growing equity, and had a job he loved which was compatible with his creative ability. He had friends he enjoyed spending time with and parents and a brother who, although he didn't see them too often, stayed in regular contact and were supportive of him. All in all, there was much to be grateful for.

It was only now, with Alex hovering in the periphery of his life—though arguably, also in the very center of it—that he knew he'd simply been content. And with each moment spent in Alex's company, Nick was aware that contentment was no longer enough to satisfy him.

In the days and weeks that followed their first meeting, their friendship escalated, and they found each other's company intoxicating. They grabbed every available opportunity to spend time together, from meeting for lunch to walking with each other to the tram station after work. They chatted like old friends about their schooldays, spent on opposite sides of the world, and the ambitions they had yet to fulfill. And at times, it was simply enough just to be with each other without needing to say a word.

Alex spoke candidly about his father's battle with dementia and how his medication was keeping him on an even keel. However, his mother had warned it was a temporary measure and it wouldn't be long before they'd lose him to the disease. And that was the very reason that their relationship was destined to remain temporary, because Alex's and his girlfriend's flights to New Zealand were booked for six weeks' time.

Along with their girlfriends, Alex's imminent departure was the second subject the two didn't refer to often. Each time the elephant tried to barge its way back into the room, they'd fix another padlock to the door. And both of them could feel the hinges creaking under the elephant's weight.

"What the hell? How can you suddenly be a gay?" Deepak exclaimed.

"I'm not."

"Well, bisexual, then."

"Again, I'm not and that's the point, and that's why my head is screwed." Nick sighed and held his face in his hands as Deepak opened the top off yet another bottle of beer and handed it to him. "You can't tell Sumaira any of this, by the way. You know what she's like. She'll be straight on to Sally, and I'm not ready to have that conversation yet."

"Of course I won't," Deepak reassured him. "I don't tell her everything. But when you say 'yet' do you mean you're thinking of leaving Sal?"

"What? No, of course not. We're getting married in a few months. How can I?"

"Mate, you can't really marry her if your heart isn't in it. You two won't stand a cat in hell's chance."

"But it is. I swear to God, I love that girl. It's just that what Alex and I have is...different."

"Different how?"

"You must know what I mean—you and Sumaira have been Matched, haven't you?"

Deepak nodded, though there was something in his expression that didn't reach his eyes.

"It's that feeling you don't get when you're around anyone else, like nobody in the world matters when you're in their company. Like you and them are this one, solitary...thing... And no matter what crap the world throws at you, you can get through it because you have them on your side."

Nick took a long swig from his bottle and placed it on a coaster on the table.

"You're stuck in a shit storm, dude," Deepak said. "I don't know why you're fighting it, though. If he's your Match, don't you owe it to yourself to follow it through?"

"I don't want to cheat on my girlfriend."

"You already are, mate. And it's not as bad a thing as you're making out. Sometimes you've got to put yourself first and go with the flow. You know she'd do the same if she found her Match."

"You think?"

"Of course. It's ingrained in everyone, isn't it? Everyone wants to cheat, but it's whether you've got a good enough reason to do it."

Nick had often suspected his friend hadn't always been the most monogamous of husbands, but he left it at that.

"Anyway, enough about me. What is it that you wanted to talk to me about? You said you had some news."

"Oh, it can wait until another time."

"No, tell me. I could do with something to take my mind off my own problems," Nick pressed.

"Okay. Well, it turns out I'm going to be a dad. Sumaira's pregnant."

"Oh, Deeps, that's fantastic!" Nick said with genuine enthusiasm. He leaned across to shake his hand, delighted for his friend. "How far along is she?"

"She just got past the first three months, and they're all doing great."

"All?"

"She's expecting twins. Apparently they run in Sumaira's side of the family."

"That's incredible! I can't wait to see you juggling one dirty nappy, let alone two." Nick joked. "That's no more five-a-side for you, no more getting hammered on a weeknight, no more sneaky spliffs on the balcony when you think she isn't looking..."

"Tell me about it. She's already started putting on weight, and our sex life has gone to nothing. If this is the future, I'm going to be hammering the hell out of Tinder."

Nick waited for Deepak to laugh or indicate he was joking, but he didn't.

"Well it's going to be a hell of an adjustment for the both of you, but I'm sure you'll get through it," he added.

"I reckon my life's in for a bumpy ride from here on out."

"You're telling me," Nick replied, and downed the rest of his beer.

50

Ellie tapped her restless foot absent-mindedly against the mat in the Range Rover's rear footwell.

In ordinary circumstances, her first trip home to see her family in almost a year was enough to make her anxious. But for this outing she had brought Tim. Sensing her trepidation, Tim placed his hand over hers, gave it a squeeze and smiled to offer his reassurance.

"You know I've been certified as a safe bet to introduce to parents?" he began. "Honestly, I've been tested and probed and it's highly unlikely I'll steal anything or call your nana a whore."

"My nana's dead."

"Then she won't care what I call her, will she? Come on, give me a smile."

"I'm sorry, it's just that I haven't seen them for a while, and, the longer the gap between visits, the harder it is."

"How painful can it be? They're your family."

Ellie sighed. "We don't have much in common these days,

and it's not their fault—it's mine. When my business started taking off, I had less and less time for a private life.

"I began to think that to be a successful businesswoman, I had to put my personal life on hold. I assumed that to be taken seriously I had to act in a certain way or be seen in the right places and with the right people, and that came at the expense of my family. Then by the time I realized I was being an idiot, I'd missed too many weddings, christenings and Christmases. I bought them cars, paid off their mortgages and set up trust funds for my nieces and nephews, but it didn't make up for it."

"But what they really wanted was for you to be around, right?"

"I suppose, yes."

"Well then, let's make tonight the start of a new chapter. You're lucky you have a family. It was just my mum and me my whole life until she died, and now it's just me." Tim gave a meek smile.

"No, you've got me, too," Ellie said, and tilted her head to rest on his shoulder.

It had been almost four months since she'd appeared on Tim's doorstep and revealed she was the scientist who discovered the Match Your DNA gene. He'd forgiven her for lying about it, and, now with the playing field leveled, the two tentatively embarked upon their relationship. Tim was a little rough around the edges and certainly wasn't her usual type. But once she'd allowed herself to open up to him and let their genetic link lead the way, none of their contrasts mattered. She had been drawn to him like a magnetic field, and it felt wonderful.

They spent many of their after-work hours living a comfortable, pedestrian life at Tim's Leighton Buzzard home. Twice a week she'd send a car to pick him up, so they could stay at Ellie's London townhouse. However, she often felt self-conscious spending time in the home she'd created for herself. The £5,000 spent on a single roll of wallpaper, imported Italian marble flooring, the basement cinema she rarely used, were all reminders of a time when she assumed that a beautiful home was the equivalent of a meaningful life.

Along with curtailing her working hours—she'd imposed a new rule to leave the office at six o'clock—Ellie had also turned her back on the trendy London eateries she frequented in favor of small, provincial pubs, watching Sunday league football games and nights spent curled up on the sofa watching box sets. Only the presence of Andrei and his colleagues, keeping guard in their vehicles outside Tim's home, reminded her that their relationship was out of the ordinary.

"We're almost here," Ellie announced, as they pulled into the street where she'd spent her childhood. Little had changed in the Derbyshire suburb of Sandiacre, where she'd spent the first eighteen years of her life; the 1950s-built detached houses remained virtually untouched by progress, with the exception of replacement PVC windows and block paving over lawns to make room for more cars. It had been a safe, nurturing environment for her, and she was ashamed for having turned her back on everything that made her.

"Oh my God, make way for the Queen's arrival!" yelled her sister Maggie from the doorstep as she flung her arms open wide and squeezed her younger sister. "And she's brought someone with her!"

A cheer rang out from the living room of Ellie's mother's house as her family and neighbors descended upon their guests. Take That's *Greatest Hits* blared from a hi-fi system, and there was a sign that read "Happy 70th birthday, Mum." The dining room table was pushed against the wall and was covered in napkins, party foods, plastic cups, cutlery and paper plates.

"Ooh, let me get a look at you," Maggie continued and grabbed Tim, spinning him around like a lazy Susan so everyone could size him up. "You've done well there," she said to Ellie and clutched her sister's arm.

"Come here, girl." Her mother grinned as she walked in, eyeing her daughter up and down. "You need a bloody good meal inside you. You're looking right skinny. And who's this handsome lad?"

"This is my boyfriend, Tim," Ellie said.

"Nice to meet you, Mrs. Stanford," he began, and went to shake her hand.

"Call me Pam," she replied. "Now let's get you a drink, and you can tell me all about yourself. At least you look normal. You should have seen the last one she brought home—he spent the whole day eyeing up the whole estate, working out how much he could buy it for. Cheeky bugger."

For the next hour, Tim was paraded around the house from room to room, having drinks thrust into his hand by strangers and being introduced to family members he likely wouldn't remember the names of the next day. He danced with her two youngest nieces, chatted football with her brothers-in-law and was given a guided tour of her father's newly erected shed. Ellie watched proudly from the sidelines as she reminded herself that she could have the best of both worlds.

"I'm sorry, has she been giving you the third degree?" Ellie asked cheekily, as her mum led them to the kitchen.

"Not at all." Tim smiled. "I've been getting all the gossip about what you were like as a kid—and you were a right little geek by all accounts. And no boobs until you were seventeen?"

"Mum!"

"Don't try to deny it, Ells," she said, and turned to Tim. "Flat as an ironing board until she could learn how to drive. But even as a girl, she always had her nose in a book. Then when she discovered science, that was it. She once set fire to her curtains in her bedroom with magnesium and a test tube she stole from school."

Ellie shook her head and felt herself blush, much to Tim's amusement.

"I'm just going to borrow your bathroom, then you can tell me more," Tim said, and gave Ellie a wink as he left the room.

"So?" Pam asked hopefully.

"So...?" Ellie repeated stubbornly.

"So has the woman who's fixed everyone else's love life actually found one herself?"

"Maybe." Ellie smiled.

"Well, if it counts for anything, I love him!" Maggie chipped in, who'd just returned from a cigarette in the garden. "He can hold his own with us lot, he's down to earth and funny, and he's not intimidated by you. He's a keeper in my book."

"Do you love him?" asked Pam. "If he's your DNA Match, then you must be in love with him. That's how it works, isn't it?"

"Yes." She smiled. "I do love him."

"Well, that's reassuring to hear," came Tim's voice from behind. "Because I'm kind of nuts about you, too."

51

MANDY

Mandy stared at the sepia-colored three-dimensional image of the child she was carrying.

The sonographer passed her two printouts to keep, one for herself and one for the baby's grandmother, who'd been with her in the room for the twelve-week scan.

"It looks like a tiny kidney bean but with the face of an alien," Mandy joked as she showed the photos back at Pat's house.

"It's not an alien, it's my grandchild," said Pat, who for a moment sounded hurt.

"She was only kidding, Mum," said Chloe. "Look at it, it's so cute! Did you ask if it's a boy or a girl?"

"No, I'm happy to wait."

"It's a boy," Pat added. "I can feel it in my bones, Richard is having a son."

Six months earlier, and much to Pat's and Chloe's tearful delight, Mandy had accepted Pat's offer. Mandy hadn't inquired about the legalities of how Pat came to be in charge of Richard's DNA, although she had hired a lawyer to deal with it, signing various forms filled with legalese and jargon she didn't understand. She was too giddy with excitement and trepidation at the prospect of what was to come to consider its lawful validity.

Pat paid for Mandy's pre-insemination checkup at a private fertility clinic in Harley Street where there were endless tests: Mandy underwent a hormone profile, and blood, ultrasound and STI checks, along with measures she could barely pronounce like a hysterosalpingogram and hysteroscopy.

A fortnight later, when Mandy was ovulating, a doctor had placed a small sample of Richard's sperm into the neck of her womb and sent her home to let nature take its course. When her period arrived three weeks later, she had sobbed so much. The thought of not having Richard's baby after having made the decision was too much to bear. She cursed herself for letting herself get her hopes up.

The following month she returned to the clinic for a second attempt. And before Mandy had even peed on the home pregnancy test stick and watched the blue cross form, she knew. She had fallen pregnant. The symptoms mirrored her first two pregnancies: from the first morning, she awoke with a queasy feeling and then the pressing need to vomit. As she sat on the cold slate tiles of her bathroom floor clenching the test, she thought about the miscarriages she had had with Sean and prayed that history would not repeat itself, that it would be third time lucky.

Truth be told, Mandy wasn't sure how she should be feeling. She was aware she should be delighted and excited, yet fear was the only emotion coursing through her veins, and as hard as she tried not to, she couldn't stop weeping.

The first person Mandy had called with the good news was Chloe, who she'd grown close to like a sister. She wanted Chloe to be by her side when she told Pat.

"As I'm going to be a grandma, you can call me mum if you

want," Pat had suggested through her tears. Mandy smiled politely, but it didn't sit comfortably with her. They were close, but she wasn't sure if she was there yet.

Now she was without the day-to-day grind of work in a job she'd grown to loathe, Mandy spent more time in the company of Pat and Chloe. Pat was still on compassionate leave from her work in the accounts department of a supermarket, and with Chloe living just a few streets away from her mother, the three women spent many of their days and evenings together.

Mandy often stayed the night at Pat's house, although she was no longer consigned to the spare room, having been offered Richard's bedroom instead. It was in his bed, surrounded by his smells and his invisible presence, that she was able to sleep the night through. And it was also a place where her dreams of Richard remained unsullied by the reality of her situation.

With her first trimester complete, Mandy felt more confident in telling her friends that she was expecting. But she had no idea how she was going to break the news to her family. It was her fault that they'd been estranged for so long, and she didn't know how to seal the rift.

She was caught off guard, however, when her doorbell rang, and she saw Paula's and Karen's faces.

"What's going on?" began Paula before she'd even walked through the door. "You never answer our calls, we get a text from you once in a blue moon, and you haven't spent time with your nieces and nephew in weeks."

"Is this Richard knocking you around?" asked Karen bluntly. "You can tell us if he is and we can help you. You don't have to stay with him just because he's your Match."

"No, no, look I'm sorry, I know I've been a bad sister and aunty. It's just that it's been a...*peculiar* few months."

Mandy ushered them inside and into the living room. They sat next to each other on the sofa with puzzled expressions, fixated on their aloof sister who paced the length of the carpet.

"What do you mean by peculiar?" Karen asked. "What's going on? Mum's worried about you. We all are."

With no words to describe what had been going on, Mandy simply hitched up her jumper to reveal a small but noticeable baby bump. Karen and Paula reacted just how she thought they would: they let out high-pitched squeals and jumped up to hug and squeeze her.

"Why didn't you tell us?" shrieked Paula.

"And is everything all right with the baby?" asked Karen.

"After the last two miscarriages I wanted to make sure I got through the first three months okay. And, yes, Karen, the baby's fine. It's growing at a healthy rate and everything looks good."

"And what does Richard think? Are we finally going to meet the father-to-be?"

"Where is he?" Paula turned her head to peer into the kitchen and dining room.

"I think you need to sit down again," began Mandy calmly.

"Don't tell me the little shit's done a runner? Kaz, didn't I say that's why we haven't met him? He's dumped her. How's that even possible? I didn't think you could get binned by your Match?"

"No, no, he hasn't dumped me. Richard doesn't know about the baby because…because Richard is no longer with us."

Mandy's sisters frowned and looked at each other, unsure if they understood her correctly.

"So he *has* left you?" said Paula.

"No, I mean he has left us in another way."

"What other way is there, other than he's dead?" asked Karen.

Mandy said nothing.

"Oh." Karen's face fell.

"Your boyfriend died and you didn't say anything?" Paula said quietly. "That doesn't make sense."

Mandy took a deep breath before she explained. "Richard was never my boyfriend—" she spoke slowly and deliberately

"—because he and I never met. Soon after I found out I had a Match, I learned he'd been killed in a hit-and-run."

Karen stared at her with a concerned expression, then reached for her hand. "Then how are you pregnant, hon?"

"I'm not mad, Kaz, and this isn't a figment of my imagination. Richard had cancer when he was a teenager, so he stored his sperm in a fertility clinic bank. I've been getting to know his family over the last few months, and his mum asked me if I'd consider having his child using his sperm." As she spoke, Mandy realized how ridiculous it sounded. *If only they could understand*, she thought.

Karen quickly withdrew her hand. The mood in the room dramatically shifted.

"You what? She just gave away her son's spunk to a complete stranger? And you said yes?"

"No, it's not like that."

"Then what is it like? You're carrying a dead man's baby! It's…it's *wrong*."

Mandy shook her head and ran her fingers through her hair. She wanted to convey to her sisters what it was like to feel love for somebody who was not there in person, what it was like to have a deep sense of connection, no matter the obstacles, but she could tell by their disapproving glares that they would remain unconvinced by the choice she'd made.

"I'm sorry, Mandy, you know I love you, but I think this is so, so inappropriate," began Paula, while Karen nodded her support. "Having a baby by a dead bloke you've never met with the permission of a woman you barely know? It's bloody ridiculous."

"How is it any different from women who go it alone with an anonymous sperm donor?"

"Of course it's different! Your donor's dead, isn't he?"

"But he's my Match and I love him." Immediately Mandy wanted to take her last comment back.

"You can't be in love with a man you've never met, Mandy.

You're in love with the idea of being in love, and his family have put these silly ideas into your head. You're not and you never will be part of their family. You're just their incubator…a rent-a-womb…a surrogate."

Mandy's temper rose and she struggled to keep it in check.

"How dare you say that! You don't know the first thing about them or what I've been through in the last few months. Just because it's not a conventional relationship like yours, it doesn't mean it's wrong. Not everyone can be like you…not everyone can find their Match and live happily ever after."

"I haven't found my Match," said Karen quietly, and Mandy and Paula looked at her in surprise. "Gary and I did the test, and we weren't Matched, but we told everybody we were."

"Why?" Mandy asked.

"Because when you don't marry your Match, people sit back and wait for it to go wrong. They don't mean to, they just do, it's human nature. So it was easier to just lie. But we love each other, and there's nothing stopping you from meeting the right man, too, and having what we have."

"But I don't want that. It will always be second best! He will never mean everything to you, you'll never have children with *the one*. You'll always be settling."

"Don't you dare say that about my children," Karen said forcefully, clambering to her feet. Paula tried to hold her back. "My kids will never be second best!"

"No, that's not what I meant, it came out wrong," said Mandy, her eyes filling with tears. "You're not listening to me."

"You need to come back with us to Mum's house," Karen said firmly. "Paula, go and get her some clothes, and I'll grab some toiletries."

"Stop it!" Mandy screamed. "Stop judging me and stop trying to tell me what I'm doing with my life is wrong. It's none of your business."

"You're our sister, so of course it's our business, especially when you're not right in the head. You can't be in love with a dead man... You need help."

"I need you two to get the hell out of my house," Mandy snapped and grabbed at Karen's arm, pulling her toward the front door. Paula looked at her in disbelief and followed. "Get out now!" she yelled, and her sisters reluctantly left, astonished by her outburst.

By the time Mandy reached Pat's house two hours later, she knew she was in the company of a family who really understood her. Pat gave her a comforting hug when she told them what had happened.

"Thank you, Mum," Mandy found herself saying.

52

Thirty.

A number that represents a myriad of inoffensive and mildly important things to different people. A figure that serves as a numeric milestone when it comes to one's age, the speed limit in a pedestrian zone, the atomic number of zinc, the number of tracks on the Beatles' White Album, the age Jesus was baptized and the number of upright boulders standing in Stonehenge.

But to Christopher, the number thirty would signify the completion of his work in orchestrating Britain's biggest unsolved murder case. If everything went according to plan, the bodies of thirty strangled women would be found across a variety of London locations, and no one would have the faintest clue as to who the culprit was or why they'd done it. Then, as quickly as they'd started, the killings would stop.

Amy was at work so he made the most of his time alone to reflect on the idea that first came to him a year and a half earlier. Single and with a ferocious sexual appetite, he'd grown bored of paying for the services of escorts, picking up girls in bars and visiting private members' club sex parties. Instead, he'd become curious about dating apps, downloading several and becoming astonished at how quickly, with just the swipe of screen, a sexual liaison could be organized. He soon learned their users were made up of people who were yet to find their Match, and who chose apps because they craved company or wanted to pass time with casual liaisons until their Match came along.

And he was just as surprised by how easily women gave out their telephone numbers—and in some cases, home addresses—to a virtual stranger. *Anything could happen to them if their details fell into the wrong hands*, he thought.

And it gave him an idea. What if the wrong hands belonged to him? Would it be possible for Christopher to get away with murder in an age where everything you did, every place you went and everyone you communicated with, could be monitored by just the phone you carried? The more he thought about it, the more excited he became.

For some time he'd been fascinated by what drove serial killers and how those not driven by mental illness frequently seemed to fit the psychopath bill. Experts suggested they killed to escape something in their everyday life that was stressful and, because it was such an intense act to commit, it acted as a blocker for their real problems. But Christopher had no such lingering issues. With no triggers, was it possible to just want to kill to see if you could get away with it? The more he thought about it, the more obsessive Christopher became about wanting to find out for himself.

It was Jack the Ripper's crimes that had inspired Christopher the most. It wasn't Jack's methodology, his choice of victim or even his blatant hatred for women. It was that almost 130 years after he'd terrorized London, the world was still fascinated by how he'd escaped identification following his five murders. Christopher decided he wanted to achieve the same kind of infamy, only on a bigger scale. He wanted his killings to be studied and theorized for years to come, with no one being any the wiser to who he was, what his motivation was or the significance of why they'd suddenly ceased.

His biggest challenge wasn't choosing his women or the actual kill itself, it was to avoid leaving any evidence at the crime scenes and evading the authorities. If his identity were ever revealed, there would no longer be any mystery to it, and his murders would be forgotten within a generation. This was the last thing he wanted. And although he had no prior experience of killing, Christopher was in no doubt that ending the life of a stranger would not trouble a man like him with no conscience.

He was a competitive sort, even with himself, so to make it work he needed to set himself an ambitious goal to work toward; otherwise he'd lose interest. He would never reach the heady figures of Harold Shipman's 260 known victims, and he didn't want to either, if for no other reason than Shipman's murders required no skill and little challenge. His sick, elderly victims had been served to him on a plate. Instead, Christopher chose a challenging but manageable thirty.

Over a year later and, by his twelfth killing, he had tied with Fred and Rosemary West's death toll. Then, at fifteen, he would be two ahead of the Yorkshire Ripper and level pegging with Dennis Nilsen. While he'd actively sought to beat their tallies, Christopher would've taken offense at being put in the same category as them—they possessed neither his intelligence nor his ambition. They hadn't planned with the same depth; they lacked his thoroughness, and, instead of following their heads, they followed their base cravings.

He'd never felt such pride as when his actions became national news and the capital began to live under a blood-red cloud. Christopher had the police where he wanted them—ignorant and powerless. And because Christopher was neither greedy nor careless, yet meticulous in his devising, he'd always be one step ahead of them.

Once he reached his thirtieth kill, he vowed his mission would be complete, and, with nothing left to prove, he would simply stop. The police investigation would continue fully manned for months before gradually thinning out. Then, after a couple of years and with no new leads, the case would join the rest of the cold cases the police neglected to investigate. Meanwhile, Amy would provide him with something new to invest his time and energy in.

He sat cross-legged on the floor and carefully placed the Polaroid of Number Thirteen beneath a film sheet and onto a page inside the white album he kept in the living room, the one that Amy had come close to opening. *Keep everything in plain sight and nobody will be any the wiser,* he told himself.

He'd never learned the answer to the question of how much it would hurt the waitress if he'd ripped out her nose ring, as she'd fallen unconscious before he had the chance to yank it out. But Number Thirteen was special as she had been the first he had introduced to Amy, so he placed her ring, complete with slivers of cartilage, under the sheet and next to her picture.

He closed the book, returned to his desk, and continued to formulate his plans to visit Number Fourteen later that night.

53

JADE

How is this even happening? Jade asked herself so many times that even she realized she was beginning to sound like a broken record.

She needed to process her thoughts, so she made her way to the closest town, approximately twenty miles away. She had traveled the world to meet the man with whom she'd been Matched, the like-minded soul she thought she had fallen in love with before they'd even come face-to-face. It was only after spending time together in person that she realized there was no spark between them, at least not on her behalf. They'd held hands, they'd laughed, they'd spoken about life and death and everything in between, and delighted in each other's company. But there hadn't been so much as a kiss between them.

Now, out of the blue, everything she was supposed to be feeling for Kevin, the sparks she had read about, she now felt for his brother, Mark, instead.

No, this is wrong, Jade told herself. *You've barely even spoken to the lad. Every time he sees you, it's like he'd rather be anywhere else than with you.*

But it was then that suddenly Mark's attitude toward her made sense. He felt it, too. What she'd previously put down to some strange hatred or animosity was actually him trying to conceal his feelings. It all made sense now. He was often tongue-tied around her or ignored her completely because he was experiencing the same intense feelings of love and lust as she did, only it had hit him sooner. And, like Jade, he knew just how inappropriate it was.

Jade remembered the film she'd gone to see at the cinema with her girlfriends last Christmas, *Rebel Heart*; Jennifer Lawrence and Bradley Cooper played a couple who had been DNA Matched but didn't get on, and Jennifer fooled herself that she'd fallen for his best friend instead. Transference, is what they called it, Jade recalled and picked up her phone to Google the word. "Transference is a phenomenon characterized by unconscious redirection of feelings from one person to another."

"Yes!" she said out loud. Somewhere in her mind, she was scared of loving Kevin because he was terminally ill. There was only ever going to be one outcome. And by the way his physical health had been deteriorating of late, they might not have much time left together at all. It made sense that her mind, or her heart—or even her DNA—had latched on to Mark as a sort of coping mechanism.

She leaned her head back against the car's headrest. With this realization she felt much less disgusted with herself. She wasn't the coldhearted bitch she was worried she was becoming, merely someone who had been put through the wringer and had subconsciously found a way to cope with it.

Jade knew what she must do—she'd follow Mark's lead and keep her distance. Whenever they crossed paths he always looked awkward. She would stop trying to engage him in conversation and try to keep away from him in general.

Hopefully her unwanted feelings would disappear with the same speed with which they had arrived.

Upon her return from the town stores, and after having unpacked the groceries, Jade made a beeline for Kevin's room. "What do you think would have happened between us if I hadn't been sick?" Kevin asked as she browsed through the many films on Netflix.

The question made her bristle. "I don't know."

"You once said on the phone that because we were destined to be together we'd probably get married and have kids and stuff."

"Yes, if everything had been normal, then that's probably what would have happened."

"I'm sorry I can't be that man for you."

"Don't be daft."

"I know I can't give you a happy ever after or a family, but I can give you this." Kevin removed a small, velvet covered box from his oversized jogging bottoms. "Here," he said, passing it to her. "Open it."

Inside, Jade found a silver ring inset with a small cluster of diamonds. She looked at him, puzzled.

"Jade, I know this isn't what either of us planned, but the last couple of weeks have been the best of my life. I love you and I'd like to marry you."

She swallowed hard and stared at the nervous young man in front of her. His fingers had trembled when he held the box to her. She wanted so desperately to love him, but here, at his most vulnerable, she knew that she did not.

"I mean, you don't have to say yes or anything because you feel you have to…" Kevin continued.

But Jade had already made her decision, and wore her best smile. "Yes," she replied. "I'd love to marry you."

54

NICK

The guests around the dining table laughed heartily at one of John-Paul's anecdotes involving a young reality star his PR agency represented and the result of too much cocaine.

John-Paul and his wife, Lucienne, a tabloid journalist, were always a worthy addition to their dinner parties with the salacious celebrity gossip they entertained them with, much to the amusement of Sally, Sumaira and Deepak. It was only Nick who wasn't laughing. Instead, he sat at the table staring out through the floor-to-ceiling window as he often did, wishing he were anywhere but there.

His ambivalence toward the company and the Malaysian food Sally had spent much of the day preparing hadn't gone unnoticed. Several times Sally placed her hand on Nick's arm, and while it used to make him smile, now he just wanted to recoil at her touch. He was also drinking more than usual, knocking back the Chardonnay, undeterred by the hangover it would inevitably give him the next day.

"How are the wedding plans going?" asked Lucienne. Nick was just sober enough to stop himself from letting out an audible groan.

"There's not much left to do now really," said Sally, a sudden edge to her voice. She was probably annoyed by the way Nick was acting. "It's just going to be the two of us in New York. All we need to find is a photographer now, and we'll probably have a party when we get home."

"I wish we'd done that," Sumaira said, glancing at Deepak. "It would've saved my parents a fortune. And you haven't had any more thoughts about doing the Match Your DNA test first?"

"Oh, don't start on that again," Deepak interrupted. "They're happy as they are. Leave them be."

"I was only asking."

Nick's eyes flicked toward Sally's, but she didn't return the look. She was too busy topping up Deepak's drink, visibly flushed by Sumaira's question. He was surprised she hadn't told her best friend they'd taken the test or about his results. He was thankful to Deepak for keeping the information between just the two of them. But there was something about Sumaira that night that was winding him up. Her pregnancy gave her a boastfulness that irritated him, as if she was rubbing her and Deepak's perfect marriage and impending parenthood in his face. He felt like his world was on the verge of collapse, and he couldn't stand looking at her smug expression.

Several times he bit his tongue to stop himself from saying something inappropriate, and, instead, he continued to stare blankly out the window, refusing to add anything to the conversation. There was an air of tension around the table, and poor Lucienne and John-Paul kept quiet.

"We decided not to take the test in the end," Sally lied. "We know everything we need to know about each other, right?" She looked imploringly at Nick for reassurance, but he gave none. In fact, he had given her little of anything in the last fortnight. He left no affectionate messages pinned to the fridge with magnetic letters, his daytime texts were humorless and to the point, and he'd led her to believe that he was spending more and more time in the office beyond his contracted working hours. Whenever she confronted him about his aloof behavior, he simply blamed it on a couple of particularly stressful accounts, an excuse she'd at first accepted. But she wasn't stupid, and he knew she understood there was more to it than that.

"Well, let's see if you can buck the trend of rising non-Match divorces," Sumaira added. "I'm rooting for you guys."

"Remind me again about how it was when you and Deepak first met," Nick asked suddenly, the first words he'd spoken for a good half hour.

"I've told you before," she replied hastily. "We were at my cousin's wedding in Mumbai—"

"No," Nick interrupted. "Tell me how you *felt* when you first saw each other, or when you had your first conversation. How did you know that Deepak was *the one*?"

"It was a gradual thing, wasn't it?" Sumaira said, blushing from Nick's interrogation. "A couple of dates in I had a feeling he was the person I was going to spend the rest of my life with. Then the DNA test confirmed it." Deepak nodded in agreement, but something inside Nick knew it was halfhearted; Nick had become the master of halfhearted of late.

"Only it didn't, did it?" said Nick, leaning over the table to grab the bottle and refill his glass.

"What do you mean?" Sumaira asked.

"I mean there were no fireworks or explosions or thunder and lightning bolts like other Matched couples talk about."

"It's not the same for everyone."

"No, Sumaira, you didn't feel any of that because there's no Match between you and Deepak."

"Nick, what are you doing?" Sally asked, darting a horrified look to their guests on the other side of the table. "I'm so sorry, you two."

John-Paul and Lucienne also glanced at each other, evidently feeling equally uncomfortable but quietly fascinated.

"You either didn't do the test because you were too scared to find out the results, or you did it and discovered you weren't compatible," Nick continued, a grimace on his face. "You've lied about it ever since because you want everyone to believe you're this perfect couple destined to be together. I've seen Matched couples, and the way they behave is nothing like the two of you act. Really, you have no idea how it feels when you meet *the one*, do you? How, when you're with them, the whole world melts away and you feel like you've been hit by the force of a tsunami. And how nobody else in the world exists in that moment apart from you and him."

At the word "him" Sally took a sharp intake of breath.

"You don't know how any of that feels because you have never experienced it. So don't try to tell me or anyone else how we should live our lives when your own is just as messed up."

And with that, Nick grasped the rest of the bottle, pushed his chair out from behind him and stormed up the stairs to the bedroom, slamming the door shut.

55

Ellie slammed the cubicle door behind her and breathed a huge sigh of relief. It was her company's Christmas party, and each time she'd attempted to make her way toward the restrooms, she'd been yanked in all manner of directions by staff wanting to bend her ear.

Until Tim had arrived in Ellie's life, she hadn't been so much aloof as she had been wary of people, and she very rarely attended events like this. She found it awkward to relax in public—speeches or lectures were a different matter as she attended those with a purpose—but mingling and small talk made her feel self-conscious. However, with Tim's encouragement, she had come on in leaps and bounds, confronting her shortcomings, and despite her employees competing for her attention, she was actually enjoying herself.

She recalled how at Christmas the year before she had been consumed by work and little else. Business had been booming, but she had no one to share the spoils with. And as 25 December approached, she hadn't given a second thought to the fact she'd inadvertently taken her joyless life out on her employees, signing off on a very impersonal sit-down dinner in the ballroom of a generic hotel. She might have footed the bill, but she had also sucked the fun out of Christmas. "I was the Grinch," she'd since told herself, and had vowed to make this year different.

This year, she'd given the company's social committee a blank check and permission to hire London's historic Old Billingsgate, a former-fish-market-hall-turned-events-venue by the River Thames. Christmas-themed props, including giant toy polar bears, snow-clad trees, ice sculptures and sleighs, were hired to give it a winter wonderland feel, and her employees enjoyed a luxurious five-course meal. Afterwards, roulette wheels, card tables, slot machines and a swing band would keep them entertained into the early hours.

Every so often, Ellie glanced across the room to make sure Tim was enjoying himself. But each time she saw him he was chatting to someone new. She liked that he was a sociable sort and that she could leave him to his own devices without worrying.

As an early Christmas present, Ellie had sent him to Savile Row to be measured for his first tailor-made suit. After its fast-track completion and delivery, he'd refused to take it off since. She hadn't minded as he looked sexy in it, and she'd have gladly paid for a whole wardrobe of them if it made him happy. But based on past lessons learned, Ellie knew how easy it was for someone with money to smother someone without it.

Her bathroom break over, she flushed the toilet and made her way to the sink to wash her hands.

"Hi, Ellie, what an amazing night!" said Kat, her head of personnel, one of her longest-standing employees. Her half-moon eyes were a telltale sign that she was drunk.

"It seems to be going well, yes." Ellie smiled.

"I think there might be a few sore heads being dragged around the corridors tomorrow. Especially mine."

"Well, that's what tonight's for."

"Your new guy seems to be going down well with people."

"I feel a bit bad actually. I've left him to fend for himself most of the night."

"Well, I think he can hold his own. At least, that's what I remember about him."

"Sorry, do you know him?" Ellie asked.

"Of course," Kat said, surprised by the question. "But I must admit, I don't recall him making it to the second round of interviews."

"I don't think I follow you."

"I interviewed him for a job about a year or two ago—Matthew, isn't it?—it was for something in computer programming, you know, about the time Miriam went on maternity leave. He was very nice and relatively experienced, but there were better candidates, so I didn't recommend he went any further. That's how you met, right? At a second interview?"

"I think you must be mixing him up with someone else."

"Oh, well, maybe I'm wrong. Nice man all the same. Anyway, I hope you two have a lovely Christmas together."

"And you," Ellie replied, and felt a slight sense of unease.

56

MANDY

"Not long now, my little kidney bean," Mandy told her baby bump, as she rubbed moisturizer into her expanding breasts and belly. "Everyone's really looking forward to meeting you and, in a few weeks, you'll be here causing me sleepless nights for the rest of my life. But I don't care. You can throw anything at me, and I'll always be there for you."

She glanced into the bedroom mirror to check on her stretch marks, and was grateful to see they hadn't extended any further.

Mandy was now staying full time with Pat, and living off her severance money. With all the big changes in her life, she was grateful to Pat for helping her. She had registered Mandy with her own doctor, enrolled her in antenatal classes at her local health center, assisted her with her birth plan and even volunteered to be her birthing partner. She'd also kept the cabinets stocked with everything she needed: vitamins, minerals and folic acids. At times, Mandy would've preferred for Pat to take a step or two back, but with nobody else but Chloe on her side, she was reliant on her for support.

It had been five months since she'd had the altercation with Paula and Karen, and she didn't wish to speak to them. She'd ignored all the texts and phone calls, even those from her mother and Kirstin. She was still angry and disappointed that they hadn't tried to understand her point of view and recognize her need to have this child. But along with her rage there was an underlying sadness that they weren't there to experience her pregnancy with her, like she had been with them.

"You're doing the right thing," Pat had assured her. "With your history of miscarriages, you need to stay away from anything or anyone that causes you stress."

Mandy agreed, but it didn't stop her from feeling sad.

Pat's and Chloe's almost constant presence helped to offset Mandy's loneliness, and they'd been by her side through everything: her hormonal tears, her mood swings and her morning sickness. They were her family now, she realized; a hermetically sealed unit joined together by a man who no longer physically existed.

Now permanently living in Richard's bedroom, her clothes hung next to his in his wardrobe and her perfumes sat beside his aftershaves. She slept only on one side of the bed, leaving room for where Richard would have been, and she cuddled his favorite jumper through the night, bringing it close to her face in the hope that somehow the baby might catch his scent.

Pat and Chloe had assembled a wooden cot one afternoon, and this now stood at the far end of Richard's room. Next to it was a stack of blue-and-white-colored baby clothes that Pat had bought, convinced that Mandy was carrying a boy.

Mandy screwed the top back on to the bottle of moisturizer and slipped her shirt on. She realized they had never discussed how long Mandy would live with them after the baby arrived, but she already knew she didn't want to leave. She felt safe in that room, as if Richard's spirit was there with them, keeping them comfortable and protecting them from the people outside. They had all been concerned that the media might find out about the story, and based on the way Mandy's family reacted, she knew the world would view her as a freak.

She lay on her side trying to find a comfortable position, and looked up as she often did at the collage of photographs Richard had pinned to the wall. Each night she'd pore through them, as well as others in albums, to learn more about him. There were photos from when they'd visited Disneyland and also at the family's cottage in the Lake District. In one photo, Richard and Chloe perched on bikes below a tiled house sign reading Mount Pleasant. It looked like such a calming place, and she wondered, had he had the chance, if Richard would have taken her to the family cottage, if he would have shared that special place with her. Mandy had seen so many pictures, with such regularity, that she felt like she knew his facial expressions and mannerisms as well as she knew her own.

Three other photos featured a teenage Richard in a hospital bed, surrounded by his friends. She assumed they must have been taken during his chemotherapy.

Her attention was drawn to two images of a young woman whose face seemed familiar. Mandy tried to remember why she recognized her, and then it dawned on her—she was the girl who'd sent Richard nude pictures of herself, the ones she'd seen on his old phone. Mandy grabbed the phone back to check, and sure enough, the girl was there in all her nakedness.

She was about Richard's age, so about a decade younger than Mandy, and it showed. Her breasts were perky, her stomach washboard flat, and she pouted her lips in a way that only a young woman can get away with. Mandy felt an instant dislike for the unnamed girl, particularly at a time when she felt so dowdy and profoundly pregnant. But she'd rather have her swollen, lumpy and stretch-marked body than be a collagen-plumped stick insect, she thought bitterly.

However, it didn't stop Mandy from wondering how close the girl and Richard had been; clearly they were intimate enough to send each other naked selfies and for her to be on his wall, but had there been anything more between them or was it just sex-text fun? Was she the girl he'd used over half a pack of condoms with? Mandy felt an overriding, irrational need to know who this girl was.

She turned on her iPad and headed to Richard's Facebook page. It didn't take long to find her—Michelle Nicholls. She discovered she lived in a village around ten miles from Pat's house. Michelle hadn't set her profile to private, so Mandy was able to scroll through all her posts. The more she read, the more begrudging she became. She managed to establish that Richard and Michelle had been in a relationship for about ten months, possibly only ending shortly before his death. Mandy wondered if it had been around the same time he had sent his swab to Match Your DNA.

But while Michelle had kept many of their photographs on her Facebook page, Richard had deleted most of hers from his. It was a small triumph for Mandy, but she did wonder why Chloe or Pat hadn't mentioned her.

As the next few days passed, Mandy couldn't stop returning to Michelle's profile and skimming through her most recent posts. She and Richard appeared well suited to each other; in her pictures she was always smiling on nights out at bars, with friends in restaurants or on holiday. Mandy wondered what Richard saw in her, apart from the obvious. Was she intelligent? Did she make him laugh? Could she hold herself in a conversation? Or was it just that she was good in bed? Why wasn't this gorgeous girl enough for him? She was clearly besotted with him. Why did he feel the need to get his DNA tested to find his real Match?

At first, Mandy put her curiosity down to her hormones, but

she gradually accepted that there was more to it than that. Pat and Chloe had told her so much about Richard but there was a side to him that only a girlfriend would know. Mandy wanted to know what kind of man Richard was as a partner and how it felt to be loved by him.

She needed to meet Michelle, so she opened Facebook Messenger and began to type.

57

"Where've you been? I've been trying to get hold of you all morning." Amy sounded frustrated when Christopher finally answered her call. He glanced at his phone and saw he'd missed eleven calls from her that day. He slipped the plastic mask from his face so he wouldn't sound muffled; his skin felt clammy and was greasy to the touch.

"Sorry, I fell asleep at my desk," he replied. He had fallen asleep, but it was actually on the sofa belonging to Number Fifteen. Dazed, he wiped the sleep from his eyes and looked around her sunlit room and then at his watch. It read 10:47 a.m. His heart sank.

He'd never been this careless at a murder scene before, but juggling the two aspects of his life—Amy and his thirty killings plan—had left him physically exhausted. He was reliant on a diet of protein bars, energy drinks and coffee to keep him awake and functioning, but they left him feeling restless and with frequent stomach cramps.

Christopher's double life was taking a mental toll, too. He had so much to hide from Amy, yet there was so much about his work that he longed to share with her. It left him divided; there'd even been moments when he'd contemplated disclosing his plans in an attempt to convince himself that, if she truly loved him, she would understand. But when it came to it, he couldn't trust that he had read her correctly, that she would forgive him. And she was hastily becoming too integral a part of his life to risk dispensing with.

"They've found a thirteenth body," Amy whispered down the phone. "The papers don't know and I'm not supposed to tell anyone, but you will never guess who it is."

The waitress who served us at the restaurant last week, he wanted to say. *That pretty girl with the nose ring. I was going to kill her anyway, but I like to think I killed her for us as something to share. Now you have blood on your hands, too.*

"I've no idea," he said, and rose to his feet to stretch his spine and stiff neck.

"It was the waitress from the restaurant we went to last week, do you remember?"

"No, I don't think so."

"Pretty girl with dark hair and a nose ring."

"Ahh yes, I do now. Shit, what happened to her?"

"Same as all the others. She was strangled and laid out in her kitchen. He tore the ring out, too, the sick bastard."

Christopher made his way into the kitchen and glared at Number Fifteen lying in the same position he'd left her on the floor. Seven hours after her death her face had sunken, her skin was gray, and for a reason he couldn't explain she had already begun to attract flies. He checked his pocket to make sure he had taken the two photographs of her, and, to his relief, he had. A picture of how she looked right now would ruin his album's aesthetic.

"Poor girl," Christopher said, and flicked through his backpack to make sure he had packed everything he'd brought. He removed a lint roller and began to maneuver it across every inch of the sofa where he'd slept.

"I recognized her as soon as I saw the photograph, which at least sped up the identification process."

"And are you okay?"

"I think so, it just brought the investigation a little closer to home."

You have no idea just how close to home you are already.

58

"Not bad, eh?" Dan asked, standing back and admiring his work. "Not how I imagined my kid's wedding reception to be, but then nothing's how I imagined it to be anymore."

He looked to Jade as if he was hoping she could say something that would make everything okay. The best she could offer was putting an arm around his shoulders in a silent show of solidarity.

She had spent much of the previous day assisting Susan, Dan and their farmhands in erecting a white tarpaulin over a grassy stretch of the garden. They'd plugged speakers into a sound system to play music, unfolded wooden chairs and tables, and on these they laid linen table covers and placed pink-and-white posies in jam jars, arranging them in clumps. The next morning—a little over a month since she had arrived so unexpectedly at their farm—Jade was to become Mrs. Kevin Williamson.

The venue Kevin had chosen for the ceremony was the old cinder block church in the town nearest to the farm. It was unlike any other house of worship Jade had ever visited, and with-

out the wooden crucifix planted in the ground by the road with
the signpost reading Baptist Church, most passersby would assume it to be a dilapidated storage building. Inside the altar was
made from an old porch door on bricks, the seating consisted
of faded-white patio chairs, and the single window had been
decorated with colored tissue paper so as to resemble stained
glass. But as derelict and shoddy as it appeared, there was a certain quirky charm to it. Nothing about her life in the last few
weeks had been ordinary, so why should the venue of her wedding be any different?

The ceremony was held in front of an intimate congregation,
consisting of just Kevin's immediate family, his last remaining grandparent, two cousins and some of their farmhand staff.
Quite selfishly, she hadn't even informed her parents, but it had
happened so fast and they wouldn't have flown over anyway.

The ceremony was as brief as the time it took Jade to choose a
dress from the slim pickings her suitcase held. As the elderly and
affable reverend began reading passages from the well-thumbed
pages of a Bible, Jade made sure to maintain eye contact with
her husband-to-be, even when she could feel Mark's eyes gaz-
ing at her. She knew that if she so much as glanced at him, she'd
have put the whole charade in jeopardy. As Kevin's best man,
he stood behind him in case his arms grew too weak to lean on
his crutches. However, Kevin was a stubborn soul and refused
to remain seated. He couldn't stop grinning at Jade.

Her parents had texted her frequently during her trip, de-
manding to know what the hell she thought she was doing. If
they could see her now, she thought, standing at the altar in a
makeshift church about to marry a terminally ill man when she
was actually in love with his brother, they'd have tried to talk
some sense into her. She wouldn't have listened, but she did feel
a tinge of regret that they weren't there.

Although it was merely part of the ceremony, when the reverend asked if there was any reason why the couple shouldn't

marry, a tiny part of Jade hoped that Mark might take it as a prompt to profess his undying love for her. But that only happened in rom-coms, and she knew she wasn't going to get her happy ever after.

Once they'd been declared man and wife, Jade braced herself before she kissed her husband, under Mark's watchful eye.

Jade had come to Australia by following her heart. But in marrying Kevin, she had followed her head—or, more specifically, her conscience. She had put someone else's needs above her own, and, for a moment, she allowed herself to feel proud of that selfless act.

However, it didn't stop a little voice in the back of her mind from telling her she'd made a mistake. She'd married the wrong brother. But there was little she could do about it now.

59

NICK

The fairy lights pinned around the window gave the bedroom a warm, buttermilk glow, but they didn't help Nick to relax or calm down.

He felt more tightly wound up than he could ever recall. Moments earlier, he'd made a scene and stormed away from the dinner party he and Sally were hosting, after assassinating the characters of Sumaira and Deepak. Now he lay on his bed, propped up against the headboard, and took another swig straight from the wine bottle he'd brought up with him. He checked his mobile to see if Alex had texted, and at the blank screen he threw the phone down on the bed in a rage.

"You said 'him.'"

Nick was startled by Sally's sudden appearance in the doorway. He hadn't heard her enter their bedroom. He wondered if their guests were still downstairs or if they'd left.

"What?"

"Downstairs, when you were tearing a strip out of our best

friends. God knows why you did that." She gave a small hysterical laugh. "You said, 'Nobody in the world exists right at that moment apart from you and him.' You were referring to Alexander, weren't you? When you went to that appointment, you felt it, didn't you? All that stuff you said about love being like a tsunami… You've fallen in love with him."

Nick said nothing. He couldn't bring himself to raise his head to look Sally in the eye. He'd already lied to her enough of late.

"I'm a fucking idiot." She laughed. "Have you been seeing him?"

Again, Nick didn't reply.

"Of course you have," she continued. "All those late nights at work, the weekends where you and your boss were supposed to be laying out new campaigns and strategies. You were with him, weren't you?"

Nick nodded reluctantly.

"So you *are* gay."

"I don't know what I am or what this is, Sally."

"But you have feelings for him."

Nick paused before saying, "Yes."

"And does he have feelings for you?"

"I guess so."

"You mean you're unsure?"

"We haven't discussed it."

Sally laughed again, a dangerous glint in her eye. Her voice was getting louder and louder as she questioned him. "How come, because you spend all your time screwing and not talking?"

"We don't do that."

"You really expect me to believe you?"

"No, but I'm telling you that nothing has happened between us…nothing like that."

"But you'd like it to."

"I don't know what I want."

Nick was telling the truth. The line between what he felt for Alex emotionally and physically was starting to blur, and there had indeed been times where he had imagined what it might be like to be intimate with him. He'd even watched a couple of porn clips on his laptop to see how same-sex sex worked, and while he wasn't turned on by it, he wasn't repulsed either.

"Even if it's not physical between you two, it is emotional, and that's the equivalent of an affair."

"I'm sorry," Nick muttered, and held his head in his hands.

"How could you do this to me?" Sally cried and sat on the end of the bed, staring at the exposed brick in front of her. "You know I grew up in a family where all my parents did was lie to each other about fidelity, and you *know* what honesty means to me. Then you do this—"

"I didn't start it," Nick interrupted. "*You* were the one who wasn't happy with the way we were. You were the one who kept scratching and scratching until you created a sore, and now I've picked at the scab and this has happened. You should have left things the way they were."

"But I was right not to because we weren't Matched! We were in love, but deep down we both knew there was none of that 'fireworks' stuff like you spoke about earlier. We don't have the 'explosions' like you have with him."

"We could have been happy if you'd just left us as we were, and we hadn't done that test in the first place," Nick said, resigned to her anger.

"Then you should never have seen him again!" she yelled.

"You don't know what it's like to meet someone you are Matched with because you don't have one!"

Sally's anger was brimming at the surface, and she opened her mouth to retort, but then stopped herself. She dropped down to the floor and began to cry, her body wrapping itself into a protective ball.

Sally was the backbone of their relationship, and he'd never seen her like this before. Nick was scared that he'd broken her. He placed his hand on her shoulder, but she recoiled from his touch, just like he'd done to her earlier.

"I'm sorry, I shouldn't have said that. I didn't mean it."

"Yes, you did," she replied. "And you're right—I pushed you into this, and now I don't know how to make it stop."

"Neither do I."

Sally wiped a tear from her cheek and took a shuddering breath. "There's only one way this can go, Nick, and although it kills me to say it, for my own sanity, I have to let you go. If it was another person you weren't Matched with, then I'd put up a fight. But I can't battle with genetics. It's a war I'm never going to win."

Nick felt tears streaming down his face. "What are you saying?"

Sally took a deep breath before she spoke. "You should be with Alex and not me."

60

ELLIE

It was at Tim's suggestion they spent Christmas Day with Ellie's family in Derbyshire.

She'd dreaded the thought of being stuck in slow Christmas
traffic for much of the 130-mile journey, so as a special treat,
she had Andrei drive them to a private Elstree airfield where a
waiting helicopter flew them to a school playing field close to
her parents' home.

For the last five years at least, Ellie had invented a variety of
excuses not to spend the festive period with her family, concerned that after the initial flurry of excitement upon her arrival, she would run out of things to talk about. But Tim had
helped her to understand that to feel part of something she had
to be part of it, too.

Once their clothes were unpacked in Ellie's old bedroom,
they joined the rest of the family for Christmas Eve drinks at
the local pub, and the following day they celebrated Christmas
Day at home. It was much like the Christmases she had enjoyed

as a child, only now the family had extended to include partners and excitable nieces, nephews and grandchildren. It was a far cry from Ellie's last Christmas, where much of it had been spent in the office working on the coming year's growth strategy reports.

With a traditional lunch finished, the kids were busy playing a combat game on a console Ellie had bought them, while her parents were fast asleep on the sofa. Ellie cleared the table and carried the dirty dishes toward the kitchen. She paused for a moment under the architrave of the doorway and watched Tim and her sister Maggie, where they were washing dishes at the sink, taking on the parts of Kirsty MacColl and Shane McGowan as "Fairytale of New York" played on the radio.

The conversation with her head of personnel, in which Kat had said she'd once interviewed Tim for a job, was playing on her mind. But as Ellie watched him interact with her family with such ease and confidence, she knew it was wrong to doubt him. She was no longer willing herself to fall in love with her Match—she was already there.

She wished she hadn't sidelined her family for so long, especially as Tim no longer had one of his own after losing his mother, his one and only relative, to a heart attack.

Ellie wasn't sure if it was the warmth of the central heating or the platefuls of food in her stomach that made her feel like she was glowing, and she didn't care to question it. For so long she'd wondered if it was possible to have it all, and if she even deserved it. Now, looking at the people she loved the most, she knew the answer.

By the morning after Boxing Day, Tim and Ellie were strapped into their helicopter seats and on their way back to London. Tim had insisted they stay at her townhouse for a few days instead of his Leighton Buzzard home, but wouldn't elaborate as to why.

"Christ, if this place was any more sterile you'd be able to operate in it," he teased when they arrived.

"What do you mean?" Ellie replied defensively. The first time he'd visited her he'd also mentioned something similar. She didn't have any photographs on the walls or knickknacks on windowsills. Tim had called it "utterly immaculate but soulless," so at Christmas, she'd made sure to make much more of an effort.

"Don't you think the Christmas decorations look pretty?"

"Ells, when I suggested we put some up, I meant that you and I go out and buy them. Not commission a stylist to go to Liberty and bring home a massive fake tree and a ton of baubles which she then put up for us."

"Oh, I'm sorry, I didn't realize that's what you meant."

"I bet you haven't even read the books on that case, have you?" he continued, purposely striding toward one of the eight chunky floor-to-ceiling shelves.

"Um, some of them I have."

"I don't believe you."

Ellie perched in front of the case with her hands defiantly on her hips. Her eyes darted back and forth to take in the titles one by one, desperately searching for a familiar book to prove him wrong. However, one spine that she didn't recognize caught her attention—it was titled *Ellie & Tim*. She glanced at him, puzzled, and he beckoned her to take a closer look.

She picked it up and read aloud. "Ninety-five things I love about Ellie Stanford."

"Come, let's sit down," Tim suggested, and she carried the book over to the sofa.

"What's this?"

"Open it and have a look."

Inside, handwritten on each colorful page was a reason why Tim loved her, along with a photograph of something relating to it.

"'Number one—I love the way you clear your throat when

you're pretending not to cry at *The Notebook* or *The Fault in Our Stars*,'" she read out. "That is so not true! 'Number two—I love the way the only shape you ever doodle is a DNA double helix'... Where did you get this?" she asked, pointing to a picture he'd scanned of a page from one of her notebooks. "How long did this take you to make?"

"I struggled to find ten things, let alone ninety-five, to be honest," he joked, ignoring her question. "Anyway, keep going."

Ellie devoured each page, frequently laughing at the pictures Tim chose and wondering how he had noticed so many of her quirks, habits and foibles when others hadn't. He really *got* her, she realized.

She turned to reach the final page. "'And it's for all of these reasons that I'd like to ask you...'" Ellie gasped. "'Will you marry me?'"

She drew her hands up to her mouth and looked at Tim. She hadn't noticed he'd slipped his hand into his pocket and removed a small black box and opened the lid. Inside, on a chiffon bed, sat an engagement ring with a central diamond.

"I asked your dad's permission on Christmas Eve, and he said yes, but I draw the line at getting down on one knee." He smiled. "However, I'd love it if my Match would do me the honor of being my wife."

Ellie threw her arms around Tim and sobbed into his shoulder.

"Shall I take that as a yes?" he asked.

"Yes!" she bawled and slipped the ring on her finger. "Yes, yes, yes!"

61

MANDY

Mandy recognized Michelle from her photographs—and of course the naked selfies—as soon as the café door opened.

She was immediately irked that Richard's former girlfriend was even prettier in the flesh; her hair was now shorter and blonder, and she wore skinny jeans with a figure-hugging top. Her tan gave her a healthy glow and emphasized her white teeth. "Bitch," Mandy mumbled to herself, and subconsciously wrapped her coat tighter over her pregnant belly. As much as she was looking forward to the prospect of impending motherhood, the sacrifice of fashion for elasticated comfort clothing was getting on her nerves. She longed to slip on a pair of heels or find a pair of skinny jeans that could fit over her swollen ankles.

She waved at Michelle and feigned a smile, beckoning her over to the table at the rear of the café. It had taken a week of messaging to persuade Michelle to meet Mandy. And even now, Mandy didn't know why she wanted to meet her either, but some invisible force inside her told her to pursue it.

"Can I order you a coffee?" Mandy began.

"No, I can't stop for long. I'm on my lunch break," Michelle replied, politely but curtly. "I'm still not really sure why you wanted to meet me."

"Well, like I said in my messages, I was Matched with Richard, and I wanted to know more about him. We never got the chance to meet, and I know the two of you were...close."

Michelle cautiously eyed Mandy before she leaned forward on to the table. "All right then, what do you want to know?"

"What was your relationship like? Did you love each other?"

Michelle smiled at this. "Rich and I had an on-and-off relationship. I was in my last year at university when we first hooked up, and he was working at the gym." She paused, clearly wondering how much she should say. "I was pretty much in love with him, but Rich? Well, I reckon he might have been at first, but then he started pulling away. In the end, I felt like he was just using me for hookups."

"Really?" Mandy said. She was surprised, but deep down secretly satisfied that even pretty girls sometimes got used.

"Yeah, and I got the feeling he had a few of us on the go, like some of the older women he trained at the gym. They were always flirting with him, especially the married ones. I just don't reckon he was the type to settle down and have one regular girlfriend."

"Oh." Mandy suddenly felt very deflated. "Maybe that's when he did the Match Your DNA test. He knew you weren't the one and didn't see any point in continuing it." She regretted her choice of words as soon as she saw a glimmer of hurt in Michelle's eyes.

"Maybe," Michelle conceded. "But I was surprised when you said you'd been Matched. Rich was adamant he never wanted to do the test."

"Really?"

"He said something like it'd take all the thrill out of the chase and that life without risks wasn't a life at all. So there was no way in hell he'd be told who he was supposed to fall in love with."

"Maybe he changed his mind."

"Possibly, but I doubt it."

Mandy leaned back in her chair and stared at the table as the mental picture of Richard she'd spent months painting, with the help of Pat and Chloe, faded before her.

"I guess I knew in my heart he wasn't the one," continued Michelle. "I've read about how it feels when you meet your Match, and I didn't get any of that with him. But he was a nice boy, and we had a lot of fun. And can I be honest with you?"

"Please, do."

"And I'm not saying this because I'm jealous you've been Matched with him or anything, but if things had been different, no matter how much the two of you might have been in love, I still don't reckon Rich was the type of guy who'd throw all his eggs in one basket. He'd have played around on you."

"Really," Mandy said, her tone flat. "Now you just sound bitter."

"Honestly, I'm not. He was just too much of a free spirit. He wanted to travel the world again, and the last thing on his mind was settling down and having kids. He didn't even like them that much."

"Didn't like what, children?"

"Uh-huh. They got on his nerves. We once had to walk out of a TGI Friday after our starters because there was a children's party at the next table. They drove him mad. He even said—although he did admit he was ashamed of himself—that he was glad his sister didn't have kids, so he wouldn't have to pretend to like being around them."

"Why did he get his sperm stored, then? Pat and Chloe told me all he wanted was a family of his own."

Michelle's eyes suddenly widened. "You know Pat and Chloe?"

Mandy nodded.

"Then take my advice and steer well clear of them. They're a couple of freaks, those two. No wonder Rich never wanted me to meet them."

"Freaks? Why, what did they do to you?"

Michelle moved closer to Mandy, her voice low and her expression grave. "So, you won't believe this. A few weeks after Rich's accident, they found out who I was and that I'd been seeing him, and they turned up at my house. The conversation began a lot like this one actually—wanting to find out more about Richard that maybe they didn't know—but by the end of the night, they were offering me his sperm to have his baby. What the hell is that all about?"

Mandy felt the hairs on the back of her neck stand to attention. "They wanted you to have his baby?" she asked quietly.

"Wanted? They became pretty bloody insistent. It was the most awkward conversation I've ever had in my life."

Mandy clenched her fists. She couldn't believe what she was hearing. She tried to control her breathing so she didn't break into a panic attack.

"When I said no, they got a bit...I don't know...pushy about it, and even offered me money to do it and cover the cost of everything," Michelle continued. "They'd really thought it through and said I could move in with them until I had it. It went on for weeks—calls, texts, emails...in the end I threatened to go to the police if they didn't leave me alone, and they finally stopped. It weirded me out, though, and that's why I was reluctant to meet you at first."

"I guess that's understandable," Mandy said, and desperately tried to justify the actions. "They probably weren't thinking straight and were still grieving Richard's death."

"Death?" Michelle looked confused. "Who told you Rich was dead? He's still very much alive."

62

CHRISTOPHER

"Jesus Christ, how much do you weigh?" Christopher panted as he dragged Number Twenty across the hallway floor and toward the kitchen.

He was a physically fit man, but he felt the sweat beading above his brow absorbing into his balaclava. Her profile pictures weren't reflective of her true size. Even when he'd followed her around Top Shop, Zara and H&M one afternoon in a pre-strike reconnaissance mission, he assumed she had bulked up on clothing because of the unusually cold snap. But in the comfort of her own home, it turned out that she was a girl with an ample amount of flesh.

The unusual layout of her two-story flat meant the kitchen was located on the floor above the bedrooms, so Christopher adapted and changed his kill pattern. Once he'd let the billiard ball drop on to the vinyl flooring outside her bedroom and she'd come out to investigate, he enveloped the wire around her neck as usual. But when it became lost in her excess skin, he yanked it harder, knocking her off balance. Her weight thrust him into the wall, causing two framed paintings to fall. There he remained pinned behind her, using every ounce of strength to keep them both upright or risk ending up on the floor like he had with the thumb-biting Number Nine.

Fortunately, Number Twenty lost consciousness within a minute, as he compressed both carotid arteries that carried blood from her heart to her brain. But it still took a further three minutes before she completely ceased to breathe.

She'd drained Christopher of all his energy, leaving his biceps and forearms sapped and strained. After giving himself time to rest and regain his strength, he secured a plastic bag around her head and neck with rubber bands, took her wrists with his gloved hands and began to drag her along the corridor, past the living room and up the stairs toward the kitchen. He paused a third of the way up to catch his breath before he finally laid her body out symmetrically in the kitchen.

Christopher's need for order dictated that each woman must be left in exactly the same position in exactly the same room. It hadn't commenced like that; it just so happened that the first three girls' homes all had kitchens with alcoves that provided the perfect place for him to lie in the shadows and wait. Number Four had been a dining room murder, and he considered leaving her there, right up until the moment he was about to exit. But he knew that for the rest of the night, then the following day and right through the rest of the killings, it'd irritate him that her alternative positioning might make her an exception. She wasn't—he treated each of them with the same lack of regard.

Once he'd removed the plastic bag that captured any stray drops of blood from her neck wound, he straightened her clothing so there were no rolls or bunches to indicate that she'd been dragged into position. He took his lint roller and applied it to her clothes to pick up any stray hairs that may have fallen from under his balaclava or from his eyebrows or eyelashes.

Then, armed with his plastic spray bottle of luminol, he retraced his steps. When in contact with the iron in blood, the chemical emitted a blue glow allowing Christopher to locate trace elements of blood she might have shed. Finally, with his antiseptic wipes, he cleaned the whole area and replaced her paintings before going through his mental checklist one last time.

With two Polaroids taken and carefully pocketed in an envelope, Christopher was ready to leave when he suddenly stopped in his tracks. He realized he hadn't smelled Number Twenty's hair. It was another of his rituals regardless of who the girl was or what she looked like. He'd inhaled Amy's hair that morning when she surprised him by joining him in the bathroom as he showered. He'd made his way behind her, massaging the shampoo into her scalp and watching as the suds poured between her shoulder blades and oozed down to the arch of her back. Then he'd crouched down and run his tongue from her buttocks up to her neck. Nothing and nobody in the world smelled or tasted as satisfying as Amy. Was that why he hadn't smelled Number Twenty?

No, it's not the only reason, thought Christopher. He knew there was something else about Number Twenty's death that wasn't sitting well with him. It was more than just the kill location or being unaware of her true size; it was that for the first time he hadn't enjoyed any part of this murder. He used to savor the anticipation of returning a few days later to place photographs of his next killings on their chests and view their decomposition rates, but even that wasn't holding the same appeal as it once had.

His heart wasn't in it anymore; it was somewhere else and with someone else instead. Amy was changing him. But into what, he didn't know.

63

Jade was beginning to feel overwhelmed by the number of people gathered in the garden for her wedding day, and, by the exhausted look on Kevin's face, he was feeling the same.

"Let's get you back inside to chill out for a bit," she said to him, and the two made their way slowly back to his bedroom.

More than a hundred of Kevin's friends, relatives and neighbors turned up for the hastily organized reception, carrying food on trays and bottles of beer, which were stored in cooling barrels of ice. A barbecue roared to life near the garages where her new father-in-law, Dan, was flipping burgers and turning sausages.

Jade could smell the meat cooking and listened to the chatter outside Kevin's window.

"Thank you," he muttered, his eyes closed and his breath shallow.

"For what?"

"For marrying me. I know how hard you found it—and I know why."

Jade's eyes opened wide, and she tried not to panic. The last thing she wanted was to hurt Kevin, but had he guessed she was in love with his brother and not him? "What do you mean?" she asked tentatively.

"Knowing I'm your Match and that I'm not going to be here for much longer…you could have just turned your back on me and gone home. But you didn't, so thank you."

Jade bit her lip and squeezed Kevin's cold hand. She knew she had done the right thing, and she waited until Kevin fell asleep before going back outside to meet the guests.

It was clear that despite the remote location of the farm, Kevin and his family were well thought of by their neighbors. She was introduced to so many enthusiastic people who loved Kevin and had heard all about her. They were quick to shake her hand, to hug her or kiss her on the cheek, and offer their congratulations. But behind their smiles she knew they disguised an underlying feeling of pity for the young widow-to-be.

Mark was the only person who'd failed to approach her, yet he was also the person she had wanted to talk to the most. They had both given each other a wide berth, and the farther apart they were physically, the more frustrated she became with herself for what she was feeling for him.

"Kevin is lucky to have you, love," began Dan, placing his arm around Jade's shoulder. "No, let me correct myself—*we* are so lucky to have you. I've never seen him happier than he's been in the last few weeks. And I know the next few aren't going to be easy for any of us, but they are going to be easier for Kevin knowing that you're with him."

Jade offered a mandatory smile and thanked Dan for his kind words, but inside she began to feel the immense weight of her actions pressing down on her shoulders and crushing her under its might. She made her excuses and worked her way through the marquee, away from everybody, where she could be alone.

She reminded herself of how, only a month ago, meeting her Match in the flesh had seemed like a pipe dream. She'd made it a reality, but somewhere along the line it had gone awry. Now she desperately wanted to gain control of the runaway train she'd found herself on, but she had no idea how. Instead, she was clinging on for dear life.

She approached the patio quietly, pleased to have some time to herself. But she wasn't alone. Before she could see him in the dusk, she felt his presence. Immediately her pulse quickened, and the fine hairs on her arms rose.

"Hello," Jade began shyly.

"Hi," Mark replied.

"What are you doing out here?"

"I needed a time out."

"Same here."

"Do you want me to go?"

"No, no," she said, a little too ardently.

Jade sat in the farthest chair away from Mark, and looked out into the dusky distance. Each of them was unsure what to say next or how to break the tension.

"It was a nice ceremony," Mark began. "I forgot what it was like to see Kevin smile that much."

"Yes, it was beautiful." She held the hand with her wedding ring finger behind her back out of view.

"I know none of this is what you expected when you came over here, but Kevin and Mum and Dad are all glad you came."

"What about you?" Jade asked, and held his gaze. "Are you glad I came?"

"I'd better get back," Mark said abruptly, and got up from his seat.

"Mark," Jade called, as he began to walk away. Her voice was impassioned. "What are we going to do?"

He turned his head and stared at her with such longing in his eyes that she felt like weeping for the both of them.

"We're not going to do anything," he said softly, before slowly turning his back on her and walking away.

64

NICK

Nick was slumped on the floor of his budget hotel room in the city center, propped up by the wardrobe and reeking of the minibar shots he'd single-handedly finished off. He ignored the no-smoking sign, and flicked the ash from his lit cigarette into the torn-off lid of the packet of Marlboro Lights.

The clothes he'd worn over the last three days were heaped in a bundle in the corner. The television was turned on but muted.

Since he and Sally had met almost four years ago, this had been the longest period they'd gone without talking. Even when she'd taken a detox holiday with her old university friends on the Thai coast, she'd still found a way to email him. But since Nick agreed to leave their flat by mutual consent, contact had come to a sudden halt.

Alex stood over him, and passed him a bottle of Fosters from a six-pack he'd brought. He'd used the top of the chest of drawers to pry the lid off.

"How are you feeling about it now?" he asked.

"I don't know," Nick replied. "A month ago I was planning my wedding, and now I'm living in a hotel room. All I can think about is what I've done to Sally and how much I want to be with you. How did Mary react when you told her?"

"She was pretty aggro… She kept telling me how much she'd given up to go to New Zealand with me and how I was breaking her heart and shitting on her from a great height. And she was bang on the money about everything. She slapped me round the face a couple of times, too, told me I was a bastard and that she hated me. But I think deep down she knew it was pointless to fight. We've all read enough about DNA Matches to know once it's there, it's too powerful to beat."

"I think Sally feels the same, although in the end she was supportive. Doesn't stop me feeling like crap, though."

"I hear you."

They clinked their bottles together.

Alex moved to join Nick on the floor. Both men stared ahead of them at the Andy Warhol reproduction print on the wall. The artist's impression of the tin of Campbell's soup made Nick's empty stomach rumble.

"There's something we should probably discuss," Alex began carefully.

"There's probably a lot we need to discuss."

"Do you want to go first?"

"No."

"Neither do I, but I will," Alex said. "You and I know that at the moment, this…whatever it is…"

"…relationship. Of sorts."

"That this…relationship of sorts…has a time limit. I'm booked to fly home a couple of months from now, and, until my old man passes on, I don't know when I'm coming back. If I come back at all."

This wasn't news to Nick, but, regardless, it felt like the wind had been knocked out of his sails.

"And if I did come back," Alex continued, "or if you came to see me, then that brings me to our next dilemma. Is it enough for us to just be together like we are now, or are we prepared to take it a step further?"

"You mean physically?"

"I guess that's what I'm saying." Alex's face reddened, and an awkward silence hung between them.

"Is that what you want?" Nick asked. "Don't we have to be, like, sexually attracted to each other?"

"That's how it usually works, yes."

"And...are you?"

"I'm not going to lie to you—I don't know one way or the other, mate. This is unchartered territory for me, well, both of us. I mean, I like sex, well, to be honest, I bloody love sex, and I reckon it's a huge part of a relationship. And if you and I aren't doing that, then can we actually be together? Is what we have between us now enough for sex not to matter? Are we supposed to live like monks for the rest of our lives, or do we get our rocks off somewhere else with women?"

"That's a lot of questions."

"Imagine what it's like being in my head right now."

"I have a fair idea," Nick said. "What if we do, you know, try...*it*...and one of us finds we enjoy it but the other doesn't? Then what happens?"

Alex rubbed his eyes, turned his head and shrugged. "This is so screwed up."

"You can say that again."

Alex let out a long breath, then ran his hands through his hair. "No," he said firmly. "I'm not going to 'say that again.' We've done enough talking to last us a lifetime."

Nick watched as Alex tilted his head and slowly moved toward him. He closed his eyes and reciprocated.

Alex's lips were much softer and warmer than Nick had imagined a man's to be, but his stubble was more prickly. Instinctively Nick moved his hand up to Alex's face as they continued to kiss silently. He felt Alex's hand on his thigh and pushed himself closer until their chests touched, connecting and slotting together like they'd been designed to do.

And in that moment, as they felt each other's hearts racing, yet beating at exactly the same speed, they felt as if they were two halves of a whole.

65

ELLIE

Tim appeared puzzled at first when Ellie had suggested they keep their engagement under wraps for the time being.

"Please don't think it's because I don't want people to know," she was at pains to point out, "but believe me, when the creator of Match Your DNA announces she's found her own Match, things are going to get pretty crazy for the man involved."

"Like, how crazy?" Tim asked. His naïveté made her want to protect him all the more.

"The press are going to try to find out everything there is to know about you. They'll track down your ex-girlfriends and one-night stands."

"As long as they say I have a big cock and I can go like a steam train, I don't care."

"I'm being serious, Tim! They'll write about your late mum, they'll find your dad—if he's still alive—and they'll offer money to anyone who ever knew you in the hopes of some scandal. Trust me, I'm not exaggerating. I've been through this before, and it's not pleasant."

"Shit," Tim said and rubbed his eyes. "Will they find that porn film I did when I was at college?"

"What porn film?" Ellie asked, a look of dismay spreading across her face.

He laughed. "You know, for an intelligent woman you can be extremely gullible."

She gave a sigh of relief and thumped his arm.

"Don't worry. The only skeletons in my closet belong to the mice."

When she'd informed Andrei, he had nearly broken into a smile. And when she'd told her family that they would be gaining a third son-in-law, she'd had to ask them to promise not to tell anyone outside their circle.

"I thought Tim would be more old-fashioned than that," her sister Maggie had said.

"In what way?"

"I thought he'd ask for Dad's permission to marry you first."

"He did, when we came up at Christmas."

"That's not what Dad said. It's not a big deal or anything, we were just a bit disappointed."

"I think he's getting confused," Ellie said. *Tim has no reason to lie*, she told herself.

To date, she had successfully shielded her fiancé from the unwanted gaze of the paparazzi by withdrawing from public life. On their rare excursions, they entered restaurants or theaters at different times and through different doors. She enjoyed having Tim all to herself and was pleasantly surprised the media hadn't discovered their relationship, especially after taking him to her work's Christmas party.

Ellie adored the engagement ring Tim had slipped on her finger, an unobtrusive diamond set upon a white-gold band. She assumed it hadn't cost the earth, but it meant more to her than any of the jewels she kept in the safety deposit box at her bank. At work and in public, she kept Tim's ring on a gold chain around her neck, buried under a blouse. Every now and again, she'd catch herself playing with it. And each night, as soon as she got back in her car on her way home, she'd slip it onto her finger and examine it from all angles.

On one rare evening not spent in each other's company, Ellie arrived back at her London home and immediately it felt empty without Tim. They'd FaceTimed before he went to play his five-a-side game of football, and he'd scoffed as she flipped the phone to show him the mountain of paperwork she had to get through.

But before she set about tackling it, she heated up the meal her housekeeper left for her in the oven and sat in the kitchen, listening to a Spotify playlist of 1990s indie bands Tim had made for her. The engagement book he'd created sat on the counter top. She couldn't stop herself from rereading it.

"Number forty-two: I love the way we shared the same hair-cut when we were kids," she read and took another look at the pictures on the page. On the left-hand side was a school pho-tograph he'd borrowed from her mum, of her as a seven-year-old and when she sported an unfortunate pudding-bowl style. And on the right was Tim with an almost identical haircut. He looked adorable in his school uniform.

The way Tim had proposed with his book was so personal, so thoughtful and so romantic, it was worth more than any gift she'd ever received. In fact, throughout their relationship, it had always been Tim who'd been the one to wear his heart on his sleeve, while she was aware she appeared more detached. She didn't feel like that, and she sometimes worried if Tim ever found it a turnoff.

Suddenly, she had an idea. If Tim could make a book of what he loved about her, she could do something for him, too. She would piece photos and mobile phone video footage of them together and create a mini movie.

She found a website on her laptop that would allow her to create her project, and she set to work harvesting media from her phone and iPad. As she went to log in to her cloud account, she noticed her iPad was already logged in to Tim's. He must have borrowed it recently. She wondered whether she could pilfer anything.

It contained images from the Christmas they'd shared with her family, a spontaneous weekend getaway to Berlin and some old photos of him as a schoolboy. She smiled as she flicked through the variations of him and wondered if or when they had children together, who they might look like. She came across several childhood photos of a young Tim with a woman, and by the various places and span of time they'd been taken, she assumed it was his mum. That puzzled her—when she'd asked to see a photo of her, Tim had claimed he had none and that they'd been destroyed in a fire.

In one, she was kneeling down with her back to the camera, holding a birthday cake with five candles in it. In another, she had her hand on his shoulder, but she was out of focus. Ellie kept swiping through the photos, trying to find one where her face wasn't blurred. It was like someone had deliberately kept her out of focus.

Finally, when she could clearly see the woman's face she let out a loud gasp. She knew exactly who Tim's mother was.

66

MANDY

Mandy sat in her car outside the café where she had met Richard's ex-girlfriend Michelle and wound down the window in the hope the cold air might cool her down.

She hadn't suffered a panic attack before, but the sudden heart palpitations and dizziness plus the feelings of intense apprehension certainly felt like the makings of one. She tried to calm herself down by remembering her antenatal breathing exercises. And if ever she had wanted to start drinking again, it was now.

"Richard is still very much alive," Michelle had said.

Richard is still very much alive.

"Are you okay?" Michelle had asked when she saw the color drain from Mandy's face. Mandy had nodded, but it was clear that she wasn't.

"What do you mean Richard is alive?" she'd asked eventually. "He was hit by a car, wasn't he? I went to his remembrance service."

"But the accident didn't kill him," Michelle had replied. "He's in a private nursing home somewhere in Wellingborough. I mean, the poor boy's as good as dead. He's got severe brain damage."

"Then why was there a service for him?"

"From what I can gather, when his mum and sister knew they weren't going to get their perfect Richard back, they shipped him off to the home. They told his friends not to visit because it would be too upsetting for them to see him, and they said they'd have a memorial of hope service for him instead, where everyone could get together to remember him. Only when it came down to it, the word 'hope' never came into it."

Mandy racked her brain thinking back over the Facebook messages left after Richard's accident and to the speeches given at his service. She'd been so anxious she couldn't remember what had been said. For all she knew, it may not have been mentioned that Richard had died. The only people to have definitely used the word "death" and blatantly let her believe he was no longer with them were Pat and Chloe.

"I don't understand. Why would they organize something like that for someone who wasn't dead?"

"It didn't make sense to us either, but who's going to question a grieving family? His friends weren't allowed to go and see Rich, so I suppose it was their way of coming together and thinking of him. When his family came to me, it was almost as if they wanted to forget about him and just find some poor cow to give them a baby as a replacement. It sure as hell wasn't going to be me."

Mandy would never forget the look on Michelle's face when, at the end of their meeting, she rose to her feet, letting her coat fall open to reveal her pregnant stomach.

"Shit," Michelle had muttered.

Mandy just wanted to get out of that café as quickly as possible.

In her car, when she had finally pulled herself together, she reached inside her handbag for her phone and Googled "private nursing homes" and "Wellingborough." There were five places in the search results, but it was the third one she called that confirmed what she already knew was true.

She typed the postcode in to the car's sat nav, put her key in the ignition and set off. She was about to meet the man she'd been made for.

67

CHRISTOPHER

"Psychopaths won't often fall in love in the same way normal people do," Christopher read aloud to himself in his empty office, "but they can still fall in love."

Too vain to wear reading glasses and having run out of disposable contact lenses, he inched his face closer to the computer screen to gain a better view of the text.

"Psychopaths prefer to become involved in time-limited sexual liaisons on the condition that they are the ones pulling the strings," he continued. "These flings don't often lead to further contact, because psychopaths see their sexual partner's eagerness as promiscuity. Yet they'll justify their own similar actions quite easily. In their minds, they can cheat and engage in intercourse with multiple partners, but if their partner does the same, they place themselves as superior and take the moral high ground."

Christopher nodded and couldn't see the problem with that. He thought back to Holly, a girl he'd dated back in his early twenties. She had the audacity to take revenge on Christopher's infidelity by doing the same herself, and she couldn't understand why Christopher had severed all ties with her, even after he broke her nose.

He took a swig from one of a dozen cans of Red Bull he'd purchased from a news agent on his return from leaving the Polaroid on Number Twenty-Two's chest. He'd later become annoyed with himself for taking his eye off the ball and visiting a shop that might have had CCTV cameras.

"The only way to successfully engage in a relationship with a psychopath is to achieve a balance in power and control," he continued reading. "Psychopaths make intense, talented and passionate lovers, but if they begin as the dominant partner, this is a pattern that will continue. When they understand they can dominate their partner or if their partner has relinquished control, they frequently lose interest and look elsewhere for sexual contact. There are, however, some psychopaths who enjoy sharing their partners with friends. For them, a partner is an acquisition whom they can lend as they see fit."

Tori was like that, Christopher recalled. She'd reluctantly attended a swinger's club at his insistence, and he watched as, one by one, seven men had sex with her that evening. He'd begged her to do it, informing her it would arouse him and strengthen their relationship. Tori was so young and naive, she'd believed him. Afterwards, in the car outside her house, he'd called her a filthy slag and ended it.

One by one, Christopher made his way through a mental Rolodex of women he could recollect having sexual relationships with, and he'd treated almost all of them in the same demeaning manner. He'd marched through life dominating his affairs and manipulating his partners to carry out whatever new deviancy excited him. But the only person he had not degraded or abused in any way was Amy.

Outside the bedroom, he reserved the slight upper hand as he had his secret which he was not ready to share, but inside, they were equals. And it was his realization of this that made him want to know more about relationships with psychopaths. A web page entitled "So you think you're in love with a psychopath?" explained it all.

He scrolled down to read on. "Once a psychopath is allowed to have double standards, then the relationship is likely to fail. The partner is not their equal and cannot expect to be treated like one. It is a fruitless endeavor to try to regain their interest. The only way a romantic relationship can flourish is if the partner does not allow themselves to become manipulated and preserves their self-respect."

Christopher jiggled his feet up and down, unable to keep himself still as he recognized a lot about himself, and in turn, about Amy.

"Because Match Your DNA studies only date back a decade, conclusions have yet to be made to determine the scale to which a psychopath can feel love for his Match. But early indicators reveal the attraction could mean a psychopath is as able to love another person just as deeply as a non-psychopath."

Christopher let out a long breath and sat back in his seat, rubbing his eyes. So he *was* capable of falling in love. It was proof that, buried among all his urges, his maliciousness and his cruelty, there was still some normality to him.

68

It was as if Kevin had saved up every last piece of verve and strength for his wedding, because fifteen days after saying "I do," Jade buried her husband.

His decline had been noticeable by all, although none of the family spoke of it. Instead, they went about their day-to-day duties of running the farm and helping to make him as comfortable as possible. Jade aided him with his multiple medications, and the town doctor visited twice daily to administer extra pain relief when necessary.

When Kevin's matchstick-thin legs finally gave up, rendering him completely immobile, she kept him company in his bedroom, whether he was conscious or not, stroking his arm and occasionally being rewarded with a gentle hand squeeze in return. She'd read that a person's hearing can be one of the last things to go, so she'd talk to him about nothing in particular. She didn't want him to leave the world with a melancholic silence for a soundtrack.

Jade felt helpless for much of the time, watching her best friend slowly slip away. In his final days, and with the use of his body almost at an end, she would dab the inside of his mouth with a wet cotton swab to put some moisture back into his tongue and applied Vaseline to his chapped lips. She'd assist her father-in-law to change Kevin's soiled bed sheets and bathed him with wet wipes. She couldn't help but wonder that if the unthinkable ever happened to her, who would love her in the same unselfish way Kevin had? Her family aside, there'd be no one, she realized.

It was Kevin's death rattle that scared Jade the most: an awful crackling, cackling noise in his throat and chest as his lungs brought to the surface a putrid-smelling liquid that made his breath reek. In his remaining hours, the whole family sat around his bed, waiting for his chest to fall one last time.

When that moment came, Jade almost thought she could feel Kevin's soul quietly leave his body and move on to its next journey. The morning sun outside was beginning to rise. It would be the first in twenty-five years without Kevin beneath it.

Susan and Dan held on to each other, quietly mourning the loss of their son, and, without thinking, Jade instinctively reached out to comfort Mark. To her surprise, he reciprocated, wrapping his strong arms around her. In that moment, she could feel everything that he felt, absorbing his months of pent-up frustration as his body and mind surrendered to grief. She could feel his longing for her. She felt it, too. Unable to act upon it, he hung on to her with all his might, scared to let go of a second person he loved so soon after the first.

The funeral was conducted by the same reverend who had married Jade and Kevin. But instead of cramming themselves into his tiny, occasional church, they congregated on the farm, as per Kevin's wishes. Mark and his father had dug the grave themselves under the shade of trees, next to the headstones of his grandparents about a mile north of the house.

The reverend made it clear to Kevin's mourners that they were there to celebrate Kevin's life and not to dwell upon how short it was. He spoke of what a wonderful young man Kevin had been and how many lives he'd touched. But when Jade heard her name mentioned, she felt like an impostor. She had no regrets about being Kevin's friend, but she could never have loved him in the same way he had loved her.

As her husband's coffin slowly descended into the earth, only now could Jade admit to herself how much she had fallen for Mark. She hadn't merely transferred her affection from Kevin to Mark; everything she felt for him was genuine. Even in the worst of circumstances, when they were side by side at his brother's grave, his presence made her stomach flutter. She was aware it was completely inappropriate, but, by the way he couldn't bear to make eye contact with her, she knew he shared what she was feeling.

However, with the exception of the moment immediately after Kevin's passing when Mark unraveled, he'd since held a tight grip on his emotions and prevented himself from unspooling any further. Any communication between them returned to limited, polite smiles and acknowledgements—and she was growing to hate him for it.

"It's good to have them here when they're so far away," explained Susan, as the mourners began to disperse. "Kevin always loved spending time with his grandparents, so I'm glad they're together, looking out for each other. Like the reverend said, let's go and celebrate Kevin's life, not mourn it."

Jade smiled and held Susan's hand as they walked the rest of the way back to the house. But before she joined the others in the dining room for food and drink, Jade made her way to Kevin's bedroom. She felt eternally grateful for having got to know Kevin and for him asking her to be his wife, but even more so now that she would never have to break his heart by telling him he wasn't *the one*.

She lay on his bed and remembered her friend who'd made her

feel so special. Theirs was the only relationship she'd ever been in where she'd felt truly loved, and it pained her that she could not reciprocate. She had given it her best shot, but the moment she felt the explosions there was no denying who she wanted to be with. The only way she could handle her suppressed emotions was to either furiously punch the pillows until the stuffing came out or, for the first time in her adult life, simply cry. She chose the latter.

69

NICK

Nick's final week at the advertising agency moved cripplingly slowly.

He sat at his desk looking over a spreadsheet on his monitor, reminding himself of what he had left to do both in and out of work before he could take his leap of faith. Often he became distracted, Googling images of the new town in New Zealand where he'd be living.

With the exception of his remaining workdays, everything in Nick's world felt like it was traveling at the speed of light, and he buzzed with the thrill of trying to keep up with it all. The most difficult and gut-wrenching parts of it had been dealt with—not for a moment did he doubt his decisions were right—and now he could look forward to the thought of his future with Alex.

Just days after he'd finalized his separation from Sally, Nick and Alex had consummated their relationship. They'd known each other's personality almost as well as they'd known their own, but exploring each other's physicality had been a completely different ball game—quite literally. There were awkward fumbles, new tastes and strange maneuvers to discover, but there'd also been incredible sensations to enjoy—while others he wasn't so sure about. And he realized that just because they were the same sex, it didn't necessarily mean they knew how another man's body worked. However, they both agreed it was something that they could and would work on.

It was Nick who had tentatively suggested that he join Alex on his return home to New Zealand. Of course Alex was delighted by the proposal, although he confessed to being daunted by the thought of introducing his family to a man called Nick when they were expecting a girl called Mary. But they would cross that bridge when they came to it.

Nick's boss agreed to him taking a six-month sabbatical. Nick hadn't explained the real purpose behind it, only that since his breakup from Sally, he needed to go traveling and "find himself." However, with Alex, he knew exactly where he was.

Nick had broken the news of his split from Sally to his disappointed family, but chose not to reveal that it was because he'd been Matched with a man. Once the half-year trial period he and Alex had set themselves had passed, he would tell them the truth.

The most onerous part of Nick's plan had been breaking the news that he was leaving to Sally. She hadn't looked as pained as he thought she might, but he was sure that it must be a front. Of course she would still be grieving their lost relationship.

He was grateful that she hadn't sought to make him feel guilty for his decision; it was as if she knew how it felt to be Matched and was aware that sometimes you have no choice but to follow the path your heart leads.

They'd taken a pragmatic approach to dividing up the life they'd shared together. Their savings were split fifty-fifty, and Nick offered her the flat until she was ready for them to sell it. All he needed were his clothes, books and the portfolio of his work—everything else he'd decided could be replaced. He'd spent the last six weeks temporarily living in Alex's flat, and he'd not spoken to Sally since.

After the monotonous day at work finally came to an end, he prepared to take the train he had booked from Birmingham New Street to London in order to update his travel documents at the Passport Office. He arrived earlier than the train's scheduled departure so he passed the time in Starbucks with a hot chocolate and a snack.

He picked at the dome of his blueberry muffin and grinned to himself. In the space of just a few months his whole life had been flipped on its head, and he'd survived it. And he'd previously had no idea how much joy there was to experience because of it. With a new chapter of his life fast approaching, he couldn't wait to see what was coming next.

The phone in his pocket vibrated, and taking it out, he saw Sally's name with a text message.

I need to see you, it read.

Nick rolled his eyes. He didn't wish to be cruel, but he had nothing left to say to her.

I don't think that's a good idea, he replied.

Please.

What's this about?

Her reply came in the form of a picture, and the bottom fell out of Nick's world. It was an ultrasound scan.

70

An agitated Ellie drummed her fingernails against her glass-topped desk and stared at the painting on the wall ahead of her. She'd spent £40,000 on the canvas two years earlier, purchased on impulse when she spotted it on an easel in the window of a Knightsbridge gallery. It was a painting of a little girl with huge green eyes, dressed in a blue coat, who stared beyond her framed confines and out into the world. A group of adults surrounded her, standing with their backs to her like they hadn't noticed she was there. She was very skinny, almost waif-like, and through the gap in her unbuttoned coat, under her top, the outline of her heart was barely visible. You could only see it if you looked closely. There was something about the forlorn expression in the girl's face and in the depth of her eyes that Ellie often lost herself for moments at a time. Almost everyone failed to notice the child's heart, and Ellie never felt the need to point it out. But for Tim, in fact, it had been the first thing he'd spotted when he first visited her office.

When Ellie stared at the painting now, she thought of Tim, and more precisely, why, like the girl, he had chosen to hide something.

The moment she saw Tim's mother in the photos he'd kept hidden from her, she recognized her. She was someone she'd worked closely with some fifteen years earlier. Samantha Ward. Though much younger in the pictures with her son, she was a lab assistant in a team Ellie had put together when she first discovered the Match Your DNA gene. Ellie was sure Samantha was one of the members of the group she'd nicknamed "the seedlings"—a batch of colleagues she'd tested her theory on. Only back then, when Ellie was desperate for guinea pigs, she hadn't necessarily followed the rules.

Ellie knew Samantha as a gray-haired, softly spoke middle-aged woman. She'd said little, and as Ellie outgrew the lab and her staff, Samantha, like most of the others back then, slipped from her radar after they were no longer of use to her.

She had saved the photo of Tim and his mother on her iPad and opened it up once again. There was an unquestionable resemblance between mother and son, and they shared the same warm smile and hazel, almond-shaped eyes. Tim didn't talk of her frequently, but when he did it was always in glowing terms. He was grateful to her for working ludicrous hours in multiple jobs so that she could afford to send him on school trips and to help support him at university. Ellie knew he still felt the pain of his loss from her sudden heart attack.

Ellie was positive it wasn't coincidence that the son of one of her former employees had come into her life, and she was desperate to know why. Did she really know Tim at all? The simplest solution was to question him face-to-face, but Ellie wanted to find the answers herself.

"Is something wrong?" Kat asked, when Ellie walked into her head of personnel's office unannounced.

"I need your help, and I need to keep this between the two of us," Ellie began, and they sat down on the sofa. Ellie inched closer to Kat and spoke quietly. "You've told me before that you pride yourself on never forgetting a face, is that right?"

"Um, yes," Kat replied nervously.

"The night of the Christmas party, you told me you thought you recognized my partner from a job interview here, only he had a different name—Matthew, I think you said?"

Kat nodded.

"How sure are you?"

"Please, don't be angry with me," Kat said, her voice trembling.

"I'm not, why?"

"The day after the party, I went back through Matthew's file and called up his interview notes and his CV. It was just irritating me that I might've got him mixed up."

Ellie's heartbeat quickened. "And what did you find?"

Kat moved quickly across the office, her high heels clicking against the marble floor like tap shoes. She flicked though folders in a filing cabinet, then passed one with a white sticker on the front to Ellie. She felt her heart sink when she read the words "Matthew Ward." He was definitely Samantha's son.

"I'm sorry, I should have come to you sooner, but I didn't know how to approach you about it. His online record has been deleted from our files, but I always keep a hard copy, too. There's no photograph of him in here, though. Each time I tried to use the digital camera, the picture came out blank. I tried with my iPhone, but that was blank, too. I remember joking with him about it."

"Have you told anyone else about this?"

"Oh God, no, of course not."

"Thank you," Ellie said, then left Kat's office and hurried back to her own. Ula glanced up at her from her laptop and was about to ask her a question but stopped herself as Ellie closed the door firmly behind her.

She sat behind her desk and opened the folder apprehensively. She scanned the copy of Matthew Ward's CV, and compared it to the details her researchers had compiled about Tim when she first learned of her Match. Both worked in the computing field, but that's where the similarities ended. Everything from the location of where they were schooled to their dates of birth, home town, exam qualifications, email addresses and National Insurance numbers were different.

Next, she needed to see photographic evidence of the Matthew Ward who'd visited her building some eighteen months earlier. She logged in to the online check-in system where visitors to the company's reception desk signed in and out electronically. She checked the names of visitors on the day he'd been interviewed but found no one of that name.

She asked Ula to contact the company's head of buildings security to request footage from the time and date of Matthew's visit. She paced around her office as she waited, looking out across the London skyline and trying to quell the rising anger inside of her.

Once the time-coded security footage arrived in her inbox she played the files in order. Cameras covered the building's ground floor entrance, lifts, the reception desk and the main corridors, but there was no footage of anyone who resembled Tim or Matthew.

She rewound and fast-forwarded for the best part of an hour, desperate to find something, when suddenly, she spotted an inconsistency in the footage at the reception desk. The time code at the top of the screen flickered ever so slightly to reveal that a full minute of film had disappeared. Ellie felt her stomach knot. Someone had accessed and edited the clip she was watching. It was the same for the images taken inside the lifts and the ground floor; they all missed approximately sixty seconds.

The last file she opened was of the corridor leading to the interview suite. She watched in dismay as, moments before Kat's time-logged interview with Matthew, the man she knew as Tim appeared dressed in a smart, tailored suit. He was walking confidently along the corridor with a satchel over his shoulder, and as he approached the final camera outside the interview room, he paused and looked directly into it.

She felt her blood run cold when she saw him clearly mouth the words "Hello, Ellie."

71

MANDY

"He doesn't get many visitors," the young nurse said, as she led Mandy along a corridor.

The nursing home where Richard was being looked after smelled of antiseptic and air freshener. The linoleum on the floors was clean and unblemished, and reproduction watercolor paintings of historic British landscapes hung on the walls. At the end of the corridor there was a spacious, open-plan, brightly lit day room, where Mandy could spy residents sitting in wheelchairs in various states of consciousness.

"How long has he been kept here?" Mandy asked.

"Around ten months now, I think. His family used to visit quite often at first, but not so much anymore. It's a pity."

"Did they give any reason why they stopped?"

"No, but you'd be surprised by how many of our patients don't get any visitors. For some of them, once they're dropped off at the gate, they don't see anything of their families again."

"Someone told me Richard's family banned friends from visiting him?"

The nurse nodded. "It wasn't an official order, but we were asked not to encourage it."

"Well, thanks for allowing me in."

"I'm sure being his Match must give you some rights."

Mandy assumed it was nerves making her stomach anxious, and then she felt a sharp kick from inside. She rubbed her belly to reassure her baby everything would be all right, but, secretly, she was terrified by how she would feel when she saw Richard.

"Right, here we are," said the nurse as she opened the door. "There's a chair by his bed, and just speak to him normally, like you would to anyone else."

Mandy mentally prepared herself before entering, and when she walked in, she waited until the last moment to turn her eyes in the direction of the bed where Richard lay.

He bore little resemblance to the photographs on his bedroom wall or to those in the folder she kept; the handsome, toned, angular man she'd become accustomed to staring at and fantasizing about was now a shred of his former self—more skin and bones held together covered with plastic tubes and breathing apparatus.

His arms were sapling thin, and there was a rash under his chin where someone had shaved him too closely. His hair was long and clumsily combed into an old-fashioned side parting. His skin was gray, and his pajamas were hanging off him. But despite his appearance and the strained noises that came from his throat as the ventilator pumped oxygen into his frail body, Mandy knew for certain she was completely in love with her Match.

She pulled up an armchair and sat down; the closer their proximity, the faster the rhythm of her heart became. And when—instinctively—she reached to hold his hand, it felt like an electric charge was running through her veins.

"Hi, Richard," she began, her voice quivering, unsure what

to say. "I'm Mandy. You don't know me, but I know a lot about you."

Mandy didn't know what she expected to happen; the last few months had shown her that the impossible could become possible, and deep down she hoped that maybe some miracle might occur—he would react to her sound, her smell or just her presence. But he didn't stir.

"It seems pretty nice here," she continued, looking out of the window at the gardens surrounding the home. "And the nurses seem very friendly. I hope they're looking after you."

Without warning, she felt her eyes brimming, and once the first few tears fell down her cheek, she couldn't stop the rest.

"I'm sorry," she said. "It wasn't supposed to be like this... I was supposed to meet you and we were going to fall in love like they do in the films and in those real-life stories you read in trashy magazines in doctors' surgeries. And even though I know it's never going to be like that with us, I still can't stop myself from thinking about what could have been. I've spent God knows how many hours looking through old photographs of you and watching your childhood videos. I feel like I know you even though I thought you were dead. And now here we are together, and you're still alive and I have your baby inside me. It should be the happiest time of my life, but it's not. Because you have no idea who I am or that I'm even here."

Mandy brought Richard's palm up to her cheek. He felt cold, she thought, and held it tighter in an attempt to warm him up. His touch was like nothing she had ever felt before. It was as if his skin was permeating hers, and she could feel his, her own and their baby's heartbeats all inside her body.

Then for the briefest of moments, Richard's body jolted as if it had been struck by lightning. Mandy stared at him, sure that her eyes were playing tricks on her, but again, his body jerked as if his heart had been restarted with defibrillators.

She couldn't take her eyes off his face, staring as his eyelids blinked, languidly at first and then more rapidly. The corners of his mouth under the breathing apparatus lifted, turning upwards ever so slightly. Mandy held her breath as she waited for his pupils to focus and see her for the first time. This was it. The moment she'd been waiting for.

Mandy dashed out of the room into the corridor frantically searching for assistance.

"Richard Taylor, he just moved!" she blurted out to a confused nurse. "He needs help."

"He just moved?" the nurse repeated.

"Yes, I put his hand to my face, and his body moved and then his arm and his eyes opened. Please, can you call a doctor? I think he's waking up."

72

CHRISTOPHER

For precisely eighty-two days, Christopher juggled his mission to kill thirty women while maintaining his burgeoning relationship with Amy.

It hadn't been easy to devote time to either, particularly when he and Amy spent every other evening and weekend together. And it didn't leave him with many opportunities to keep regular tabs on the remaining five women. He'd check his computers when possible and occasionally resorted to drugging Amy's drinks with a small measure of propofol he'd purchased from the dark web, which rendered her unconscious for up to seven hours at a time. That left him undisturbed to continue his research at home until the early hours or, in the cases of Numbers Twenty-Four and Twenty-Five, snuff them out before a groggy Amy awoke.

Amy had been the first to hesitantly use the "L" word, surprising him as they took her sister's dog for a walk across Hampstead Heath one morning. Oscar, the scruffy, ginger border terrier, had been staying with her for a week while her sister was away on holiday, and, while Christopher didn't see the point in pets, he liked how he felt when the three of them went for long walks together, their arms linked. He told her that he loved her, too, and, while he'd said the same to several partners over the years, it'd always been in order to get something from them. With Amy, it was the first time he had meant it.

He permitted himself to imagine what it could be like if they remained this way for the rest of their lives. Maybe one day they could even buy a dog of their own, he thought, or a house in a countryside village? A marriage and a family of their own might follow. Everything he'd assumed he didn't want or need was now appearing very likely, and it was all because of his DNA Match.

When Amy wasn't around, he found himself thinking about her, and when she was in his vicinity, he felt something he could only compare to the thrill of killing. Or at least how killing used to feel when he'd first started all those months ago, because now it was different; Amy had made everything different. She made his skin feel tender to the touch even when she wasn't touching him; his eyes softened as they followed her around a room, and he longed for the nights he could finally complete his project so that he could spend undistracted time with her instead.

Even the act of murder no longer felt as joyous as it once had. The final gasps that had once been music to his ears were now simply a means to an end. Revisiting the women's homes days later to leave a photograph of his next victim was a chore. Everything that did not involve Amy was burdensome.

Their lives together were quite secluded—neither had yet shared the other with an outside party. Christopher had no one to call a friend, but he'd lied and told her how his university pals were now spread out internationally and that it was problematic for them to see each other regularly. In truth, he had never been to university, and the only people he had occasional contact with were his two older brothers. And, if put on the spot, he wouldn't be able to remember the names of all five of his nieces and nephews, or who was the offspring of whom.

Likewise, Amy hadn't mentioned Christopher to any member of her family. She'd explained that being the only girl and the youngest of five children, her protective parents and siblings didn't approve of her dangerous job as a police officer. And they couldn't understand why she, as yet, had no desire to marry, settle down and start a family of her own.

"I want to continue with my career for at least another three years," she'd explained. "My parents are from a different generation and haven't done the test, but they believe in it, and, if I told them I'd met my Match, the pressure they'd put on us would be relentless. I'll tell them about you eventually."

"Do your work colleagues know you're seeing me?" Christopher asked, hoping she'd boasted about her wealthy, handsome boyfriend—who just so happened to be the police's most wanted man.

"They know I'm dating, but I haven't told them it's anything serious. I like keeping you as my dirty little secret."

Christopher smiled to mask his disappointment. The mischievous side of him wanted to meet her colleagues, especially those investigating his case. He'd pictured himself enthusiastically shaking their hands without them knowing just how close they were to the killer they were hunting.

"That's fine," he replied. "We all have our dirty little secrets, don't we?"

73

JADE

It had been close to a fortnight since Kevin's funeral, and Jade was feeling increasingly claustrophobic living in the confines of his family's farm.

To watch someone die so young was both heartbreaking and inspiring. Kevin had wanted so desperately to embrace life but had been robbed of the opportunity, and the best way that she could pay tribute to him was to begin the next chapter of her life by immersing herself in what the world had to offer.

Kevin had left no will and owned very few possessions, but on his parents' suggestion, she would return her rental car and take Kevin's old four-by-four on the journey she'd planned down the east coast of Australia. "It'll be like he's with you," Dan had told her. She planned to stay in backpacking hostels rather than hotels, so she could meet other people her age and experience the kind of traveling she had missed out on when her uni friends had gone to America.

Jade estimated five weeks would be long enough to see what

she wanted to see, then she'd drive back toward Victoria, drop Kevin's truck off and bid one last farewell to his family before returning to England. Only once she was home, she wouldn't simply go back to her former life—she could never do that now—she would begin a brand-new one. If Kevin's death had taught her anything, it was that life should be lived, not viewed from afar.

Mark's refusal to acknowledge her since the funeral wounded her. She'd offered his parents support and a shoulder to cry on whenever they needed it, but she and Mark had not shared a moment since those first few minutes after Kevin's death.

Being in his proximity was a Herculean task. Every time she saw him, or even sensed his immediacy, she had to hold back the urge to confront him—or throw herself at him. The fireworks were still there when she looked at him. At certain times, like when he was lifting bales of hay for the cows or finishing the day with a dip in the pool, and when she thought he wasn't looking, she'd snatch a glimpse of his firm frame and strong muscles.

Jade, too, had grown accustomed to going for a cooling swim before heading to bed—a treat she knew she'd miss when she left the farm to begin her travels. And, she had to admit to herself, she'd taken to her nightly swims in the hope that she'd bump into Mark, although this hadn't happened yet. On this particular night, as she turned underwater to begin her fifth length, his figure at the other side of the pool caught her attention.

Mark stood under an open parasol, watching her every stroke. She stopped and wiped the chlorine from her eyes in case she was imagining his gaze. She stood on her tiptoes in the middle of the pool, and the two stared at each other in silence until Jade could no longer control herself.

"What?" she shouted. "What do you want from me?"

"Nothing," Mark replied, a surprised look on his face.

"Then why are you staring at me?"

"I'm not."

"You barely talk to me for days, you walk past me and ignore me, you leave the room as soon as I enter. Clearly I've offended you, and now you're standing there watching me swim. You're doing my head in, man. So I'll ask you again, what do you want from me?"

Mark paused and stared at her intently, then opened his mouth as if to speak but stopped himself. He turned to walk away but again stopped himself. She watched as he pulled his T-shirt off over his head and threw it to the ground. He dove in and swam toward her, stopping inches from her waist. He cocked his head to one side and kissed her, tentatively at first, but then more fervently.

Jade felt dizzy as Mark's lips touched hers, and try as she might, she couldn't close her eyes because she wanted to see his longing. She kissed him back with an equal measure of passion, her arms gripping him tightly and her fingertips fizzling like sparklers as they ran up and down his back.

When they finally separated, Jade took a small step backwards and looked him in the eye. "Why now?" she asked. "Why after all these weeks?"

"Because my parents said you're leaving." Mark ran his hands through his wet hair. "And I couldn't let you go without knowing what I was going to spend the rest of my life missing."

Before Jade could answer, Mark turned and swam back to the edge of the pool, lifted himself out and returned to the house, leaving her alone.

With no idea what just happened, Jade closed her eyes and slowly sank to the bottom.

74

NICK

"How long have you known you're pregnant?" Nick asked, trying to keep the tone of his voice measured.

He paced the length of his former apartment with his arms folded while Sally remained on the sofa, wearing an oversized woolen jumper and covering her stomach with her hands.

"I found out a couple of weeks ago," she replied quietly.

"Why didn't you say anything before now? You've had plenty of opportunity to."

"What was I supposed to say? 'Oh, Nick, by the way, I know you have a boyfriend now but I'm pregnant with your baby'?"

"But why wait to tell me until just before I go to New Zealand? It's almost as if you want to keep me here."

Sally glared at her ex-fiancé. "Fuck off, Nick! The world doesn't revolve around you or your sodding love life. This isn't about you, it's about this thing growing inside me. I knew I shouldn't have said anything."

"Then why did you!"

"Because I don't know if I can do this on my own. Because I wish I was a stronger person, but I'm not. Because before I make my decision I thought you had a right to know."

"Make what decision?"

"Oh, come on, Nick, you're not stupid. You know what I mean. I don't know if I either want or can deal with having and raising a child alone."

"You can't get rid of it."

"Can't I?"

"No."

"Watch me."

He was surprised by the venom in her voice. Clearly being alone was very difficult for her. "What's that supposed to mean?"

"It means you don't get to tell me what to do. You made your choice when you left me for someone else."

"You agreed I had no choice! You told me to go!"

"That was before I realized I was pregnant. Before *you'd* made me pregnant."

"*Made* you pregnant? It takes two, remember?"

"I didn't see you throwing me off you when we were in Bruges."

"Is that when it happened? Jeez, Sally, that was ages ago. Why didn't you figure it out sooner?"

"I've been counting back, and it must have been," she huffed. "I knew I should have gone with my gut instinct and kept my mouth shut."

There was a selfish side to Nick that also wished she had kept quiet. That way he could fly to the other side of the world in blissful ignorance.

"What do you want me to do, Sal?" he asked.

"I don't want you to do anything. I just wanted you to know." She looked at him. "I thought you'd want to do the right thing, but clearly I was mistaken. I can deal with this by myself."

But Nick knew that doing nothing wasn't an option he could, with a clear conscience, take.

"I don't want you to have an abortion."

"Neither do I, but you can't have it both ways, Nick. Either you stick around and we try to find a way to make this mess work, or you go away and do your thing while I do what I have to do. The choice is yours."

75

Ellie and Tim went about their day-to-day routines like everything in their world was perfectly normal. For all intents and purposes, they were a typical, contented couple—but for one difference: Ellie knew that her relationship with her Match was a sham.

At 5:30 a.m. each day, Andrei picked Ellie up from Tim's house and drove her to work in London, and each evening, Tim cooked them dinner. Then they'd either settle down to watch a drama Tim had recorded on his DigiBox, or retreat into their own online worlds on their tablets.

Ellie hated that she had fallen in love with a man with a hidden agenda. Before she had found footage of him mouthing the words "Hello, Ellie" into the security camera, a tiny part of her had clung on to the hope there might be an innocent explanation for all his lies about his mother, like he'd only discovered that she'd worked for Ellie after they'd begun dating or that he didn't even know himself. But the footage confirmed what her gut told her. There was nothing innocent about Tim or his motives. Everything he had done was deliberate and well-rehearsed. And the burning question that dominated Ellie's every thought was, why? She knew Tim had only just registered with Match Your DNA; otherwise she would have been notified of the Match earlier. Yet he'd been interviewed for a job more than a year ago. Was he an undercover journalist? Or employed by a rival company trying to infiltrate her ranks? Had he just gotten lucky being Matched to her? It was too far-fetched a theory to make sense, but she was struggling to find an alternative.

What she did know was that at some point long before they met, Tim had anticipated that she'd find the footage of him for an as yet unknown endgame. And until she knew exactly what he was hiding, their uncomfortable charade would continue.

The suite in London's Soho Hotel was ready for Ellie as she entered through the glass doors and was escorted up to the third floor.

She'd hurried inside before the paparazzi could recognize her. Andrei walked ahead, and Ellie was flanked by two of his team, all briefed on her predicament with Tim. She had declined Andrei's offer to elicit Tim's information by force, and she refused all his demands to sever ties with him. Getting to the bottom of the situation without violence was her priority, and she pursued her quest with a dogged determination. However, she did agree to carry a panic alarm when she was with Tim.

Once inside the plush modern suite, Ula greeted her and took her jacket. A woman and three men she didn't recognize sat at a table in the middle of the room. Ellie took off her sunglasses and joined them.

"Ellie, this is Tracy Fenton and her team—Jason, Ben and Jack," Ula said. "They've been looking into Tim's background for you."

Ellie had never met the team of private investigators her company used. Their services bent many privacy and information

security laws, but this had never worried her, and this particular investigation was paramount.

"Shall we get started?" Tracy said matter-of-factly, and opened
the colored folders that lay on the table. Ellie was surprised by her
appearance—considering how borderline-legal her techniques
were, she had a very unassuming, mumsy look about her. But
she spoke with directness and efficiency. "Firstly, on behalf of my
team I'd like to offer my sincerest apologies for us dropping the
ball the first time round. The timescale we were given to complete
our work didn't allow us to do a thorough enough job, but that's
no excuse. I can assure you personally it will not happen again."

Ellie nodded but didn't offer any outward signs that she for-
gave their error.

"Details about your fiancé are scant, and it's our opinion that
he has buried himself very deeply," Tracy continued. Already,
Ellie felt her stomach knot. She dug her heels into the rug to
maintain her composure. "But let's tell you what we know about
him so far. Timothy Hunt, real name Matthew Ward, was born in
St. Neots, Cambridge, to parents Samantha and Michael Ward."

"He told me he didn't know his father. His parents were
married?"

"They were," Tracy said, and passed copies of marriage and
birth certificates to Ellie across the table. "The couple had no
further children. Matthew was educated in Cambridge until at
least sixteen—an average student with mediocre GCSE results.
But we cannot ascertain if he continued into further education
or university. Meanwhile, his parents divorced, after twenty-
six years of marriage, eight years ago. Both went on to remarry,
and his mother died three years ago in a house fire in Oundle,
Northants. The coroner's cause of death was smoke inhalation.
The CV he provided you with for his job application includes a
selection of fictional businesses, none of which check out. And
we cannot find any current record of employment."

"So for almost twenty years, Tim… I mean Matthew, hasn't existed?" Ellie asked.

"It appears that way. He has erased all traces of himself." Tracy opened a second folder and passed Ellie more printouts and photocopies. "Timothy appears to have made his first appearance in your life at his job interview—we can find no record of him before that date. Everything we learned upon our first investigation was created, faked or manipulated. We have spoken to his football teammates who informed us he joined them just over a year ago, but rarely attends social functions. None of them know much about him."

"But if he got the job with us, he must've known we'd discover his CV and references were faked?"

"I'm sure he did."

"Which leads me to believe his sole purpose for applying was to gain access to the building, look into a camera and mouth my name in the hope that one day I'd see it."

"He's playing a long game, but for what purpose, I cannot say."

Ellie shook her head. "And if you can't find a current employer, then what's he doing when he says he's going to work each day?"

"I can put together a team to follow him if that's what you decide."

"Can we go back to his father? Is he still alive?"

"He is alive, but he's now living in a home for stroke patients in Galbraith, Scotland. He's recently been widowed. According to the manager, he can no longer converse."

"And you haven't been able to discover anything else about Tim, not even from his DNA?"

"Nothing, not even when we ran his picture though facial image recognition software. His DNA information is no longer on the company database, but we ran a trace on the fingerprints we obtained from your property. They revealed nothing of interest. It's as if he's left behind a trail of crumbs only leading in the direction he wants you to follow."

"Damn it," she whispered, and sat back in the chair. Her back and underarms were wet with perspiration and she pressed her wrists into the leather arms of the chair to try to cool herself down. Everything she feared about her fiancé was coming true, only it was worse than she'd imagined. Tim wasn't just her Match; he was also her enemy.

She suddenly became aware of the silence in the room and that everyone present was avoiding eye contact. She felt foolish and humiliated, and wondered if they'd all had a laugh at the gullible rich girl behind her back. She rose to her feet, slipped her sunglasses and jacket back on, and thanked Tracy and her team. She left swiftly, followed by Ula and Andrei.

As she was driven back to her office, attempting to dodge the mid-morning London traffic, Ellie's sadness gave way to anger. She felt like someone who had been bereaved and cheated out of a future, and she was furious because of it. She had lost her loving Tim to a stranger with an agenda.

By the time the car had snaked its way through traffic across London Bridge and pulled up outside her office in The Shard, Ellie had already begun to bark orders at Ula, who furiously typed them into her iPad: changing all the locks and security codes to Ellie's home, organizing a new mobile phone number and private email address, deleting all of Tim's text messages and photographs they'd taken together, and erasing any contact there had ever been between them.

By the time the lift reached the lofty heights of the seventy-first floor, Ellie was mulling over how and when she would confront Tim. She eventually settled on that night; she would return to his home, and, with Andrei and his team's assistance, she would learn the truth, no matter what means were used to get it out of him.

Only, the element of surprise had been taken away from her. As she closed the door to her office, Tim was sitting behind her desk, his feet resting on the top.

"Hello, Ells, I think it's time we talked, isn't it?" he said, smiling broadly.

76

MANDY

Mandy faced an anxious thirty-minute wait while Richard was examined in private.

She couldn't stop her imagination from working overtime, convincing herself that it was her and the baby's presence that had brought him back to consciousness. After an unbearable delay, his doctor finally called Mandy into Richard's room.

"I'm sorry," he began sympathetically. "But I can't see any substantial signs of brain activity."

"I've heard that sometimes people come out of a coma when they hear a song they like or a familiar voice. Maybe that's what happened to him?"

"That can certainly be the case for some coma patients, but your friend isn't in a coma," the doctor said. "Please, take a seat."

As Mandy lowered herself into an armchair, Dr. Jenkins perched on the edge of Richard's bed.

"Let me explain. Coma patients are totally unresponsive. They don't move or react to sounds and can't feel pain. Their brains have simply shut down to deal with the trauma they have been put through, but research shows that they are still aware of their surroundings. The severe brain injuries Mr. Taylor sustained in his accident pushed him from a coma into a prolonged vegetative state, which is quite different. He's unconscious and has no awareness of anything around him. However, parts of his body can still move like you witnessed—his arms and his eyes. He can yawn and may even utter the odd word, but it's not *him* in control of it. It's a natural reflex. If it continues much longer— which we suspect it will—the chances of him recovering are virtually nil. I'm sorry, Ms. Griffiths…"

Mandy dabbed at her eyes with the sleeve of her top. "There was more to it than that," she said. "You said he's not aware of anyone around him, but I'm sure he was—is—aware of me. It was only when I held his hand to my face that this happened."

Dr. Jenkins paused and frowned. "I understand you are Mr. Taylor's partner. You are both Matched, I believe?"

"Yes, but I'd never met him before today." Mandy felt almost embarrassed. But she was eager to impress on Dr. Jenkins the uniqueness of the situation. "I'm also carrying his baby."

Dr. Jenkins looked at Mandy with a confused expression, likely thinking she was mad.

"It's a long story," she added quickly.

"Well, I have read about cases where patients respond to their Matches, and it can certainly become even more intense when a child is involved. Researchers believe it is because a pregnant woman's hormones contain certain properties that can stir senses in the unconscious. However, it's probably an exaggeration to call them restorative or healing. It's not impossible, but it's more of an involuntary chemical reaction than a cerebral one."

"I don't understand."

"It's not Richard, per se, who is responding to your touch. It's his body—his receptors, his pheromones, his nerves, his muscles—recognizing the feeling and the presence of its Match rather than his brain."

Mandy sank back into her chair, feeling deflated. For a moment, she'd let herself believe that the impossible had happened; that the power of their Match had woken the man she had been destined to spend her life with. But it was just their shared chemistry playing tricks on her.

When Dr. Jenkins left the room, she spent another hour or so sitting in silence with Richard, her hands clasped around his, praying that his body might react to hers again. But there wasn't even as much as a twitch. Then, giving in to defeat for now, she kissed him on the forehead and promised to visit him again.

"I'm sorry," she said to her baby bump, as she made her way out of the building and back toward her car. She felt a twinge inside as the baby shuffled into a different position. Mandy knew the stress of the day was going to get worse before it could get better. After packing her clothes and belongings, she was going to confront Pat and Chloe, then disappear from their world of deceit for good.

77

CHRISTOPHER

Amy wound her arm around Christopher's as they plodded along the bleak, pebbled beach.

The gray skies, howling wind, drizzle and encroaching tide hadn't put her off suggesting a long walk along Southwold beach back toward Aldeburgh, so they'd donned their thick jumpers and covered up with the matching blue raincoats they'd purchased from a shop in town.

They passed a paddock by the side of the path with three large, black horses sheltering behind a gate under a tree. Christopher remembered when he was a teenager he'd unlocked a similar paddock gate by the side of a busy road, just to see what might happen. He'd sat by a ditch on the opposite side and didn't have to wait long as the travelers' horses in the field bolted to freedom. It was the second one to escape that had collided with a VW Beetle, its head crashing through the driver's side of the windshield, killing both of them instantly. Ever since, he'd held a soft spot for horses.

"Shall we go somewhere for a coffee and warm up?" Amy asked, and Christopher nodded his head sharply. He despised being cold, and he loathed long hikes. Unless they had a dog on a lead or a specific destination to reach, he didn't see the point of just going for a walk. But he enjoyed spending time with Amy, and as being outdoors appeared to make her happy it gave him an equal satisfaction.

They made their way along the beach, past the brightly painted chalets, up a concrete ramp and along a high street framed by clothing boutiques, galleries and fish and chip shops, before choosing a cozy-looking café.

A young woman with wet hair and an irked expression pedaled furiously on an oversized bike to escape the drizzle, and, for a split second, Christopher pondered how she might look if he pushed her under a passing car. He used to fantasize about that kind of thing frequently as he traveled on the London Underground escalators. He'd look at the opposite side of the moving staircase and play "fuck" or "kill" with anonymous female faces, and it almost always resulted in more kills than fucks. However, Christopher hadn't felt motivated to play since he'd met Amy.

Once inside the café, they sat by the radiator, draped their wet windbreakers across it and waited for a member of staff to take their order.

"I know you're a posh city boy at heart, but this isn't too bad, is it?" said Amy, glancing out the window as the drizzle turned into a downpour and lashed against the glass. "Well, apart from the weather."

"No, it's nice," Christopher replied, and he meant it. He couldn't have given two hoots about the town, but he was appreciating her company.

"It's good to get out of London sometimes just to get your head together."

Christopher knew precisely what she meant, although when she'd suggested taking their first weekend away together in her parents' static holiday home by the coast, he felt something akin to anxiety. With just four women left on his list before he reached his goal of thirty, he didn't need any further distractions. Distractions meant mistakes, and he'd already risked losing sight of the endgame by falling into a relationship. But his desire to spend an undistracted long weekend away with Amy was greater than his need to reach his target.

Christopher had contemplated finishing prematurely after Number Twenty-Six. At that point, he'd have still accomplished what he'd set out to do: sending a city of seven million into panic and generating news headlines worldwide. The killings and the faceless madman behind them had fascinated everyone. "What are his motives?" they asked. "How is he targeting them?" "Is there a pattern to where they lived?" "What is the significance behind the stencil mark?"

Christopher was the only person able to answer each question, and on occasion it stymied him not to be able to do so or to take any credit for it. However, that was the sacrifice that needed to be made for his crimes to become a thing of legend.

"Can I ask you a question, Chris?" Amy said, as their whipped-cream lattes were placed on the table. She appeared a little nervous.

"Go ahead," he replied, as he arranged the mugs symmetrically. Her abbreviation of his name no longer seemed to bother him. "What's on your mind?"

"Nothing really," she said, and placed her hand upon his in a reassuring manner. "Well, I just need to know—and I hate to be that person who brings this up—but where do you see us going? Am I *the one*? Do you want to settle down with me and do what every other couple does?" Her cheeks were beginning to redden, which made Christopher smile. She carried on, her words getting faster and faster. "I know we're Matched, but is that enough for you? Because if that's what you want, you've not actually told me. I know you're a bit different from the other guys I've been in relationships with, I get that, but sometimes I find you so hard to read."

Christopher frowned. "What do you mean by 'different'?"

"Well, you play your cards pretty close to your chest, don't you? It's like there are things going on under the surface that you keep from me, and, once upon a time, with other boyfriends, that would have been excuse enough for me to have walked away. I mean, I'm a police officer, for God's sake. It's my job to be suspicious even with my nearest and dearest, but with you, it's...it's different. It's like whatever you are not telling me doesn't really matter." She paused for a second, and Christopher really hoped she was right, that his secret didn't really matter. "It isn't something that's going to change my opinion of you. It's hard to explain, but rather than making me feel insecure, it has the opposite effect—it makes me trust you more. I trust you to have your secrets and that they won't hurt me."

Christopher felt a sudden urge to strip away the layers he'd spent years building and explain everything about who he was and what he'd been doing. He wanted her to know that while people had loved him in the past, he had never known how to accept it until now; how before Amy appeared he was merely living to type, but now the dark side of his nature, which formed so much of who he was, was diluting. And for the first time in his life, he wanted to be completely honest and vulnerable for someone.

He paused and closed his eyes, opening his mouth for the big reveal. But self-preservation prevented his voice from escaping. He reminded himself that if he gave up on his mission now, then for the rest of his life it would become his only regret. A tiny portion of him would resent Amy for coming between him and his killings, and gradually that rancor would grow from a seed into a tree that would eventually block out the light that shone from her. And it scared him what he might do to her if he ever felt himself begrudging her.

"I want everything that you want," he said quietly, and meant it.

Then he stared at the table, afraid to look her in the eye in case she saw straight through him and realized the man she loved had no soul.

78

With just two days until she began the next leg of her Australian adventure, Jade was no longer as eager to leave Kevin's family farm as she had been.

Mark's kiss had changed everything. Loyalty and common decency had initially kept them apart, but after giving in to their emotions that one time in the pool, they were now making up for lost time, stealing as many moments as they could when nobody was looking. Jade would accompany Mark to town to pick up supplies, holding his hand on the gearshift; their arms would brush up against each other's at the dining table, and she'd assist him herding the cows into the sheds before fixing them up to the milking machinery. Every minute spent with Mark made Jade's heart threaten to beat its way out of her chest.

He was an addiction she didn't want to be free of. And the more she had of him, the more she craved.

As she packed her suitcase and prepared herself for her forth-coming solo journey around Australia, the need to be with him was the strongest it had ever been. She felt short of breath when she thought of what the next five weeks might feel like without him nearby, and an ever-growing part of her wanted to stay on the farm.

Then, on Jade's final night, she decided their kisses, hand-holding and infrequent frissons were no longer enough. She slipped the silver band from her wedding finger and left it on her bedside table, then closed the door to the guesthouse and silently padded toward Mark's bedroom in the main house. Her hands felt clammy as she reached for the handle, and she prayed to God he wasn't going to reject her advances. But his door was already ajar, and, when she pushed it open, she found him lying awake facing her, as if he'd been expecting her to come.

He pulled the sheet to one side to invite her in.

"Come with me tomorrow," Jade whispered afterwards, her body exhausted and her lungs close to breathless.

"You know I can't, it's too complicated."

"Don't you think I know that? I was the one who married your brother."

"And I'm the one who's just screwed his wife."

"What did you just say?" she asked, pushing herself away from him. "Is that all I am to you, a shag?"

"I'm sorry, it's not what I meant."

"It's what you said, though. I'm not some cheap slapper who jumps into bed with any lad."

"I know, I know, and I shouldn't have said that." Mark reached out to hold her hand.

"You and I know there's something here that's bigger than both of us."

Mark nodded.

"So come with me. It doesn't have to be tomorrow. It could be in a week or a fortnight's time. Just tell your parents you need to get away from here to clear your head. Give us some time together on our own to figure out what this is. You owe us this chance."

"Jade, I'm needed here."

"And I need you."

"I can't do that to my family or to Kevin's memory. How can I tell people…people who came to his funeral two weeks ago, that I'm in love with my sister-in-law?"

Mark's use of the word "love" made her blush, and her body felt as if it was burning up. "But if I feel the same, how can it be so wrong?" she asked.

Mark shook his head apologetically, and threw himself flat against the bed, staring up at the ceiling, as if waiting for divine intervention to tell him what to do. Jade suddenly felt awkward and very naked. Rejected and frustrated, she slipped her T-shirt and underwear back on and opened the door to go back to her room.

"I am worth more than this, Mark," she snapped. "And if that doesn't sink into your head pretty bloody soon, it's going to be too late."

As she turned back toward the door she was shocked to see Mark's mother Susan glaring at them both from the corridor, her face a mixture of fury and disappointment.

79

NICK

Nick's appetite had all but disappeared. Each time he tried to fill his empty, rumbling stomach, he felt like bringing it back up again. So instead he stuck to his diet of cigarettes, chewing gum and bottles of flavored water.

His initial reaction to discovering he was going to become a father was to shy away, and he'd checked himself into the central Birmingham hotel room he'd stayed in when he and Sally first separated. Unlike Alex's apartment that was littered with his possessions, this anonymous room would help him think without his judgment being clouded.

Hour upon hour of solitude followed, as he stood at the ninth-story window, taking in the city's diverse skyline. He'd discovered that by removing the four screws from the window frame, he could disable the safety catches that prevented the window from being opened fully. The first two screws he held in the palm of his hand, and an idea came to him. He quickly dismissed it, yet still he continued to turn the remaining two with a teaspoon. It was a solution that could put a stop to him being everyone's problem, he reasoned.

Nick chose not to respond to any of Alex's text messages that evening. He didn't know how to tell him that instead of traveling to London to renew his passport, he'd actually spent the evening with his ex-girlfriend trying to come to terms with the fact that he could have a child by the end of the year. As the tone of Alex's unanswered texts became more and more concerned, and the calls and voice mails more frequent, Nick decided to switch his phone off.

A gentle breeze drifted through the window and reached Nick's face, but he didn't register it. Instead, he recalled how he'd always wanted children, but it was Sally who hadn't been so sure. They'd reached a compromise that they'd wait until a couple of years after they married and would let nature take its course. But their city break to Bruges saw an end to that, and now they were dealing with the consequences.

"You can make this happen or you can make this stop," Sally had been at pains to point out, and he believed her. "I'm just presenting you with the facts. You can either be a father or not. I just know I can't do this by myself. I'm not threatening you or giving you an ultimatum."

It didn't feel that way to Nick.

He was pragmatic in his approach and had worked through each viable way he could play a part in his child's life and still remain with Alex. He figured he could still emigrate to New Zealand, and, with flight prices falling year-on-year, he might be able to afford a return trip to the UK at least once a year, even twice if he was careful with his money. The rest of the time, he could watch his child grow up via FaceTime and Skype. It wouldn't be ideal, but it was what thousands of armed service parents did stationed countries apart from their children. And there's no reason why Sally might not also bring their child over to visit. This was all on the assumption that she'd view this idea as "not being alone." She was so scared of raising the baby by herself, and he wanted to be there as much as he could. He couldn't face thinking of the other option Sally had presented him with.

It was too big an ask of Alex to remain in London. He needed to be with his sick father. He was deteriorating by the day, and Nick knew Alex was eager to make the move to be with him as he saw out his final weeks. If the shoe had been on the other foot, Nick would've put his family's needs before his own, too.

There were other ways around the problem, but all of them ended with the same result: Nick would be a bit player in his child's life, and that would never be enough for him. If he was to be a father, he wanted an active role in raising their child.

But a worrying thought began to creep into his mind, and it frightened him. What if he resented the child for coming between him and his Match? What if every time he looked into its eyes, they would reflect the emptiness of his own? Nick shuddered.

The thought of being unable to see his soul mate for an indefinite period of time made Nick's body ache. Not being able to laugh with him, be responsible for his gawky grin when he walked into a room, or hear the rise and fall of his chest as he slept, made Nick feel physically sick. And if he felt like this while they were still in the same city, what would it be like once they were a world apart? Nick knew deep in the marrow of his bones that it would be too much to bear. Trying to come up with one answer to suit everyone was like trying to push the tide back into the ocean with a broom.

He swallowed hard and then glared at the remaining two screws in the window's safety catches and closed his eyes. He had made his decision, and there was no going back.

80

ELLIE

"Hello, Ells, I think it's time we talked, isn't it?" Tim said, smiling broadly. His voice was carefree and melodious in tone, but his superficial grin undermined it. He leaned back in her chair behind the glass desk and sipped from a tumbler, then swirled the ice around. The lead crystal decanter that contained a much-sought-after Scotch sat atop the drinks cabinet, purposely left out and unplugged for Ellie to notice.

This wasn't the Tim she'd been head over heels in love with; this was Matthew, an unknown quantity, a man she had yet to meet but one she already hated. She fumbled around in her jacket pocket for Andrei's panic alarm.

"I know about the alarm and feel free to alert the giant to my presence if you like. I'm not going to stop you."

Ellie turned to leave and press the button, but Matthew spoke again:

"But if you do, you'll never find out why I went to all this trouble to fuck with you."

She stopped in her tracks, and remained with her back to him.

"And as a scientist who has spent her life figuring out problems, I bet you're just dying to know why."

Ellie turned toward the drinks cabinet and mixed herself a gin and tonic. She straightened her skirt, sat down on one of the two sofas, crossed her legs and waited for Tim to join her on the sofa opposite. Her initial bewilderment at finding him there had been replaced by a sudden steely resolve. If he wanted to talk, he would have to come to her. She would not pander to any man.

"How did your meeting at the Soho Hotel go?" he asked as he walked over. His knowledge of her whereabouts took her by surprise, but she refused to let it show. "You should get a better password for your cloud account. I always know where you are and where you've really been when you've been telling me you're at work."

"Likewise, you shouldn't have left your account open on my iPad."

"You think that was by accident? There are no accidents, Ellie. Only carefully constructed plans."

"Do you want to get to your point, Matthew?" she asked calmly.

"Ahh, it's the first time you've called me that. I think I like it, Ells. Do you know why I picked the name Timothy, by the way? It's biblical, apparently. It means 'honoring God.' And that's who you think you are, isn't it? Some God-like figure who should be honored?"

Ellie raised her eyebrows, and he paused for a reaction before continuing.

"Discovering your little gene, telling people who they should be spending the rest of their lives with…it certainly appears that you have a God complex."

"This kind of accusation is nothing new." Ellie sighed dramatically. "So let's not waste any more time. What do you want from me? There has to be a point to all this, and money is the obvious motive. You're probably expecting me to pay you off, or you'll threaten to sell your story to the papers."

Matthew took another sip of his drink. "Nope. I'm not the kiss-and-tell type. Try again."

"I have no idea what 'type' you are."

"No, you don't, so let me tell you. I, my darling bride-to-be, am the type of person who is about to change your life in a way you never dreamed possible." He gave her a grin and held his glass aloft, like he was offering her a toast.

"And how will you do that?"

"We'll get to that in good time. But first I have to say, I wish I'd been there to see the look on your face when you recognized my mum in that photograph."

"I don't actually remember her very well," Ellie lied. "She was only a junior member of staff. Quite insignificant and nondescript, if I'm being honest."

"She was one of the first to take your test, wasn't she? I'd have thought that would've made her a little more memorable, especially as she didn't know she'd taken it."

Ellie shot him a glance. She knew exactly what he was referring to.

"I see you're not jumping in to correct me," he continued.

"There were some people whose DNA I…borrowed…to build up the database in the early days," she conceded.

"Some? One of your old colleagues told me you were nicknamed 'Oscar the Grouch' because you spent so much time ferreting around the bins looking for used plastic cups and forks. By all accounts you'd be sneaking them out and swiping their DNA to add to your collection without their permission."

Inside, Ellie seethed. She'd been assured that those in her inner circle had been paid generously to remain silent about those murkier early days. "And?" she asked. "Hardly the crime of the century, is it?"

"Not only is it illegal, but it's also unethical."

Ellie laughed. "*You* are about to give *me* a lecture on ethics? Come on now, Matthew, you can do better than that."

"Okay, shall we discuss how later, once you had a bit of money behind you, you hired a team to bribe government employees into allowing you access to records from the National DNA Database? Or how they paid off staff in clinics, hospitals and mortuaries for samples?"

"I can't be held responsible for the methods of a third party."

"You took the DNA of the dead, the dying, sick people and criminals to bolster up your numbers in order to get more financial backing and expand your business. I found the details of known pedophiles, sex offenders and killers buried deep in your files, some of whom you actually found Matches for. And when I trawled a little deeper, you had the DNA of the severely mentally handicapped and even dead children on your database. Dead children, Ellie! How the fuck can you justify that?"

"Show me one successful global company that hasn't blurred the lines in its early days to get a foot on the ladder."

Ellie looked away, refusing to feel shame for what she'd turned a blind eye to. "The end justified the means," she replied. "My discovery changed the world, so what harm did it do?"

"Do you recall what the results of my mum's Match Your DNA were?"

"Of course not—it was very early on, so I can only presume that she had no confirmed Match back then."

"And what about my dad?"

"Your dad? I didn't even know he existed until two hours ago."

"My dad was also one of your early test subjects. He was working for the government when you stole his details. Then when you made the test available to the public, a woman got in touch with him after discovering she was his Match. At a time when my parents should have been thinking ahead to their retirement, he was packing his bags to move to Scotland with a complete stranger."

"Matthew, I am not responsible for—"

"I'm not interested in hearing you toe the corporate line or your usual bullshit about how you're not to blame for destroying people's lives. I'm here to tell you how I'm about to destroy yours. Now, do you mind if I help myself to another drink?"

81

MANDY

Mandy was relieved to find Pat's house empty when she returned from visiting Richard at the nursing home.

She needed space to formulate a plan before she was ready to confront Pat and Chloe about why they'd lied about Richard's death. But first she needed to get out of Pat's house. She made her way upstairs to her bedroom—his bedroom—and fought the urge to cry again. She was concerned about the effect her afternoon of stress might be having on her baby.

What had begun as an ordinary day with so much to look forward to had taken more twists and turns than a James Patterson novel. She was exhausted, and couldn't wait to return to the safety of her own home and its familiar surroundings. Once there, she'd lock the doors, slip into a deep, soapy bath and begin to come to terms with everything she had learned. And then, in a couple of days when the dust had settled, she'd visit her mum and sisters in the hope of making amends. It had been the best part of a year since she'd seen them properly, and she needed her real family now more than she could've ever imagined.

She grabbed her clothes from around the room, and threw them into two suitcases. Everything baby related she left where Pat had hung it, alongside bags of toys, nappies and a stroller. She could buy these things for herself, later.

The sound of the front door opening gave her a queasy feeling, and she quickly slammed the lids of her cases and zipped them up.

"Hiya! Are you upstairs, Mandy?" yelled Chloe. "We've brought fish and chips from the takeaway as Mum couldn't be bothered to cook…"

Her voice trailed off as Mandy appeared on the landing lugging her cases behind her. "Is everything okay?" asked Pat.

"I'm going home for a few days," Mandy replied. "I just need a bit of time to myself."

Pat and Chloe looked at each other, a baffled look crossing their faces. "Has something happened? Is it the baby? Is he okay?" asked Chloe.

"Yes, the baby's fine."

"Then why are you leaving? I thought you were happy here?"

Mandy paused and stared at the two strangers below her, realizing she didn't really know them at all. They had lied to her from the day she'd first met them, and she resented them for every mistruth they'd sold her and every fake promise they'd made.

"I know about Richard," Mandy said slowly but firmly.

"What do you know?" Pat asked.

"I met Michelle Nicholls today, Richard's ex-girlfriend. She told me a lot of interesting things about him, like that he was quite the ladies' man and that he didn't want kids of his own. But that's not even the half of it, is it?"

"Whatever she's told you, she's lying," said Pat immediately. "Michelle is a bitter little tart, angry because Richard didn't want her anymore."

"So you didn't beg her to have Richard's baby and then harass her when she said no?" Mandy fixed her glare on Pat.

"No, of course we didn't, darling. Before he died, Richard told me he never loved her."

"'Before he died'! Pat, stop it. I know the truth. I just spent the afternoon with him in his nursing home."

Pat held her hand to her mouth in surprise, and Chloe looked away.

"Why did you lie to me?" continued Mandy. "Why did you tell me he was dead?"

"We didn't mean to," Chloe interrupted, her voice trembling. "When you turned up at the remembrance service, we assumed you knew he was alive. Then when you came to the house, we realized you thought he was dead and..." She glanced at Pat. "Mum thought it best not to upset you any further. I wanted to tell you the truth, but then it all went too far." Again, she exchanged an uneasy look with Pat.

"You even showed me where you had sprinkled his ashes, Pat. What kind of mother would do that? When her son is still alive?"

Even Chloe looked surprised at this. "Mum?" she said quietly, but Pat ignored her.

"For all intents and purposes he is dead," said Pat. "I lost my little boy, and I wanted him back. And you, you wanted a child. I'm sorry I lied to you, but it's worked out for all of us, hasn't it?"

"That was the plan then, to replace Richard with my baby?"

"No, we could never replace him," snapped Pat.

"Then what? Because from what his nurse told me, you never go and visit him. You pay for his care, but you've had nothing else to do with him since before you met me."

"It's too hard," said Chloe. "To see someone who was so full of life, drained of everything that made him exist. It's just too bloody hard."

"Oh, poor you. What about your brother? He's the one who's

all alone up there. You've even banned his friends from seeing him."

"Don't you dare judge us," Pat said, making her way up the stairs toward Mandy. "You're lucky you've only seen him the way he is now—that body in bed who needs a ventilator to breathe, a pipe down his throat to feed him and a catheter to piss through. You have no idea how fortunate you are not to have known him back then, because you have *nothing* to compare him to now. That boy is not my son anymore. That *body* is not him, so don't tell me what I should and shouldn't be doing, because you are clueless."

"Mum, Mandy, please calm down," said Chloe, but she was ignored again.

"So what am I to you, then? Just a vessel to carry his baby?"

"No, of course you're not. If we'd just wanted that, we'd have found a surrogate."

"But that's what you wanted from Michelle, wasn't it? You asked her first."

"We weren't thinking clearly back then," added Chloe. "We were grieving and still in shock. We understand that now, don't we, Mum? That's why we sent Rich's DNA swab to find his correct Match, to find the person to have his child with. And that's you."

"What?" Mandy lost her grip on the suitcase handle, and it fell to the floor. "You did the test for him?"

Chloe hesitated. "You make it sound worse than it is," she said, and lowered her head. "Mum was just doing what she thought best. Please, Mandy, just leave your cases there and come downstairs and let's talk about this. You're part of our family, just like the baby will be."

Mandy shook her head and laughed. "You're wrong. I am not part of this family, and I'll be damned if my baby will be either. You've lied to me from the word go, so how can I ever trust you? I need to go home and start putting my life back together, without you two in it." Mandy grabbed her suitcases and pulled them toward her and started making her way down the stairs.

"Like hell you are," yelled Pat and ran up the last few stairs until she was face-to-face with her. "You aren't taking my grandchild away from me." As she said this she yanked at her arm, which made Mandy lose her balance.

Mandy fell forward. She managed to grip the handrail just before her legs gave way, but with the force of her giant body falling, she didn't catch herself in time to stop her forehead from cracking into the spindles. She felt the warm trickle of blood run down her face. She held herself steady with one hand and with the other Mandy reached to touch her wound. When she realized it was a deep cut, she immediately felt faint.

"I'll call for an ambulance," yelled Chloe, and ran into the living room for her phone.

"Don't move, you stupid girl," said Pat. She pulled a tissue from her sleeve and placed it on Mandy's injured head. "How could you put my grandchild at risk like this?"

"You and your lies did this," Mandy wept.

"We could have been happy, just the four of us. You were honestly like another daughter to me, but you shouldn't have gone sticking your nose into business that didn't concern you. Whether you like it or not, I am going to be a part of this baby's life. Nobody—not you or any court in this land—is going to keep me from my grandson."

Scared and disorientated, Mandy wanted to get as far away from Pat as possible. She pushed away Pat's arm which was supporting her and once again reached for her suitcase. But as she tried to descend the staircase her legs buckled, and she tumbled, cracking her already injured head against the bannisters and spindles, before falling down the remaining steps and landing in a crumpled, unconscious heap, facedown on the floor.

82

CHRISTOPHER

The odorous molecules of Number Twenty-Nine's auburn hair charged up Christopher's nostrils and dissolved in his mucus, creating a signal to his brain.

But there was something about the fruit-infused ingredients in her generic brand of shampoo that repelled him, and, to the best of his recollection, it was the first time a smell had ever had a negative effect on him.

Christopher wanted to get through this as briskly and efficiently as possible, but the skin around her neck was thin and he'd wrapped the wire around it too tightly, causing it to penetrate. He loosened the slack a little, concerned that it might pierce her jugular and release a jet of blood across the room. Cleaning up each microscopic droplet would be far too time consuming, and Christopher wasn't in the mood.

His partly released grip meant he had to wait an agonizing eight minutes—he had counted—for her to finally lose full consciousness and slip to the floor. She'd put up a brave fight, he conceded, with her futile attempts to kick, scratch and bite him. But he'd learned from the thumb incident of Number Nine not to be that careless again. And in the end, experience and the element of surprise were on his side, and the duel was weighted in his favor.

Christopher followed the unconscious girl to the ground and wrapped the wire around her neck again, using just enough pressure to completely starve her brain of oxygen. For a moment, in the reflection of the bifold doors, he watched the hunter take down his prey in an ill-fated tango, before turning away. He no longer resembled or recognized his old self.

The squelch emitting from Number Twenty-Nine's throat as she slowly died was just as unpleasant as the odor from her hair, and he chose to ignore the mucus dripping from her nose and the frothy white bubbles pooling in the corners of her mouth.

With her life finally expunged, Christopher released his grip and lay by her side, shattered, staring at the ceiling as images of another woman on his list flooded his head. Number Twenty-Seven had haunted him for days and had been a turning point for him; between her and Amy, the psychopath was developing empathy and a conscience.

Twenty-Seven had been dead for the best part of three days when he'd returned to her kitchen to leave a Polaroid snapshot of Number Twenty-Eight. And it became the one and only time in Christopher's life that he'd been truly shocked and mesmerized by what he saw.

Lying between her swollen, discolored legs was a small, perfectly formed, lifeless fetus, no bigger than an apple. To begin with, all Christopher could do was stare at it transfixed, wondering if the pressure he'd placed upon himself to reach his goal was causing him to hallucinate. But each time he held his eyes shut and released them again, the fetus remained.

Number Twenty-Seven's name was Dominika Bosko, and he wouldn't forget it, because she and her baby were the only two Christopher considered victims. He felt compelled to wrap the fetus in a tea towel and gently move it into the crook of its mother's arm.

Christopher imagined how he might feel if he were looking at Amy and their child lying before him, cold and lifeless, and with all their potential quashed because of the actions of another. And for the very first time in his adult life, he could feel tears forming in the corners of his eyes. It was too late to stop the first few from splashing mother and child.

It was only when he arrived home and researched it on the internet that he discovered that her unborn child had been a victim of a rare occurrence named coffin birth. The pressure of abdominal gases inside Dominika had built up as she began to decompose and forced the child from her body.

Christopher spent the rest of the day working his way through every piece of information he had on her, trawling her emails, text messages and social media interactions. Then in four separate emails to friends back home in Syria she revealed she was pregnant. He cross-checked the dates—they'd been sent the weekend he was away in Aldeburgh with Amy.

His relationship with Amy had made him complacent. He'd invested more time in her than keeping up to date with other aspects of the women's lives; if he'd known of Dominika's pregnancy, he'd have removed her from his short list.

There was only one more left before Christopher's work was complete, but whether he could stomach it was up for debate.

83

JADE

Jade had never felt more heartless as when she stood partially clothed before her mother-in-law, still flushed from having made love to her son, and not the one she married.

The light from Susan's bedroom illuminated the distress on her face, the shadows accentuating her formidable presence. She glared at both of them in turn, disgusted by what she saw, then turned and walked toward the living room.

Mark scrambled to find the underwear Jade had stripped from him and thrown across the room. Pulling them on, he grabbed a T-shirt and pushed past her to follow his mother.

"Mum," Jade heard him say, as she reached for the terry cloth dressing gown which hung from the back of Mark's door. With her legs wobbling, she went to join him. They'd face this together.

"How could you both?" Susan exclaimed, tears already streaming down her face. "Kevin is your *brother*, Mark, and your *husband*,

Jade. How could you do this to him?! We've only just buried him, he's not even cold in the ground."

"I'm sorry," Mark said desperately. "I didn't mean for you to find us."

"Oh no, of course you didn't, it's pretty bloody obvious that you wanted to carry on behind everybody's backs."

"No, it wasn't like that."

"And you!" continued Susan, pointing her finger at Jade. "We welcomed you into our *home* and treated you like a daughter. And this is how you repay us? Sleeping with your brother-in-law the whole time?"

"It hasn't been the whole time," began Jade. "This was the first time."

"You expect me to believe that?"

"Yes, because it's the truth."

"You two don't know what the bloody truth is. Mark, I thought we raised you better than this."

"You did… You have," Mark tried to explain.

"Clearly I didn't… You're disgusting!"

"There was never anything physical between Kevin and me," Jade said firmly, hoping to defuse the situation. "We didn't have the chemistry, and…I don't know why."

Susan's eyebrows knitted together as she glared at her. "Yes, there was, he was your Match! I saw how he behaved around you. He loved you."

"And I loved him, but I wasn't *in love* with him. I know we were Matched, but there was no romance there, at least not on my part. I guess that must sometimes happen…"

"What you mean is that as soon as you found out he was sick, you lost interest."

"No, that's not it, honestly, Susan. If I didn't care about him I wouldn't have stayed."

"He was besotted with you, Jade. I could see it in his eyes.

You were his Match, so why didn't you feel the same way? You were *supposed* to feel the same way!"

"I don't know, please, believe me. I tried so hard to fall in love with him... I wanted to love him like he loved me, but... but I couldn't."

"I don't think you tried at—"

"She's being honest, Mum," Mark interrupted. "Jade couldn't fall in love with him. She wasn't his Match."

Both women turned their heads quickly toward Mark.

He swallowed hard before he spoke. "And I know that Kev wasn't her DNA Match because...because she's Matched with me."

84

ALEX

It was Alex who had found the note waiting for him in Nick's empty hotel room.

When he had still not heard from Nick the morning after sending him so many texts and voice mails, he'd canceled his clients' appointments and took a taxi to the hotel where Nick was staying. He knew his train back from London was scheduled for that morning, so he would wait for him, but hours later, when Nick still hadn't returned, Alex, full of worry, talked the receptionist into letting him in.

As the electronic key card opened the door, Alex held his breath, scared of what he might find. Inside, the room was empty and tidy, but the bin was full. Crammed along with cigarette packets and minibar bottles were scraps and scraps of paper, curled up into tight balls, having been tossed away.

The security man stood by the wide-open window looking puzzled. While the breeze violently blew the curtains back and forth, it did little to take away the smell of stale smoke that clung to the material. "He'll be fined for that," the man mumbled in broken English.

Alex glanced around the room and eventually spotted the sealed envelope which sat atop the pillow on the neatly made bed. He felt a sudden chill from the wind when he recognized his name and the handwriting, then held his breath as he dashed to the window and looked to the concrete roof of the building below.

85

ELLIE

Matthew brought the decanter of whisky from the drinks cabinet back with him to the sofas where Ellie sat.

As he poured himself another glass, Ellie tried to disguise that
she was becoming increasingly agitated by his accusations and
threats. But they were both aware that he knew her well enough
to see straight through her titanium veneer. He sat down opposite her and took an overexaggerated breath.

"After my dad left my mum—thanks to your test—in the
space of a few months he forced her to sell the family house, so
all she could afford was a flat miles away from her home and
her friends," he continued. "She was lonely, humiliated and iso-
lated, and over the years she turned to booze to blank it all out.
It was just a matter of time before she lost her job because of al-
cohol dependency. Do you have any idea what it's like for a son
to have to change his mother's underwear because she shat her
knickers when she was paralytic? Or to pick her up from the
police station when she was arrested for being drunk and dis-
orderly in a supermarket?"

Ellie wanted to shake her head but refused to give him the gratification.

"Of course you don't know," he said. "Then, just when she reached her lowest ebb, she was Matched with somebody."

Ellie paused and placed her glass on the table. "Well, what's your complaint, then? Everything worked out for her in the end."

"You'd think so, wouldn't you? Bobby Hughes was his name," Matthew said. "He seemed like a good guy at first, and she fell for him hook, line and sinker, just like Matches are supposed to. But he was a manipulative bastard, and she was so desperate not to be alone that she agreed to do anything he asked, including turning a blind eye to the fact he took a fancy to young girls. *Very* young girls, judging by the three thousand or so images the police found when they seized his laptop. He tried to claim they were already on the computer when he bought it on eBay, and Mum was stupid enough to believe him—she paid his legal bills and took out loans for him right through his court case. But when he was put behind bars, she was left with nothing but final demands she couldn't pay back. And all of this, everything that went wrong in her life, was because of a test that she and my dad had no knowledge of taking, because you'd decided to play God. You, sitting here in your ivory tower up in the clouds, have never had to watch someone you love transform into something else right before your eyes."

Ellie shot him a withering glance. "You think?"

"I'm not talking about me, this is different," he continued dismissively. "I'm talking about watching a strong, intelligent woman disintegrate into a physical and emotional mess. You know she was passed out drunk when she set herself on fire with a cigarette? She burned alive. She was so badly injured that I couldn't even identify her body."

He folded his arms defiantly while Ellie took a sip from her gin and tonic. He appeared to be counting on her feeling pity toward his unfortunate mother. But the more accusatory he became, the more she quietly seethed.

He had underestimated her. He hadn't known her back then when she was an ambitious young woman trying to convince a scoffing scientific community of her DNA discovery; she hadn't told him of the sacrifices she'd made to be heard and how much of her old self she had been forced to surrender to become the powerhouse she now was. While Tim had certainly softened her, Matthew was a fool if he thought she couldn't snap back into her previous shape in a heartbeat.

"There are millions of couples across the world who have taken the test and found they aren't Matched," she began firmly, "but they've stayed together because they're in love. I may have taken certain shortcuts back in the early days, but I won't be held responsible for the decisions those Matched people eventually made. I didn't force your dad to leave your weak-willed mum, and I didn't put a bottle in her hand or pour booze down her throat. At some point, people have to take responsibility for their own actions."

"And at what point do you take responsibility for *your* actions, Ellie?"

"My actions have put homophobia, racism and religious hatred on the edge of extinction—a Match doesn't recognize sexuality, color or whatever God you choose to celebrate. It has united people of all faiths and persuasions in a way we never thought possible. Show me what you have done to make this world a less hostile place."

"But you've divided just as many people by creating a 'them' and 'us'—those who are loved by design and the rest who've been made to feel like their relationships are less worthy. Do you not see a parallel between what you've done and what Hitler did to the Jews? The Nazis eroded them, one by one, until they were a ravaged minority, treated like vermin. Is that your aim for un-Matched people? To gradually break them?"

Ellie laughed. "You're more deluded than I thought."

"Matches are better off financially than the un-Matched. Matched couples get bigger tax breaks, better life insurance deals, they're more productive at work because they're happier at home so they're offered better jobs. For the un-Matched, suicide rates are higher, as are divorces and depression—"

"Both of which actually fell last year as more and more people are finding happiness with those for whom they were designed. Domestic violence against both men and women has also dropped."

"Only because people are too scared to report those kinds of crimes against their physically and mentally abusive Match. They don't want to risk a *better* relationship with a non-Match."

"Immigration and emigration are no longer such contentious issues," Ellie continued, getting into the swing of her arguments. She was going to take this Matthew down. "People are fast-tracked through red tape and are allowed to travel worldwide and settle with their Matches in other countries."

"And that's damaged almost a fifth of businesses across globe who have lost key members of staff because they've relocated to another city or country."

"You can throw as many figures at me as you want, Matthew, but you cannot deny one thing. Match Your DNA exists, whether you like it or not."

He gave her a knowing look. "I don't deny it, but I predict it's not going to be around for very much longer."

"That's not your decision to make."

"That judgment belongs to the people," he continued. "And the people always prevail."

"What are you talking about?"

He stood up and stretched his arms behind him. "Another drink?"

Ellie shook her head. She watched as he helped himself to a third whisky, unable to recognize the man before her as the one she had loved. Everything about Matthew was different from Tim, from his arrogance to his mannerisms and even the way he sat. She wondered how hard it must have been to maintain the facade in her presence for so long.

"Even now that you know what kind of person I am, you're still in love with me, aren't you?" Matthew said, the ice cubes cracking as whisky oozed over them.

Ellie didn't respond.

"I thought so. It's not much fun having someone play God with your life, is it?"

"Don't kid yourself, you're not playing God. You're being just as manipulative as the man who conned your gullible mother. Only I'm not pathetic like her, and I'm not going to let this little blip shape the rest of my life. I'm always going to love you because it's in my DNA to, but I'm never going to like you, and, after today, we will never see each other again."

"With all the contempt you have for me, you still have faith we're a Match, don't you?" he said scornfully.

"Yes, of course we are, and Christ knows I wish we weren't."

"You see, that's the funny thing, Ells. Because we aren't Matched, and we never have been."

Ellie narrowed her eyes. "What do you mean?"

"You're a woman of science, yet you were so desperate to be coupled that not for a single moment did you doubt your results."

"I was not 'desperate to be coupled.' I had a perfectly happy life before you."

"You were, and still are, an ice-cold corporate whore who dated a series of wealthy idiots. You made up excuses not to see your family, and all you had to keep you company was your work. With me you had everything, which is ironic because, in reality, I am nothing to you."

"Of the 1.7 billion people who've been tested, there hasn't been one reported mis-Match—"

"Until now. You and I are a mis-Match, Ellie, because I hacked into your servers to manipulate our results."

"Rubbish," Ellie said, secretly balking at the notion. She folded her arms indignantly. "Our servers are more secure than almost every major international company across the world. We receive so many hacking attempts, yet no one gets in. We have the best software and team money can buy to protect us against people like you."

"You're right about some of that. But what your system didn't take into account was your own vanity. Do you remember receiving an email some time ago with the subject 'Businesswoman of the Year Award'? You couldn't help but open it."

Ellie vaguely remembered reading the email as it had been sent to her private account, which only a few people had knowledge of.

"Attached to it was a link you clicked on and that opened to nothing, didn't it?" Matthew continued. "Well, it wasn't nothing to me, because your click released a tiny, undetectable piece of tailor-made malware that allowed me to remotely access your network and work my way around your files. Everything you had access to, I had access to. Then I simply replicated my strand of DNA to mirror image yours, sat back and waited for you to get in touch. That's why I came for a job interview, to learn a little more about the programming and systems you use. Please thank your head of personnel for leaving me alone in the room for a few moments with her laptop while she searched for a working camera to take my head shot. That was a huge help in accessing your network. Oh, and tell her to frisk interviewees for lens deflectors next time—they're pocket-sized gadgets that render digital cameras useless."

Ellie wanted the ground to open up and swallow her whole. She felt her cheeks glow red, a combination of regret for allowing him into her life without question and fury for trusting him.

"You fell in love with me through your own free will," Matthew continued. "You so desperately wanted it that you talked yourself into it. You can't blame your DNA for getting you into this mess—you can only blame yourself."

Ellie took a moment to regulate her shallow breaths.

"There are several reasons I did this," Matthew continued, sinking deeper into his sofa. "Humiliating you was one of them. But I also wanted to demonstrate how greedy we are as human beings. How willing we are to give up everything and anyone we hold dear on the suggestion there might be something better around the corner. What you felt for me wasn't a DNA Match; we weren't designed for each other, we weren't written in the stars. It was mind over matter that made you fall in love, not science. It was a good old-fashioned boy-meets-girl relationship, nothing more and nothing less. And once I tell everyone how I fooled the woman who 'discovered' Matches, you'll be a laughingstock and your credibility ruined."

Ellie gripped the arms of the sofa as her temper got the better of her. "So what? Go ahead. Go public with it, be my guest. I'll survive it. In the end, plenty of others have found a true happiness they never thought possible because of me."

"Oh, Ells. Still so naive. Have you not learned anything from this?"

She glared at him, not knowing what he was talking about.

"You're not the only one to have the rug pulled from under your feet. Millions of your subscribers are about to have their lives turned upside down, too."

"What do you mean?" she asked hesitantly.

"Did you think I'd simply mis-Match you and me? Of course not. I rewrote your whole coding so that, over the space of the last eighteen months, at least two million people on your database were Matched with the wrong person."

Ellie swallowed hard, and her heart beat so fast, she thought it might break her chest bone.

"My mis-Matches are so completely random, even I don't

know who's been affected," he continued. "Anyone signed up and Matched in that time period—which by your company's growth rate is around twenty-five million people—could be one of my mis-Matches. Because of me, your business has just become completely worthless. Nobody will know if their Match is for real or if they've just talked themselves into it. I told you I was going to destroy you, and I never make promises that I can't keep."

86

MANDY

It was the pounding in her forehead that eventually woke Mandy from her unconscious state.

With her eyes still closed, she reached her right hand slowly toward her face and felt the egg-shaped lump. It was tender to the touch. She could feel a line of stitches holding it together. Slowly, she attempted to open her eyes, but her eyelids felt as if they'd been glued. She tried to move her left hand, but it was too heavy and she was too weak. She went to grasp it with the other and realized it was encased in plaster that stretched toward the middle of her forearm.

As she gradually came round, Mandy couldn't fathom out where she was or why the smell reminded her of bleach and mouthwash. She guessed she must be in a bathroom until she turned her head and squinted through the window. As her eyes focused, she recognized the built-up landscape outside. She had been here before; she recognized that view. Both times she'd lost her children, she'd been here. She was in a hospital.

Suddenly, a rising sense of panic engulfed her. She moved her hands under the sheets to her pronounced belly. It was much flatter than before. *No, please not again*, she prayed helplessly.

"Is somebody there?" she croaked, her throat bone dry, but she was alone in the room. Mandy tried to pull herself up in the bed and lie back against the metal frame, but a sharp, shooting pain wrapped its way around her stomach. She grimaced, and her hand flailed against the side of the bed, looking for the button she knew should be there. She jabbed at it hard.

It took a few moments before a nurse with ponytail appeared at her door. "Ah, you're awake. How are you feeling?" She spoke in a foreign accent and made her way to Mandy's side.

"My baby," Mandy mumbled, and tried to clamber out of the bed. "Where's my baby?"

"Let me get the doctor," the nurse said, and left the room.

Mandy's body trembled involuntarily as she took in her surroundings. The nagging pain in her forehead compounded with the pain in her stomach and wrist made her nauseous. She only just managed to lean toward the edge of the bed before she vomited on the floor. The doctor arrived.

"I need to see my baby…" she mumbled.

"No, no, no, you must stay where you are Mrs. Taylor," he replied, as the nurse helped to clean her up. Mandy was too panicked to even notice he'd called her Mrs. Taylor. "Your little boy is safe and well."

"Little boy?" she asked. Pat's prediction had been correct.

"Yes," he continued, glancing at a chart which he'd pulled from a hook at the base of her bed. "You gave birth prematurely to a boy five days ago. Four pounds, four ounces. He's safe and healthy and just down the corridor."

"What happened to me?"

"We were told that you fell down a flight of stairs. You sustained a head injury and a fractured wrist along with a minor swelling to the brain, which put your body into shock. You've been kept sedated for the last few days, and your baby was born by cesarean section as a precautionary measure. Now you need to take it very, very easy for the next few days. You'll be of no use to him if you try to rush these things."

"When can I see him?"

"I'll ask one of the nurses to bring him to you in the next few minutes."

"Thank you."

Mandy leaned her head back against the pillow, and she sighed with relief. She could just about remember tumbling down the stairs during her confrontation with Pat and Chloe, but could recall little else. It wasn't the ideal way for her baby to come into the world, but he was here nonetheless, and he was healthy. It hurt her head to smile and cry, but she did both regardless. She was a *mother*.

However, her delight quickly turned to concern when she saw the doctor's face when he returned minutes later.

"I'm sorry, Mrs. Taylor. It appears your son is elsewhere in the hospital with your family at the moment. They've probably just taken him for some fresh air around the grounds."

Mandy's eyes widened. "My family?"

"Yes, they've been here most days waiting for you to wake up. They've been spending a lot of time with him."

"Who? Who is it exactly that has him?"

"Your mother and sister, I believe. They called the ambulance that brought you in."

Mandy's body filled with an ominous dread before she grabbed the perplexed doctor's arm.

"Call the police right now," she growled.

87

CHRISTOPHER

The rear entrance to her ground floor flat was shabby. A dust-
ing of fallen rendering was scattered across the pavement below
and cracked putty held the window frames in place.

But the age and the lack of maintenance to the property were
an advantage to Christopher, as it meant little had been updated
or replaced in the last twenty years. For a man of his experience, the basic two-lever mortice door lock was easy to pick.

Two clicks of the barrel and he was inside, quietly closing
the door behind him and familiarizing himself with the layout
of the apartment. He'd last visited Number Thirty some weeks
earlier, and she'd changed nothing since. A smell of damp still
lingered in the air, and the streetlight outside illuminated the
cheap, flat-pack assembled furniture.

Christopher's thirtieth kill should have been something for
him to celebrate; a target that at times seemed insurmountable
was now, against all odds, within his reach. Thirty corpses,
thousands of newspaper and magazine column inches, televi-

sion documentaries and appeals featuring dramatic and wide-of-the-mark reconstructions, and all because of his efforts. And still no one was any the wiser as to who was behind it or their motivation.

However, Christopher was in no mood to commemorate his achievement or rest on his laurels. He just wanted to get his last kill over with, leave his mark on the pavement outside and return home. Then tomorrow night he'd be curled up by Amy's side and in her bed, his arm draped over her chest and holding on to her as if there was nobody else in the world.

They could move forward and lead their lives doing the same things other normal couples did. Once, his fantasies only stretched to killing strangers; now they were about spending his weekends with the woman he loved, wandering through garden centers and National Trust estates, deciding how to decorate the home they'd buy together, running together or cuddling up on a sofa watching box sets and eating junk food. He used to revel in being different, but not any longer. Everything that had been alien to the psychopath before he met Amy now appealed to him because she had made him feel *normal*.

Christopher paced silently around the flat and wondered again if one day he might tell her the truth about who he had been and who he'd become because of her. But since being part of a couple he'd learned relationships didn't need truth to make them work, they just needed one of them to possess a heart large enough to beat for both of them.

The muffled sound of a radio emanated from beneath the door of Number Thirty's bedroom. Christopher took up his position in the hallway and removed his familiar white billiard ball and cheese wire from his backpack. The final time he would do this. But he had neither the time or the inclination to be sentimental. He threw the ball against the wall and, with the taut wire in his hands, he felt almost apologetic for what was about to happen.

His heart had long since left this project, and he would gain no pleasure from her death.

But despite his noise, the bedroom door remained closed. Christopher assumed she must have fallen asleep. This was no problem; it'd happened before with Number Eighteen. But as he went to pick up the ball and repeat the process, he felt two sharp pricks to the back of his neck. He turned quickly and felt a massive electric jolt tear through his body. He immediately dropped to the floor in pain.

The last thing he saw before the crippling convulsions pushed him into unconsciousness was Amy's face.

88

JADE

Susan and Jade glared at Mark, awaiting further explanation.

"What do you mean you're my Match?" Jade asked, shaking her head. "Why would you say that?"

"Mark?" asked Susan, puzzled. "What's going on?"

Mark hung his head and closed his eyes. He took a deep breath before he spoke again. "Kev and I did our tests at the same time, and the results came back on the same day, when he was in hospital for one of his early chemo sessions," he explained quietly. "I opened my email, and I'd been Matched with you, Jade, but Kev, he didn't have anyone. Mum, you remember how desperate he was to know there was someone out there for him after the diagnosis?"

Susan nodded.

"I deleted his email and told him *he'd* been Matched, but I hadn't. I just wanted him to be happy. So I paid for your contact details, Jade, and sent them to his phone, so he never saw the original email. You should have seen the look on his face when he realized you existed, even if you were thousands of miles away. It was back when he still looked like the old Kev, remember, Mum? He even begged the doctors to let him fly to England to visit you, but they wouldn't allow it, and he couldn't get the insurance to cover the trip."

Jade could see Susan nodding, remembering when this had happened.

"As the treatment got into full swing, it was so awful to watch him starting to lose his hair and weight and become a brother I barely recognized. But I knew what I had done was worth it when I'd see the old Kev reappear in his eyes and watch him smile when he got your texts and your calls."

Jade thought back to the day she had first received confirmation of a Match. The notification had come through during her lunch break at work, and she'd been so thrilled that she'd paid for her link's details without giving much attention to his name. Almost immediately, she'd received a text from Kevin introducing himself and, from their first conversation, she just assumed he was her Match. She liked his warmth and enthusiasm, and immediately warmed to him. It was a stark contrast to her feelings of failure for having a job she hated and living with her parents.

"We just started talking and hit it off," Jade said quietly. "I didn't think to check it was the right name."

Jade felt her mother-in-law's disappointment dissipate, but for her, her anger only grew.

"I'm so sorry, Jade," Mark said. "But believe me, I know how hard it's been for you over the last few weeks. From the moment I opened the front door to you, I felt those explosions they talk about. And I hate that I've hurt the one girl in the world I love."

"You have no idea how much you've hurt me," Jade replied solemnly, and dug her fingernails into the palm of her hands to hold back her rising temper.

"I do know, honestly...hearing Kev talk to you on the phone every night and watching him in the living room grinning as each of your messages came through, knowing it should have been me reading them and not him...it was hell. I'd wonder what you were saying to each other and what you felt about him, and I couldn't say a damned thing. But I never expected you to actually turn up at the house. And then when you did it was both my worst nightmare and the best thing ever at the same time. Suddenly here you were, the one I was supposed to be with, on my doorstep and staying under my roof, but it was my brother you were here to see, and he was head over heels in love with you."

Jade could feel her eyes pooling, and she blinked the tears back, trying to keep a handle on her emotions. Part of her wanted to slap Mark, but the other part wanted to hold on to him for dear life.

"You lied to me...you lied to Kevin...you lied to the people you say you loved—how could you do that?" she asked. "I've spent weeks trapped in this nightmare, beating myself up over why I wasn't in love with him and thinking I was this selfish, heartless bitch. And you watched me going through absolute shite, but you didn't say a word. You didn't even try to hint that all wasn't as it seemed—you just let me deal with this all by myself. If you'd just given me a clue and let me work it out, then I could have at least decided if I wanted to go along with it or not. But you took the choice away from me. You used me, Mark, and that's what hurts the most."

"Please, try and understand why I did it."

"I do, and that's the only thing stopping me from punching you right now. I get it, you had to put Kevin first. But it takes me a long time to trust someone, and, no matter what my body feels for you, I don't think my head or my heart will ever trust you again."

"Please don't say that," Mark begged. "Just give us a chance."

"I'm sorry, I really don't think I can."

Jade hurried out of the living room and back to the guest-house, slamming her bedroom door shut behind her, along with all the feelings she'd ever held for her Match.

89

NICK

After another night of fitful sleep permeated by dreams of Alex, Nick left the spare room and made his way into the kitchen to make himself a cup of coffee. Sally was already sitting at the breakfast bar, pushing a partially eaten chocolate croissant around on a plate. The hem of her T-shirt was no longer able to cover her pregnant belly.

"Morning," he mumbled, and made his way to the coffee machine.

"Hi." She winced and shuffled from buttock to buttock.

"Can't you get comfortable?" he asked.

"No," she replied. "It's been like this all night. The baby's either been pressing on my bladder or kicking me."

"Has your headache lifted?"

"Not really, no. There's nothing I can take for it but the occasional aspirin, and they're doing little to help."

"Is it worth mentioning to the midwife this afternoon?"

"Probably not. She'll only tell me it's high blood pressure or chronic hypertension again and that I've got to chill. You try relaxing when there's a jackhammer going through your head."

"Can I get you anything?"

"A herbal tea would be nice. One of those lemon and jasmine ones in the cupboard."

Nick put the kettle on the stove, and they sat quietly, both staring ahead at nothing in particular while they waited for it to whistle.

Five months had passed since Nick had left Alex; the letter saying he was choosing Sally and the baby. It was long and heartfelt, and he hoped that he would understand the decision he'd made. He'd known how much it would hurt him, but he'd tried to tell himself that if Alex had been in an identical situation with his ex-girlfriend, Mary, he'd have done the same thing. This hadn't done much to assuage his guilt.

It had been the hardest thing Nick had ever had to do, much tougher than admitting to Sally he had fallen in love with a man. This unborn baby he had sacrificed everything for would grow up having no idea what its father had given up for it.

Nick reluctantly moved back into their apartment, although now he spent his nights in the spare bedroom. He hoped that a clean break from Alex, rather than a painful, lingering one, would be easier to handle, but he'd been fooling himself—barely an hour passed without him dwelling on his lost love.

A handful of days before Alex's departure, Nick had found himself on Alex's doorstep, apologizing.

Alex had given him a frosty reception, berating him for being such a coward. But he couldn't maintain his animosity for long, and they agreed to enjoy their last few days together.

However, no matter where they went or what they did, their relationship was no longer the same. The intense feelings remained but gone was the laughter, the spontaneity and the fun, all being replaced with an eye on the clock as they watched and waited as it counted down to the day Alex would leave Nick's life.

And when that day arrived, it was even worse than Nick could have ever imagined. He insisted on accompanying Alex to the airport, but, at the last minute, a distraught Alex changed his mind, begging to be allowed to go alone. Their goodbye consisted of a long, silent embrace until they could no longer ignore the taxi driver blowing his horn. Then, when the cab turned the corner out of sight, Nick sat on the steps outside Alex's apartment and sobbed. He only returned home when his eyes were so tender he couldn't cry any longer.

He canceled his sabbatical from work and returned to the advertising agency a week later, his colleagues none the wiser as to Nick's heartbreak. He threw himself into his work to busy his mind, and, at weekends, he and Sally would shop for baby-related necessities as if they were any other expectant couple. He accompanied her to Lamaze classes, stayed at home for health visitor appointments and massaged her feet and ankles when they were swollen.

To an outsider, Sally and Nick's life resembled what it had been like before they'd known about Alex's existence. But in reality, the shadow he left continued to loom over them.

"Have you spoken to Sumaira recently?" Nick asked. "How are the babies?"

"I texted her yesterday," Sally said with little enthusiasm.

"Something's definitely gone on between you two that you're not telling me about. She had them four weeks ago, and you still haven't been to visit."

"I told you before, we're good. I'm just giving her time to settle down."

"You barely saw her while she was pregnant. Is there something you're not telling me?"

"Nick, my head hurts and I'm tired. I'm not in the mood for this."

Steam blew from the kettle's nozzle and brought both of them back to reality. Nick dropped a tea bag into Sally's cup and filled it with boiling water, but a dripping sound somewhere else in the kitchen caught his attention. He examined the bottom of the mug to see if it was cracked, but then a sharp intake of breath made him turn his head.

"My waters," Sally began nervously, "they've just broken." Her pajama bottoms were wet, and a look of fear warped her face.

"But you're not due for another fortnight," Nick replied.

"Try telling the baby that."

90

ELLIE

Ellie was suffocating. She felt as if someone was kneeling on her chest, restricting each breath and refusing to allow fresh air into her lungs. Each of her body's ten pulse points vibrated like the woofers in a stereo speaker. But the only noise in her office was the echo of Matthew's confession.

Pull yourself together, Ellie, she told herself. *He's lying.*

"What does it feel like, knowing you've been duped?" Matthew asked softly, like a therapist would to his patient. He arranged his fingers in a steeple-like formation in front of his mouth to add to the fake sincerity of his question. "How does the puppet master feel having her strings pulled by someone else?"

"I wouldn't know," Ellie replied, "because nobody pulls my strings. Everything you've said is bullshit."

"How can you be so sure of that?"

"My IT department will prove it." She reached for her phone, but there was no signal. She grabbed the telephone on the table but could hear no dial tone. She glared at Matthew. "What have you done?"

"A signal blocker and two phone jammers. Like a modern-day Faraday cage."

"What do you want from me?"

"Believe it or not, absolutely nothing. Not a single penny, not an apology, not an explanation. I'll get enough gratification over the next few days when this becomes public and the world will begin to doubt whether the person on the other side of their bed really is the one who's supposed to be there."

Something inside Ellie suddenly snapped. Her self-preservation instinct, built from so many years as a woman in a male-dominated corporate world, kicked in with glaring speed. She rose to her feet with such force, it took Matthew by surprise.

"I'll deny your claims. Who's going to believe you?" she snarled. "My press department is built for damage limitation, and we'll spin this so you come across as a desperate, two-bit systems analyst who wasn't qualified enough to get a job here. Then we will find everything there is to know about you to discredit what you have to say. I'll savage what's left of your dead mother's reputation by dragging her and her pedophile boyfriend's name through the mud, alongside any friend or acquaintance you may have. The Sunday League football team you play for? None of them will have jobs by the end of the week, I guarantee you. Then I'll tie you up in court with so much litigation and private prosecutions that you won't be able to afford a bed to sleep in. By the time you have left this building, we'll have found whatever wormhole you claim to have discovered and seal it up, so there will be no proof you ever broke into our system."

"I'm your fiancé," Matthew said confidently. "That'll give me a lot more credibility. Especially when I tell everyone that the woman who's amassed a personal fortune out of predetermined love is willing to hide the fact there are two million people out there who have been Matched incorrectly. There'll be an investigation at the very least. There is no way out of this for you, Ells."

"They won't believe you."

"Ah, well I hate to disappoint you, but I think they might. I have everything I've done saved on backup hard drives and memory sticks hidden across the city, all waiting to be sent to WikiLeaks, who'll expose the story. They love a whistle-blower, especially when it's about corporate misconduct."

"I am not going to lose everything I have built because of you," Ellie spat.

Matthew smirked as he rose to his feet, straightened his tie and winked at Ellie. "Let's see about that, shall we, Ells? For the rest of your life, people will be queuing the length of the Thames to sue you for your flawed results and their failed relationships. Then, when everything you have cherished has been taken away from you, you'll know how my mother and countless others felt because of what you did. You, my love, are *fucked*."

It was the clear, crisp way in which Matthew delivered his final statement that convinced Ellie everything he'd told her was true. In an instant, she saw all she'd accomplished being yanked from under her feet. She'd survived a decade of abuse and criticism, and sacrificed her family, friendships and lovers, all for nothing because of a man who'd duped his way into her life.

It was the straw that broke the camel's back.

As Matthew made his way toward the door, he turned his head to look at Ellie one last time. But he couldn't have anticipated what Ellie was about to do.

Without thinking, she picked up the lead crystal decanter from the table and hurled it at him. The weight of it collided with his temple and knocked him to his knees.

Ellie's shadow loomed over Matthew where he cowered helplessly on the floor. For the briefest of moments she saw the Tim of old in his eyes, the man who had brought out a side to her that had lain dormant for so long. But allowing her warm, loving side to shine through her thick skin had made her vulnerable. All that she had forfeited for her discovery would not be for nothing, she vowed. She would not allow the feeble creature before her to take anything away.

Matthew's eyes rolled as he struggled to focus, then he glared at her in disbelief, clutching the side of his head. He watched, helpless and disorientated, as she coolly and calmly picked up the decanter and swung it for a second time with great force, hitting him squarely in the same part of his head.

She could almost feel his skull split as the decanter shattered, spraying fragments of bone, glass and whisky across the floor.

Ellie stood motionless as she watched Matthew's body convulse and his blood seep into the rug. His eyes opened wide, and her mis–Match was suddenly erased.

91

MANDY

Mandy stood rigidly at the foot of the drive of the home where she'd lived with Pat for five months.

"The door's unlocked, you can go in," urged Lorraine, her police liaison officer. "Just take your time."

Mandy hesitated and glanced over her shoulder to check her sister Paula was still in the police car they'd both arrived in. Paula had offered to go inside with her for support, but Mandy was too embarrassed to show her the home of the family she had chosen above her own.

Lorraine went inside first, and Mandy followed apprehensively. Together they paused in the hallway, and Mandy's eyes shot to the bottom of the staircase where she'd fallen some five weeks earlier.

She looked at the open doors leading to the rooms off the hallway and took a deep breath, covering her stomach with her arms. Where a baby bump had once protruded, there was now just loose skin, and Mandy felt her cesarean stitches tug sharply each time she made a sudden movement. Yet she cherished the horizontal scar above her bikini line—it was the only physical proof she had that she and her baby boy had ever been together. He'd been removed from her unconscious body and then stolen by her twisted in-laws before she'd had the opportunity to even catch sight of him. Every morning after showering, she wiped the steam from the full-length bathroom mirror and traced the red, raised scar tissue with her finger, imagining what her son might look like.

It had been a very difficult few weeks. She regularly pumped her breasts to keep them lactating in preparation for the time she would be reunited with her boy. She cursed the breast pump for not being her child clamping upon her nipple. She hated that they were losing this precious bonding time, and she prayed that the police would find a lead to his whereabouts.

Pat's house hadn't been aired in the best part of a month and it was beginning to smell stale. Mandy gave the living room, kitchen and dining room a cursory glance before following Lorraine up the staircase. She liked Lorraine; her softly spoken approach was at odds with her masculine appearance, and under different circumstances she'd have tried to match-make her with Kirstin.

Once Mandy had alerted the hospital staff to her missing child, they had contacted the police. A warrant had been issued to search Pat's home, where they'd found that everything but her clothes and gifts she'd purchased for the baby had been left. Chloe's house was in a similar state, and their bank accounts had been emptied. Along with the baby, they had vanished into thin air.

Mandy's worried family insisted she return to stay with them. The tragedy had rebuilt their bridges without need of a word of apology from either side, and they supported her as she anxiously awaited police updates. Together they prayed that Pat or Chloe might develop a conscience and return the baby, but in the month following their disappearance there had been no contact whatsoever. There had been some potential sightings following her appeal in the national newspapers and a televised press conference, but they'd turned out to be false leads.

Mandy had run the full gamut of emotions: from anger toward the hospital for allowing her son to be placed into the hands of those who had no business touching her child, to frustration at the police for failing to develop any fresh leads, to herself for her post-op body not allowing her to become more physically proactive in the search. Her still-tender wound and limited mobility gave her too much time to dwell on the guilt she felt for failing to do the one thing a parent must do—protect their child. No matter how many times her family, Lorraine or doctors tried to convince her she was blameless, Mandy refused to believe them. It was her fault because she'd tried to chase the impossible—the love of a man who could never love her in return—and she'd lost her baby because of it.

"I want to go back to her house and look around," Mandy had informed Lorraine after much internal deliberation. She wasn't sure why, but it was something she felt compelled to do. Lorraine wasn't convinced of the benefits of this to Mandy's healing, but she had persisted, threatening to go alone if necessary.

Mandy stood in the doorway of Pat's bedroom. It wasn't very different to how it'd always been, with the exception of the empty drawers and clothes rails inside her open wardrobe. She made her way into Richard's room where she'd spent much of her time. Like Pat's, it had been ransacked by the police who had been hunting for clues. For a moment, it saddened her that her sanctuary had been soiled as part of a criminal investigation.

Stay strong, Mandy told herself, and balled her fists.

Her eyes made their way across the collage of photographs spread across Richard's wall. Each snapshot of his life had once made her wish they'd found each other earlier. But from what his ex-girlfriend had revealed shortly before Mandy's accident, Richard wasn't the man of her dreams. He wasn't the monogamous type, and he had little desire to settle down and have a family of his own. He was a human being, and he was flawed, not a fantasy, and she could see that now.

As her eyes skimmed across the photographs, Mandy went back to one in particular. Richard and Chloe were still children, probably aged around ten, and were on oversized bikes outside a cottage surrounded by rolling green hills and woodland.

Suddenly Mandy felt like someone had woken her with a slap across the face.

"I know where my baby is!" she said out loud, and stared Lorraine in the eye. "I know where to find him."

92

CHRISTOPHER

Christopher suddenly awoke to the sensation of cold liquid being poured over his head.

He opened his eyes, but everything had a misty haze and he couldn't make out where he was. The left side of his body ached where the Taser gun's darts had made contact, and his whole body stung like he'd fallen onto a bed of nettles. He wasn't sure if it was the force of his head colliding with the floor that had rendered him unconscious or the fifty-thousand volts that'd traveled through his body.

As he came to, he was engulfed by a wave of nausea and retched several times before spewing bile down the front of his jumper. He turned his head and spat a foul-tasting mouthful to his side. Blurry images flashed from a television attached to the wall with what sounded like newsreaders recapping the day's headlines. His eyes finally focused and rested on the familiar figure standing before him, and he recalled what had happened moments before he blacked out. Amy had put a stop to the death of Number Thirty and a halt to his project.

Amy had been here. Which meant that she knew everything.

He looked down toward his wrists and saw two tightly bound ropes securing them to the chair's arms. He was still in Number Thirty's kitchen. A pair of handcuffs tightly pinched his ankles.

It was then that he noticed that Amy was still there. He stared at her trainers wrapped in blue plastic bags, moments away from him, then lifted his gaze to her dark jeans and black sweatshirt, then to her face, the balaclava pulled back to her hairline. It looked like a sweatband, and in any other situation he would have thought she was preparing to go out for a run. He couldn't read her expression, but it wasn't difficult to assume it was not favorable. His pulse quickened.

"Where's Number Thirty?" he asked.

"Is that what you do? Give them numbers? They have names, you know. They are *people*."

"They *were* people," Christopher corrected and gave a long, sigh-strewn pause. "Where is she?"

A look he recognized as shame briefly passed across Amy's face. "She's in the bedroom. When she answered the door, I pushed my way in, overpowered her and tied her up. Then I locked her in her room and turned her stereo up so she wouldn't hear us."

The corners of Christopher's mouth rose slightly before suppressing what would've under ordinary circumstances formulated a smile.

"Don't look at me like that. I'm not proud of scaring that poor girl to death. This is something that will stay with her for the rest of her life, and, thanks to you, I'm to blame for it."

"But you did it all the same. We could've made a good team."

"It's better to put her through this than do nothing and have you kill her."

Christopher shrugged.

"If I thought you were capable of feeling anything I'd say that it's disappointment you are trying to hide."

"I can *feel*. I feel things for you."

Amy let out a forced laugh. "No, you don't! You played the part—I'll give you credit for that, and you played it well—but I was always just a pawn in your sick little game."

"Is that what you really think?"

"What am I supposed to think? My boyfriend is a fucking serial killer! How could you, Chris? How could you?"

"You are so much more than a pawn."

"If that were true, then why didn't you make an excuse to leave as soon I told you I was a police officer? Why didn't you just let me go about my life if you cared that much? I was just an extra challenge for you, to see if you could get away with doing this while dating someone in the police." She was fighting to hold back tears.

"That might have been the case at first, but then things changed."

"How was this ever going to end? Or wasn't it? Were you just going to keep killing?"

"The girl in the other room, she was the last. Or at least she was supposed to be."

Amy laughed. "How coincidental."

"No really, thirty, that was my target."

She paused. "Why?"

"To begin with it was a challenge I set myself. But, as much as I enjoyed it at first, it ended up becoming laborious."

Amy shook her head and raised her eyes to the ceiling, as if she were silently asking God if she'd heard him correctly. "*Killing* women...*murdering* innocent people...that was *laborious* to you? Working in a factory production line, washing cars for a living, sweeping the streets, those are laborious jobs, not taking twenty-nine people's lives, Chris!"

"When did you put everything together?" he asked, genuinely curious.

"Six days ago. You were out, killing your twenty-eighth victim, if my time line is correct. I was at yours, flicking through the psychology and serial killer books on your shelves, trying to get my head around what makes a monster tick. And among them I found your photo album."

Christopher nodded slowly, satisfied that at last he could share his work with her.

"It didn't make sense, at first," Amy continued. "Why would *my* Christopher have those pictures, and how did he get them? I went back to the station briefing room and compared them to the photos that'd been left on the bodies, and they were almost identical—*almost* identical. Because each photo had been taken from an ever so slightly different angle, meaning the ones in your album weren't reproductions or copies. Whoever took those pictures must've been at each of the crime scenes. But it was the waitress's nose ring you kept that removed the last shred of doubt."

Christopher made no attempt to defend himself. She began pacing around the open-plan kitchen and diner, shaking her head.

"Can you even begin to imagine what went through my head when I knew what you were?" Her question was rhetorical, he could tell. Christopher was quite pleased that he could finally recognize the subtleties. "I searched your house from top to bottom, and I found dozens of smartphones in a bag in your broken freezer. And I turned enough of them on to see the only app installed on them was that dating one, UFlirt, and that every victim had sent you their number. Of course, your computers were password encrypted, so I didn't get anywhere with those." She added the last sentence almost as an afterthought.

"No, you wouldn't have," Christopher replied conceitedly.

"Look at yourself, Chris," Amy replied sharply. "You're in no position to be smug. And you're not as clever as you think. You left a piece of your DNA at a murder scene."

He shook his head. "That's not possible. I was always careful, I'm sure of that."

"Number Twenty-Seven."

"Dominika Bosko."

Amy arched her eyebrows. "So you *do* know their names?"

"Only hers."

"Why, because you killed her baby, too?"

Christopher glared at Amy, and for the first time during their confrontation, she recognized regret in his eye.

"There was one tiny piece of DNA the forensics team found on the child," she continued. "At some point when you went back to the scene of the crime, you stood over her and cried. They found teardrops on his head and chest. I got your DNA results from the swab you sent to Match Your DNA, and I paid a private lab for some fast-track work to compare the tears on the baby to your results. They were 99.97 percent identical. I have to know, what was it about them that upset you?"

"You did," he whispered, picturing the child's lifeless body.

"Me?"

"I imagined somebody doing that to you, and me standing over your body having lost you. For the first time in my life, I had no control over my emotions, and they got the better of me."

Christopher watched Amy's arms begin to unfold and her shoulders droop slightly. Then, just as quickly, she tensed up again.

"You almost got me there. But do you know why I can never believe a word you say? Because I've read passages in books that you highlighted and then quoted to me *verbatim* about how you feel, and passed them off as your own. You tell me what you think I want to hear."

"It's only because I'm not used to expressing myself. This is new to me, Amy. I didn't even know people like me could fall in love."

"People like you. You mean psychopaths, right?"

Christopher nodded.

"My boyfriend, the psychopath. The one thing your books have taught me is that psychopaths are master manipulators."

"That's true, but not when it comes to you. How have I ever manipulated you?"

"You knew what you were and what you were doing, and you still let me fall in love with you."

"Be honest with yourself, I didn't do anything. We were Matched. We were predetermined."

"You chose to take the test and to meet me. If there was any humanity inside you at all, you would have stayed the hell away."

"I'm sorry, but I was curious to see who'd be Matched with me, and then when I met you, I felt something I'd never experienced before…something that was completely alien. I needed to get to know the person having that effect on me to try to understand why it was happening. I even read up on it because I didn't think it was possible to…but I'd fallen in love with you."

Amy shook her head. "Please stop lying to me," she said, but from the quiver in her voice, Christopher knew she was beginning to believe him.

"I know what I am, Amy…or at least I know what I *was*. I was a man who craved infamy for my crimes, and I felt a pleasure I can't describe from ending other people's lives. I was selfish, I was devious, I cared for nothing and no one, I was everything that you were not. But when I am with you, I'm…better. At least, you make me want to be better."

Amy wiped her eyes with her sleeve as she listened, then took a few hesitant steps forward and crouched down so their eyes were level.

"Do you love me, Chris?" she asked. "Do you, in your heart of hearts, really love me?"

"Yes," he replied firmly and without missing a beat. "Yes, I do love you."

For once, Christopher had let himself be vulnerable. It wasn't because he was securely fastened to the chair, or that he had been caught. He could tell that Amy saw this. She saw that he was a lost little boy, someone who had spent his life unable to fit into society, someone who was aware of the difference between right and wrong, but chose to do wrong anyway. He wanted to change for her, and she saw someone who needed her stabilizing influence. She saw their shared future.

Amy slipped her hand in her pocket and pulled out the keys to the handcuffs.

93

JADE

Jade took the keys to Kevin's four-by-four from the hook in the kitchen cabinet and climbed into the truck.

After the revelation that Kevin wasn't her DNA Match and that Mark was, she'd stormed back to the guesthouse and spent the next hour pacing the bedroom, trying to get a handle on her mixed emotions. She was furious with herself for having allowed things to have gone so far with Kevin when she knew that she didn't love him. But she was also furious with Mark for lying to her. It was because of him that she'd felt like such a rotten person for so long, being attracted to someone who was out of bounds. Without trust and honesty, was being Matched enough to keep two people together?

With the clothes she'd thrown into a duffel bag on the passenger seat beside her, she drove along the dirt track driveway toward the highway. The radio played the opening bars of a Michael Bublé song, and it reminded her of how she'd used to tease Kevin for having the musical taste of a housewife double his age. He didn't care, he said, music was music and, as long as it made you feel something, it didn't matter who was singing it. Jade turned up the volume to "You're Nobody Till Somebody Loves You."

She followed the road signs back in the direction of Echuca Moama on the Murray River, and an hour later checked herself into a budget hotel. She knew that eventually she'd have to return to the farm and face the Williamsons, but for the next few days she needed respite from them all, and especially from Mark.

Jade tried to stop herself from thinking about him by taking in the local sights, going on a trip along the water on a historic paddle steamer, joining thousands of strangers listening to blues and roots music at the annual Winter Blues festival and exploring nearby towns, red gum forests and wetlands. But nothing worked. Her anger toward Mark remained ever potent, despite the fact that she knew his actions had come from a selfless place.

After a fourth fitful night of sleep, she awoke early to the sound of birdcalls. She climbed into Kevin's truck and from memory drove to where he'd taken her to watch her first Australian sunrise the day after she arrived on the farm. She hoped the calmness of the arrival of a new day might help slow her brain from racing at a hundred miles an hour.

She sat on the vehicle's front bumper, watching the sun begin its ascent into the sky, when a noise on the gravel disturbed her. She turned her head. It was Susan.

"I hoped you might be here," she began. "Do you mind if I join you?" Her tone was much softer and less confrontational than it had been a few days earlier. "I've been back here every morning since you ran out, just in case you came. I used to bring Mark and Kevin up here when they were boys. Kev liked to see as far into the distance as he could. He wanted to travel the world one day."

"I remember him saying," Jade murmured. "He wanted us to do it together."

She closed her eyes and tried to recall Kevin's voice. It had only been a few weeks since his passing, and already she was beginning to forget how it sounded. Despite everything she felt for Mark, she still missed her daily conversations with his brother. Susan stretched her arm out and wrapped it around Jade's shoulders. "So you married my son even though you didn't love him."

Jade nodded.

"Why?"

"Because I knew how happy it would make him. I was very fond of him, and I wanted his last days to be happy."

"You wanted the same thing for him as Mark did. And Kevin's last days *were* happy, and for that I'll always be grateful. The both of you placed his needs above your own, I see that now. Please don't hate Mark for it."

"I don't hate him, Susan, but that's not to say I haven't spent the last few days pissed off beyond belief. I'm usually pretty sure of myself—normally it's one strike and you're out. But Mark has my head all over the place, and I don't know what to think or how to feel. The only thing I know is that, after everything that has happened since I got here, I need some space and to get away from your family. I don't mean that to sound as nasty as it does."

"No, it doesn't sound nasty at all, love. And I'm not going to pretend I know what it's like for you. But please take some advice from an old 'un. Don't let the chance to be happy pass you by. I had to let go of my anger at the disease that was killing my son, as the only person that hate was hurting was me. Now you've got to let your anger toward Mark go. I'm sure that's what Kevin would have wanted. If you've got the opportunity to love someone as much as they love you, then grab it with both hands and hold on to it for dear life."

94

NICK

Nick didn't understand why Sally was so averse to accepting pain relief to make her labor a little more bearable.

For the best part of a month she'd complained of crippling headaches that had made her feel sick, but she'd been unable to take anything stronger than acetaminophen. Now she was being offered a cocktail of drugs, but she refused to accept any. Nick knew, in her position, he'd have taken enough to knock out a hippo, especially after the twentieth hour passed.

Watching Sally's body contort in pain, he wondered if she was trying to prove a point. Nick had been hurt mentally by sacrificing his Match for her and the baby. Was she voluntarily going through such physical discomfort to prove she could hurt, too? He shook his head and decided he was being foolish—nobody would put themselves through that just to make a point.

"That's it, Sally," said the midwife confidently. "Keep pushing when I tell you, and don't worry, you're doing great."

"I can't," yelled Sally, and looked at Nick with such desperation in her eyes he felt bad for being responsible for so much of her pain. He regained his composure, held her hand firmly and rubbed her shoulder.

Nick realized that, no matter what had happened in the past or what had been taken away from him, at that moment the only two people in the world that mattered were in that room with him. He made a silent vow to make the best of their relationship for the sake of Sally and the tiny person about to make its way into the world to join their unconventional unit.

"You can do this, babe," he said softly. "I'm here, I'm not going anywhere again."

"But what if—"

"There's no what-if," Nick interrupted. "I'm in this with you for the long haul. I promise."

During a break in her contractions, the midwife suggested Nick take a break. It had been twenty hours—he needed something to eat. Sally was the one doing all the work, yet supporting her had left him shattered, and he desperately craved something sweet. A £2 coin bought him a Snickers bar and a Coke in the hope that the sugar rush might perk him up. Then, with nobody else in the corridor to catch him, he took a few sneaky drags from the e-cigarette he had tucked inside his pocket while they had been waiting for the taxi to take them to the hospital.

For a moment, Nick allowed thoughts of Alex to creep into his head, and he wondered how he might be coping back home in New Zealand. They had both agreed to block each other on Facebook so neither could see the other getting on with their life. But that didn't stop him wondering if Alex had started dating again and, if so, who the lucky person was—and whether they were male or female. He couldn't imagine what it might be like to be with someone new after losing the person you were designed to be with. How could any potential relationship stand a hope in hell when you know you've loved somebody else with every inch of your being?

He threw his empty can and sweet wrapper into a bin, but as he made his way back to the ward he heard a loud alarm and beeping sounds coming from the direction of Sally's room. He quickened his pace until he spotted her midwife and two nurses pushing Sally and her bed out of her room, into the corridor and toward a sign which read Theater.

"Sal?" Nick yelled, but she didn't respond. She lay motionless with her eyes closed. "What's happening?"

"There have been some complications, Nick," the midwife explained calmly, as a porter took her place. "Sally has fallen unconscious and is not responding to our attempts to revive her."

The color drained from Nick's face, and his legs threatened to buckle. "And the baby?"

"Our first priority is Sally, but an obstetrician is on her way now to perform an emergency cesarean while we work on Sally. There's a team in theater ready."

"Can I go with her?"

"I'm afraid you can't. Let me take you to the waiting room, and as soon as I get any news I'll come and find you."

"She's been having headaches for weeks…"

"We're doing all we can for her. Now let's get you into the waiting room."

As the glass door closed behind him, Nick stood helpless and stared at the midwife as she hurried down the corridor and out of sight.

He was too numb to take in his surroundings, but stood in the empty room bolt upright and motionless, his brain whirring ten to the dozen as he tried to make make sense of what was happening. He'd already lost Alex; losing both Sally and their child was unthinkable. Without them, he would have nothing. He would *be* nothing.

The midwife returned fifteen minutes later, accompanied by the obstetrician. He knew by the look on their faces what they were about to say, long before the words fell from their mouths.

95

ELLIE

Ellie stood over Matthew's lifeless body, frozen in a moment that would change everything.

Her hand began to tremble as she covered her mouth with it, suddenly struck by the enormity of her actions and petrified she might let out an involuntary scream. She glanced around the office, unsure of which way to turn as the shaking spread to her legs. She was scared that if she dared sit down to steady herself, she might never get back up again. She wanted to escape her office, jump into her car and drive home to the safety of Derbyshire and her family, leaving Matthew hundreds of miles away. That would have been possible had she not just deliberately killed him.

Ellie took several deep breaths and tried to focus her mind on her now limited options. Andrei would help her, she reckoned. She felt for the panic alarm and pressed down hard. Less than a minute later, she heard his shoes running down the marble floored corridor before he burst through the door with a baton in his hand. He stared at her and then at Matthew's body on the floor, his head now framed by a halo of blood.

Andrei's face remained expressionless.

"I need your help," she said, her tone hushed but panicked.

He checked around the room for any potential threats and pulled out his mobile phone.

"You won't get a signal," she continued. "He saw to that."

"Change into clean clothes, and then we are leaving," Andrei said gruffly, gesturing to the spots of blood splattered across her clothes. "I know people who can make it look like this never happened."

Ellie glanced at him with nervous gratitude.

"Change now," he repeated, his voice more authoritative.

She hurried to her adjacent bathroom and dipped into her wardrobe where she kept a selection of spare clothes, pulling out a virtually identical blouse and skirt. She rinsed her face under the tap and the remaining blood from her hands. For a moment, stared at her reflection in the mirror, unable to fully comprehend her living nightmare. "He did this to himself, he gave you no choice," she said out loud. "You're a good person who has done amazing things for the world. He didn't just want to take it away from you, he wanted to take it away from everyone. He did this to himself, not you."

A thud from the office brought her back to reality, and she returned to find Andrei rolling up Matthew's body in the rug he'd died upon.

"We leave this room for my people to clean up," he said, and dragged Matthew into the bathroom out of sight. "Do not allow anyone else in."

Ellie obeyed, and Andrei escorted her into the corridor just as Ula ran toward her.

"You weren't answering your phone!" she said, concerned.

"I have a meeting I need to—"

But Ula cut her off. "Your office, it's being streamed online."

"What?"

"Look," she yelled, then pulled Ellie by her arm into her room. "You and Tim are all over the internet. Everyone can watch and hear you arguing. But I don't understand. How can you be here, and yet on my computer you're still in there?"

Ellie looked at the video footage of her and Matthew. By her estimation it was time delayed by approximately fifteen minutes—to the beginning of their confrontation—as Matthew was pouring his second whisky. She watched as he carried the decanter back to the sofas, and inwardly shuddered at the thought of what the object would be later used for.

"Who can see this?" she asked, alarmed.

Ula checked. "I think it's automatically playing on every employee's computer or tablet through the internal messaging system."

"Get hold of IT and tell them to shut it down."

Ula left the room to use her own phone while Ellie looked at Andrei for reassurance, but for the first time since he'd begun working for her, she witnessed concern in his steely gray eyes.

"They're saying the IP address is from the desktop computer in your office," Ula said, "and it's also being sent as a live feed to dozens of other online sources. YouTube, Vimeo, Facebook, Twitter... Anyone in the world can watch right now, and it's all coming from your computer's webcam."

Andrei ran back into the office with a terrified Ellie in pursuit. She shut the door behind her as Andrei yanked all the leads from the iMac, then picked up the machine, lifted it over his head and hurled it to the floor. He slammed his foot into it a half-dozen times.

As she and Andrei left her office for a second time, she saw that a small group of secretaries had now huddled around Ula's screen. They took an awkward step backwards when Ellie reappeared.

"It's still showing," Ula said. "I'm sorry, but IT says it's not broadcasting from the servers in our building so there's nothing they can do to cut the feed."

Ellie froze. In approximately five minutes, the world would watch as Matthew explained how he'd compromised her database and how two million people who'd trusted her were the victims of mis-Matches. Then they'd see one of the world's most prominent businesswomen beat her unarmed fiancé to death. And she was powerless to stop it.

All eyes, with the exception of Ellie's, were on Ula's computer screen. Ellie took a succession of deep calming breaths and leaned against the wall of her office, slowly sliding her back downwards against the glass until she reached the floor.

At Andrei's order, Ula ushered everyone else out, leaving just the three of them. Ula and Andrei were finding it hard to draw themselves away from the screen, and Ellie didn't try to stop them. She was forced to listen again to the dull thwack of the decanter as it hit Matthew's head, the sound of him collapsing to his knees, followed by that of her hitting him a second, fatal time.

Ula gasped and glared at her in disbelief.

"Come," said Andrei in desperation and held his hand out toward Ellie. "Let me take you out of this building."

But Ellie shook her head politely, then looked at them in turn and spoke calmly. "Thank you both for everything you've done for me. I'll make sure you're well recompensed for it." She patted out the creases from her skirt and tucked her hair behind her ears. "Ula, after what you've just seen, if you are able to assemble my legal team and have them meet me in the boardroom, I'd be grateful. I assume the police will be here very soon. Then clear my schedule for the foreseeable future."

Ellie paused and looked up at the Match Your DNA logo etched into the smoked glass of her office wall. She pictured the inert figure of Matthew on the other side, wrapped in a rug on the bathroom floor. She'd been happier with him than she had ever thought imaginable, but only now she understood it wasn't because their DNA had dictated it, but because she'd opened herself up to the concept of love.

She picked herself up from the floor and began to walk in the direction of her office, closing the door behind her. She poured herself a gin and tonic and took a seat behind her desk. From down the corridor, she heard the first of many pairs of feet making their way out of the lift and toward the office.

She took her iPad and swiped the screen to take one last look at the extensive list of tasks she'd always begrudged yet needed to complete before her working day was over. But it was blank— Ula had already erased it.

96

MANDY

"Stay in the car until I know what's happening. Promise me you won't move from here."

It wasn't a question; it was an order. Lorraine, Mandy's police liaison officer, was firm in her demand and didn't wait for a reply before jumping from the driver's seat and hurrying toward the front door of the cottage.

Two other police cars and a van were already on the scene, parked on the cobbled road next to two ambulances. Mandy hunched forward in the rear of the car, barely breathing, and craned her neck to see past the headrests to gain a clearer view of what was happening in the house. It was a frenzy of activity, with uniformed police officers coming and going, speaking into walkie-talkies and mobile phones.

Eventually, a frustrated Mandy couldn't wait any longer, so she clasped her fingers around the doorframe and pulled herself out.

The journey from Essex to the Lake District had taken five hours, and, on occasion, the vehicle's motion combined with the stress had made her so uncomfortable that Lorraine had been forced to pull onto the hard shoulder so Mandy could vomit onto the grass verge. Her head was spinning with adrenaline, and nothing was going to prevent her from being reunited with her child if he was indeed being kept there.

The picture of the family's Lake District cottage had jolted her memory, and she'd remembered Pat mentioning how much Richard had loved it there. Detectives had quickly discovered the title deeds to the home buried away in Pat's files, and an immediate operation had been launched, beginning with officers inside an unmarked police car scoping out the property. When they confirmed a woman matching Chloe's description had entered the home, the rescue plan had begun in earnest.

"Where is he?" shouted a panic-stricken Mandy as she made her way toward the front door from which Lorraine was exiting.

"Mandy, I need you to stay calm," she said, and took hold of her arms. "Chloe has already been arrested and was taken away earlier. Your son is with Pat. However, she's barricaded herself in the bathroom."

"What's she doing in there?"

"He's safe as far as we can ascertain, but Pat wants to talk to you before she unlocks the door."

"I don't have anything to say to that woman, I just want my baby back."

"It goes without saying that we want a positive outcome from this, so let's give it a try. I'll be by your side, so please don't worry."

Mandy wiped her eyes with the back of her hand and was led inside the small, thatched cottage, up a narrow carpeted stairway and toward a paneled wooden door. Dusty framed photographs of Richard and his family hung from the walls, partially hidden by the half-dozen police officers crowding the corridor. One held a black metal battering ram, ready to break down the door if necessary.

"Relax, take deep breaths and talk to Pat in the same way you used to before all this happened," Lorraine began. "Nice and calm, okay? Don't get involved in an argument or lose your temper with her. Do you understand me?"

Mandy nodded, unsure how she was going keep a lid on her emotions when she'd spent so much of the last month waiting for this moment to tell her baby's paternal grandmother what she thought of her.

"Pat, I have someone here who wants to talk to you," Lorraine said, and nodded at Mandy.

Mandy paused and took a few breaths before she spoke. "Hello, Pat, it's Mandy."

She could hear movement, a shuffling sound, in the bathroom, and for the very first time, she also heard her son make a noise, like a delicate whimper. She closed her eyes and wanted to cry—suddenly her son was real, and all that separated them was a few feet of wood and plaster. It was all she could do to stop herself from tearing down the door with her bare hands.

"Is my baby safe, Pat? Can you just tell me that he's safe?"

"He's fine," Pat's voice inside replied. She sounded exhausted, Mandy thought.

"Pat, I need to see my son."

"I know you do. I just need a little bit longer with him."

"You've had long enough, Pat. I haven't seen him at all yet."

"He looks like his daddy, don't you, little man? You have the same eyes and the same coloring."

"I can't wait to meet him."

Mandy looked toward Lorraine for confirmation that she was saying the right things, and Lorraine nodded encouragingly.

"Why did you take him, Pat? Why did you run away with him? We've all been so worried."

"I'm sorry, but we had no choice. You weren't going to let us see him."

She was right, Mandy thought. Once she'd learned how Pat

and Chloe had lied to her about Richard's death, she wanted to get herself and her baby as far away from them as possible.

"Of course I would," she lied. "You're his grandma. Why would I keep him from you?"

"I don't think I believe you, darling, but we had to see if it worked..." Pat's voice trailed away.

"What worked?"

Both the bathroom and the hallway fell silent. "Pat, what do you mean? To see if what worked?"

"We didn't want to replace Richard like you think we did..."

"Then why did you take my baby? I don't understand."

"Chloe read somewhere that the children of Matched couples can be powerful enough to bring a parent out of a coma... He was our last hope."

Mandy looked at Lorraine to see if what Pat was saying was true. Lorraine shrugged.

"But Richard's not in a coma. He's in a permanent vegetative state. They're two very different things."

"I know, but don't you see, we had to try. We took Richard's son to the nursing home, and we sat with them both for hours, but nothing happened. He didn't move. My boy just didn't move..."

Mandy thought she heard gentle sobs coming from behind the door.

"So why didn't you bring him back to me, then?"

"I don't know," she whispered. "I don't know. We need to rest now, I'm sorry."

Mandy felt herself growing more and more anxious. "Can I have him back now please, Pat?"

There was no response.

She repeated herself. "Pat!" she said again, raising her voice.

"I just need to sleep," Pat replied quietly, her voice barely audible. "My grandson and I, we need to sleep. When Chloe finds out the truth, please tell her I'm sorry."

"What's she talking about?" Mandy asked Lorraine, who turned to look at another detective. "Lorraine!" yelled Mandy. "What's going on?"

Mandy felt someone pull her backwards by the shoulders, and the police officer with the battering ram slammed it against the door handle, breaking the lock. As three officers charged into the bathroom, Mandy rushed in after them to locate her son.

Slumped on the floor against the side of the bath were the motionless bodies of grandmother and grandson, both with closed eyes and skin as white as snow.

97

CHRISTOPHER

Amy knelt before Christopher as he sat restrained in a chair inside the home of what should've been his final kill. In her tightly clenched palm Amy held the key that could unlock the handcuffs keeping his ankles bound tightly together.

For a moment, the connection they shared was so powerful, it was like Christopher could read Amy's mind: when Christopher admitted she was responsible for making him a better person, she believed the sincerity of his words, and he didn't doubt that she still loved him despite the evil inside.

"The only small mercy I can get from this awful, awful nightmare is that it's not me who triggered this side of you," she said, slipping the key in the lock, "because when I pieced together the dates of each murder, they started about three weeks before we met."

Christopher nodded. "This…*thing*…in my head, that makes me…well, it has nothing to do with you. When we first started dating, I did get a buzz from doing it behind your back, not just my girlfriend's back, but a police officer's back. But the more I got to know you, the deeper I fell and the less of a thrill it became. Believe me, I could feel myself becoming someone else the longer we were together."

Amy stopped turning the key and paused. "Then why did you keep killing if you didn't get a thrill from it anymore?"

"Sorry?"

"If I made you a better person, why did you need to keep killing?"

"Because my goal was always to reach thirty people."

"So it wasn't that you felt a compulsion to do it anymore, you just made a choice to do it? It was a conscious decision and nothing to do with what you are?"

"I guess so."

"And then, what? You were just going to stop?"

"Yes."

"What did you hope to get out of it? Recognition? Would you have turned yourself in to the police? Or to me?"

"No. It was enough knowing that nobody would ever have any idea who I was, why I started and why I stopped just as suddenly."

"And what if you didn't reach thirty? What if you'd put our relationship first and quit? Then what would've happened?"

"I don't know. I did consider it, but I feared I might grow to resent you for coming between me and what I had planned and that I might—"

"—kill me, too?"

Christopher nodded, and something in Amy's eyes shifted. In a moment of clarity, she removed the key from the still locked handcuffs and rose to her feet. "There are so many things I want to ask you, but I don't know where to begin, and I'm afraid of what I'll hear."

"Try me."

"Were you born this way?"

"Yes."

"Have you always been a killer?"

"No."

"Why do you hate women?"

"I don't. They're just easier to overpower than men."

"Why did you start killing?"

"To see if I could get away with it."

"Why? You're an intelligent man—that's one of the things I love about you. Why not put your efforts into something that helps people?"

"That's not how my brain works. I don't care about people. I only care about you."

"Why did you take me for dinner at the restaurant where the young waitress with the pierced nose worked?"

"I don't know."

"You do know, Chris. It was to get some perverse kick from having her serve us, knowing that later you were going to murder her. It was like a cat leaving a mouse at its owner's feet. You were showing off."

Christopher averted his gaze from Amy's.

"What does the symbol you leave spray-painted on the pavements outside your victims' houses mean?"

"It's a Saint Christopher, the patron saint of travelers. He's carrying Christ, as a boy, on his back, over a river."

"And that's what you think you are? Saint Christopher, leading these girls from life on one side into death on the other?"

"Kind of, but they're never really going to remain dead. They are always going to be associated with this case, and, when you're remembered, you're never truly dead."

"Don't kid yourself, Chris, they are truly dead."

"Can I ask you a question now? Why didn't you just turn me over to your colleagues when you discovered who I was? That would've been the obvious thing to do, not...this."

Amy turned her head from side to side and was about to run her fingers through her hair. "Don't do that," Christopher ordered. "If even one strand falls out, you'll be leaving your DNA." His concern surprised her.

"We are supposed to be living and working in an age of equality, and I have just as many opportunities to climb the promotional ladder as any of my male colleagues. But if I told them what I know about you, then to my friends, my family, to strangers in the street, in books that'll be written about you and television dramas that'll feature the two of us, I'll always be the policewoman whose boyfriend was one of the country's worst serial killers; the detective whose Match murdered twenty-nine women right under her very nose. As well as ending the lives of those girls and ruining their families, you will have destroyed me, my career and any chance I might find of happiness with another man, because the world will know I'm damaged goods."

Christopher felt something akin to jealousy by her mention of other men. For the first time, he began to imagine how he might feel if Amy was with someone else, and he didn't like it.

"So let me go, and you'll still have me, albeit a flawed me," he reasoned. "Untie me and let's make this work. Now you know everything there is to know about me, we have nothing to lose. You think I've ruined what we had, but it doesn't have to be that way. I won't ruin what we could have from here on in."

"You can't ask me to do that, Chris," Amy replied, her voice weakening. Her face began to screw up as she fought to hold back the tears, desperately wanting to believe him. She was evidently torn by the love she had for her Match and knowing the right thing to do. She began to pace around the room again, cautiously sidestepping him.

"And what happens when your true nature rears its ugly head again? What happens when you need to find that thrill you get from killing again, that project, that buzz, that I can't give you? You didn't love me enough to stop killing when you had the chance. And as much as I want to believe that this won't happen again, it won't be love or our shared DNA that keeps us together, it will be my fear that you will strike again and hurt another person."

"You don't understand," Christopher replied sharply. He was becoming increasingly frustrated that he was losing his battle to convince Amy. As long as they were together, he'd never need to hurt another soul. "I love you, Amy."

The voice of a male news presenter on the television interrupted Amy before she could react to Christopher's words. "Breaking news in the story we have been following this evening," he began. "After the streamed footage we saw earlier, allegedly showing Match Your DNA Chief Executive Ellie Stanford involved in a fatal altercation with a man believed to be her fiancé, an official company statement has confirmed it has launched an immediate investigation into revelations that Matches worldwide could have been tampered with."

Amy and Christopher glared at the screen and listened carefully as the news anchor continued. "Up to two million Matches are thought to be affected in one of the highest profile data breaches of the last decade, throwing into question the relationships of all couples that have met in the last eighteen months."

Christopher turned to Amy, his brow knitted as he tried to process the news. Although he wasn't good at reading people, he knew what the expression on Amy's face meant.

"Amy," he pleaded, his voice trembling as she stepped out of his sight line. "This doesn't change anything, we know that we are meant to be…"

But before he could continue, he felt the cheese wire he had used on twenty-nine separate occasions wrap around his neck and tighten. He rocked his body back and forth and then sideways in an attempt to free himself, but Amy refused to let go of her grip. He knew she was strong, but she must have been using every muscle in her arms and torso to the point of bursting as she held firm trying to restrain him.

As the wire began to penetrate his skin, he suddenly stopped fighting, and allowed a feeling of calm to take over his body and mind. He snapped his head backwards and stared Amy in the eyes, watching as the tears fell from her chin onto him and merged into his own until, eventually, everything became black.

98

JADE

Jade spent much of her final day on the farm preparing for her trek around Australia's east coast.

By the time Jade returned from the store picking up food supplies, Susan had washed, dried and ironed all of her clothes and left them neatly pressed by her suitcase. Dan had taken the keys to Kevin's truck and made sure the tires were full of air, that a spare wheel was in the boot and that the oil, water, coolant and brake fluid were all topped up. He loaded the vehicle with seven two-liter bottles of water just in case of an emergency and gave Jade a spare phone charger in case she needed it. He made her promise to email them photos she'd take en route.

Before leaving, Jade took time out to visit Kevin's grave and sat before the temporary wooden cross that'd been erected while they waited for a headstone to be fitted. If she closed her eyes and became mindful of her surroundings, she could feel Kevin in the breeze, and when she took a deep breath she could smell him in the flowers. He was in the trees and a part of every sunrise she'd ever wake up early to see. He'd always remain inside her, no matter where her journey took her.

She scrolled back through her phone, reliving the hundreds of conversations they'd had over the six months she'd known him before she came here. DNA Match or no DNA Match, she missed him terribly. There was no one else in the world who'd known her better than Kevin had.

Jade made her way back to the farmhouse where Susan and Dan were placing Tupperware boxes crammed full with sandwiches and salads in the rear passenger footwells.

"Are you all set?" Susan asked.

"Pretty much."

"I've put a road map in the back with your route plotted out just in case technology lets you down," said Dan.

"Thank you," Jade said, and leaned in to hug him.

"No, thank you for everything," said Susan. "I know it's not been easy, especially the last few weeks, but I'm glad we're still friends. Now promise me one more thing, will you?"

"Of course, what is it?"

"Promise me you'll look after my boy."

"Mum, I'll be fine." Mark smiled and kissed her on the cheek, before throwing his rucksack across the backseat.

"I promise," Jade said. "Neither of us are leaving this family anytime soon."

99

NICK

Nick's eyes fixed on the doorway as he waited for the undertakers to carry the coffin into the crematorium.

A song he'd chosen by Amy Winehouse played through the speakers, as the wicker coffin was placed on a table in front of the packed room and the minister took her position. Nick's parents stood either side of him, each holding on to an arm as Sally came to a rest before them.

The coroner had released her body to the family eight days after her death, and, although the inquest had been opened and adjourned, Nick had been informed off the record that a previously undetected aneurysm in Sally's brain, the cause of many of her recent headaches, was likely to have been to blame.

Her sudden loss was a shock to Nick's system, but it wasn't the only one. Sally's baby boy had been taken from her womb by emergency cesarean section as she died. He was alive, and his skin was as dark brown as his hair.

★ ★ ★

"How many times did it happen?"

"A few."

"How many is a few?" Nick repeated, more firmly this time.

"I don't know, I didn't count. Quite often, though, I suppose."

"Was it just sex?"

"No."

"What else was it, then?"

"She was my Match."

"What?"

"We did the test, and Sally was my DNA Match. At least, that's what we thought."

Nick stopped pacing the living room and stared at Deepak. Baby Dylan slept close to his chest, his head resting on a towel draped across his shoulder.

It had been impossible for friends and family who'd visited Dylan to see anything but the difference between his dark skin compared to Sally's and Nick's chalky pallors. After the shock of Sally's death, and the subsequent realization that his son was not biologically his, something told Nick that the boy's real father was close to home.

Shortly after, Sumaira and Deepak, recent parents themselves, arrived at the flat to offer their condolences and meet Dylan for the first time. The panicked look on Deepak's face was enough to tell him what he had feared was true. They said little and didn't stay for long. Nick later noted their absences at Sally's funeral.

Now Deepak perched stiffly on Nick's sofa, his eyes bloodshot and underscored by dark bags.

"So all those months ago, the night it all kicked off between Sally and me, I was right when I said you and Sumaira weren't Matched?"

Deepak nodded. "We did the test after we got married, but

Sumaira was too ashamed to admit it to anyone. You know how some people can look down on couples that aren't Matched."

"But what makes you think Sally was your Match?"

"Sumaira and I took the test a couple of years ago and found out we weren't Matched. My email came, and it was her. Sally. It turned out she worked with Sumaira—coincidence, huh? I wanted to meet her, so eventually I made Sumaira arrange that night we all went out for Chinese…"

Nick nodded slowly. "That was the evening we had to leave early because Sal wasn't feeling well."

"Yeah." Deepak laughed, but tears were still in his eyes. "We all had a lot to drink that night, didn't we? I had a lot of beers, but I felt it—you know what I mean. It was as if all these light-bulbs had been turned on at the same time in my head."

Nick did know what he meant. He tried not to think of that first day he met Alex. "She'd felt the same thing as you, hadn't she?"

"Yes."

"So you started sleeping together."

"No, not for a long time after that. We became friends on Facebook first, then we started Instant Messaging, and met for the occasional lunchtime coffee or dinner. But that wasn't enough, so gradually it escalated."

Nick knew how hypocritical it was for him to feel animos-ity toward Sally for her lies, when his and Alex's relationship had followed almost the exact same pattern, but still he found Deepak's words hard to swallow.

"She was going to leave you," Deepak added hesitantly. "And I was planning on leaving Sumaira. We'd spent too long going behind your backs, and we wanted to be together out in the open. Then Sumaira got pregnant with the twins, and I came to my senses. I knew I couldn't just walk out on my wife. So I ended it with Sally. I don't think Sally was too happy, but I was certain that I wanted to stay with Sumaira and I told her that.

That's when she booked those tickets to Bruges, to try and re-connect with you."

Nick had known there was something off about Sally's sudden desire to go away together. "Go on," he said to Deepak.

"When Sally thought she might be pregnant, she started panicking because she didn't know which one of us was the father. She was scared if she told you the truth you wouldn't want to stick around and that you'd leave with Alex. She was so petrified of ending up a single mum."

"So she used me."

"I guess so."

There was something that had been bugging Nick about Deepak's story. "You chose Sumaira, and it sounds like Sally chose me. How the hell did you two deal with not being together? I know how powerful it feels when you meet your Match..." It had been six months now since he'd last seen Alex, and it was physically killing him to not be around him.

"I don't think we were actually Matched," Deepak admitted reluctantly. "I saw the news in the papers. I think we were one of those false Matches. It's only when I look back on it that I realize after those initial few months of excitement, the spark gradually vanished, and we became like every other couple cheating behind their partners' backs. And even thinking back to that night we first met and the 'explosions' people talk about. I think we were just drunk and got carried away with it. I'm really sorry, mate."

Deepak's apology was in earnest, but Nick couldn't bring himself to accept it.

"We both knew it, but because we thought we were Matched, we thought we had to stick together. In the end, all we had was an affair."

"There's something else that's been bothering me," Nick interrupted. "If Sally thought she was Matched with you, why did she want us to take the test?"

"I think she wanted to give you an 'out'…letting you go and be with your Match meant she wouldn't have to break your heart and look like the bad guy when she left you. Instead, she'd be the victim in all of this. Then when you found out you were Matched with a bloke, it was just as much a shock for us as it was for you, and we never thought you'd want to meet him. She was surprised she managed to talk you into it."

"Well, I'm glad her *plan* to get rid of me went well for her," Nick said sarcastically.

"Don't be like that, mate. After all, it all turned out okay in the end, right?"

If by okay, he meant a dead fiancée, a child that wasn't his and his soul mate lost forever on the other side of the world, then yeah, he was great, Nick thought bitterly.

The look on Deepak's face showed that he realized the stupidity of his words. He looked down at the floor.

Nick was stunned by the lengths Sally had gone in her desperation. "I had no idea how manipulative she was," he muttered. "And what does Sumaira have to say about her husband fathering a child by her best friend? Your wife tends to have an opinion on most things."

"She's gutted. She hasn't kicked me out, but she doesn't want me to see Sally's baby."

"What about you? What kind of future do you want with him?" The task of raising the baby had fallen to Nick, and he loved him to the end of the world, but he did sometimes wonder if it was better for Dylan to be with his real father.

Deepak paused and looked away, but Nick held firm, desperately trying to disguise how concerned he was about the answer to come. He knew that many men would've discarded a child that wasn't biologically a part of them, but Nick had sacrificed too much already to give up on Dylan. The delicate little boy who slept so peacefully in his arms had lost his mother even before his birth, and Nick would not allow him to lose the

man who had hoped to be his father. He felt an overwhelming amount of love for his son, as he had come to think of him.

"I don't think the kid and I have any future together," Deepak
eventually replied.

"You don't *think*, or you know for sure?"

"I know for sure."

"Do you feel anything for him at all?"

"No, and I'm not ashamed to admit it either. I'm sitting here
looking at him, and I don't feel a thing. All I see is trouble and
complications. I don't even have an urge to hold him or cuddle
him like I do with my girls. Even if Sumaira hadn't rejected
him, I still wouldn't want him."

Nick was disgusted by this admission. "You and Sally were
better suited than you think. You both only care about your-
selves."

"If you want him to stay with you, I'll sign whatever papers
you need me to sign to make it official." And, with that, Deepak
rose to his feet and walked toward the front door. "Nick," he
said, without turning around. "I really am sorry for everything,
and I hope you believe me."

Nick didn't reply. When the door closed, he held his son
tightly and planted a long, gentle kiss on his forehead.

100

MANDY

"We don't think it's the first time Pat's taken a child that wasn't hers," Lorraine said. "Neither Richard's nor Chloe's DNA results match each other's or hers. They're all unrelated."

"Could she have adopted them?"

"We've checked European and American databases, and so far we can't confirm that. Now we're looking into cold cases of children reported missing around the time Richard and Chloe were born."

"Jesus." Mandy shook her head in disbelief, and her heart sank at the thought of what could have happened had she not identified the Lake District holiday cottage in Richard's photographs. She clutched her son a little closer to her chest, wondering how Richard's and Chloe's biological parents must have felt not knowing what had happened to their babies.

"What's going to happen to Chloe?" she asked Lorraine, who sat opposite her. It was the first time they'd met face-to-face since Mandy's baby had been rescued a week earlier.

"She's been charged with kidnapping a child, but as she has no previous convictions she's been released on bail pending further inquiries. We predict her defense will plead insanity. But don't worry, she has restrictions preventing her from going anywhere near you or your home. Pat is being held in a psychiatric unit following her overdose, but it's going to take some time before we find out the full story."

Mandy found it difficult to erase the image of the moment she saw her child for the first time. He was wrapped in a towel, held loosely by Pat, who was unconscious and surrounded by empty blister packs of tablets. Everything else slipped into slow motion as Lorraine held Mandy back, her flailing arms reaching to grab her child. He was scooped up instead by a paramedic, whisked to the safety of the landing and placed upon the floor, his towel removed and his body checked for any signs of injury. It was only when it was confirmed there were none that Mandy was permitted to hold him for the very first time.

She'd fallen to her knees when he was placed into her arms. She smelled his head and ran her fingers across his soft chest, and held him close to her body so that he could feel her heartbeat against his skin.

She didn't notice the paramedics rush to Pat's aid or watch as they turned her on to her side and shoved piping down her throat, forcing her to vomit. Every voice that spoke to Mandy was muffled because all she could hear was the delicate sound of her baby breathing.

"There's something else I should tell you that I'm not supposed to," continued Lorraine, "something that was discovered in Pat's medical records. Apparently she has a history of psychotic episodes that doctors who treated her believe stemmed from multiple miscarriages and at least two stillbirths. At some point these episodes appear to have ceased, which match up to the time Richard and Chloe came into her life."

Mandy couldn't help but feel sympathy toward Pat for the

torment she must have suffered all those years ago. She knew how awful miscarriages could be and how they can ruin your life. It didn't exonerate her subsequent behavior, but it went a little way to explaining it.

Mandy embraced Lorraine before she left the private room in the care home, and she thanked her for all she had done. Then, she picked up her son and made her way to see Richard. She took a moment to compose herself, and then slowly opened the door to where Richard was lying in bed, where he'd been when she'd first greeted him six weeks earlier.

"Hi, Richard," she began gently, and took a chair by his side. "I've brought somebody to see you. This is your son, Thomas. I named him after my dad who died a few years ago, I hope you don't mind. I know you've met him before when your mum brought him, but I thought it'd be nice if it was just the three of us together."

Mandy gazed at father and son in turn, and admitted to herself that Pat was right—there was a palpable resemblance between the two. They shared the same coloring and even the positioning of dimples in their cheeks.

She thought back to the news headlines regarding the Match Your DNA falsified results scandal, which she'd heard earlier as she drove to the nursing home. If hers and Richard's had been faked, she'd decided it didn't really matter. The result was still this beautiful child buckled into the baby seat next to her. Once, she'd worried that she couldn't love a child who wasn't born out of a Match as much as one that was. But now she knew that not to be the case.

The strong smell of disinfectant in the room made Mandy's nose tingle, and she sneezed twice, which made Thomas giggle. She rose, placing him on the bed inside the safety railing next to Richard's forearm, which lay poker straight by his side, and fumbled around in her pocket for a tissue.

But when she turned back to pick up her son, something was

different. Richard's arm was no longer by his side. Instead, his palm was face up and his baby son's hand was pressed firmly inside it.

Mandy took a sharp intake of breath, not believing what she was witnessing. She watched as Richard's fingers slowly and purposefully entwined with his son's.

101

AMY

Amy couldn't bring herself to look at the blank, motionless face of the man she'd loved and whose life she'd ended.

Slumped in the chair she had tied him to, Christopher's head tilted backwards, and tears were still visible in the corners of his bloodshot eyes. She desperately wanted to bring the man she had adored back to life, but even if she could raise the dead, he'd bring with him the compulsions that she loathed.

For the sake of every other woman and herself, it had to be this way, and it had to be Amy who'd set his tortured soul free. "Hold it together," she told herself and clenched her fists into tight balls so as not to give in to sorrow. Her body still shivering, she clambered back to her feet and sifted through Christopher's backpack, using his equipment to clean up any trace of her presence in the home of the terrified woman she'd left tied up in the bedroom, oblivious to what had just happened under her roof.

Amy harked back to just a few days earlier when, after discovering the love of her life was a serial killer, she'd put on a brave face in front of him while silently beginning the grieving process for what she was about to lose. And just as Christopher had planned to kill his final victim, after much soul-searching and internal deliberation, Amy had decided to kill him.

She'd followed his car one night as he drove to a quiet residential street in Islington, and she'd watched from a safe distance as he patrolled the road on foot, making mental notes of the position of streetlights, access to the rear of a ground-floor flat and a probable escape route. She placed her hands over her mouth to stop her sobs from being overheard outside her vehicle.

If she'd followed his time line of kills correctly, his next strike would be within the next forty-eight hours. And when he canceled their planned evening together, blaming a rushed editorial deadline, she knew exactly where he was going and arrived there before him.

Once inside the property, she'd watched in horror as he revealed his true nature, a ruthless, efficient psychopath gearing up for the kill. She'd waited, buried in the shadows inside the girl's home, as he made his way into position and placed his bag by his feet, removed the cheese wire and then a billiard ball, which he'd thrown at the wall to gain Number Thirty's attention. Standing behind Christopher with the Taser gun in her hand, she could smell the adrenaline flowing through him, and it had made her nauseous.

Now with the crime scene cleaned up, Amy searched Christopher's pockets. All they contained were two phones—his regular mobile and a burner he'd used to check Number Thirty's location. Neither contained any clue of their owner's identity, but she took them anyway.

Amy stood in front of Christopher and took a deep breath. Then with all her strength she dragged him and his chair, inch by inch, through the kitchen, toward the rear door that Christopher had broken through, and out into a courtyard. She went back inside and took a duvet from the spare room and covered

Christopher in it from head to toe. She dialed 999 from the girl's landline, asked for the police and whispered "help me" when connected with an operator. Then she discarded the phone on the kitchen countertop and assumed the police would arrive within the hour and find the girl.

Outside, she removed two liter bottles of white spirit she'd brought with her in her own kill kit and poured them over Christopher's shrouded frame until the duvet absorbed the liquid. Then she stepped away, lit a match and threw it at him. She turned her back and walked away as Christopher caught light— she had no desire to witness the flesh melt from the bones of the man she had loved.

Given what you've just heard about those fake Matches, was he really the one or were you just in love with the idea of finding your Match? she asked herself suddenly. *Think about it, surely to God someone like you who wants to do good couldn't have been Matched with a man like that? Your results must have been hacked. You just got caught in the moment.*

Amy nodded and decided it was the only logical explanation, even though deep down she wasn't sure. The thought of choosing to love a man who turned out to be a serial killer was just bad judgment, and far better than having her DNA Matched to him. It was the lesser of two evils, and, in time, she might just about live with it.

As Amy left a painted stencil mark outside Number Thirty's home, she knew it could be months before Christopher's body was positively identified. She drove back to his home and let herself in with his keys and planned to clean the place from top to bottom over the following week to remove as much of her DNA as possible. Then she would leave his car with the keys in the ignition in a South London crime hot spot, certain it wouldn't remain there for long.

There were very few ways Christopher and Amy could be linked once the police discovered who he was. He'd always paid cash, so there'd be no credit card trail of where they might have eaten or visited together. His computers were heavily password controlled, but she would destroy them with a hammer anyway and dump them. And as they hadn't met each other's friends, families or colleagues, there'd be nothing tying them together as a couple—with the exception of their Match Your DNA link. However, no proof would ever be found that they'd taken it a step further. Even their few introductory text conversations were to Christopher's anonymous pay-as-you-go phones, which she would also smash to pieces.

In the months to come, Amy's colleagues would never discover why the last person to die in the baffling, unexplained serial killer case was male, why he'd been chosen and his body set ablaze. It would be an added twist to the story, and she was sure Christopher would approve of her self-preservation skills.

Christopher had reached his target, only *he'd* been the thirtieth kill. He'd also kept the anonymity he so desired, and the only thing his story lacked was the nickname he'd been affronted not to have been given. Suddenly, it came to Amy.

When I go to work tomorrow, I'm going to suggest they call you The Saint Christopher killer, she said to herself, imagining him watching her and picturing his smile. *Thirty kills and a name...you got your wish in the end, didn't you?*

102

NICK

The town was more grand and picturesque than Nick had given it credit for after having looked it up on Google Street View.

The climate was balmy and almost Mediterranean, and he wore his cargo shorts, a T-shirt and flip-flops as he'd wandered around the well-kept streets that surrounded the town's Spanish mission-style architecture. He now sat on a wooden bus stop bench, taking in the hot December morning. The rows of shops he faced were tidy and organized, and there appeared to be enough there to satisfy each of the town's seventy-three thousand inhabitants.

Every now and again, Dylan made a cheery gurgling noise from his stroller, both amused and excited by the plastic ring of colorful farm animals attached to his wrist, which rattled every time he waved his hand. He had coped with the twenty-three-hour flight remarkably well for a four-month-old, with only the occasional outburst of tears during some particularly troublesome turbulence.

After checking into their B and B, Nick had been too ani-mated to give in to sleep, so they made their first excursion to the park to explore the winter gardens and to feed the ducks. Then they stopped off for a snack in a café before making their way to their Russell Street destination. Ahead of them and three doors to the right was the building which held the man they had flown twelve thousand miles to see.

The street in Hastings, New Zealand, was becoming busier as the lunchtime trade picked up and the staff left their work to grab a snack or meet with friends in cafés. Nick bided his time, trying to remain calm, but really all he wanted to do was run through the shop door to announce his arrival.

Even moments before he opened the door, Nick could feel *his* presence, and a kaleidoscope of butterflies had, en masse, risen up from the pit of his stomach and taken flight inside his body. When the man appeared, Nick's breath was well and truly taken away.

Alex stood still for a moment, not seeing him, and Nick noted that his wavy hair was shorter than when he'd last seen him, almost nine months earlier. He'd shaved off his stubble, too, revealing a clean-cut, more angular face. Suddenly, Alex looked flustered, as if he knew something was out of kilter but he couldn't pinpoint what it was.

Nick knew what he was feeling because he felt it, too.

Then, as their eyes locked, Alex took a step backwards in shock. The stroller especially must have been quite the surprise, he thought.

"Hello, stranger," Nick began, making his way toward him.

Alex was too stunned to reply.

"Alex, meet Dylan. Dylan, meet Alex." Alex moved his dis-believing eyes from Nick's toward Dylan. He took in the boy's darker skin and looked at Nick, bewildered.

"It's a very, very long story," Nick continued, "and I have to warn you now, he and I only come as a package. But if you'll have us, we're here for keeps."

Alex tried to cover his mouth with his hands but it was too late to hide his huge, white smile or to stop the tears from falling down his face. And he gave Nick the firmest, most longed-for hug he'd ever received, which Nick took as a yes.

103

ELLIE

Ellie sat behind the desk in her office and stared at the spot where, seventeen months earlier, she had bludgeoned her fiancé to death.

She'd heard whispers that some members of staff who'd remained within the company had questioned why she would stay in an office where such a violent act had occurred. And when her refusal to budge from that space was leaked to the press, they, too, branded it ghoulish and macabre. But Ellie would not allow anyone to bully her from the seventy-first floor of the tallest building in London. What happened the day Matthew was killed would not define the work for which she had sacrificed everything to call her own. He had deserved to die, and she didn't regret that decision for a second. Now, alone in the room, she had earned the right to remain head and shoulders above everyone else.

Since that day, Ellie had effectively erased the man she had known as Tim from her memory. Even when being cross-examined in the witness box at her trial, she was vague about their life together despite her barrister's attempt to paint her as human and not as the monster millions witnessed online committing a lethal act. *That* Ellie was woeful and powerless, and had convinced herself to fall in love with a man she had no business loving. *That* Ellie had been the architect of her own misery, and *this* Ellie had no desire to ever meet or replicate that woman again. So she spent seven days a week working in an office with a ghost to remind her never to be that pathetic.

She took a moment to note how hushed it was in the corridors and offices surrounding hers. Not so long ago it had bustled with life, from Ula and her assistants fielding telephone calls and chatting together. Now, with the business scaled back and a third of staff having quit and not been replaced, the floor was silent. Even her own office was quiet, with her computer switched off, her landline removed and her mobile phone switched to airplane mode.

Her eyes glanced across the room to a stack of the week's newspapers and magazines piled upon the glass coffee table. From day one, the media's reaction to her arrest and charges was as she expected. The tabloids went to town with predictably savage character assassinations, and they frequently crossed the line when it came to what they could legally report on in a case that had yet to come to trial.

The images of the twenty minutes that changed Ellie's life had been repeated so often on the news and online that they had become iconic. Like constant replays of the Twin Towers collapsing or the Sri Lankan tsunami that swept thousands to their deaths, viewers gradually became desensitized to the crux of the story—that they were witnessing the murder of a man. But it had worked to her advantage because, to an ever-expanding majority, Matthew had become the enemy.

Media commentators and psychologists analyzed the footage in depth to judge his character, body language, lies and motivations, and had labeled him borderline psychopathic. It was Twitter, Facebook and other social media platforms that took it a stage further, making her a poster girl for the victims of mental and emotional abuse. For the first time since she sprang to fame, more than a decade earlier, those who once described Ellie as a ruthless businesswoman, unafraid to trample over anyone to get what she wanted, had now been referring to her as an ordinary girl who'd been cruelly manipulated. The PR company she was paying hundreds of thousands of pounds had done a sterling job. Ellie loathed how she was being perceived by the public, but her extensive legal team had frequently reminded her, if it kept her out of prison, then it was for the greater good.

However, while Ellie's popularity rose, confidence in Match Your DNA was at an all-time low. All these months later and, despite robust marketing campaigns, it continued to suffer the aftershock of Matthew's two million mis–Matches. In the first month, the number of new testing kit applications dropped by 94 percent. The weeks that followed saw the steep downward curve lessen, but potential customers were no longer willing to place matters of the heart in tainted hands.

The lawsuits arrived thick and fast, and TV channels worldwide broadcast adverts from opportunist law firms offering no win, no fee representation to those who believed they were part of the two million. Match Your DNA's insurers were threatening to not cover any successful compensation claims, accusing the company of being negligent for its ineffective online security that had allowed Matthew to hack into. Without the insurers' backing, Match Your DNA would end up in inevitable bankruptcy.

Ellie looked at her watch: 2:00 p.m. She stood up, applied fresh lipstick, slipped her sunglasses on, threw her handbag over her shoulder and made her way out of the office. As she moved into an elevator and down to a floor housing one of The Shard's six restaurants, she was flanked by her recently appointed trio of bodyguards and took a moment to think about her former head of security, Andrei. For his own sake, it was best that he disappear from her world rather than face charges for assisting her in disposing of Matthew's body. She assumed he'd gone back home to Eastern Europe; the payoff was generous enough to allow him not to work for many years to come.

She walked confidently through the bustling dining room, noting the hushed tones and cocked heads as she brushed past each table. She was no longer concerned by what people thought of her; she'd let her PR team take care of that. That extended to her family, too, who she hadn't seen since Matthew's death. There had been intermittent contact with them through Ula, and she had felt huge waves of guilt when their home had become besieged by reporters. But by accepting Tim into their lives, they too had been complicit in breaking down her barriers and allowing him to poison the waters. In Ellie's mind, Tim and her family were intrinsically linked, and, to cut him out, she had to cut them out, too.

She kept her sunglasses over her eyes as the maître d' led her to a corner table overlooking the Thames. She ordered her usual Hendrick's gin and tonic and thanked a nervous young waiter whose hand trembled as he filled her glass with sparkling water. She could smell Ula's perfume before she reached Ellie's table.

"I'm sorry to bother you, but your barrister's just called," Ula said, unable to disguise her concern. "The jury is ready to return with its verdict."

Ellie nodded, took a sip of drink and followed Ula and her bodyguards into the lift, toward where her car was parked by the service entrance. They sped off in the direction of the Old Bailey courts where she had spent every day of the last four months on trial for Matthew's murder. She had pleaded an assertive "not guilty" on the grounds of diminished responsibility.

"Have you made a decision about the re-tests? Will we be offering them to those unsure if they're a Match?"

"No, I don't think we will," Ellie replied coldly. "Everyone included in that time frame who may or may not have been mis-Matched will have to follow their instinct. Sometimes, the grass isn't greener on the other side, and we should stay in the field where we belong. And sometimes we just need to take a gamble and hope for the best."

"And if you don't get the verdict you hope for?" Ula asked. "What then?"

"You know what to do," Ellie replied. "Press the button and let the world start making its own mistakes again."

★ ★ ★ ★ ★

ACKNOWLEDGMENTS

The first person I'd like to offer my thanks to is John Russell. Much gratitude comes to you for allowing me to bounce so many ideas at you over Oscar's dog walks, and for coming up with some alternative twists and turns of your own. For a man who rarely reads a book, your ideas and suggestions were amazing! Thank you also for your patience while I hid myself away in our office as you kept me fed and watered.

Thanks to my mum, Pamela Marrs, for being my most loyal supporter and the inspiration for my love of books. And a huge thank you to Tracy Fenton, Queen of Facebook's THE Book Club, for her advice and frequent abuse. To writers both experienced and new to the game, you're a Godsend.

I'd like to offer a massive shout-out to members of the aforementioned and largest online group of like-minded readers. There's no other group out there like you and I'm grateful to every one of the thousands of you who have downloaded my novels to date.

Special thanks to the wonderful Randileigh Kennedy and governess of grammar Kath Middleton (fantastic authors themselves), Anne Lynes for your eagle eyes and the inimitable Samantha Clarke. Also thanks to my early readers/self-titled groupies Alex Iveson, Susan Wallace, Janette Hail, geography expert Michelle Nicholls, Janice Leibowitz, Ruth Davey, Laura Pontin, Elaine Binder, Rebecca Burntin and Deborah Dobrin. And a special mention to my friends Rhian Molloy and Mandie Brown, both early days readers.

Gratitude goes to my fellow writers Andrew Webber (your enthusiasm helped so much) and James Ryan. Thanks to Peter Sterk for his advice when it comes to DNA and genetics; Angela Holden Hunt; Chloe Cope Neppe for medical advice and use of Aussie slang; and Julie McGukian for her crime scene cleanup suggestions—Christopher couldn't have got away with murder without you.

Thanks to my friend Adam Smalley from thedesigngent.co.uk for the mock-up web pages that even I believed existed. I also found the website psychopathyawareness.wordpress.com very useful when examining Christopher's psyche.

A whopper of a thank you goes to Emily Yau, my commissioning editor at Ebury. Of the hundreds of new books popping up online every day, you came across mine and took a punt on downloading it. You have changed everything, and for that you'll have my eternal gratitude.

Thank you also to Peter Joseph and the team at Hanover Square. I am delighted you chose *The One* and it's been a pleasure working with you. I am so grateful for your enthusiasm.

Finally, my thanks go toward you, whoever you are, for taking the time to purchase this book. You'll never know quite how much this means to a writer.